THE SINNERS

ALSO BY ACE ATKINS

QUINN COLSON NOVELS

The Ranger
The Lost Ones
The Broken Places
The Forsaken
The Redeemers
The Innocents
The Fallen

ROBERT B. PARKER'S SPENSER NOVELS

Robert B. Parker's Lullaby
Robert B. Parker's Wonderland
Robert B. Parker's Cheap Shot
Robert B. Parker's Kickback
Robert B. Parker's Slow Burn
Robert B. Parker's Little White Lies
Robert B. Parker's Old Black Magic

NICK TRAVERS NOVELS

Crossroad Blues
Leavin' Trunk Blues
Dark End of the Street
Dirty South

TRUE CRIME NOVELS

White Shadow
Wicked City
Devil's Garden
Infamous

THE SINNERS

ACE ATKINS

G. P. PUTNAM'S SONS / NEW YORK

PUTNAM

G. P. PUTNAM'S SONS
Publishers Since 1838
An imprint of Penguin Random House LLC
375 Hudson Street
New York, New York 10014

Library of Congress Cataloging-in-Publication Data

Names: Atkins, Ace, author.
Title: The sinners / Ace Atkins.
Description: New York : G. P. Putnam's Sons, [2018] | Series: A Quinn Colson novel ; 8
Identifiers: LCCN 2018022151 | ISBN 9780399576744 (Hardcover) |
ISBN 9780399576768 (ePub)
Subjects: | BISAC: FICTION / Crime. | FICTION / Thrillers. | FICTION /
Action & Adventure. | GSAFD: Suspense fiction. | Mystery fiction.
Classification: LCC PS3551. T49 S56 2018 | DDC 813/.54—dc23
LC record available at https://lccn.loc.gov/2018022151

Printed in the United States of America
10 9 8 7 6 5 4 3 2 1

BOOK DESIGN BY MEIGHAN CAVANAUGH

For Burt Reynolds

To understand the world, you must first understand a place like Mississippi.

—*William Faulkner*

Have your musket clean as a whistle, hatchet scoured, sixty rounds powder and ball, and be ready to march at a minute's warning.

—*Rogers' Rangers Standing Order No. 2*

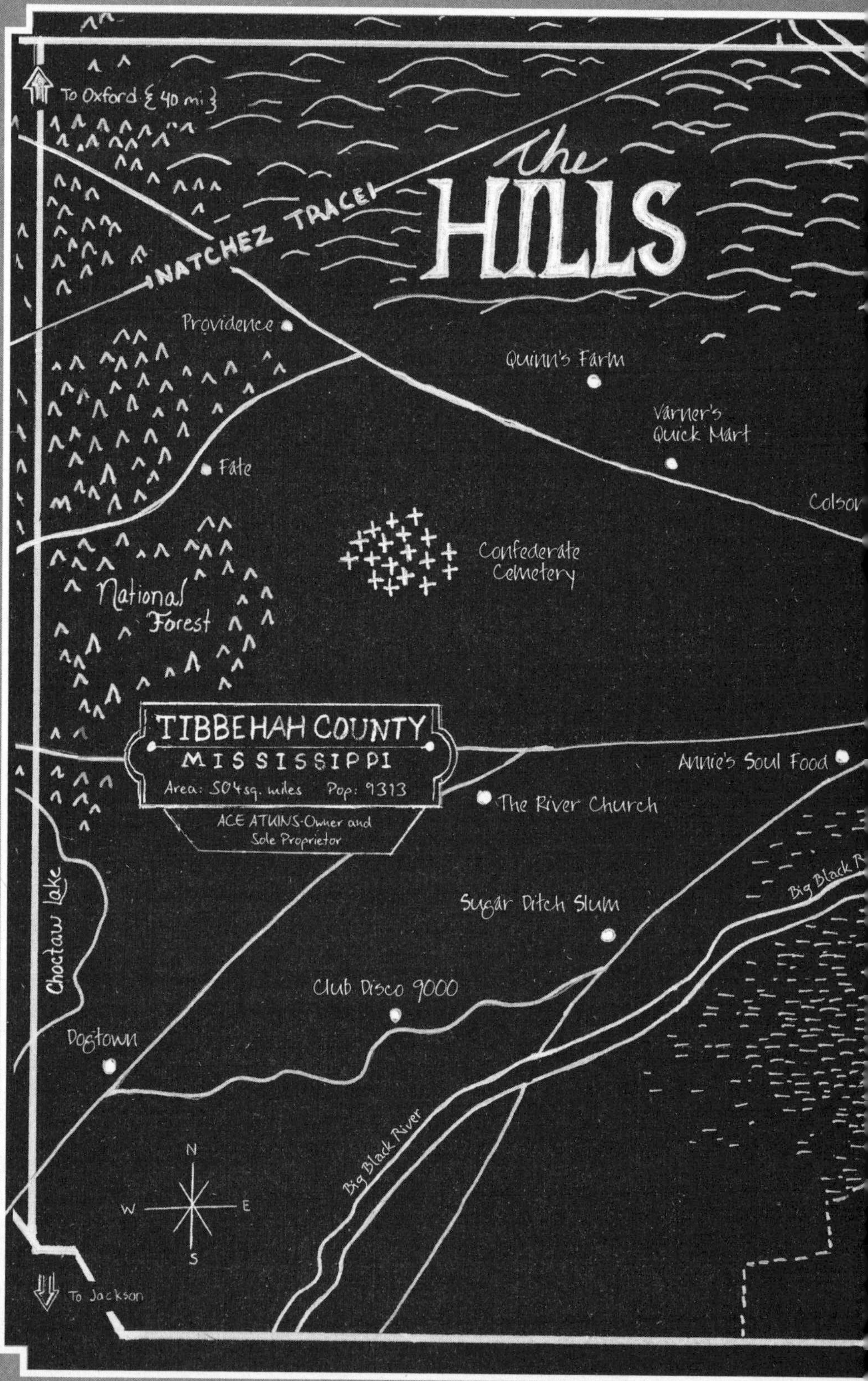
To Oxford {40 mi}
NATCHEZ TRACE
the HILLS
Providence
Quinn's Farm
Varner's Quick Mart
Fate
Colson
Confederate Cemetery
National Forest
TIBBEHAH COUNTY
MISSISSIPPI
Area: 504 sq. miles Pop: 9313
ACE ATKINS-Owner and Sole Proprietor
Annie's Soul Food
The River Church
Big Black R
Sugar Ditch Slum
Choctaw Lake
Club Disco 9000
Dogtown
Big Black River
N
W
E
S
To Jackson

TO MEMPHIS
{99mi}
Carthage
Big Black River
HWY 45
Yellowleaf
Rebel Truck Shop
JERICHO
Post Office
Fillin' Station
The Tibbehah Monitor
Sheriff's Office & Jail
General Store
Sonic
Piggly Wiggly
Hollywood Video
Dollar General
Driver's Flat
Traveler's Rest Motel
Farm Supply
the BOTTOMLAND
INDIAN CASINO
CHOCTAW LANDS

THE SINNERS

1

"YOU SURE YOU WANT TO DO THIS?" E. J. ROYCE SAID.

"Yes, sir," Sheriff Hamp Beckett said, reaching for the cigarette lighter in the patrol car dash and setting fire to the end of a Marlboro Red. "Damn straight."

"Good and goddamn sure?"

"No, Royce," Beckett said. "I'd rather sit here and play with my goddamn pecker while Heath Pritchard keeps making those Memphis runs with enough pot in that Ford Bronco to keep half of Tennessee stoned. You know that son of a bitch waves at me every time he sneaks back across the county line? Like me and him are big buddies. He might as well be saluting me with his middle finger, that big shit-eating grin on his face."

It was late June of 1993, growing warm and muggy at first light, while he and Royce parked the cruiser right beside the Jericho Farm & Ranch, waiting for Pritchard to speed on past, scooting back from a midnight run, hightailing it to the big farm he shared with his two spinster sisters. Pritchard sure was a bastard, wasn't a doubt in Beckett's mind. He'd been busting that boy since he'd been elected sheriff back in '74, on everything from aggravated assault to public drunk. He once shot a neighbor's dog with a crossbow and several times had been caught in intimate acts with girls too young to know better.

Pritchard sure loved those teenagers, cruising the Jericho town square in his growling truck, window down, hairy ape arm out the open window with a lit cigarette. He was a real hillbilly hero to those kids. All Levi's, sideburns, and a big thick roll of cash.

"You know," Royce said. "The other night, I was watching this movie on the HBO. Had Robert Duvall and that fella who was married to Madonna. They was cops out there in Los Angeles fighting a bunch a gangbangers. Anyway, him and Duvall are sitting in their squad car and Duvall tells the other fella a story about an old bull and a young bull sitting on a hill."

"I heard it."

"I don't think you have, Sheriff."

"How the hell do you know what I heard and not heard?" Beckett said, spewing smoke from the side of his mouth, weathered old hand tapping the wheel, nervous and expectant.

"'Cause you ain't got the HBO out there in the country and probably never will," Royce said. "So, the old bull and the young bull are looking down at a herd of heifers and the young bull says, 'Why don't we go down and screw one of them big fat cows?'"

"That ain't how it goes," Beckett said. "Christ, Royce, you'd fuck up your own funeral. Way it goes is, the young bull says, 'How about me and you run down there and fuck a heifer?' and the old bull turns to him and says, 'How about we just walk on down there and fuck 'em all.'"

"I don't see no difference," Royce said. "Story's the same. Just a couple damn animals shooting the breeze."

Royce was a rail-thin, leathery old bastard in his tan deputy uniform. What remained of his gray hair had been Brylcreemed down to his head in a sad attempt to cover up a freckled bald spot. Beckett was a large man, barrel-chested and big-bellied, what his wife Halley called sad-faced but handsome. He was tall and lumbering, smelling of cigarettes and whiskey breath from the night before.

"Are you trying to make a point to me about patience?" Beckett said. "And me dealing with Heath Pritchard? 'Cause if you are, you're doing a horseshit job."

"Hold up there, Sheriff," Royce said, holding out the flat of his hand. "Just hear me out. We got the whole damn department and them boys from the DEA descending on Pritchard land this morning like a wave of locusts. But what if we got fed some bad intel and we don't find nothing? One of those shit-in-one-hand, wish-in-the-other situations. Me and you been lawmen too damn long to rush in without being damn sure what we're gonna find. Someone like Pritchard will take some serious offense if we're wrong. I don't want truck with him or any of his crazy people."

"Oh, you don't?" Beckett said. He lifted his tired blue eyes and weathered sunburned face to the rearview mirror, rubbing his chin. He needed a shave and maybe another shot of Jack Daniel's in his morning coffee to steady things. "That's mighty interesting. Ain't it about time for you to put in your retirement?"

"Shit," Royce said. "I'm just watching your back, Hamp. I've been doin' it half my life. Don't go on and get a sore ass about it now. There's just been a lot of talk in town."

"I know too damn well," Beckett said. "I heard all that shit."

"Pritchard ain't like other folks," Royce said. "Something is broken in that fella's head."

The dash radio squawked, the deputy watching the county line letting them know that Heath Pritchard was inbound, rolling fast and steady back to his family's land. Beckett gave a big 10-4, sitting there, sweating and waiting, his heart pumping fast in his tired old ribs. This was it. They finally were going to put that crazy bastard in the cage where he belonged. Beckett flicked the Marlboro out the open window, dusted the ash off his wrinkled uniform, and cranked the ignition. Royce leaned into his shotgun like a cane, waiting for Pritchard to zip past the Jericho Farm & Ranch, racing to his two hundred and fifty acres. Every inch was fenced off with barbed wire or half-buried truck tires painted white, a Confederate flag flying high above the front gate, letting everyone know that Pritchard land was as free and sovereign as any country down in South America or Walt Disney World in Orlando.

"I once seen this monkey at the Memphis Zoo," Royce said. "Wadn't a hell of a lot of difference between him and the way Pritchard acts when we get him in the cage. That damn ape stared at me like he wanted to rip my arms from their sockets and my eyes from my head. All I know is, Pritchard won't go quiet."

"Then my Sunday prayer will be answered."

"You gonna try and kill him?"

"Deputy Royce?"

"Yes, sir?"

"Don't you ever ask me a question like that again."

The Ford Bronco flew on past, buggy antennae whipping about, and Sheriff Beckett pulled out fast and hard behind. Beckett didn't hit the lights, just keeping a good even pace behind Pritchard to let him know they were all over his ass. They'd run him back to his foxhole, where the DEA boys were already waiting out down that county road. The plan was for everyone to hit the farm at the same time, Beckett getting to Pritchard first as he walked from his truck to that old house of his. If he wanted to make a play, Beckett was the man to finish the business. Four miles down, Pritchard slowed his Bronco and pulled quick into his land, closing the gate behind him, and trailed off in a billow of reddish road dirt.

"What now?" Royce said.

"We got cutters, don't we?" Beckett said.

Royce hopped out, cut the chain, and then climbed back into the sheriff's car, barely getting the door shut before Beckett was off again, this time joined by a half-dozen black cars and three more deputies following. He was reminded of that old Waylon song: "Jack of Diamonds. Jack of Diamonds. I still got my Ace."

"'But you cannot take my soul,'" Beckett sang, holding the wheel tight, back end bucking up on the dirt road.

"What'd you say?" Royce said.

"There he goes, sprinting like a jackrabbit," Beckett said. "Hit the goddamn lights, Deputy."

E. J. Royce flicked on the blue lights and the siren, lighting up the summer dawn. Dust flew into the open windows, tires hitting a few potholes, until he skidded to a stop and tossed open the door. Beckett was an old man but not a slow man, and he was within ten paces of Heath Pritchard quick, with his .44 out and drawn.

"Hold up, Pritchard."

Pritchard stopped at the steps of his rambling one-story farmhouse, one foot on the first step, as the screen door was flung open by one of his crazy sisters, standing tall and proud with a shotgun up in her skinny arms. With his back turned, Pritchard raised his hands and faced Beckett slow and easy. He gave a look only a Pritchard could with a dozen lawmen with guns trained on him, a big old cocky smile and a silly-ass laugh. "You boys lost?" he said. "'Cause my other sister got my Jew lawyer up in Memphis on speed dial."

"Get your ass down here, Pritchard," Beckett said. "And I'd appreciate it if your dear sweet sister drops that twelve-gauge at her feet or she's going to be shellin' peas at the state pen until the Second Coming."

The woman was as short and wiry as the other Pritchards, with a sallow face and sunk-in black eyes but with the big belly of an expectant mother. Her jaw set as she looked down at all the lawmen out on the gravel road, blue lights flashing and a dozen guns trained on her and her brother. The door flew open and the other sister, with the same look only fifty pounds heavier, rushed out carrying a black skillet in her hand, seeking to do some battle or fry up some eggs for breakfast.

"Morning, Missy," Beckett said.

The big girl looked dazed. She nodded slow. "Sheriff."

"Anybody else in the house?"

She shook her head. Royce and two more deputies walked up and grabbed the woman as Beckett kept his eyes and his gun on Pritchard. Hell of thing to be run so ragged by some shitbird like Heath Pritchard. Black-eyed and black-haired, he had on a dirty V-neck T-shirt, jeans, and rattlesnake cowboy boots that must've cost five hundred dollars. He saw Beckett eyeing his feet and grinned even more.

"I know what you're thinking," he said. "And, yes. They do look damn sharp on me."

Beckett reached around the man and pulled a Browning 9mm from the back of his Wranglers.

"You ain't gonna find nothing here," Pritchard said. "Look all you want. I'll wait here all day. And when you're done, I'll make sure this is your last term as sheriff. You're a goddamn dinosaur, Hamp. A damn ole toothless T. rex that don't know he's already extinct."

The DEA boys already had the Bronco's doors and tailgate open. Men searched under the seats and pulled back the bloodred carpet trying to find Pritchard's hidey-holes. The two sisters had found a secure spot on a metal glider on the porch, gliding away, looking worried as hell, while their brother seemed amused by the whole situation. The deputies had gone on into the old house to rifle through closets and peek under beds, while Hamp turned his attention on a big rickety barn on the edge of the property. Barely red, sun-faded and busted, leaning a lot to the right.

"I know how much you like that Gunsmoke, *Sheriff," Pritchard said. "But don't you know the ladies love outlaws?"*

"Why don't you shut your hick mouth."

"Missy?" Pritchard said. The woman coming to attention and stopping the motion on the glider. "How about you get on in the kitchen and fry up some bacon. It's gonna be a long morning."

"Stay where you're at," Beckett said. "Where you been, Heath?"

He shrugged. "Shooting pool."

"Up in Memphis?"

"Good a place as any."

"After you made that delivery."

"I don't know what the hell you're talkin' about."

Beckett spit on the ground as E. J. Royce walked out from the old barn with another deputy, shaking his head. A moment later, he heard heavy shoes on the stairs and the screen door squeaking open as two DEA men in khakis and black windbreakers walked out and showed their empty palms. Beckett nodded to the men, in both directions, letting them know to keep on looking. He had to keep that goddamn stash somewhere.

"Johnny Stagg tugging your leash, Sheriff?" Pritchard said. "He sure would like to put me in my place."

Beckett gave him a hard look and shook loose a Marlboro from the pack. Everything soft and quiet in the early-summer morning. He could feel the heat coming on, smell the manure in the pasture, see the red pops of color from the sisters' canna lilies planted along the steps.

They ransacked the house, the barn, and two machine shops where Pritchard claimed to repair appliances for a living. About the best the men could find was four gallons of moonshine, a stack of nudie magazines, and a Thompson machine gun. Pritchard had pulled out an old wooden chair and sat in the middle of the gravel path, smoking a cigarette, smiling at all the confused and frustrated lawmen as they turned his own private world inside out. Beckett walked up to him and looked down on the grizzled little man.

"Where is it?"

"You been after my ass a long while," he said. "Blaming me for things I'd never do."

Beckett wanted to snatch up the cocky son of a bitch by the front of his filthy T-shirt and kick the everliving shit out of him. But he just smiled and walked back to his patrol car, calling dispatch to send in some dogs from Lee County to assist. That's when Beckett felt the morning coffee kicking in and he wandered away from the cars, Pritchard laughing and grinning, telling stories to the DEA boys about how he'd been three-time dirt track champion of the Mid-South. "The King," Pritchard said, "Jerry Lawler himself, sponsored my team before the wreck."

Beckett wasn't listening to any more horseshit, heading toward the big cornfield, the cicadas coming alive as the soil started to get warm, growing crazy and wild, humming and clicking way out into the trees. He stepped up to a row of Silver Queen higher than his head and started to piss into Pritchard's crop. Those DEA boys had flown over the land twice since spring, not being able to find where he'd gotten that weed.

But standing there that morning, he saw something through the corn that caught his eye, deep in the fourth row, a darker shade of green that made him rush his business and zip up, and drew him, kicking and stumbling through the corn, pushing the leaves away from his face, busting stalks, and tromping through the rows until he found what everyone had told him wasn't there. Either those DEA boys were goddamn blind or Pritchard was smarter than he thought. Four rows of corn in the middle of the big field with marijuana planted between them, big, healthy plants with those wild razory leaves. Out of breath, Beckett pulled a blue bandanna out of his pocket and wiped his sweating brow. He walked for twenty minutes straight through the cornfields to find the whole maze and precise coverage of the crop. Goddamn, he had the bastard.

Beckett reached for his radio to call Royce. This was more goddamn pot than he even knew how to calculate.

"What you got there, Sheriff?"

"Tell Pritchard to wipe that grin off his hick face and tighten up his asshole," Beckett said. "Parchman Farm ain't no county-line beer joint. He ain't gonna get to choose his own dance partner."

2

"EVERYTHING WAS DONE WITH SECRECY," JEAN COLSON said, frying bacon on the old gas stove as her son, Quinn, watched her and drank his morning coffee. "Elvis and some of the boys in the Memphis Mafia snuck over the fence of his house in Palm Springs to throw off the press. Frank Sinatra even let him use his private plane to Las Vegas, where Priscilla was waiting."

"We don't plan on getting married in Vegas," Quinn said. "And I'm not Elvis. And Maggie's not Priscilla."

Quinn was a hard-looking man, not yet forty, tall and lean with a face made of bone and sharp angles. He was clean-shaven as always, with his dark hair cut less than an inch on top and buzzed short on the sides. He wore Levi's and cowboy boots, the tin star of the Tibbehah County sheriff pinned to his khaki uniform shirt and the Beretta 9 he'd carried on thirteen tours as a U.S. Army Ranger on his right hip. His mother was in her mid-sixties, wide-hipped and blue-eyed. Her hair was the color of copper and she had a smallish nose and a wide mouth. She wore an old apron over a faded denim dress. The apron read I LIKE PIG BUTTS AND I CANNOT LIE.

"He and the Colonel kept it to just fourteen guests," Jean said, removing the bacon and setting it on a paper towel to soak up the grease. "George Klein and Charlie Hodge acted as his best men. His tuxedo was designed by his friend Marty Lacker. Marty sketched it himself, black with paisley designs. Some man who worked at MGM made it for him. I can't recall his name. But did you know that Priscilla's wedding gown was just off the rack? You might tell Maggie that. She went to the Neiman Marcus in Beverly Hills and found the perfect one."

"Next time we're in Beverly Hills, we'll make sure and check out the Neiman Marcus wedding department, Momma," he said. "We only need family and some good friends to get hitched. Right now, I'm thinking fourteen may be a little too much."

"Fourteen?" Jean said. "Elvis invited a hundred folks to join him and Priscilla at the Aladdin Hotel for the reception. They had a four-tiered wedding cake made of yellow sponge cake and filled with apricot marmalade. The frosting was some type of Bavarian cream on account of them meeting over in Germany. Did you know Elvis brought her to Memphis to finish out her senior year of high school until she came of age?"

"I always found that part kinda little creepy," Quinn said. "Some good ole boy from Tupelo tries to pull that in Tibbehah County and I'll put his ass in jail."

Jean shook her head, calling for her grandson Jason and her soon-to-be stepgrandson, Brandon. Quinn's nephew Jason was nearly ten now and Brandon had just turned seven. They'd become good buddies over the summer break. Jason had shown Brandon all the back paths and secret hiding places out on the old Beckett farm. They ran wild in the woods. They fished for bass and bluegill. They shot cans with a .22 rifle with Quinn when their grandmother wasn't around.

The boys ran down from upstairs and took a seat on each side of Quinn. Jason smiled up at him. A good-looking boy, with the eyes and smile of his once-famous grandfather and the dark brown skin of a father that his sister never acknowledged. Brandon was lighter, towheaded, with Maggie's bright green eyes and freckled face. Quinn didn't see a bit of his father in him and hoped to God that he never would.

"I heard Miss Maggie won't let you smoke in the house," Jason said.

Quinn nodded.

"My momma hates smoke," Brandon said.

"You keep that up, Uncle Quinn, and you'll give Hondo the cancer," Jason said. "I saw it on television. You shouldn't smoke around children or pets."

"I'll keep it outside," Quinn said. "Where is Hondo anyway? You boys seen him?"

The boys pointed out the front door. Quinn picked up his coffee mug and headed out to the front porch, where he lit up his first Liga Privada of the day. The farmhouse was an old classic tin-roof job, built in pieces by his great-grandfather starting back in 1895. His mother had been raised there and came over most Saturday mornings to make breakfast and talk about old times or, most often, Elvis Presley. The front and back doors were wide open, screen doors shut over the openings, creating a cooling shotgun effect even on the hottest days.

After a few moments, his mother came out to join him. "Why do you continue to smoke those nasty old things?" his mother said.

"I get shot at for ten years and you never say a word," he said. "I get back home and you don't want me to relax?"

Quinn whistled for Hondo, the rangy cattle dog soon trotting in from the cow pasture, holding a deer bone in his mouth. He was a patchwork of blacks and grays with two different colored eyes. Shaking his dusty coat off on the porch, he set the bone down at Quinn's boots.

"Did you find a band yet?" Jean asked. "Time's growing short, son."

"Working on it."

"Working on it ain't gonna get it," she said. "You yourself said there's only three weeks until the big day. And unless you want me to buy one of those karaoke machines at Walmart and start practicing 'Can't Help Falling in Love,' you better get going."

"What about Uncle Van?"

"Good Lord," she said. "Your Uncle Van would just show up with a guitar and a pint of Wild Turkey, singing some off-key Merle Haggard about how tonight the bottle let him down."

"I heard about a good bluegrass band out of Oxford," he said. "Some man named Ed Dye who used to play with the Nashville Jug Band. Don't you remember that version of 'Blue Moon of Kentucky' that has kind of a reggae beat? They put out a record of it. Maggie has a copy."

"Son," Jean said, placing a hand on her hip. "There's only one version of that song."

"Momma," he said. "Before you say anything else, you really need to know something."

Jean looked over at her son with some concern, waiting for him to ask some delicate question or relay some bad news she didn't want to hear. Quinn tapped the end of the cigar and smiled at her. "Elvis ain't coming back."

Jean frowned and opened her mouth just as Quinn's cell phone started skipping and skittering on the porch railing. Quinn saw it was Reggie Caruthers, now his number one deputy since Lillie had left for a better job in Memphis a year ago. He picked up the phone and read his text. He stood up, placing the cigar on the rim of his coffee mug.

"I gotta go," he said, kissing his mother on the cheek.

"Music," she said. "A wedding has to have music."

"Working on it, Momma."

"Are you're absolutely sure Boom will be back?" she said. "We can't miss the music and the best man."

"Boom said he'll be there," Quinn said, walking down the front steps, heading toward his new F-150 and whistling for Hondo. "Nothing could make him miss it."

You a goddamn inspiration," the man said. "People out here be mopin'. They ain't got no job. They ain't no opportunity. But here you are, driving the ass crack of America in an eighteen-wheeler with one goddamn arm."

Boom was a big man, six foot six and two-sixty, bearded with dark brown skin and built like an Abrams battle tank. People didn't often approach him at truck stops for a handout or a hand job, so when the two boys ambled up to the diesel pump in Meridian, he knew they were about to talk about the prosthetic arm. Everybody wanted to know about the arm.

Where'd you lose it?

Iraq.

Were you in a big battle?

Nope. Delivering water north of a Fallujah and hit an IED.

Did you get a medal and shit?

Purple Heart. If you're wounded, you get a Purple Heart.

And then folks, mainly kids, wanted to know how he grabbed things with the hook.

Takes practice.

One dumb son of a bitch at Club Disco 9000 wanted to know how he still jacked his monkey without his right hand. Boom didn't answer that. He just coldclocked the motherfucker and knocked his ass out. But that was back when he was drinking too much.

"Yes, sir," the man said. "You an inspiration. You know that?"

"OK, man," Boom said. "OK. It was good meeting you."

He gripped the billy club in his hand and started a slow, steady walk around the truck to thump tires and check the pressure. As he made his way, the man and his pal followed. Both of them black. The one doing the talking was a stocky little shit, wearing a wife-beater tee and saggy-ass jeans. His friend was just a teenager, skinny, wearing a blue tee that advertised THE PITTS FAMILY BBQ 2010. WHAT IT'S ALL ABOUT.

"Zero excuses. Zero," the man said. "Ain't none in the world. You mind if I video you working? I got to throw this shit up on YouTube."

Boom shrugged and kept walking around the trailer, thumping the tires, waiting to hear a dull thud and not that tight thwack of the proper inflation. The two men followed, one praising Jesus as he filmed, telling everyone how this no-excuses man was getting it done.

It had hit ninety-two degrees at the truck stop pumps and Boom paused and wiped his forehead with the bill of his CAT hat. He had on a pair of khaki pants with work boots and a blue mechanic's shirt cut off at the sleeves, hot wind billowing up off the roadside ruffling the material.

"Just doing my job, man," Boom said.

"'Just doin' my job,'" the man said, laughing. "Damn. Ain't that some real old John Wayne shit? *'That's just my job, sir.'* Look at you. You giving me some real joy today. The Lord done brought me some joy at the motherfuckin' Magnolia Truck Stop."

Boom thumped a big ole tire behind the passenger side of the cab. The two watched his every movement, the older one walking backwards to get the whole scene in the frame. "Out there, working a Kenworth, with one goddamn arm."

"It's a Freightliner," Boom said. "Classic XL. With a 515 Detroit engine."

The man looked over at the younger kid, hands in his pockets, head down. "What's your excuse, man?" he said. "You see this shit? You see what this man's doin'? The Lord put him here for you to see. A living example."

Boom reached up with his hook, grabbed the door handle, and hoisted himself to grab the logbook. He stood by the pumps, writing down with his left hand the mileage, hours, and the weight he was hauling. In Amarillo, he'd picked up a refrigerated trailer full of produce he'd drive back to the docks in Tupelo. All the paperwork was a safety; he'd have to reload the same shit into the computer and GPS on his dash.

"You own that truck?" the kid asked. "That's a big-ass truck."

"Naw, man," Boom said. "I work for a company. I just drive."

"But could you own your own truck?" the kid asked. "Someday, you make enough money?"

"Yeah," Boom said. "Someday."

"Who's that you working for?" the kid said. "Sut-pen?"

"Yeah," he said, looking at the hand-painted name on the semi's door. "Sutpen Trucking. They based out of Tupelo but roll all over the country, mainly down South."

"What y'all haul?" the kid said.

"Every damn thing," Boom said.

"You get your own truck," the stocky man said, "make sure you get a bunch of flashing lights, neon and shit. Women go crazy for that stuff. You get a tricked-out truck and you get some pussy at every stop."

"Pussy at every stop?" Boom said. "Yeah. OK. I'll keep that in mind."

The man fist-bumped his hook and the young dude nodded at him, heading back to their car parked outside the truck stop diner. The stocky man was praising Jesus the whole time. The fuel pump clicked off at one hundred and fifty gallons, the other tank still full. Boom moved around to the back of the trailer to check on the load, make sure the boxes hadn't shifted too much and the temperature was still under seventy. They'd told him not to worry about it, but his own AC had crapped out back in Shreveport and he wanted to make sure he was straight.

Boom unlatched the back door and hefted himself up into the trailer, where hundreds of boxes had been stacked nearly to the roof with only narrow spaces to walk between. Everything felt cool and good inside the dark trailer, the thermometer showing seventy on the nose, but as he was about to hop down he spotted the names on the long, narrow boxes: SONY. TOSHIBA. VIZIO. LG. When he opened up a large box by the doors, he found a fat stack of PS4 game consoles. Another box had some drones, computers, and tablets. The more he looked, the more Boom felt like he'd picked up a truck headed for a Best Buy.

"I think something got messed up," Boom said, calling to the Sutpen dispatcher. He told him all about the trailer. "This ain't no avocados."

"Nothing's wrong," said the dispatcher, a gravelly-voiced country man. "Don't worry your pretty little head about it. Just don't fuck up your delivery, Mr. Kimbrough. You got two hours."

"'Pretty head'?" Boom said. "Hey, man—"

The line clicked off and Boom got back up into the cab. He looked all around the truck stop to see if anyone was watching, rolled down the windows, and cranked that big engine, the seat shuddering under his ass.

He drove careful and slow all the way back to the Tupelo city limits.

What's he on?" Quinn asked, driving and talking on his cell.

"Not really sure," Reggie Caruthers said. "Man's just been hooting and hollering, sitting there, dragging his ass down Jericho Road like a dog with worms. You can't really talk with him or reason with him. He's making some weird sounds. It's hard to explain, Sheriff."

"What's he sound like?"

"Well," Reggie said. "The man kinda sounds like Michael Jackson. No other way to say it. Lots of high-pitched screams and moans, grabbing his pecker ever so often. Dude is definitely way messed up."

"You know him?" Quinn asked, turning off the Square and now heading west toward Choctaw Lake.

"Never seen him before in my life," Reggie said. "I don't think he's from Tibbehah. Maybe he scooted his ass down from Lee County. Hard to know, on account of the limited communication."

"Just what's he saying?"

"Don't really know," he said "Lots of *hee-hee*s and *'Sha, mon'* and all that shit. He told me he was the light of this world when I brought out the cuffs. That's when he started moving on me, real aggressive-like. Tried to bite my damn ankle. May have to tase him."

"I don't like to tase," Quinn said. "Unless we don't have a choice. Especially on the King of Pop."

"Kenny said to talk to you before we did anything," Reggie said. "Man's not armed and not dangerous other than stopping traffic. Kenny said it's pretty much the same when we get a cow loose and got to call animal control. You think that's maybe something we could do, get animal control to slip that wire over this man's head and give him a tranquilizer?"

"Y'all just hold up," Quinn said. "Almost there."

"Good," he said. "Might need a few more hands, too."

"You don't think me, you, and Kenny can control one man?"

"He ain't feelin' much pain," Reggie said. "You'll see when you get here. Dude is flying on those eleven different herbs and spices."

"Roger that," Quinn said, hitting the siren and the lights on Jericho Road. Since the spring, they'd been getting more and more wild calls about folks being strung out on drugs. When Quinn had first come home it'd been bathtub meth, then bootleg prescription pills, and lately folks had been dipping into some mind-corrosive crap called bath salts. You could inject it, smoke it, snort it, or all three. The bitch of it all was that you could buy the shit at your local convenience store in the pharmacy aisle. The stores knew what they were selling and didn't give a good goddamn, except for

Luther Varner at the Quick Mart, who ran folks out of his store just for asking about it.

Quinn got about six miles out of town when he saw the gathering of patrol cars on the side of the highway. He pulled in behind Kenny's vehicle, which he'd parked sideways with the lights flashing, and walked toward Reggie Caruthers. Dave Cullison had taken a position on the far side of the road to direct traffic around the man, who, true to Reggie's word, was indeed dragging his ass down the road and making sounds not unlike Michael Jackson, with a few more grunts and growls in there.

"How we doin'?" Quinn said.

"Man tried to bite my damn leg again," Reggie said.

"You up on your rabies?"

"Not funny, Sheriff."

Kenny ran up, red-faced and sweating, as Kenny still hadn't dropped the thirty extra pounds he'd been carrying for several years. He was a chubby, plain-faced country boy with a brownish crew cut and a constant dip in his lower lip. Reggie Caruthers was a few years younger, in his late twenties, lean and baby-faced, with light brown skin. Like Quinn, his ticket out of Jericho had been the U.S. Army, and, exactly like Quinn, family had brought him back home. Both deputies were hard workers and loyal to a fault. He needed a few more like them, with Lillie, his former assistant sheriff and trusted friend, now up in Memphis working with the federal marshals.

"Damn," Kenny said, watching the man scooting closer and closer down the highway's white line. "That boy's higher than a giraffe's pussy . . . He really bite you, Reggie?"

"Y'all watch your ass," Quinn said. "But try not to hurt him. It's gonna take six months to get a psych eval at the county jail."

The man was shirtless, shorts hanging down loose past his boxers. It was easy to tell he wasn't armed, but you never took any chances. Quinn went for the guy, again telling him to lie down, but instead of complying, the man pushed himself into a crouch, chewing on his bloody lower lip, and tried to make a sprint for it. Quinn grabbed him by one arm and the crazed man turned for him, knocking him hard in the right eye, taking off. Kenny ran after him, tackling the man to the ground, while Reggie stood over him with a taser, letting him know either he calmed down or he was gonna light his ass up like a Christmas tree.

Quinn felt the blood trickle down into his eye. He was more embarrassed than pissed, as he pressed the flat of his hand to the wound and made his way to where his deputies surrounded the man. The guy looked like a cornered dog, hissing and chomping his teeth, making a few more high-pitched MJ sounds, playing some kind of wild movie in his head that only he could see. Up in Memphis, they'd send an emergency response team to help out. In Tibbehah, it was up to him and his two deputies to clear the damn road and lock this man up for his own good and the good of the community.

"Hold it," Reggie said, aiming his taser. "Don't you move. Don't you dare move."

The man turned and spit at Reggie and then broke into another sprint. Reggie fired his taser and hit the man square in the back, the click, click, zap sound sending fifty thousand volts into him.

The man kept on walking, impervious to the zaps. Quinn wiped the blood from his brow and shook his head.

"Dang," someone said from the roadside. "That man don't give two fucks."

Reggie followed the man, wires hanging from his bare back,

Reggie trailing the way you take a dog for a walk. Reggie kept on telling him to comply as Kenny ran up after him with his hand on his holstered pistol. He looked back to Quinn, obviously a little thrown that Quinn could actually bleed, and tried to grab the walking man by the arm. The man turned and pushed Kenny to the ground, Reggie jumping onto the man's back and wrapping his forearm around his throat. The man just kept on walking, whistling, and hooting, the few people on the side of the road laughing and taking video. Quinn knew none of this was gonna look good out on social media.

You don't shoot a head case. You don't beat one up. But the man sure didn't mind being tasered, and whatever shit he was on seemed to give him lots of strength and no pain. The three of them could take him down with some rough moves, but Quinn didn't want that. This guy wasn't resisting arrest. He was just flying high. They just needed a way to hold his crazy ass down long enough to cuff him.

Down the road, he saw Dave Cullison hold up his hand to stop a big red Dodge Ram. Dave was leaning into the window to explain something to the driver. Quinn saw the truck door swing open and big Chucky Crenshaw crawl out. Quinn hadn't seen Chucky's new truck, but the vehicle had to have a hell of a suspension to handle the added weight. At best guesstimate, Chucky was pushing the hell out of four hundred pounds, making Kenny look downright svelte. His big belly stretched his MISSISSIPPI STATE T-shirt for all it was worth, the trucker hat on his head looking like it belonged to a doll.

"What you got there, Sheriff?" Chucky said, yelling over Dave's shoulder. "Y'all need some help?"

Quinn looked at his two deputies trying to subdue the crazed man. He was still walking, moving ahead, with Kenny following, zapping him a second time. While Reggie yelled for him to get down and stay down, Quinn turned back to the big man standing by his idling red truck.

"You know what, Chucky?" Quinn said. "You just might be the right man for the job."

3

MAGGIE POWERS CHECKED OUT THE CUT ABOVE QUINN'S right eye with a flashlight. She had a soft touch as she moved his face from side to side, her fingers long and narrow in the latex gloves. "Jesus," she said. "You're gonna look like hell in the wedding pictures."

"Aren't you going to ask me what happened?" he said. "Aren't you worried about all the blood on my face and shirt?"

"Nope," she said. "Not a bit. Let's get that wound cleaned and that eye sewn up. You think you can handle the prick of a little needle?"

"I'll try not to cry."

Maggie pressed some gauze to his cut and began to flush it with some saline. He smiled at her as she worked under the harsh hospital lights. It was hard not to smile at Maggie Powers. She had the most wonderful face, pale green eyes, a strong but delicate jaw, and a smallish, imperfect nose that she'd broken playing softball in high school. Her skin was fair, almost milky, but in the summer turned a reddish gold color, with freckles sprinkled across her nose, cheeks, and forehead. She hated those freckles and always tried to cover them up, saying she looked like a goddamn spotted cat. But Quinn loved them. The green eyes, the busted nose, and that mess of freckles hit him just right.

"Why are you giving me that goofy look?" she said. "Did you already take some painkillers before I saw you?"

"No, ma'am."

"Damn you," she said. "Quit smiling and let me work. Are you sure you're not feeling dizzy? Do I need to check you for a concussion?"

"I've had lots of concussions," he said. "This is just a cut. There's three of you, right?"

She pricked him with the needle again to numb the skin and then started to sew up the wound. As she worked, Quinn reached around and placed his arm around her waist. Her scrubs were a black print with little panels from comic books. Wonder Woman, Supergirl, Batgirl. GIRL POWER written in a big white bubble. Quinn's hands moved off her waist and down onto her butt. It was tight and high under her scrubs, and he squeezed it a little.

"I swear to Christ," she said. "I'll poke you right in the eye. Don't you ever stop? This morning in bed and then later in the shower?"

"Do you want me to stop?"

"Hold still," she said. "Don't grab my ass at work and I won't grab yours at the sheriff's office."

"You know I wouldn't mind."

Maggie rolled her eyes but grinned. "Yeah," she said. "You would. What the hell happened?"

"We had this fella under the influence walking down the center of Jericho Road," Quinn said. "He could not, and would not, be subdued. Reggie tased him twice and it only seemed to make him madder and stronger. He was yelling and screaming, making sounds like Michael Jackson."

"Come on," Maggie said. "Michael Jackson?"

"Yep," Quinn said. "He also let us know that he was the Second Coming of Christ and that we all needed to repent. We figured that's why he was crab-walking down to Jericho, scooting his butt down the center line."

"And he hit you?"

"I don't know if he meant to," Quinn said. "It was my own damn fault. I should have been more careful. The son of a bitch was strong. You can't beat up a crazy man. You do your best to restrain him and make sure he doesn't hurt himself or you."

"How'd y'all finally get him down?" Maggie said, tossing away the bloody gauze and the syringe.

Quinn smiled. "You know Chucky Crenshaw?"

"Big Chucky?" Maggie said. "He's kinda hard to miss."

"Well, he rolled up on the scene and offered his assistance," Quinn said.

"So he gave y'all an extra hand?"

"He gave us an extra-big ass," Quinn said. "Reggie and I finally got the man facedown on the roadside. Chucky walked on over and sat on this crazy SOB until we could get him cuffed and transported."

"That's some sharp police work there, Sheriff."

"Yep," Quinn said. "Thank the Lord for Chucky's momma's fine cooking."

Maggie smiled and stepped back, crossing her arms over her smallish chest as she checked out her handiwork. She nodded, which

Quinn took to be a damn good sign. "You know I don't cook," Maggie said.

"I do."

"And I don't care for that 'honor and obey' shit in the vows."

"Reverend White told me she doesn't go for that part, either."

"Most of this town has an issue about how we met," Maggie said. "Lots of talk about my former husband and your wanting him to stay in jail."

"It's tough not having hard feelings for a man who blew up my favorite pickup truck with an RPG," Quinn said. "I loved the Big Green Machine."

"He nearly blew you up."

"And now his ass is in Parchman and his ex-wife is in my bed."

"I hope I'm more than a nice piece of tail."

"You're a nice piece of tail I've known since I was ten years old," Quinn said. "I love you and I love your son. I can't wait for both of you to be part of the Colson family. Although, full disclosure, the Colson family is bat-shit crazy."

"Funny," she said. "I keep hearing that. But I don't see it."

"Stick around."

"We've been together a year now," she said. "I know what I'm getting into."

"Always time to back out," Quinn said.

"You're stuck with me, Ranger."

L. Q. Smith was a shit talker of the first order. Boom hadn't been back at the Sutpen Trucking docks two minutes when Smith came ambling out from the back office with a phony smile on his face, offering a pat on the back for doing another fine job. As with most folks, Smith was a few inches shorter than Boom. He had stooped shoulders, longish brown hair, and a droopy cowboy mustache. His face was pockmarked with acne scars and he had a voice like he'd once gargled with broken glass.

"You're doing real fine, Mr. Kimbrough," he said. "Come on back and let me get you paid."

Boom nodded, holding his logbook in his good hand, heading onto the trucking company docks, not looking back once at the load of electronics he'd picked up in Amarillo and not saying shit about it. Smith knew what he'd been carrying, and if Boom had done wrong, or picked up the wrong load, he'd damn well mention it. But instead, he just headed through the maze of folks working in little cubicles and back into his glass office. He reached into his desk and handed Boom an envelope.

When Boom held on to it and sliced it open with his hook, he found a check that was five hundred dollars more than he expected.

"I hadn't even turned in my receipts yet."

"We know where you been," L. Q. Smith said. "We know the fuel costs on the GPS. One thing that we don't fuck around with is getting our boys paid."

"Appreciate that," Boom said.

They headed back outside to the docks, where five more trucks were being unloaded. Smith pulled out a pack of American Spirits and plugged one in the corner of his mouth. He fired it up with a Bic, cupping his hand around the flame even though there wasn't a speck of wind.

"Jerry Colson told me that we'd get along fine," he said. "Said you're in real tight with his family. And if there's anyone in this world I trust, that'd be Jerry Colson. He's been trucking since CB radios and Billy Beer were cool. That boy used to wear the biggest gosh dang belt buckle ever seen. Indian silver with turquoise and bigger than a dinner plate. He still have it?"

Boom shrugged, placing the check in the front pocket of his old shirt.

"I never for a second doubted you could run that rig," Smith said, flicking a long ash with his middle finger. "Jerry told me about your arm. But also told me about your experience working on engines and running trucks over in Iraq. I thought, if that ole boy can stomach folks shooting at him over there in that sandbox, he sure can handle a chicken run from Picayune to Eupora. Except for the smell. Son of a bitch, chickens smell to high heaven. Did you know those farmers snip off their beaks so they won't fight? Cut down them claws, too. No wonder those chickens are so damn mad."

"Appreciate you giving me a chance, Mr. Smith."

"I don't care what's wrong with you or what color you is," Smith said, letting some smoke out his nose. "All I care is that you can do the gosh dang job. You done good on that run. Go on, get yourself showered and rested up, and I'll have something for you Monday."

Boom nodded, watching the Mexicans in coveralls working fast on that dock, nearly unloading the whole trailer in the time it took to kill a cigarette. Smith noticed Boom watching the load and caught his eye, giving him a knowing wink. And Boom knew then that's how it all went down. You drive twenty-four hours, nearly a thousand miles, with your ass on the line and you get the wink and a little something extra in your stocking. He wasn't about to argue. Boom needed the work.

He shook L. Q. Smith's hand and headed back to the parking lot, where he'd left his old GMC truck. He'd planned to meet Quinn for a catfish fry at the VFW and maybe down a beer or two before getting some sleep. Quinn still worried every time Boom touched alcohol, not sure if he was going to go full-tilt drunk like he'd done when Quinn came home the first time. Back then, it had been a long path of clear liquor and weed. Damn glad none of that had gone on his permanent record or he'd have never found good work outside Jericho.

Boom opened the door of his pickup and tossed his road gear inside. He was thinking about a warm shower and shave when he spotted the electric-blue muscle car cutting across the lot.

Damn if it didn't look just like that galaxy-blue Nova that Ordeen Davis had inherited from his friend Nito Reece. As it slowed, Boom spotted that HERE KITTY, KITTY license tag and saw Ordeen crawl out from the behind the wheel. He'd known Ordeen since that boy was born. Boom's daddy was a deacon at the church where Ordeen's momma was the pastor. Even coached the kid some when he was playing football at Tibbehah High.

Boom called out to Ordeen. The kid looked behind him and then back at Boom as if he might've been calling to someone else. But since no one else was in the lot, Ordeen knew he was caught and he strutted, cocky and cool, over to Boom's truck. Boom slapped Ordeen's hand back and forth and pounded his fist. Kid had a Grizz jersey over a white T-shirt, worn long over his shorts and down to his knees.

"What up?" Boom said. "Thought you still working over at the titty bar."

"Yeah," Ordeen said. "Just had to make a pickup for Miss Hathcock. Some new rubbers machines for the bathrooms. French ticklers, horny goat weed, and all that shit."

Boom nodded. Ordeen not looking him in the eye, not wanting to get into why he won't get his ass straight and get away from Vienna's

Place. There'd been a time when Boom thought that boy would go straight D1. But Ordeen hadn't grown those extra two inches his junior and senior years and never could get faster than a four-eight forty. Two years back, his old friend Nito almost got both their asses thrown in jail. Ordeen broke free and got with Fannie. Nito got his ass killed.

"See you at church tomorrow?" Boom said, sliding it right in there, both of them knowing everything was about Ordeen getting right.

"I'll be at church," Ordeen said. "It bein' Homecoming and all. Momma said it's gonna be a throwback service. She wants folks to dress up like it was a hundred years ago. I don't know about all that mess. I don't think I want to step back a hundred years. Not a good place for a black man."

"It's Tibbehah County," Boom said, grinning. "Not much has changed."

Boom, leaning on the door, watched Ordeen head on up the ramp at Sutpen Trucking to talk to a couple guys working the docks. He hung there for a moment until Ordeen turned back his way and noticed him watching. Boom didn't say a word, just got into his truck and headed on back to Jericho.

He figured he needed just to do his own thing and tend to his own damn business.

Fannie Hathcock tried not to think about the shoot-out at her titty bar too much. Dwelling on the past, talking about old events, wasn't good for business. She'd cleaned up the blood, patched up the bullet holes, and hired some new and better men to watch the door. Since she'd taken over the bar, when it had been known as the Booby Trap, she'd had some nasty-ass bikers keep order. It'd been a fine and decent agreement until a couple U.S. Marines with a headful of snakes busted in the door, started shooting up the place, and ran off with every nickel in her safe, before they got caught.

They pretty much wiped out the entire Jericho chapter of the Born Losers MC. The only son of a bitch left, her buddy Lyle, aka Wrong Way, had shagged ass down into Lafayette, Louisiana, with rumors he'd kept on riding clear over to Yuma, Arizona, before he finally returned to Memphis. They'd shot four of his buddies dead, even shooting her damn DJ in the head. Who the hell shoots a DJ?

Fannie sat at the bar that afternoon, watching the last of the lunch crowd leave Vienna's Place, picking all those free chicken fingers from their rotten teeth. Sometimes she didn't know why she put up with this shit. She fired up a cigarillo with a gold Dunhill lighter. Neon beer signs and stage lights dimly lit the big, cavernous space, where two girls twirled around their brass poles to Taylor Swift's "Ready for It?"

"Miss Fannie?" Ordeen Davis asked. He was a good kid, not more than twenty years old, in his red VIENNA'S PLACE tee, long cornrows shining in the neon light. "I took care of that business in Tupelo, got you set up out back. Is that it?"

She nodded, blowing smoke from the side of her mouth. He'd been a big help since her right-hand man, Mingo, had turned on her and, as a result, fell off the face of this Earth. Ordeen now managed the bar and took care of her personal errands. He helped in the count room and was trusted to make pickups and deliveries. She trusted him, and Fannie didn't trust anyone.

"Good," he said. "Some motherfucker just threw up all over

Damika's titties. She in the locker room, crying, getting her nekkid ass cleaned up."

"What'd you do with the guest?"

"Tossed him out," Ordeen said. "Did I do right?"

"You did," Fannie said. "Does he need some attitude adjustment? 'Cause I'll get out my framing hammer and knock that pervert senseless."

"No, ma'am," he said. "He was real sorry about it. Said he'd hit the buffet at the Rebel and ate a dozen fried pies. Midnight Man's back there with the Purple Power and a garden hose."

Fannie nodded, ashing the cigarillo. The goddamn hospitality business. There was a time when working with gentlemen meant custom suits, Sazeracs, and deluxe suites at the Roosevelt in New Orleans. Now it was fuckin' Chicken Strip Saturday. That's what happens when a girl hits forty, even though she still had the mouthwatering tits and natural red hair, with just the faintest crow's-feet forming around her eyes whenever the Botox needed a refresh.

"I'm going to need you tonight," she said. "How about you go on over to the Rebel and get something to eat? We just put the country-fried steak back on the menu. Johnny Stagg's momma's recipe. Or so he says."

"Stagg wasn't a bad man," Ordeen said. "He treated me fair. Paid me on time."

"He was a crooked and twisted old motherfucker, Ordeen," Fannie said. "You think he would've ever trusted you the way I trust you?"

"No, ma'am."

"Since Mingo ran off, you really stepped up, kid," she said. "Maybe old Johnny Stagg wouldn't be in federal prison right now if he'd trusted you with more than just cleaning toilets. He got sloppy as hell, trusting those shit-for-brains rednecks out in the county to keep his secrets. We keep a tight circle of trust. Me and you. You keep that going and there's no stopping you, kid."

"Yes, ma'am," Ordeen said. "What do you need me to do?"

"We'll talk later in private," she said. "I need to know more about some folks giving me an ass ache."

"Those goddamn Pritchards again?"

Fannie nodded, replacing the cigarillo back in her wide red mouth. "They've busted up our agreement."

"I knew it," Ordeen said, grinning. "I never did trust those motherfuckers."

4

THERE WAS NOTHING IN THE WORLD LIKE FLYING AROUND A dirt track at a hundred miles an hour with only a steering wheel and a prayer between you and the goddamn wall. It was a mud-flying, death-defying, corn-dog-smelling race against the pack and yourself. Tyler Pritchard knew that if you didn't beat yourself, you'd get your ass ate up real quick. Every week was about counting down the hours until you were back on the track, the minutes spent taking apart your car and putting it back together. He and his brother Cody could build a car blind, from the transmission to the tailpipe. Both of them worked on the car and whoever was flat-out crazier that week would drive it. Someday, they hoped they'd get up to Oklahoma and race the Chili Bowl on the sprint track. But right now, they were late-model boys, about to run a twenty-lap on a third-of-a-mile oval track in Columbus, Mississippi, known as the MAG.

Tyler was the taller of the two, bald-headed and brushy-bearded, with the build of a Russian basketball player. Cody was short and thick, with a full head of brown hair, and, truth be known, probably the better racer of the two. It wasn't so much on account of him fitting better in the car as it was mainly 'cause the boy was born without a lick of sense. He was all speed and snatching up that checkered flag. The kind of man who'd be shot out of a cannon with a smile on his face.

Cody kicked back in the long, empty trailer, smoking a little weed to calm his nerves before that first race. He had his fire suit unzipped, and sat bare-chested in a folding aluminum chair with his shades on, listening to some country music. If the rain didn't stop soon, they'd be calling off the whole Possum Town Grand Prix.

Tyler finished up grooving that last tire and slapped it back on the hub, zapping on the lug nuts. He walked to Cody and reached for the weed, took a long hit, and handed it back. The music on the earbuds was turned up so loud he could hear a little bit of Luke Bryan singing "Light It Up."

"Man," Tyler said, ripping a bud from his brother's ear. "Why do you listen to that shit? That ain't country. Sounds like a lot of nigger music to me."

"Why don't you eat my ass," Cody said, snatching back the earbud. "I'm sitting here trying to cool out, go through the fuckin' race in my mind, get everything set, every straightaway and drift, and you got to mess with me."

Since Cody got to drive, Tyler got to party. He'd already seen those two hot things from Lucas Oil hanging out there in their tight tees and Daisy Dukes. One of them gave him the eye when he walked past, the girls digging his big, wild mountain man beard and his sleeve tats. One of his arms was a damn history of dirt track racing from Jack Boggs to B. J. Parker and on to Bud Lunsford and Carl Short. He'd had most of his tats done at the parlor in Jericho and a few down in Gibtown, Florida, where they raced when the weather got cold.

That was it. That was their life. Tyler and Cody Pritchard didn't hunt or fish or give two shits about SEC football. Ever since they could crawl, both boys wanted to go real fast. Tyler once broke his arm in two places going down a big ole hill in his Radio Flyer, hitting a pothole and bucking up about ten feet in the air. When his momma saw his arm hanging all crooked, she began to scream. But, goddamn. It sure was worth it.

"Hey, monkey nuts," Cody said, standing up and stubbing out the joint for later. "How about you run and get me a hot dog before the race starts? Or some boiled peanuts. I'm hungry as shit."

"There's a cheeseburger in the truck, fuck brain," Tyler said. "I picked it up on the ride down while your ass was sleeping. And you call me monkey nuts again and I'll make sure to loosen one of them wheels."

"You do that and I'll gut you in your sleep."

Tyler toyed with his beard for a moment, breaking his hand free with a long middle finger.

"How's the track?" Cody said, hopping out from the long black trailer and looking up into the spitting skies. "Slick?"

"Wetter than an otter's coot."

"You seen him yet?"

"Yeah," Tyler said. "That bastard's here. Drove in about five minutes before he'd get his ass disqualified. Damn. I hope you blow that motherfucker's doors off tonight."

"You know I will," Cody said. "If he rubs my ass once, I swear to

God I'm gonna punch that fucker right in the face. I don't give a shit if he is sixteen years old."

"He's a dirty little shit," Tyler said. "Booger Phillips. What the hell kind of name is that?"

"I heard his folks thought he was some kind of retard," Cody said, looking out across the pit at the dozens of race teams who'd come from all over the state and Deep South. Little tow-behind trailers to big fucking eighteen-wheelers. Low-money and high-dollar—they were all here at the MAG on race night. Lights glowed from all the trailers, and the smell of cigarette smoke and burning oil blew across open lot.

"Did he used to eat his boogers or something?" Tyler said.

"All the damn time," Cody said. "He ate 'em like they was chocolate-covered raisins. I never liked that midget. He's got no business being on a man's track."

"Me and you got started that young."

"Yeah?" Cody said. "Well, me and you were different. We come from a racing family. Everyone still knows Charlie and Uncle Heath. If you come from dirt royalty, like me and you, you start early. If you're just some little sawed-off bastard from Florida, it's best to stick to go-carts until your pecker grows. He hadn't even got his dick hard yet."

Tyler walked over to their truck, a big-ass white Chevy, unhitched from the trailer, and opened the driver's-side door still thinking about being a kid and going to all those races with their stepdaddy.

"Where the hell you goin'?" Cody said.

"Make us some gas money," Tyler said. "Unless you think you're really gonna win?"

"Hell, yeah, I'm gonna win," Cody said. "Did you see the damn

Lucas Oil girls are here? I win and they'll be presenting me with that big-ass check. I'll tell 'em one for me and one for my brother. We'll buy 'em a steak dinner with all the rolls they want over at that Logan's Roadhouse. Get them panties wet talking about flying wild and fast and take their sweet little asses back to a Motel 6."

"Those girls don't give a shit about boys like us."

"Says you, monkey nuts."

"Goddamn right, says me, fuck brain," Tyler said. "Last time you won, you tried to steal that girl's bikini top on your victory lap. Remember? She had on that Confederate flag bikini and kept on calling us the Duke boys? Your dumb ass nearly got us arrested. No, sir. No thank you. Go check on that wet track, see about race times. I'll be back."

"Don't forget my damn boiled peanuts," he said. "And get me a Coke, too."

Tyler drove on out the security gate and behind the grandstands. It was still early, but the fans were already crowding toward the ticket booths, cars and trucks jammed end to end in the wide, grassy acres of parking. He picked up his cell, driving with one hand and texting with the other, letting Levi know where to meet. He drove real slow, his eyes on the rearview searching around for any police. He'd seen one cop up by the ticket booths and another by the entrance, but out in the parking lot it was just speed freaks and good ole boys sipping iced-down beer before they waved that green flag. Off to the west, he could see the skies starting to clear, a beautiful bloodred-and-orange sunset forming through the clouds.

He turned on the wipers just as he got a text back, Tyler searching through the lot for Levi's cherry-red '69 El Camino. That boy had refurbed it himself, slapping on sweet white racing stripes and those SS stickers. That thing had a 454 V-8 under the hood that could move like a scalded cat.

Tyler parked far down the dirt road, Levi standing by the ride drinking a cold one with a tall-ass blonde in a black T-shirt and tiny jean shorts. She wore black boots up to her knees, and the T-shirt had been tied up high around her titties. Tyler parked beside them, keeping the engine and the AC running. He got out of the truck and looked over at the El Camino and the girl. He stroked his long beard, thinking on the night's race, the deal, and now this smoking-hot piece of ass.

"This here's Rhonda," Levi said. He was a beady-eyed, narrow-faced peckerhead with thick eyebrows and a weak chin, sunglasses up on top of his MONSTER ENERGY cap. "She came all the way from Indiana to promote those Hoosier tires. Ain't she something?"

"Are we gonna get high or not, Levi?" she said. "I can't face these toothless motherfuckers with a clear head. They put their damn filthy hands all over me."

"Sounds like you don't care for Mississippi," Tyler said, noticing her shirt read DISTURBED. When she turned to the grandstands, motors growling and gunning, he saw a nice little dreamcatcher tat at the small of her back. "What makes Indiana so damn high-dollar?"

Levi laughed and shoved a fat envelope in Tyler's hand. Tyler didn't flinch, taking the money and sliding it down the front of his Wranglers. A Glock 9mm tucked in the rear of his pants just in case someone tried to interrupt their business. He looked over at the fine-ass girl and then Levi. He tilted his head, looking at the lights above the grandstands, the sunset off to the west, and spit into the dirt. "Maybe we should do this later."

"She's cool," Levi said. "Ain't you, Rhonda?"

"Yeah," the girl said. "I'm fucking ice cream. Now, where's that killer fucking weed you've been talking about all day, Levi? Or was that just your dick hopping out of your shorts while singing me a damn slow jam?"

Tyler pulled at his beard some more and studied on the situation. Levi wasn't the type to fuck him over and this girl didn't look like no cop. If she was a cop, then he'd gladly let her frisk the ever-living shit out of him. She placed a hand to her bare waist and chawed on some gum, not really thrilled with the whole situation. "What's that shit on your arm?"

"Legends of Dirt," Tyler said.

She laughed, nearly spitting out her gum. "Yeah," she said. "That sounds about right for deep down South. You boys are country as hell."

Tyler smiled with pride and walked over to the panel of the truck bed and pushed into the magnetic catch, a hidden panel popping open to a medium-sized lockbox. He pulled out a half-dozen gallon bags of Pritchard family weed and handed them to Levi like a delivery boy from Papa John's. Levi zipped open the baggie, put it his nose to it, and inhaled deep. "Good Lord Almighty."

Levi passed it to Rhonda. She sniffed deep but didn't look impressed at all. "Smells like dog shit to me," she said. "What makes this shit so damn special?"

"Try it," Tyler said. "I ain't had no complaints yet."

Rhonda shrugged, still holding one bag as Levi slid the others under the seats of his El Camino, looking around to see if anyone noticed the little transaction. But there wasn't anyone within a hundred yards paying a damn bit of attention. The sun had gone down now and the track was lit up in that beautiful bright white glow. Tyler could hear the motors starting up, purring and and gunning, burnt rubber and smoke drifting over their way. He knew he needed to get on back before the prelims started.

"You think Cody'll beat that smartass kid Booger Phillips tonight?" Levi asked.

"Hell no," Tyler said. "But he's sure as shit gonna try."

"Why's this say 'Thunder Road' on it?" she said, not listening, just studying the baggie. "What the hell's that mean?"

"It means it's gonna blow your damn tires off," Tyler said. "I done left my card with Levi in case you're wanting more. He knows where to find me."

Levi just stared as Tyler walked around to the driver's side of the truck, knocked her in neutral and hit the gas, glass packs growling. As he drove off, he could tell that wild bitch was interested, Rhonda studying that sweet-ass THUNDER ROAD label and looking in his direction.

Women just couldn't shake them Pritchard boys.

Fannie and Ordeen stood inside the center of the truck wash, out back of the Rebel, Ordeen unloading the cash he'd picked up from Tupelo and handing it over to Midnight Man. Midnight Man would make sure the two big crates of bills went through Vienna's Place. Ordeen did right, but, damn, if Fannie didn't miss those Born Losers. When Wrong Way and the Losers did the money run, you knew sure as shit no one was going to fuck with those boys. Even state troopers were known to squirt in their uniforms just a bit.

"How'd we make this kind of cash?" Ordeen said.

"You really want to know?" Fannie said. "That might make you complicit in this little arrangement."

"I don't care," he said. "I'm up to my damn neck in this shit already."

"Mexico," Fannie said. "We got a nice deal worked out with some *muchachos* down there. Before things got settled, those boys had tried to bust their way into Mississippi and up to Memphis. You ever hear that story of how Craig Houston lost his fucking head? It got to be a real sloppy deal, before the borders were drawn. Now none of 'em get up this way unless they want to pick some sweet potatoes and collard greens."

Ordeen nodded. Midnight Man, who was so black she could barely see him behind the wheel of his truck, backed out of the truck wash and drove off into the night. The big bay door closed behind him. Now it was just Ordeen and Fannie, the concrete floor wet, the hoses still dripping off the walls. Everything echoed and pinged around them. It was as humid as the basement of hell.

"You got it all figured out, Miss Fannie," Ordeen said. "I respect that."

"The thing about those Mexicans is, they know a deal is a fucking deal," she said. "It's all that Latin honor and big-dick shit down there. But the fucking rednecks around here? These rednecks don't give a shit about honor anymore. You make a deal with a man one day and the next he's trying to stick his dick down your throat. You know what I mean?"

"You talking about those Pritchard boys?"

"Just good ole boys meanin' us a lot of harm."

"You say they're back on it?"

"I don't think they ever stopped," Fannie said. "One of them, the tall one with the nasty-ass beard and smart mouth?"

"Tyler."

"Yeah, Tyler," she said. "That son of a bitch told one of my girls that growin' weed was a goddamn family tradition and he just couldn't help himself. I guess his uncle had been some big swinging dick around here a hundred fucking years ago. I don't go in for any of that Hank Williams, Jr., bullshit. In fact, I fucking hate Hank Williams, Jr. I have people in Alabama who know for a goddamn fact that Hank Williams, Jr., didn't come from Hank Williams's loins. I heard that Audrey fucked so many servicemen she should have been given a Congressional Medal of Honor."

"Miss Fannie."

"Yes, sir."

"I don't know none of those people."

Fannie nodded. "Those Pritchards are cutting into the bottom line," she said. "Goddamn them to hell. We had a fucking deal."

"How much they runnin'?"

"I can tell you it ain't just Granddaddy's ole family farm."

"How do you know?"

"Neither one of those useless shit-for-brains work," she said. "They're running a race team on what? They don't have sponsors. They drive a nice Chevy Silverado, got a bunch of four-wheelers, couple boats, and a WaveRunner for when they head to the Coast. Where's all that coming from?"

"Sounds like Memphis to me."

"You're damn right, kid."

"Working with the new crew," he said. "Probably that goddamn Marquis Sledge."

"They're growin' something we can't."

"I've had it," Ordeen said. "And I don't mean no disrespect, Miss Fannie. But, *whoo-wee*, that shit is good."

"How good?"

"Like that ole Meow Mix," Ordeen said. "Your damn pussy ask for it by name."

"Girls like it?"

"Everybody like it," he said. "What we getting from your people in Mexico ain't shit but dirty twigs. You told me to speak free, Miss Fannie. And I'm gonna speak free. What y'all truckin' in is weak-ass. The Pritchards' shit is dank."

"Can you find out how big?"

"Ain't no way to find out without getting on their land," he said. "And there ain't no way gettin' on their land without gettin' your ass kilt."

"You can't get killed if they're not around."

"Can't be too damn sure."

Fannie reached into her purse and handed Ordeen a racing bill announcing the thousand-dollar purse for the winner of the 19th Annual Possum Trot Special, with special guests the All-American Skydiving Team and eight-year-old wonder Miss Lucie-Ann Chisholm singing the National Anthem.

"What's this shit?"

"While the Pritchard boys are away," she said.

"You sure?"

"I need to know what I'm dealing with here," Fannie said. "Every man has a price and I don't want to pay any more than I have to."

"You gonna buy out their asses?" Ordeen said. "Again."

"Sure," Fannie said, rubbing out her cigarillo under a stiletto. "Something like that."

. . .

The VFW Hall, just north of Jericho, was one of the few places Quinn could have a couple drinks and not get the Baptists all over his ass. He sat at a corner table, well away from the Saturday-night catfish-and-hush-puppy buffet, sharing a little Wild Turkey that Luther Varner had brought in. The older man was weathered but hard, with ramrod straight posture and a silver crew cut. He sported a faded skull tattoo on his right arm, the skull's helmet reading USMC. Varner had served in Vietnam, and now, besides running a little convenience store, helped Quinn out on occasion.

Varner refilled both their coffee mugs with a little more barrel-proof Rare Breed. "See if this don't put a little wobble in your gobble."

Quinn took a sip and nodded at the older man. Two paper plates of cleaned catfish bones sat between them. The corner jukebox played Charlie Feathers singing "I've Been Deceived."

"Wish ole Donnie could make your wedding," Varner said. "He thinks the damn world of you, Quinn, and is sorry as hell for all the mistakes he's made."

"You'll be there."

"Wouldn't miss it for nothing," Varner said, raising his mug at Quinn. "You talked to your old man about things?"

"I haven't heard from my father in more than a year," Quinn said. "I heard he'd gone back to that horse farm in Pocahontas. I also heard he went back to L.A. and was living out back of some big-time producer's house."

Varner took a long pull. "Darlene drove down from Nashville

last week," he said. "Brought those grandkids with her. Funny how those things work out. Me and my wife raised her and Donnie just the same, but, I'll tell you what, kids just come out the way God wired them. Got one child who's a solid citizen and another in a federal pen. Lord help me."

"He'll be coming up for parole sometime," Quinn said.

"Try ten years," Varner said, pulling out something from his back pocket. "But he's taken up leatherwork while he's there. Made me a damn fine wallet for Christmas. Just look at the stitching on it. Built in a little hidden compartment in back as some kind of joke. Just like the way he'd smuggled them guns."

Quinn nodded as Boom Kimbrough walked into the cinder-block building, greeting the old white woman who ran the buffet. The old woman placed four large pieces of catfish and countless hush puppies on a plate, patting him on the back as Boom headed their way. Quinn stood up as Boom set down the meal, giving him a welcome hug. Varner winked at Boom and shook the silver hook.

"We got started without you," Varner said. "Can I pour you a bit?"

"Staying off that brown liquor," Boom said. "Might have a beer. Been a long-ass day. I drove all the way back from Texas."

Quinn walked up to the bar and got Boom a bottle of Bud. When he sat back down, he caught Boom telling Varner about the drive to Amarillo and back. "Ate at this place called the Big Texan," Boom said. "Ole-timey restaurant with a big-ass dinosaur out front. They had this steak on the menu that was seventy-eight ounces. I shit you not, Mr. Varner."

"One of them deals that if you eat it, it's free?" Varner asked.

"Yes, sir," Boom said. "But that means you got to eat all that fat and gristle or it was all on you."

"Don't seem worth it," Varner said.

"Damn, Quinn," Boom said, turning toward him. "What the hell happened to your eye?"

"The King of Pop."

"Damn right," he said. "Popped you right in the fucking eye."

Through the window, Quinn could see the mobile road sign out front, a flashing arrow pointing to tonight's BIG BUFFET and a special appearance by TUPELO'S OWN "COUNTRY QUEEN" KAY BAIN. Boom picked up a whole piece of fried catfish and started eating, tail first. Quinn reached for his whiskey, feeling relaxed and happy, glad to be back in company of his good friends. Charlie Feathers was replaced by Johnny Cash singing "One Piece at a Time." The familiar, steady, driving drumbeat reverberating off the cinder-block walls and over the scuffed checkered linoleum floor.

"How's your momma and them?" Boom said, setting down the empty skeleton and picking up a second piece of fish.

"Momma's been getting on me about the wedding," Quinn said. "Wants to invite half the county. Says if I don't find a band quick, she's gonna sing all the Elvis hits on a Walmart karaoke machine. And I'm pretty sure she means it."

"What's your sister think about all this?" Luther asked.

"Caddy's got her hands full out at The River," Quinn said. "She's been taking in some of the migrants, making sure they don't get hassled by Ole Man Skinner and his folks wanting to call ICE on them. She knows her law, I'll tell you that much."

"That's one curious old cocksucker," Mr. Varner said. "I've known Skinner my whole life and can't figure out what makes that man tick. He got out of being drafted on account of sayin' he's got flat feet. Now he's wearing that American flag lapel pin and leading the Veterans Day Parade. I didn't say a word about it, but it didn't set well with me."

"He's bringing back old-time values to Tibbehah County," Quinn said.

Varner looked at Quinn dead-eyed and said, "Right."

"Maybe he can get us old darkies back working in the fields where we belong," Boom said. "I heard he said this county was better before the Civil War, that we had better families and stronger traditions then."

"What I can't figure, amongst many things," Varner said, drawing on the whiskey, "is if he's all for these family values, the Christian way, why the hell doesn't he try and pass some new ordinances? Get rid of the titty bar and all those hot pillow joints. This county is known as the armpit of Mississippi, a trucker's wet dream, and no one seems to see any shame of it. Most of all, the man could put some teeth in them old laws and make your job easier."

"Can't figure it out myself," Quinn said. "I enforce the laws. I don't make 'em."

"That Fannie Hathcock got somethin' on his old ass," Boom said, pointing a hush puppy on a hook right at Quinn. "Some real sick shit."

"I always took Skinner as a horsefucker," Varner said. "What happened is that he put his old dick somewhere it didn't belong and that Hathcock woman's got pictures. Ain't no other reason why she got him by the cojones."

"Some folks think The Rebel and Vienna's are the only things keeping Tibbehah going," Quinn said. "Skinner may change his tune if we can get some more business around here. Maybe when Vardaman's business park finally opens up."

"I still say he's a horsefucker," Varner said, turning up the coffee mug and finishing the whiskey. He reached for the bottle and said, "Reload?"

Quinn nodded and Varner refilled his mug as Boom pushed away the catfish, waving off another helping from the women working the line. He picked up his beer and twirled it in his hands, mouth pursed, something turning over in his mind. Quinn had known Boom so damn long that he could always tell when something was bothering him. He'd get a lost, faraway look in his eyes. All Quinn had to do was watch him from across the table. Boom knew it, looked at him, and just nodded back.

"You all right?" Quinn said.

"Fine and dandy," Boom said, tilting back the beer and taking a long pull. "Just fine and fucking dandy."

5

ORDEEN WAITED UNTIL DARK.

He parked his electric-blue Nova a half mile down the road from the gate to the Pritchard land, where he'd found an old filling station that had long since gone out of business. The place was falling in on itself, nothing but broken windows and toppled concrete blocks, with kudzu and shit climbing all over it. The Pritchards and most folks in Tibbehah knew that HERE KITTY, KITTY ride, and he sure as hell didn't want anyone talking about seeing his ass. Ordeen wanted to get in and get the fuck out, take some cell phone pics of what he saw, and get on back to Vienna's Place. Ain't no way he could turn down a request from Miss Fannie. You do that once and you end up like ole Mingo. No one had seen that boy since last year.

He jogged on down the road, cutting into the piney woods whenever he saw headlights coming fast on him. He'd lay down in a ditch or behind a tree, sweating like a motherfucker, his heart beating fast as hell. *Damn.* He had no reason to be scared of them two peckerwoods except for a few stories he'd heard about that land. He'd heard they ran booby traps, trip wires and shit, all around their property. He heard they had some mean-ass dogs, pits or Rottweilers, roaming free and ready to tear a man's dick clean off. One nigga even told him that he'd been on the land, delivering a truckload of cow shit for those boys' crops, and he saw all kinds of video cameras and high-tech shit around their house. That spread was legendary, and Ordeen figured maybe half that shit was true. Just to make sure, he'd wear his hood up, slide on through that land and see just how much weed they was growing down on the farm.

At the turnoff, he hopped the cattle gate, watching his feet for wires and looking up into those tall pines for cameras, and headed down a curvy dirt road, rocky and potholed, in the moonlight. It was bright as hell, what the old people called a Buck Moon on account of that's when you first spotted new antlers on a deer. He kept moving in the ditch, just in case he heard someone headed his way. Ordeen knew Miss Fannie was right about those boys not missing a race, but what she didn't know is who they might've left behind to watch that land. If they was running an operation as big as she believed, someone would be keeping an eye out, maybe making night rounds with them mean-ass dogs.

Ordeen followed that curving sandy road, walking for about a half mile. Every fifty feet, there were bright yellow signs reading NO TRESPASSING. One hand-painted sign nailed to a tree showed a sloppy ole skull and crossbones with the words IS THERE LIFE AFTER DEATH? KEEP COMING AND YOU'LL FIND OUT! But Ordeen kept on coming. It was warm that night, the day hitting ninety, and he'd about soaked through the thin navy hoodie. He'd want something to hide his face if what they said was true, especially with this damn Buck Moon shining high as hell and silver, keeping everything in a bright white glow. He kept his ears open for dogs. If one came on him, *man*, he'd shoot any animal with his Glock 9 and wouldn't think twice. Ordeen never liked dogs. One bit his ass when he was a kid and he hadn't trusted them since.

He didn't know how far he'd come from the road when he saw the artificial light coming through the pine trees. He walked on, making out the shiny metal roof of a house or a barn. He could hear crickets or a damn owl someplace, and bullfrogs making a racket out in the creek. The Glock heavy in his side pocket as he reached for the hood to cover his face, stepping onto the lonesome dirt road and heading toward all that bright light.

Two telephone poles stood between an old one-story farmhouse and a big metal barn. He listened for animals and didn't hear a thing. He looked for cameras and thought he spotted something on a telephone pole but couldn't be too sure. He turned back to the front porch of the house, the place dark as hell, not a single light on, as he headed toward the barn and a big sliding door. The door was cracked, the chain cut with a lock hanging loose.

Maybe he wasn't the only son of a bitch in Tibbehah who knew them Pritchard boys were gone to the races.

He looked inside and saw a couple trucks, a race car up on a jack, tilted sideways, nothing under the hood. Outside, he'd seen some boats turned upside down on blocks, a couple of them Wave-Runners, a Polaris, and three four-wheelers. Rednecks sure as hell loved their toys. Ordeen squeezed through the sliding door, careful not to make a sound in case whoever had come was still around. The barn was big, metal, and about thirty to forty feet high, with a concrete floor splattered in little grease spots. A big-ass workbench waited down at the end, small lights on over the tools, lots of banners and stickers for car parts. Two long shelves held a bunch of gold trophies and plaques, checkered flags, and what looked to be dozens of pairs of satin panties. A big framed poster said IF YOU AIN'T ON THE GAS, I'LL BE KICKING YOUR ASS.

He turned around and listened. A mangy little dog had come in after him, sniffing the ground, and headed over to a couple big silver bowls by the tools. He made a racket lapping up some water, turning to Ordeen, looking him right in the eye, and burping. Ordeen kept searching but found nothing but engine parts, axles, bald tires, nudie calendars, and a half-dozen shotguns. If someone came in to steal some shit, they sure left some good stuff behind. Looked like the Pritchards got lucky. Maybe he scared off some thief.

Ordeen checked out two refrigerators loaded down with about a hundred cans of Keystone Light, and studied a big wall of old photographs. Pictures of the Pritchards when they were boys, running go-carts, winning races, sitting in the booth of a Waffle House with some skinny white woman who looked to be their momma. The thought struck Ordeen as odd. He never thought of those Pritchard boys having a momma. Come to think of it, he'd heard they'd been on their own since they'd turned sixteen, like a couple of feral animals. He started to wonder if Boom Kimbrough might tell his own momma he'd seen her boy in Tupelo. His momma knew about his work with Miss Fannie and said she could only pray for him. But what else could he do? Ain't nothing else to do around here except stock shelves at the Walmart or flip burgers at the Sonic, neither holding a goddamn bit of interest for him.

Ordeen heard the cool hum of the fluorescent lights over the tools, the inside of the barn dimmer than under the moonlight. He headed over to a bank of switches and cut on a few, a row of them lighting up by the door and an old jukebox over in the corner coming to life, the bright spinning lights and blare of the music just about scaring the shit out of him and the dog. The dog raced out the door, the jukebox wailing out a song about being the only hell his momma ever raised. *Goddamn rednecks.*

Leaving everything as he'd found it, he headed on back outside, and found a place on the other side of the barn, out of the glow of the pole lights and that camera. He stared out into the field and saw acres and acres of corn, coming up higher than his shoulder. The barn was up on a slight hill and he could see deep into the drop, all the stalks colored with the bright silvery light. He'd heard the Pritchard family was known to grow a little weed between those rows, and he spent the next thirty minutes walking down a few dozen rows, not seeing a damn thing but corn. He zigzagged the crops, trying to find some weed growing tall, but only found row after row of Silver Queen in the moonlight. Walking and walking but not finding jack shit.

Ordeen started to cuss himself, running out of breath, when he saw an ass crack of light coming from inside an old barn, rotten and leaning so hard it looked like it just might fall. Maybe his eyes were playing tricks, or maybe that big moon was shining light into the mouth of it. He walked toward that sliver of yellow light, pulling open a busted-ass old door and moving into the soft brown ground, smelling the old hay and manure and rotten leather. The light seemed to be coming from inside a stall. He pushed open a swinging door and saw some old wood feed bins, light shining up from the goddamn floor.

Ordeen looked down in the hole and saw a little ladder and a series of white lights headed deep into a dirt hole.

He took a long breath. "Well, goddamn."

Hondo met Quinn at his truck and trotted behind him as he headed up the steps to his farmhouse and through the front screen door. Inside, he could hear Tammy Wynette singing "I Don't Wanna Play House" as the door slammed behind him, Maggie listening to her little portable record player in the kitchen. She was at the sink, up to her elbows in suds, scrubbing clean a plate and putting it on the rack. "You just missed Caddy," she said. "I tried to get them to stay for supper but she said she had to get on back to town."

"How's Brandon?"

"Asleep," she said. "He didn't want Jason to go but I promised he'd see him tomorrow at your mother's. Are we still having lunch after church?"

"Unless you see a way out of it."

"You don't mean that," Maggie said, drying her hands. "Come here and let me see that eye."

Quinn set his green sheriff's cap on the kitchen table as the needle caught in the next track, "Take Me to Your World," and he walked into the overhead light. Maggie caught his chin and turned his head to the left, checking out her handiwork. "I did a damn fine job, if I say so myself," she said. "How's Michael Jackson doing?"

"Bat-shit crazy," Quinn said. "If it goes like it always does, he'll be with us at the jail for a long while. When I left, he was singing 'Man in the Mirror' and dry-humping a pillow."

"At least he won't be lonely," she said. "You still hungry?"

Quinn shook his head, telling her about grabbing dinner at the VFW, sitting down with old Luther Varner and catching up with Boom. "Mr. Varner was honored to be a groomsman," he said. "He looked like he just might cry."

"Luther Varner?" she said. "The Marine?"

"I know," he said. "First time I ever saw it. I don't like seeing him be sentimental. It means he's getting older. I hate to know that. I figured he was damn-near indestructible."

Maggie walked back to the sink and started to scrub another plate, dish towel thrown over her shoulder. The full moon shining bright through the window as she worked.

"Any word on your daddy?" Maggie said. "Have you decided what you want to do about that situation?"

"No situation," Quinn said. "That's just a lost cause."

"You really don't want him there?"

"Jason Colson does for Jason Colson," he said. "I thought he'd changed, and I was wrong."

"And that's it?"

"I'm not begging him to be a part of something that he doesn't deserve," Quinn said. "Besides, it's an affront to my mother and to Caddy. He can't just pick and choose when to ride back into town in his cherry-red Firebird. Do tricks for his grandkids."

"He does tricks?"

"About the only thing he's good at," Quinn said. "Sometimes I forget you haven't met him."

"What kind of tricks?" Maggie asked, drying a plate and sticking it in the wooden rack. She dumped some silverware into the sink and added a bit more soap to the water.

"All kinds," Quinn said. "He can walk around while being set on fire, drive backwards at sixty miles per hour, and with the proper equipment, jump from a twenty-story building. Things like that. He also taught his horse how to drink beer."

"Hard act to follow."

"You said it."

"You want some pie?"

"What kind of pie did you get?"

"Does it really matter?" Maggie said, walking over to the table. She had on an old ringer T-shirt with faded bell-bottom jeans and bare feet. Her tee said I'M A LITTLE DEVIL. Quinn pressed the side of his face into her chest and pulled her tight. She didn't have on a bra and smelled like fresh laundry. "How about I surprise you?"

Quinn smiled, Maggie opening up the refrigerator, an old tank of an International Harvester he'd found in the barn and had refurbed in Memphis. She cut out a nice slab of chocolate pie with a tall bit of meringue and set it in front of Quinn. She handed him a fork and a cup of coffee and sat down right next to him, resting her head on her hand and staring through him with those translucent green eyes.

"So," she said. "I need to know a little bit more about something."

"Shoot."

"I don't think you've told me everything about you and this Anna Lee Amsden."

Quinn put down his fork. He reached for the coffee and watched Maggie over the rim of the cup watching him.

"What'd you hear?" he said.

"In town?" she said. "Probably more than I wanted."

Ordeen's goddamn mind was blown.

He crawled back out from the tunnel and set his feet on

the old barn's floor, breathing hard. Walking backwards, he closed the stall doors and turned toward the loose-hanging doors. Ordeen had taken plenty of pictures down in the ground and needed to get back to Miss Fannie's as soon as he could. This was a hell of a lot more than either of them expected. A hell of a lot more than Ordeen could even imagine. His mind spun with all the details, flooded his thoughts, as he reached for the hood to cover his face since he'd have to pass back by that camera watching the property.

"Hold it right there, nigger," a man said.

Ordeen stopped, heart jackhammering in his chest. He heard the voice but couldn't see anything deep inside the barn. Off in the far corner, he saw a shape, just a shadow, and smelled the cigarette smoke, the red tip glowing hot.

"Where the hell you'd come from?"

Ordeen didn't answer.

"I seen woodchucks, foxes, and even snakes crawl from out of the earth," the man said. "But this is the first time I ever seen some thieving nigger pop his head out."

"I didn't take nothing."

"Then who the fuck are you?"

Ordeen didn't answer. He had that Glock in his pocket but knew the man was watching his hands, nothing but a cell phone in his right.

"You got permission to be on Pritchard land?" he said. "I'm betting you don't."

"No, sir," Ordeen said, then thinking he should have just kept his mouth shut. This wasn't one of the goddamn Pritchard boys. This was an older man, gravelly-voiced and country-fried. Ordeen could smell his body odor and foul breath from all the way across the barn. He didn't move, looking to the door and then back to the shadow. The shadow moved forward, taking shape and form in the sliver of light shining from the hole. He could only make out half the man's face, but it damn sure wasn't pretty. He was dusky-colored, flat-headed, with mean black eyes and a shaved head. The man didn't wear a shirt and only had on jeans and cowboy boots. He had crude tattoos all over his body like he'd been inked by a six-year-old.

"I don't like thieves," the man said. "Had to live with too fucking many over the years. Can't trust a damn one of them."

"I didn't take nothing."

"Shut your fucking mouth, boy," the man said. "Go on. Git outside."

He saw the man's hand lift, a shotgun sliding up onto his shoulder.

"You're gonna shoot me in the back."

"I wouldn't ever do such a thing."

"I didn't do nothing," he said. "I didn't take nothing."

"I know what you seen," he said. "That ain't something for no prying eyes of some wandering nigger. So you either tell me what you're doing on Pritchard land or look forward to catching some buckshot in your face."

"I came to talk to Tyler," he said. "About business. He wadn't here and I started to look around. I didn't mean nothing. C'mon, man."

"Liar," the man said, spit flying from his mouth. "Black liar. You people can't help but lie. It's in your damn blood like the mark of Cain. You better get going. *Run. Run, nigger.* Let me see if you can't get to that bend in the road before I blast your black ass back to Africa."

"I didn't come for none of this."

"Run, boy."

"You gonna shoot me in the back?"

"One . . ."

"Don't shoot me."

"Two . . ."

"I don't have no business."

"Three."

Ordeen set off running, sprinting faster than he ever did playing for the Tibbehah Wildcats, looking for that bend in the road where he could break into those woods and make it back to the highway. He got past the shop barn and the old house and had damn near made it out when he heard the shotgun blast and caught that hot lead in his back.

He kept on trying to run, stumbling and tripping, falling down onto his knees, hands, and face.

Ordeen was hurt bad.

He was bleeding out, breath coming in ragged gasps from his mouth, with his head cocked back toward the barn. Boots crunched on the gravel, Ordeen watching the man making his way, in no damn hurry, with the shotgun held in his right hand. All he could make out were the man's boots, looking to be rattlesnake skin.

The man was whistling to himself. He was bleeding to death and this goddamn redneck was whistling. He walked up and found Ordeen's cell phone that had fallen in the dust and took a long while clicking through some things.

"Please," Ordeen said.

"I've been through too damn much to take any more fucking chances."

Ordeen closed his eyes.

He heard the snick of the shotgun pump.

"Goddamn you."

"Too late," the man said, pulling the trigger. "I've been damned since I slid outta my momma's coot."

Just what did you hear?" Quinn said.

"Don't you want to eat your pie first?" Maggie said. "Chocolate. Look at the meringue on top."

"Nope," he said. "Not really. And I never kept my relationship with Anna Lee secret."

"I knew it was complicated," she said. "I knew what you had and what it had been before you left for the Army. And that you'd tried to keep it going when she separated from her husband."

Quinn nodded. He drank some coffee. He swallowed, knowing what was coming next. He had not exactly lied to Maggie, but he'd omitted some important details. He looked into her clear green eyes, pretty freckled face, and full mouth now tight, caught in a question.

"I didn't know what made her leave her husband," she said. "I've met a lot of people at the hospital who knew him before he left. They said he was a good guy, a fine man, who kind of became a mess. Made a lot of mistakes before he left town. There was talk of self-medicating."

Quinn took a deep breath. He met Maggie's eyes again and nodded. There was no getting around it, and better to get on with it here, right here in the kitchen, than some time after they were married. She should know it. Should know all of it. All the dirty laundry and all the sordid whispers she'd have to put up with for years on end because of him not being able to leave Anna Lee alone.

"We had an affair."

"How long?"

"About a year," Quinn said. "For the last six months, I think Luke knew it. He never mentioned it to Anna Lee because he figured it was something would pass, like a sickness."

"But it didn't."

"She left before you came to town," Quinn said. "If that's what you're asking. I don't think about her. I don't want her. She was never good for me, and I wasn't something she really wanted, either. Kind of like being on a merry-go-round. It was all pretty much a run-down, dirty game in the end. Lillie couldn't stand the stink of it. Ask Boom. Ask Caddy. Hell, they know all of it."

"I just wish you'd told me."

"Me, too," Quinn said, toying with the handle of his mug. "It's not the kind of thing you bring up when trying to court a woman."

"You knew all about me," Maggie said. "You knew every detail."

"Hard to keep secrets," Quinn said. "Your ex did try and kill me."

"But it was all there, out in the open," she said, fingering her bangs away from her eyes. "If there were people talking about us, they didn't have to whisper."

"It's over."

"Are you sure?"

"This may not make any sense," Quinn said. "But what I had with Anna Lee wasn't love. It was need and probably a lot of lust. But it wasn't love. Maybe it was love before, when we were kids. But when I came home after the Army, it wasn't something I needed in my life. I was wrong. I should have never started that up again. It hurt Luke and made a mess of her family."

"What if she comes back?" Maggie said. "You'll see her again.

She has a lot of family in this county. Will you be able to stay away? Even if she wants you back?"

"I'm with you," he said. "I love you."

"More than Anna Lee?" she said. "I've heard too much. I heard that's why you could never make things work with that Ophelia Bundren."

"That woman once threw a steak knife at my head."

"Because of Anna Lee."

"Because I told her I couldn't make a commitment."

"What's so different about me, Quinn Colson?" she asked. "We've only been together for a year and now I'm about to give you everything I have. You'll be Brandon's daddy for his whole life. This is some serious shit."

"People are just jealous," Quinn said. "Don't let a bunch of wagging tongues and gossips pollute what we have."

"I don't like to be be broadsided," Maggie said. "Makes me nervous."

"Won't happen again," Quinn said.

"Better not," she said, pushing the plate forward and handing him the fork. "Were there a lot of other women?"

"I once dated a hairdresser from Phenix City, Alabama," he said. "Would you like to hear the details?"

"Not really," she said. "How about you just shut up and eat your damn pie."

You did it," Tyler Pritchard said. "You couldn't get them Lucas Oil girls' phone numbers, but, damn, if you didn't edge out that fucker Booger Phillips. I got to be honest, man. I didn't see you doing it, with y'all tradin' paint going into those last four laps. That snot-nose fucker not letting you get inside. Y'all kept tight as hell on those turns, drifting all nice and pretty going into that last lap when you smoked that fucker. I still got the dirt in my teeth from watchin' it all go down."

"That boy done got cocky."

"That's what I was thinking," Tyler said. "Wait until that last lap to go all in. I thought you were done on that stretch for the line. Hitting the gas in that last turn, drifting like hell, and scooting ahead before hitting the wall."

"I never lost control."

"You about flipped the car," Tyler said. "Whole front end is fucked up where you smacked that wall, sparks flying, people all yelling in the stands."

"You do it any different?"

"I'm just saying I didn't see it goin' that way," Tyler said. "You sure surprised me, brother."

"I leaned over to that one girl," Cody said. "The one with big ole titties."

"They both had big ole titties," Tyler said. "That's why they're working for Lucas Oil. You think they'd hire some flat-chested chicks to hand out T-shirts and bumper stickers?"

"I just kind of leaned in and asked that one if she'd like to split a nice rare porterhouse with a pitcher of them prickly pear margaritas."

"And what'd she say?" Tyler said, grinning.

"Not a goddamn word," Cody said. "She just stood there smiling as they took pictures with me and the car. She presented me with that trophy and then told me to go take a hot shower. That I smelled like country-fried funk and weed. That's a damn lie. Before the race, I drowned my dang ding-dong in Axe body spray. I don't know what the hell that woman was talking about."

"When I was passing on that weed to Levi, he had this girl named Rhonda with him," Tyler said. "She was good-looking but had a real smart mouth on her. But I could tell she was interested. Levi seen it, too, and it pissed him off. Hell. I can't make women stop loving me. Once she tries some of our shit, she's gonna be calling me. I guarantee."

"Levi pay up?"

"That shithead paid in full."

"Well, then, I take back everything I said about his sorry ass," Cody said. "Except for him being stupid. He may be one of the dumbest shits I ever met. Last time I was over at his house, he tried to feed a goddamn dog on TV a Cheez-It. We were watching *Beverly Hills Chihuahua* and he couldn't tell no difference."

Tyler slowed down, getting close to their homeplace, hitting the high beams on the county road when he spotted their old silver mailbox. He turned slow into their long driveway, waiting for Cody to get out and open up the cattle gate. His brother fiddled around in the high beams, then turned back toward Tyler's open window.

"You leave that gate open?" Cody asked.

Tyler shook his head.

"Either you forgot or someone stole the damn lock," he said. "Ain't nothing but the chain." Cody hopped back in the passenger side and they drove fast over the gravel, the trailer behind them bucking up and swerving. The tall pines walled the snaking road, as they curved up and around, deep into their land, high beams still on, until they took the big, familiar turn to the house. All the lights were on, the old place looking like a big glowing yellow box. "Get your god-damn gun."

Cody reached back into the gun rack and pulled out the 12-gauge. Tyler had the Glock in his waistband and reached for it even before he stopped the truck. He pulled in right by the shop, trying to make it look like everything was cool as hell to anyone who was waiting on their asses. Cody was already out, shotgun up in his arm, watching the shop. Tyler looked into the house, seeing a figure darken a window and hearing the squeak of the front door open and then thwack shut.

The high beams had shot up onto the landing, where he saw a short, muscled man smoking a cigarette. He had a shaved head and lots of tattoos across his chest and belly.

"Get your ass down here," Tyler said. "Or I'll shoot your nuts from here to Tishomingo."

The man started laughing, keeping that cigarette loose on his lips, walking down the steps, hands held high. Tyler moved forward, Glock on the man, waiting for Cody to swing back behind him. "Damn, boys," the man said, still giggling. "You done grown. Good to see you boys. But that's a hell of a way to welcome home your Uncle Heath from Parchman."

"Fuck me," Tyler said, lowering the Glock. "Nobody told us you was getting out."

"Come on inside the old homeplace," Uncle Heath said. "I got a real funny story about this dead nigger we got out in the field."

6

"SON OF A BITCH," TYLER SAID. "THIS GODDAMN BOY'S heavy."

"Take 'em to the garage," Cody said. "Shit. We can't leave his ass out here for the buzzards."

Tyler had the black man's feet and Cody carried him under the arms. He'd bled out onto the roadside and they'd have that mess cleaned up with some dirt. If he bled any more in the garage, they'd just toss down some kitty litter like they did with the oil and transmission spills.

"If it were me," Uncle Heath said, "I'd tie that bastard down with some blocks and dump him out there in Choctaw Lake. Ain't nobody'll ever find him."

"And let everyone in town see us?" Tyler asked. "You know how many boats are out right now, fishing for crappie? Y'all the ones who wanted to have your goddang pancakes and cigarettes while we figured this out. And just what did Aunt Jemima tell us?"

"I don't know," Uncle Heath said. "I don't recall asking that woman nothing."

"This ain't our damn problem," Tyler said, he and his brother dropping the body on the oil-splattered ground where they'd just been working on their car. He stood back under those buzzing fluorescent lights and shook his head, looking to see if Uncle Heath showed any kind of remorse for the shit he'd caused. "You're the one who done killed him. Ain't nobody asked you to come back to this farm tonight. That's your own doing."

"This is family land," Uncle Heath said, looking down at the dead man and then up at his two nephews, shaking his head like he was the one disappointed. "We all own this dirt. Remember when y'all used to come over to Parchman with your momma and Aunt Missy with your damn toy trucks and little wrestling action figures? You'd always bring me a carton of cigarettes, hug my dang neck, and tell me how much you loved me. Ain't nothing thicker than blood."

"We didn't have a choice," Cody said. "Our momma made us. When she left, we didn't have to go no more."

"Just where is your momma?" Uncle Heath asked.

Tyler looked down at the dead man and then up at Cody. Cody met his stare and shook his head. "Last I heard, she was down in Florida," Cody said, shrugging. "Somewheres around Tampa."

"After our stepdaddy died, she never was worth a shit," Tyler said. "We had a lot of 'uncles' coming and going. She's somewhere, smoking her damn brains out, without anyone in Tibbehah County to tell her she ain't doing right."

"She would've listened to me," Uncle Heath said. "Pritchards take care of Pritchards. The way I see it, it don't really matter who killed this damn nigger. We just have to make sure that ole Johnny Law don't find his black ass. We all need to configure some kind of goddamn disposal operation."

Tyler mashed the heel of his hand to his eyeball, tired as hell, full of whiskey and weed. He'd been dreaming about hitting his bed the whole drive up Highway 45. Now he was talking about hiding a dead body before the sun came up. He stepped closer to the body, squatted down, and turned the man's head. He hadn't recognized him in the dark. But in the fluorescent light of the garage, he knew exactly who Uncle Heath had shot dead.

"Shit," Tyler said. "Goddamn, son of a bitch. That's Ordeen Davis."

"Holy shit," Cody said. "He was in my history class. Thought he was pretty durn smart, too. Knew all kinds of shit about the Civil War. Said Nathan Bedford Forrest was a fucking racist just 'cause he started the Klan."

"Damn good football player, too," Tyler said. "We used to get high and watch him play linebacker for the Wildcats. Tough as nails. I always figured he'd turn pro."

"I asked if y'all knew him," Uncle Heath said. "Not have some kind of memorial service. I don't give a good goddamn if we got Denzel Washington down there. We got to get rid of this mess."

"Did you really have to kill him?" Tyler said. "Couldn't you just have tied him up or something till we got home? *Ordeen Davis.* Holy hell. Maybe he just came over to see us. Get some weed."

"No, sir," Uncle Heath said, reaching into his skintight jeans for a cell phone. "Not a damn chance. Take a look at all this damn shit, all these fucking pictures, and tell me that boy wasn't all over your ass. I got to admit, I didn't see just what all you boys accomplished while I was incarcerated. I'm damn impressed. Y'all did some things down in that hidey-hole, in all those Conex containers, with all that new technology, that's just impressive as hell. Looks like fucking Epcot Center down in the earth."

Tyler didn't like Uncle Heath knowing their business and exchanged another quick look with Cody. Cody shuffled around the garage, their old dog wandering in, sniffing at Ordeen's blood. Damn if everything they'd worked for and built up was about to get split into a third piece of the pie. This land, the house, the barns, and most of what they owned legally belonged with their Uncle Heath. How come no one had told them? Why didn't Momma warn them about that little fireplug bastard getting loose?

"I can't believe that Ordeen Davis, superstar, was spying on us," Tyler said.

"Well, we know who he's working for," Cody said. "That shit says it all."

"Goddamn Fannie Hathcock."

"What the fuck is a Fannie Hath-cock?" Uncle Heath said, scratching his bare stomach decorated with prison tattoos. "Sounds like a rooster that will suck your peter."

"She's the bitch who runs the show," Cody said.

"What show y'all talking about?" Uncle Heath asked.

"North Mississippi," Tyler said. "All of it."

"A woman?" Uncle Heath said. "Holy Christ. What the hell the world's coming to?"

"We got an old truck toolbox," Cody said. "I think we could get him in there if we cut off his arms and legs. We lock that up tight and drop him downriver on the Big Black."

"Cut off his arms and legs?" Tyler said, looking his brother over like he'd just met him. "Jesus Christ. What are y'all talking about?"

"Smart," Uncle Heath said, standing back, rubbing his chin as if judging a contest. "That's a right smart idea, Cody. Can we lock that box up tight?"

"Oh yes, sir," Cody said.

Uncle Heath grinned and walked over to the workbench, where they'd plugged in their heated tire groover. He flicked it on, its sharp blade buzzing high in his hands. "Hot damn," he said. "This oughtta do the trick. Cut through flesh and bone like a hot knife through a stick of butter."

Tyler felt those pancakes rise up in his throat and he walked from the garage into some fresh air. He lit a cigarette and watched the first light peek out over the cornfields, thinking of what his momma always said about their Uncle Heath. *"Don't judge him, boys,"* she'd said. *"He was born a real prick."*

Fannie had been up all goddamn night.

She must've called Ordeen fifteen times since three a.m., staying on through the last shift of the girls, closing up Vienna's herself and sitting at the bar drinking until she could get hold of Lyle up in Memphis. Fannie hated like hell to call on Lyle, the two parting on some real rough-ass terms, Fannie telling Lyle he wasn't nothing but a worthless turd and that he and the remaining members of the Born Losers Motorcycle Club better keep the hell out of Tibbehah County or she'd nail his nuts to the wall. But it was either send in the damn clowns or call up her people on the Coast, and the last thing she needed was the old boys' club sensing she was weak.

"Can't say I'm sorry to hear from you, Fannie," Lyle said, putting his dirty biker boots up on her velvet sofa. "Me and the boys got us a new clubhouse in Memphis. Been partying like hell, recruiting new members. Drinking all day, fucking all night. You should come on up sometime. Born Losers are back and better than ever."

"Ordeen is gone."

"What do you mean 'gone'?"

"He's missing," she said. The houselights dim, a smoky haze in the dull glow of the neon over the bar. "He was supposed to be back here late last night. Won't answer his cell phone. I even called his momma to check on him and she hasn't heard a word."

"Does he always answer?"

"Always," she said.

"OK," Lyle said, firing up a cigarette and putting his boots back on the floor. He waved away the smoke and rested his elbows on his thighs. He had on leather pants and a sleeveless black T-shirt. Since she'd seen him last, he'd grown a thick black beard, with his long, greasy black hair pulled into a ponytail. "What the fuck can I do? Put out an AMBER Alert for his black ass?"

"I want you to ride over to the Pritchards' place."

"You think he's with them?"

"He was headed over there last night," she said. "Those little bastards broke our deal."

"Was Ordeen supposed to scare them?"

"Ordeen?" she said. "There's nothing scary about Ordeen. He was going to just check on things for me, see how deep those boys have gotten back in business."

"Never trusted those little bastards," Lyle said, spewing smoke from his nose. "But, damn. They sure do grow some fine-ass weed."

"Good for them," she said. "But they're now making friends up in

Memphis. We agreed for them to keep up their little nickel-and-dime-bag chickenshit business. You know, for you real connoisseurs. But working with the folks up there? That was hands-off."

"I don't see it," Lyle said, stubbing out a cigarette, reaching for the shot of Jack Daniel's Fannie had poured for him. "Those two country-fried fuckups working up in Black Town? They'd get killed in two seconds. You know they got a brand of weed called Rebel Yell? What kind of black man would smoke that shit?"

"I think they got him."

"The Pritchards?" he said. "For doin' what?"

"Sniffing around," Fannie said. "I shouldn't have sent him. Goddamn it. I should have called you boys right off."

Lyle smiled as big as humanly possible, lighting up a new smoke and settling back into the purple sofa, hands outstretched, looking as if he'd just regained his royal throne. "Shoot," he said. "Is this your way of offering the Born Losers MC and yours truly an apology? Because if it is, I am touched at the heartfelt gesture."

"No," she said. "It's not. It's a way of saying I fucked up. Soon as I knew those boys crossed me, I should've found a way to light their asses up."

"Fucking, fighting, drinking," Lyle said. "Our boys have a particular set of skills."

"Don't burn down the barn yet," Fannie said. "I don't need any shit from Preacher Skinner and the goddamn Moral Majority. I'm lucky to keep this place going by agreeing to let my girls cover up their coots."

"Either the coots or the liquor license," Lyle said. "We all got to make compromises. Even you, Fannie Hathcock."

"How about you wipe that stupid-ass grin off your face and

round up some of your cretins," she said. "I want to know what happened to my Ordeen and I want him back here today."

Lyle kept on grinning, lifting his right arm off the couch and taking a puff. He nodded along, in deep thought. "And would you think less of me if I asked what's in it for the Losers?"

"Baby," Fannie said. "It's impossible to think any less of you. But if you want to get on down to the cold hard facts of life, how about we pick up where our old agreement left off?"

"Free pussy and lap dances," he said. "With free use of the Golden Cherry Motel when we're sleeping off the fun?"

"To keep the peace."

"Unlawful order," Lyle said, blowing more smoke out his nose. "Our goddamn specialty."

Just when did we get a Chinese buffet?" Uncle Heath asked, riding shotgun in the truck with Tyler at the wheel, Cody sitting in the backseat, the body of Ordeen Davis stuffed in the toolbox in the bed. "Tanning salon, pizza joint, and, shit, even the old movie theater is open again. What the hell is a goddamn Transformer? I don't think I'd believe this was Jericho, Mississippi, if y'all boys didn't tell me."

"Even got a new Walmart out by the highway," Tyler said, rounding the Square, eyes lifting up into the rearview as he drove nice and slow around the gazebo. "It ain't no supersized one—it's what they call a Walmart Market—but it sure as hell beats driving to Tupelo every time you need ammo and Ol' Roy. Got some jobs coming this fall out at the business park."

"That your way of telling me to look for a job?" Uncle Heath said, laughing it up, still walking around in blue jeans, rattlesnake boots, and no damn shirt. "Hell. Figure I just held my own, looking after our land."

Tyler didn't say a thing, heading north on the road up to Blackjack, wanting to ask just how long Uncle Heath planned to stay in town. But he seemed to be having the time of his life, eating a second breakfast, watching some kind of titty movie on Cinemax, and wandering around their garage, talking race cars and the latest standings in the Mid-South.

"I didn't expect no balloons and flowers when I got out," Uncle Heath said. "But would've been nice to get picked up by my kin. Didn't your momma tell you I was about to get released?"

"We done told you, we hadn't heard from that woman in two years," Cody said.

Tyler kept driving, Uncle Heath craning his head out the window, checking out the yellow and red neon of the Sonic, a new AutoZone, the old VFW, and the Jericho Farm & Ranch. "Right there," Uncle Heath said. "That's where that son of a bitch Hamp Beckett and his two-bit Barney Fife waited for me. They tailed me the whole way back to our land, cutting the chain on the gate and leading a mess of folks from the DEA right to my crop. Which I'd planted just as clever as hell."

"Not clever enough," Tyler said.

"Just where you headed?" Uncle Heath said, lighting up a joint and filling the cab with weed smoke. It was first light, a gray-gold dawn breaking across the flat land of the bottom, stretching clear from the city limits down to where all the blacks lived in Sugar Ditch. "This ain't how you get out to the lake."

"We told you we weren't going to the lake," Cody said, leaning between the seats. "It's fishing season. There's a little slice of land down south where you can get to the Big Black. Daddy Charlie used to take me and Tyler down there to hunt for arrowheads after it rained."

"Your old stepdaddy sure was proud of you both," Uncle Heath said. "He got to be a real big man when y'all ended up on that TV show. What was that called again?"

"*America's Funniest Home Videos*," Tyler said, cutting off the main road and following a sandy gravel road with big oak branches overhead forming a tunnel.

"You know, I seen it at Parchman," he said. "Got permission from the superintendent to let the whole pod watch. We all crowded around some twenty-inch Sony and seen you knock old Charlie in the nuts with that baseball bat just as plain as day. I never heard as much laughing in my life with the boys. I don't know if the television wasn't worth a shit or it really happened, but we all thought your stepdaddy done turned green before he fell on his side."

"He got real sick," Cody said. "But we also won ten thousand dollars and a trip out to California."

"Sure," Tyler said. "Momma and Charlie left us in that hotel out by the airport while they took off to go get high. Me and you slept in that arcade down in the lobby, asking folks for quarters. We weren't six years old."

"Good times," Cody said.

Tyler turned off the main road onto some private land, ignoring all the NO TRESPASSING signs, passing an abandoned trailer covered in kudzu and two trucks up on blocks, rusted and useless. He had the windows down, the radio on low, and he could hear and smell the river from there. That old road, with that busted-ass trailer, brought back a lot of happy memories for him, about a year or so before Charlie got real mean and got himself killed.

"You sure ain't nobody out here?" Uncle Heath said.

"Yeah," Tyler said. "I'm sure."

He stopped the truck and killed the engine, looking out across the tall green grass and the bend in Big Black River, cotton land stretching out beyond its southern border. The sun was barely up and it had already gotten hot as Tyler jumped from the truck and made his way around to the tailgate. That dead son of a bitch was heavy as hell and it had taken him and Uncle Heath both to load that box into the truck. He wished he could drive a little closer to the river, but he could see where the mud had gotten thick. He sure as hell didn't want to get stuck with no dead body.

"Is that water deep?" Uncle Heath asked, coming around the truck and looking at the locked toolbox.

"Deep enough," Tyler said.

"How about that blood in the garage?" Uncle Heath asked.

"Nothing a pressure washer and some bleach can't handle," Tyler said.

"Why you think that nigger was out on our land?"

"You keep on saying 'our land,' Uncle Heath," Cody said, speaking up. "I think me and Tyler have what you call squatter's rights on that property. We done worked long and hard to get what we got."

"You boys each grab a handle and I'll clear a path through all this tall grass," Uncle Heath said, lighting up a cigarette and squinting into the wind. His tanned back was sweaty, with an imprint of the truck seat over his jailhouse tattoos. He smelled all musky and feral, like scat off a wildcat. "We can talk family business over supper. Maybe go out to the Rebel Truck Stop for some of that fine chicken-fried steak. Me and Johnny Stagg used to be thick as damn thieves before he done turned on me."

"Johnny Stagg's in prison," Tyler said, pulling the toolbox toward the tailgate, Cody reaching for the opposite handle. "Fannie Hathcock took over everything he owned."

"Sure would like to know more about that woman," Uncle Heath said.

"Fella in this box might could've told you," Cody said. "If you asked questions first and shot him dead later."

"You reckon that woman's gonna have some truck with us?"

Tyler grabbed the handle and pulled in tandem with his brother, the weight of the box feeling like it just might pull his arm loose from the socket.

7

SKINNER WALKED INTO QUINN'S OFFICE SHORTLY AFTER nine a.m. Monday morning, holding his pearl-gray Stetson in hand, his bald dome shining in the artificial light. Quinn had just started his third cup of coffee, working his way through the overnight reports and jail log. He had two prisoners that needed transport over to Lafayette County and a break-in up in Yellowleaf.

"Mornin' there, Sheriff," Skinner said. "Mind if I take a minute of your time?"

Quinn nodded toward an empty seat. Behind him hung a framed American flag that flew on his last deployment to Afghanistan and on a far wall several rifles and shotguns waited, locked in a wooden rack. His desk was neat and clean, with only a telephone, a computer, and a humidor filled with Undercrowns and Liga Privadas.

"I wanted to see if you're still making the community development meeting tonight," Skinner said. "Lots on our plate, with the expansion of the industrial park, patrols at the construction sites. Some folks are worried about more traffic out there on Jericho Road."

"I said I'd be there," Quinn said.

"Good, good." Skinner grinned, as much as the old reptile could, just a sliver on his purplish lips. He was a big man, taller than Quinn, but stoop-shouldered and potbellied. He wore a little gold cross and an American flag pin on the pocket of his starched white shirt. His old, weathered skin sagged at his neck like a turkey's, as dry and thin as parchment paper. "We already got half occupancy for the industrial park, with those German folks flying in next week," he said. "You know the ones who make those consoles and fancy bucket seats for off-road vehicles?"

"I met 'em when they came through to look at the facilities."

"That's right," Skinner said, twirling his hat in his hand, looking Quinn right in the eye. Quinn looked straight back at him. "You sure did. You talked some facts you knew about some Air Force base."

"Is that it?" Quinn asked.

"You don't like me much," Skinner said. "Do you, Sheriff Colson?"

"It doesn't really matter if I like you or not," Quinn said. "I got business to tend to this morning. If you want to shoot the breeze, I'm down at the Fillin' Station most mornings for breakfast."

Skinner nodded, clearing his throat. Cleotha, the office dispatcher, opened the door, peeked inside, and just as quickly closed it. Quinn leaned back in his chair and crossed his arms over his chest, waiting for Skinner to get to whatever he'd really come to say.

"Your sister," Skinner said, "has some interesting ideas about how the laws of this country work."

"How's that?"

"You do realize she's taken it upon herself to be the Mother Teresa of Tibbehah County?" Skinner said. "There's more Mexes at her little commune than in all of Guadalajara."

"I highly doubt that," Quinn said. "I imagine there are plenty of Mexican folks in Guadalajara. You ever been out of this country?"

"Me and my wife once took one of the Carnival Cruises from Miami," he said. "We went to Key West and over to Cozumel. My wife bought a straw hat and some little ole sombreros for the grandkids."

"And I've seen you over at the El Dorado once or twice on two-for-one taco night."

"That's the thing," Skinner said. "I ain't got a thing against Mexes. As long as they're here all fair and legal, you won't hear a word from me. It's when these people show up in our little Southern town, taking jobs from the workin' man, that's when you're gonna hear me raise a real ruckus."

"Well," Quinn said. "Maybe before you raise your next ruckus, you check the paperwork on the legal workers who stay down at The River. Just how many arrests did ICE get on that last raid?"

Skinner looked at Quinn, dead-eyed, from across his desk, breathing in through his nose, eyes hooded with heavy wrinkled lids. "Hard to catch these folks if they get tipped off."

Quinn had had enough. He stood up slowly, grabbed his coffee cup, and took a long sip. What he wanted to do was toss the mug at the old man's forehead and drag him from the sheriff's office. Instead, he looked over at the sorry old bastard and shook his head. "See you tonight," Quinn said. "We'll discuss the traffic out of the industrial park."

Skinner blinked and swallowed, using the armrests of the chair to push himself back to his feet. He composed himself, slipping the

Stetson back on his head, and offered his hand to Quinn. "We've been blessed with this Tibbehah Miracle," he said. "Thanks to hardworkin' men like Senator Vardaman and some good folks down in Jackson. The last thing we need is a blemish on this county."

"Nice to see Vardaman is using this little postage stamp of a community for his ads," Quinn said. "Guess I'm still waiting to see if that miracle appears."

"Already has," Skinner said. "It's all around us. This town is starting to look like it did when I was a boy. Been a long time since I could walk out on the Square with my buttons about to burst."

"Glad to hear it," Quinn said. "Now, I got some shit I need to clean up in the county."

Quinn walked over to his door and held it wide open. Skinner wished him a good day on his way out of the office.

Boom didn't have a lick of trouble with the next run. He checked the load this time in Tupelo and on the way back from Atlanta, nothing but catfish on the way over and truck parts on the way back. *Smooth and easy.* Dropped off the trailer and picked up a new one, helped with the packing and didn't stop off until he got to I-22 in Birmingham at a Flying J truck stop with a Denny's inside. He got that All-American Slam—with three eggs and cheddar, two slices of bacon, two sausage links, hash browns, and white toast—and ate while he watched the rain. That rain had been following his ass all the way from Talladega.

"How you doin' out there, young man?" said a voice behind him.

Boom turned to see an old trucker he'd met down in Biloxi. Black-skinned and gray-headed, the man took a seat at the table near him. He had on denim coveralls, work boots, and a navy ski cap. The waitress came up with a fresh cup of coffee, calling him Sugar Bear. Boom couldn't recall his real name.

"Making it," Boom said.

"Met you on your first run?" Sugar Bear said. "Somewhere down on the Coast."

"Yes, sir."

"Takes time," Sugar Bear said. "Ain't nothing good comes quick and easy. Trucking ain't no job. It's a way of life."

Boom scribbled some more figures into the logbook. The man turned away, drinking his coffee, staring out at the pumps, the rain, and the road that led back to Tupelo or I-65 up to Nashville, Louisville, all the way to Indianapolis and beyond.

"Where you headed?" Boom asked.

"Home," Sugar Bear said. "Mobile. Take a few days off. Go deep-sea fishing, maybe get me a haircut. How about you?"

"Tupelo," Boom said. "Don't know where to next. But I'll get some sleep after I drop my load and wait until I get a new schedule."

"It's hard working for someone else," he said. "I did that shit a good long while. It took time before I got to be an independent contractor. That's where the money is at. You just keep on keepin' on."

"Must be nice to have your own truck," Boom said, slicing into the eggs, yellow busting, spilling out on the plate into the bacon and sausage. "Whoever had this truck I'm driving didn't have respect for it or himself. Smells like cigarettes and body funk. Man must've hung twenty air fresheners in the cab that didn't do shit. Even left me a big old jug of piss next to the seat."

"How'd you know it was piss?"

"Jug said 'Green Tea' on it," Boom said. "Didn't look like any tea I'd seen. Got that truck cleaned out before I hit the road."

"Cleanliness being next to that godliness," Sugar Bear said. "And I am a praying man."

"Ain't nothing godly about that smell of that cab," he said. "AC busted and I'm riding with the windows down all the way to the ATL and back."

"Just who you driving for?" Sugar Bear said, slipping on a pair of half-glasses and checking out the laminated menu, all those photos of eggs, pancakes, and breakfast skillets.

"Outfit out of Tupelo," Boom said. "Called Sutpen."

Sugar Bear didn't react, didn't answer, just kept on reading, acting like he was making a decision, before taking off the glasses and placing them back in his coverall pocket. He wrapped his hands around the coffee mug and took a long sip, looking out at the pumps. "How long you been driving for them?"

"Since March."

"Mmm-hmm."

"You know 'em?" Boom said.

"Drove for them a few times," Sugar Bear said. "Damn sure won't again."

"Why not?"

The waitress walked back up to the man's table, Sugar Bear ordering some steak and eggs, wanting that steak well done and the eggs runny. He kept on drinking coffee, not answering Boom's question, and Boom wondered if the old man had forgotten. Boom didn't say anything, finishing his breakfast and asking for a cup of coffee to go. Out on the highway, the cars and trucks had their headlights on, windshield wipers working against the rain. Boom stood, laid down the cash on the check, and slipped back on his flannel shirt.

"Those Sutpen folks ain't no joke," Sugar Bear said, looking up at Boom, raising his eyebrows.

"How's that?"

"You'll know it when you see it," Sugar Bear said. "They like a godddamn water moccasin about to strike. Watch your ass, young man."

How much shit are you getting from Momma?" Caddy Colson asked, leaning against the bed of her battered GMC truck outside the Jericho Farm & Ranch. Quinn and Hondo had just stopped off to buy a sack of dog food and ran into her on the way out.

"She worked herself up pretty good," Quinn said. "Wants everything perfect, obsesses on every detail. I told her Maggie and I want a simple service. Just family and close friends. We don't need to invite the whole damn town."

"Did you expect any different?" Caddy said, grinning, enjoying the screws being put to her brother this time. "Maybe y'all should have just run off to Biloxi and got married down there. Y'all going on a honeymoon? Right?"

"Gulf Shores for a few days," he said. "Put some chairs down on the beach and drink cold beer all day. Hadn't worked out all the details. It'll depend on what happens around here. You can never predict the shit storm of the week."

"I believe it, seeing those stitches on your eye," she said. "Momma said the man thought he was Prince."

"Michael Jackson," Quinn said.

Hondo jumped up into Caddy's truck bed, letting Caddy scratch his ears, the truck loaded down with fertilizer, chicken feed, galvanized tubs, and a flat of pepper plants. Caddy was a slender girl, lighter and shorter than Quinn, with hair bleached blond from the summer sun and cut nearly as short as her brother's. She had on a man's undershirt, dirt across her arms and down the front of her jeans, which had been tucked into a pair of mud boots.

"Tibbehah County will be OK for a few days," she said, squinting into the sun. "And Jason and I'd be glad to take care of Hondo for you."

"He'd appreciate that."

"And you're still welcome to have a reception out at The River," Caddy said, talking about the property she had south of town where she operated a shelter and interfaith church. They grew food, helped battered women, and looked out for neglected kids. Some folks in town called it a damn hippie commune.

Quinn smiled and thanked her, calling for Hondo to get out of his sister's truck and back into his official vehicle, a gray F-150 with a light bar above the cab. He held open the door for Hondo, who hopped inside. "You having any more trouble with those boys from ICE?"

"Not since you explained things to them," she said. "But they'll be back. They figured coming to this county is like shooting fish in a barrel. Only, we got our shit together. Even though I had all the documentation they needed, they jammed up me and The River. Scared the shit out of our families. Where the hell is this coming from?"

"One guess."

"Ole Man Skinner."

"Yep," Quinn said. "I tell ICE folks one thing and Skinner's on the phone the next minute, calling Jericho a rogue sanctuary city. He claims the cartels have infiltrated the sweet potato pickers and are planning a drug war in our streets."

"I'll let the Gonzales family know," Caddy said. "I had to explain to them that they have rights same as folks born in this country. They came here to work on a visa and are still getting shit from some people in town and that bastard Skinner."

"Before the supervisor meeting last week, Skinner prayed for the county, saying we'd lost our moral ways," he said. "He says it's his America, too, and he wanted us to start protecting what's rightly ours."

"That for the black and brown folks, too?"

"Skinner believes in the 1950s ideal," Quinn said. "When black folks were happy being separate and not equal."

"How can a man have so much hate and ill will in his heart and still call himself a Christian?"

"Because he's not a Christian," Quinn said. "He's a liar and a hypocrite. He just likes the brand name, like some folks say they drive Chevy trucks or drink Pepsi. He cherry-picks what enforces his views from the Bible and clings to it like a life raft."

Caddy ran a hand through her short hair and shook her head. A maroon truck wheeled into the lot, backing up to the loading dock. The truck had a Mississippi State tag and a few bumper stickers, and the potbellied man who crawled out from behind the wheel had on an MSU golf shirt. Melvin Pierce gave Quinn and Caddy a two-finger salute and hobbled on up the ramp to the store.

"Thank the Lord I don't have to deal with Skinner."

"We all have to deal with him," Quinn said. "I may regret saying this. But sometimes I really miss Johnny Stagg."

"You don't mean that," Caddy said, leaning into her truck bed, chin resting on her forearms. "That's a bold statement."

"At least with Stagg you knew where you stood," Quinn said. "Skinner is ambitious as hell, rolling over on his back and showing his belly for his boys down in Jackson. He'd do anything he could to drive his retro agenda. What kind of man shows up to the polls on Election Day riding a horse?"

"I think your partner is ready to ride," Caddy said, laughing.

Quinn turned to see Hondo sitting at the wheel of the truck, resting his paws on the steering wheel. He walked over and gave Caddy a hug, squeezing her tight, and she said, "Diane Tull."

"I just saw her inside," Quinn said. "She sold me two sacks of dog food, a new pair of work pants, and some fishing line."

"You need a wedding band," Caddy said. "And Diane Tull sings just as pretty as Jessi Colter. She also might cut you a break since she sometimes plays with crazy Uncle Van. Ask her and you get Momma off your back for a minute."

Quinn nodded and opened the driver's door to his truck. He liked the idea. Diane Tull was a hell of a singer and had put together a nice little classic country band. Hondo scooted on over to the shotgun seat. Quinn waved at Caddy through the open window.

"Joys of a small town," Caddy said. "One-stop shopping."

8

A FEW DAYS LATER, REVEREND REBECCA WHITE HAD A MESS of questions for Quinn and Maggie at the Calvary United Methodist Church—*Will you tell the truth? Will you commit? Are you willing to submit to each other? Will you give the respect each other needs? Are you ready to get naked?*—the last question getting a laugh from Maggie, before Reverend Rebecca explained that real intimacy includes spiritual, emotional, and interpersonal connection. Afterward, they'd walked in the empty sanctuary and taken a seat on the front pew, staring up at the altar and the stained-glass window of a friendly-looking Jesus. His arms outstretched in welcome, sunlight shooting from his hands. He looked like a good dude, the kind of relaxed guy who'd turn water into wine for a wedding party.

"I do love this old place," Maggie said. "Simple and old-fashioned. No big-screen TVs, no big rock band or praise music. How long have y'all been going to church here?"

"My whole life," Quinn said. "I used to be an acolyte before I nearly set the church on fire when I was ten."

"How'd that happen?" she asked.

"Donnie Varner and I were using a brass candle lighter and the cross like swords," he said. "Wasn't a real good idea."

"Too bad Donnie can't make our wedding."

"Mr. Varner said he'd be sending us a handmade gift from Atlanta," Quinn said. "I'm pretty sure it's going to be a barbecue grill he welded. He's a hell of a welder."

Calvary Methodist was a white clapboard structure with heart pine floors, beaded board walls, and two dozen or so rows of weathered pews. The floors had been swept clean for the Sunday service, with neatly stacked hymnals at the end of every row. After three days straight of rain, the sun had finally shone and brightened the sanctuary, making everything seem airy and clean. The last forty-eight hours had been nothing but traffic accidents and folks stuck in gullies. Quinn looked down at his cell phone, saw a text from Reggie, and slipped the phone back into his pocket.

Whatever it was could wait.

"The pastor kept on referring to Brandon as our son," Maggie said. "I know she was just being sweet. But we can't change his name right off. I think listing him in the announcement as Brandon Colson might not be honest. Or fair."

"I want to adopt him."

"I know you do," Maggie said. "But Rick plans to fight it every step of the way. He's already got an attorney sending me nasty letters, talking about the rights and privileges of the father."

"You never showed me those letters."

"I didn't want to worry you," she said. "I know how you feel about Brandon. We wouldn't be getting married if I thought you felt any different. But this fight with Rick may get ugly. He's afraid he'll be forgotten and that he'll never see his son again."

"Rick killed a lot of folks," Quinn said. "And stole a lot of money. I think he's kind of forfeited his right to Daddy of the Year."

"You really think a guy like Rick is going to wander into prison hanging his head?" she said. "This is all he's got now. He still thinks he's a damn hero for killing some drug dealers and boys in a motorcycle gang. He doesn't see what he did was wrong, only what he calls fighting injustice in America."

"That might explain hitting a drug house," Quinn said. "Not robbing small-town banks."

"That was the PTSD," Maggie said. "Or haven't you read his profile in the *Commercial Appeal*?"

"Yeah, I read it," Quinn said. "And tossed it. Looked like the only thing he was interested in doing was selling his shitty music from inside a prison cell. I also doubt half the shit he says he did in Afghanistan."

Maggie took a deep breath and Quinn wrapped his arm around her shoulder, pulling her in tight. He leaned over and kissed her on the cheek as she stared down at her hands. She'd been biting her nails again, taking that black nail polish down to the quick.

"We can change the announcement," Quinn said. "But I prefer Reverend White calling him our son at the wedding. Most folks know the whole story."

"Can I at least decide the song list and the menu?"

"Wouldn't have it any other way."

"How about tofu and tacos?" she said. "Fresh fruit and vegetables. Skip the sappy love songs and go right for Waylon singing 'Lonesome, On'ry and Mean'?"

"Always good with Waylon," Quinn said. "But you'll have riots on the tofu. Folks expect good food that's bad for you."

"Your momma still thinking about adding a few folks to the guest list?"

"A few?" Quinn said. "How about the whole damn town?"

"Let's discuss over lunch," Maggie said. "I don't have to be back at the hospital until two."

"Just got a text from Reggie," Quinn said. "Some kids fished something out of the Big Black River and he wants me to drive over and take a look."

"What is it?"

"Probably nothing," Quinn said. "Reggie thinks everything he finds is a damn crime scene."

You always take me to the nicest places," Fannie said. "How the hell could I turn down all the goddamn egg rolls I can eat?"

Fannie sat across from Ray in a back booth of a Chinese buffet in Southaven, Mississippi. It was too late for lunch and too early for dinner and, besides the Asian woman at the cash register, they were completely alone. The buffet was in a far corner of a strip mall down from the Super Target and across the street from a Chevy dealership. Nothing but fast food, cheap motels, and endless strip malls along Goodman Road.

"You're looking good, mama."

"Don't I know it."

"Enough to make an old man blush."

Ray helped her into the life more than twenty years back. A

mentor, friend, and sometimes lover. He was a nice man, did Buster White's bidding while Buster did a twenty-year stretch in Angola, running the hot pillow joints, casinos, and other cash businesses from Biloxi to Gulfport and on to Pass Christian. He was good-looking old gent, with tan skin, silver hair and mustache, and a tailored navy linen suit.

"Perfect hair," he said. "Perfect clothes. Damn, if you don't smell like Christmas morning."

He was right. Fannie knew she looked good. She had on a low-cut white silk top with tapered black ankle-length pants and a pair of Yves Saint Laurent strappy heels. Before she'd left the club, she'd dabbed a little Chanel Gardénia perfume right behind her neck and between her breasts, where she'd hung her heart-shaped ruby pendant. "What's on your mind, Ray?" she said. "You didn't come all this way to smell my goodies."

"Our friends down on the Coast have been making a few complaints," Ray said, spreading his hands wide in a *What can we do?* gesture. "I told them they don't understand the complexities of dealing with these fucking animals in north Mississippi and Memphis. But there you are. This wasn't something I wanted to bring up over the phone."

"Why didn't Buster just call me up himself?"

"You know why," Ray said. "Shit, that guy has wiretaps all over him. He said he can't take a dump without wondering if there's a bug in the toilet paper roll. He talks to people, those people talk to people, and then they talk to me. Sorry. But that's just what we've got."

The Asian woman from the cash register walked over and asked in broken English if they wanted sweet or unsweetened tea or Coke or Sprite. They asked for the sweet tea and the woman let them know they only had ten minutes to get the buffet, after that they'd have to order off the menu. Fannie gave her a *Fuck you* smile and the woman moved off quick to fetch their tea.

"Business is down," Ray said. "Memphis seems to be a tough nut."

Fannie nodded, knowing full damn well what he wanted to discuss when he called. She just didn't know why the hell he couldn't have hinted around that his sunburned fatties down on the Coast were pissed. But Ray was old-school and he'd never deliver bad news on the phone. Besides, she knew Ray always liked seeing her in person, bringing back fun memories of when she was twenty-two and he was forty-four, balling and dining down on Grand Isle.

"I can't deal with this new guy," Fannie said. "I've tried. But he just won't fucking listen."

"Can't you charm him?"

"I can charm any fucking man," Fannie said. "But this shit, this crap you're getting from the Mexicans, ain't exactly to his liking."

"This fella has high standards."

"His name is Marquis," Fannie said. "He's a seventy-year-old black dude who's living the fucking *Super Fly* dream, driving a gold-plated Bentley and running whores out of motels down in South Lamar. Last truckload we sent up was left abandoned down on Winchester. We were lucky as hell they didn't trace the trailer back to us. He told me, and this is a direct quote, that he 'wanted weed, not seed, bitch.'"

"He called you bitch?" Ray said, eyes wide.

"He did."

"God help his black ass."

The Asian woman brought over two huge sweet teas, filled with a lot of ice and lemon. She pointed out the artificial sweetener on the table. Fannie gave her another hard, silent look and the woman scooted on back to the register. Outside, across the street, Fannie could see the multicolored flags flapping over rows and rows of pickup trucks. A sign read that it was time for the annual SUMMER SALEBRATION.

"Besides those good ole country folks trying to convert you," Ray said, "everything else running smooth through the Rebel?"

"Smooth as Grandmomma's silk panties."

"You know you can talk to me, Fannie," Ray said. "What goes between us doesn't reverberate down in Biloxi. I know you have some worries about the way they approach a woman running things, but you know I don't have those kind of hang-ups. I can't imagine anyone else I'd trust with business."

"Everything is just great," Fannie said, looking at Ray with heavy eyes. "If it were any better, I'd flash my titties at every trucker who drove past our little exit. No trouble at all. If we can just get a better grade of shit hauled on up the Coast, I'll be doing fine and dandy."

"Damn," Ray said, leaning in. "You always smell so good. You mind telling me what you have all over you?"

"Pussy and cash," Fannie said. "Few men can resist."

It was a lovely little section of river south of town, where the Big Black turned and twisted into the bottomland toward Choctaw County. Quinn knocked his F-150 into four-wheel drive and followed the ruts into the mud off the gravel road, rambling toward the gathering of other vehicles from the sheriff's department. As he walked toward the river's edge, he saw Kenny interviewing a teenage boy. Kenny caught Quinn's eye and pointed down the riverbank to where Reggie Caruthers stood, bolt cutters in his hand, speaking to another teen boy. He waved to Quinn, waiting to bust open a big truck lockbox that someone had dragged up onto the rocky little flats.

"These boys were out hunting for arrowheads," he said. "After all that rain. He says they come down here most Saturdays and saw where it had caught at the edge of those rocks. They pulled it out with their truck winch but couldn't bust it open. They didn't notice the smell until they got down to work."

"I smell it from here."

"And what are you smelling, Sheriff?"

"Same as you," Quinn said. "Glove up and cut it open. I'll video it all on my phone in case we get questions about the surprise we find inside. Cover up your face, too. You got a handkerchief or something? If it smells this bad now, God help us."

Reggie nodded and walked to his truck to get a bandanna. Quinn was left standing there with the teenage kid with an orange bucket hanging loose in his hand. The kid was white, medium height, and bone-skinny, dressed in a *Deadpool* T-shirt that said LADIES DIG CRAZY. The air was thick and still down on the riverbank, the sun high and hot. Quinn reached for the sunglasses in his pocket. "You may want to go on up top," he said to the boy. "Stay with your buddy."

"I found it," the boy said. "I'd like to see what's in it."

"Nope," Quinn said. "No you don't. You think you do. But, trust me, you don't want it on your mind. Go on."

The boy hung his head but nodded and followed the little trail up the rocky banks to where his friend waited with Kenny. Quinn pointed for Kenny to back the boys away from the river and Kenny, although confused for a short second, did as he was told just as Reggie wandered back with the bolt cutters. The cypress and cottonwood blew in the wind along the wide twisting banks of the Big Black. Reggie rolled up his sleeves and strapped on a pair of rubber gloves as Quinn hung back to get the opening up on his phone's camera.

"How's everything going with the wedding?" Reggie said, wiping his brow with his forearm and picking up the cutters.

"Church and band are booked," Quinn said. "Maggie wants to serve tofu and tacos, but I think I can get her to agree to catfish or barbecue."

"That's a tough call," Reggie said.

"They got a place up in Oxford who'll fry the catfish on-site," Quinn said. "Bring barbecue, too. Ever been to Taylor Grocery?"

"No, sir," Reggie said, gritting his teeth and squeezing the bolt cutters tight. "Can't say I have."

"Want some help with that?"

"Ain't budging," Reggie said. "Shit."

Quinn handed him the cell phone, slipped on his own pair of rubber gloves, and tried the cutters. "You know that kid?" Quinn said, motioning up the bank at Kenny.

"His momma is Tonya Boyette," Reggie said. "Works over at the western shop on the Square."

"Sure," Quinn said. "I know Tonya. She sold me a pair of boots for Brandon. Tried to get me into a new pair of Tony Llamas, but I'm kind of partial to these Luccheses. Had 'em a long time. John Wayne and Jimmy Stewart preferred them."

"I got both kids' phone numbers," Reggie said. "Addresses and all that. Both of them live in town."

Quinn squeezed as hard as he could and the bolt cutters snicked the lock apart. He reached into his pocket for a small baggie and carefully removed the lock, knowing any trace of fingerprints would long be gone. But he'd learned from Lillie Virgil, you never take any piece of evidence for granted and you tag and bag every little thing you find. He placed the baggie with the open lock on the riverbank, then turned back to the box and looked to Reggie. "You getting all this?"

"Oh yes, sir."

"You mind if I use that bandanna?"

Reggie reached into his pocket and handed it to Quinn, Kenny appearing at the top of the riverbank again. "Can I let these boys go yet?" he said, yelling down toward where the water flowed south.

"Nope," Quinn said, looking down at the metal box. "And y'all back up from here."

Quinn spit on the ground, covered his face with the blue bandanna in his left hand, and looked up to Reggie. Reggie nodded back and Quinn lifted up the top.

"Oh, damn," Reggie said. "Goddamn, Sheriff."

Quinn stood up and walked back a few steps, the smell of it all about to knock him on his ass. "Call Batesville and get some tech folks down here," he said. "Let's tape off this whole damn bend in the river."

"I know that face," Reggie said. "Damn. You see that? You see who that is?"

"Yes, sir," Quinn said. "He's been headed for this box for a couple years now."

Who said truckers are lonely?" the woman said.

"Not me," Boom said. "Not anymore."

"That bunk's not made for two people," she said. "We had to move around a lot."

"We made it work," Boom said. "You and me. Between the bunk and that chair."

"And the floor of the passenger side."

"There, too," Boom said. "You said you wanted to see how a trucker lives. I'm good to my word."

Boom had met the woman last trip through, waiting tables for her father's Vietnamese restaurant down by the Port of Houston, serving up pho and spring rolls. She was short and slightly chubby, with shiny black hair, a beautiful broad face, and large white smile. He was ten hours and seven hundred miles from home with some mandatory sleep due. So while they loaded the trailer, he decided to call her up. She'd met him where he'd parked his truck at a wide-open crushed oyster shell lot at Boggy Bayou, surrounded by nothing but endless warehouses, oil tanks, and loading docks. When she'd knocked on the door last night, she'd been carrying a cardboard box filled with about everything on the menu, including a pot of hot tea.

"I was surprised you called," the woman said. "You hadn't been by in a while."

"First time back in Houston," he said. "And you said you liked trucks."

"I love trucks." The woman sat under his bunk bed wearing one of his old TIBBEHAH WILDCATS T-shirts. "When I was a kid, I used to watch this movie that played all the time on TBS called *Black Dog*. Patrick Swayze was a trucker who'd lost his license because he'd been in jail. When he got out, his family didn't have any money and they were about to lose their house when he got an offer to run an eighteen-wheeler full of guns and explosives up to New Jersey."

Boom nodded, reaching for a pack of Kools and lighting up. In a big plume of smoke, he asked, "He do it?"

"Yeah," she said. "Swayze didn't have a choice. First, he needed the money. Then this other bad guy kidnaps his wife and daughter. He said he'd chop them up into little pieces if Swayze didn't make the delivery."

"Tough spot," Boom said. "Man's got to do what a man's got to. And all that shit."

He stood up and looked into the minifridge for the rest of that good Vietnamese food. The pot stickers and white rice wouldn't make a bad breakfast with some instant coffee.

"Do you have a wife?" she asked. "I don't care. You can tell me."

"Nah," Boom said, shaking his head. He took a seat beside her, mixing up the rice in the paper container and eating with the fork in his left hand. "I ain't been married. Don't ever want to be married. But my friend Quinn said that, too, and he's getting married in two weeks. Man don't do nothing but fly by the seat of his pants."

"What about family?"

"Sure," Boom said. "I got a family. Lots of family. My folks live in the same house my whole life. My daddy farms and preaches. My momma worked for the post office. I got three brothers and three sisters. All but two live in Tibbehah County. My family hadn't left that little county since slave times."

"That's home?"

"Yes, ma'am."

"Nice place?"

"I wouldn't say 'nice,'" he said. "But it's home. Don't plan on ever leaving, but I sure do like getting out, driving, seeing the country. When I'm home, I like where I'm at. Got a nice place on my family land, smack-dab in the middle of some cotton fields. A little old house where my granddaddy was born. And no neighbors. I don't care to hear my neighbor's toilet flush."

"Sounds good to me," she said. "All that space and quiet."

Boom nodded. It was early morning in the port, the sounds of trucks and barges already clanging to life. Folks getting out, in a hurry to make it to somewhere else. Boom checked the clock on the dashboard. He didn't have long to get that trailer and get on the road.

"I have a boyfriend," the woman said, blurting it out fast.

"That's OK."

"It's not OK," she said. "I shouldn't've come. He's a nice guy. Comes from a nice family that works with my family. If my father knew where I'd been, I think he might shoot me."

"That why you come?" Boom said. "Piss off your boyfriend?"

"He'll never know." The woman reached out with her little hand and touched his bearded chin. "You have such interesting eyes. So dark and sad. I could tell you've seen a lot."

"I'm not sad."

"Lonely?"

"Not now," Boom said, smiling. "Not this morning. I got cold food, hot coffee, and some companionship."

Boom sat next to her as she felt for the mass of scars where his elbow had once been. He turned and reached for his prosthesis on the bed and fitted it back over the old wound.

"When do you leave?"

"Soon."

"I can't see you again," she said.

"I know."

"Like, ever."

Boom nodded. She stood up, stripped out of the T-shirt, and tossed it into his lap. She only had on a pair of little white panties and ankle socks, reaching for her jean shorts and pink tank top she'd had on a few hours before. He didn't move, watching her find her purse, head up into the cab and check her face in a little compact mirror. She kissed him hard on the mouth and, without another word, left the cab.

Boom sat in the bunk for a few moments, taking long breaths, before drinking the rest of his coffee and moving back into the driver's seat. He cranked the ignition, turned on the air hoses, and checked his GPS. He'd start the clock as soon as he hooked up the load. Once that clock started running, you couldn't stop it. He knocked the transmission into first and lurched forward, starting the half-mile trip to the distribution center, feeling light and off-balance without a trailer behind him.

He'd dropped his trailer last night and was told to pick up a new one. This time he'd be hauling cars and trucks back to Tupelo, lots of old classics to be sold at auction. Two Mexican men waited for him outside the trailer, looking out of place on the docks in black rodeo shirts and hats. One of them had on sunglasses and neither of them acted like they understood English when Boom tried to make small talk as he hooked up the fifth wheel and the air and electrical lines.

"Nice-looking rides," Boom said.

Neither one of them smiled. A man in coveralls walked out on the docks, caught sight of the two men, and ducked back in the warehouse.

"You boys don't understand jack shit of what I'm saying."

They just stared at him.

"Probably put some real bad shit in those vehicles," Boom said, grinning. "And got some dumb-ass nigger to run it over two more states."

One of the men smiled back. The man in the sunglasses just stared at Boom.

"Just call me the Black Dog."

"Perro negro?" the grinning man said.

"Goddamn right."

Boom climbed up into the cab and turned over the engine. If he got back over state lines and back to Tupelo, this would be the last goddamn time.

9

"SURE YOU DON'T WANT TO STEP INSIDE, SHERIFF?" FANNIE said, standing with Quinn in the Vienna's Place parking lot, heat waves rising off the busted asphalt. "Folks might start to talk with Matt Dillon and Miss Kitty mingling on the highway. We've got air-conditioning, cold beer, chicken wings, and nekkid women."

"Ordeen Davis work for you?"

"He sure does," Fannie said, tilting her head and smiling as they stood in front of his truck. "What's the matter? Did that boy get himself in some trouble again? I thought all that mess was behind him when you shot Nito Reece. That kid was bad news, had a head full of snakes. You did good, Sheriff. I never doubted what you did for one minute. True red-blooded American male establishing that law and order."

"What exactly does Ordeen do?" Quinn said. "Miss Hathcock."

"Work at Vienna's Place doesn't exactly come with a job title," she said, cheeks growing hollow as she inhaled smoke from a long brown cigarillo. "He works the door, tends bar, takes out the trash, cooks, cleans, busts heads when the moment calls for it."

"And when did you see him last?"

"Damn, Sheriff," she said. "You're coming with a whole truckload of questions." Fannie threw her head back like a 1940s movie star, maybe Rita Hayworth or a pissed-off Maureen O'Hara, and squinted into the midday sun behind Quinn's head. Quinn had been waiting for a long while when she'd stepped out of her white Lexus, the woman seeming surprised to see him and wanting to get out of the heat and harsh light real quick.

"I appreciate all your concern for Ordeen, doll," Fannie said. "But, Jesus Christ, you got to tell me just what that boy has done. I mean, do I need to help him or fire his ass? You know how much I like to stay in the good graces of the elected officials of Tibbehah County. I really do believe that me and that old fossil Skinner could be good friends if he'd just relax a little bit. Have a drink. Have a smoke. Maybe get laid if that ole pecker of his still works."

"How about in the last week," Quinn said. "Did you see Ordeen then?"

"I'm not really sure," she said. "And I'm not a big fan of the way you're asking."

"Ma'am," Quinn said. "I've been waiting for you for nearly three hours. None of your people inside seemed to know where you'd gone or can recall seeing Ordeen in the last few days. I was hoping we could talk here instead of driving you over to the sheriff's office."

Fannie touched the center part of her chest with her long red nails, left arm dangling loose with the cigarillo. She stared at Quinn a long moment. He had his hands on his hips and stared right back.

Fannie Hathcock was a good decade older than him but not unattractive, standing there with her silk top clinging to her skin, red hair pulled up high above her head to expose a long, elegant neck.

"I don't know where that boy's gone," Fannie said. "He ran some errands for me last Saturday. I expected him to help shut down the club at midnight. The kid never showed. But I got to be honest, I'm surprised he stuck around Jericho this long. I think he's got a lot bigger aspirations than pouring out Jäger shots for drunk kids from Ole Miss or kicking some old coot in the ass for trying to titty-fuck one of my girls."

"Did y'all leave on good terms?

"Of course," she said. "He was a good boy. Good to his momma. He called her every night before he got off work to see if she needed anything from the Piggly Wiggly. Did you know she was a preacher?"

"I just left their home," Quinn said. "She's in the care of a local doctor and getting some support from people at her church."

Quinn watched Fannie pull on her little brown cigarillo, exhale some smoke, and widen her big eyes. Perfect hair and makeup. Standing outside, she'd nearly sweated out of her white silk top, the moist material clinging to her chest. She picked at it, popping it off her breasts, the makeup beginning to soften around her face.

"He's dead," Quinn said.

"Christ Almighty," Fannie said, taking in a long breath, putting a hand to her throat. "Why didn't you just start with that part of the story? *Jesus God.* What happened?"

"Hoped you might tell me," Quinn said. "Ordeen's momma said he spent all of his waking hours at Vienna's or over at the Rebel. Said you had him on speed dial, calling him up all hours at night to do all kinds of odd jobs for you."

"That was Ordeen," she said. "A jack-of-all-fucking-trades. Fixing things. Running errands."

Quinn nodded. He had a little spiral notebook out of his pocket now, writing down a few things to put in the report, still planning to pull her in a little later. But he'd wanted to catch her as fast as he could, get her talking nice and conversational before she had an idea about cooking up some more stories. Whatever had happened started right here at Vienna's.

"What time did he get to work on Saturday?"

"I don't know," she said. "About noon. I guess."

"And that was the last time you talked to him?"

"No," she said. "He made a run over to Tupelo for some supplies for the club and picked up a few things for the girls. I saw him when he got back."

"Did he leave with anything that maybe didn't belong to him?"

"If you're thinking that maybe he skipped out with some of my cash, you know I've been blamed for that kind of crap before."

Quinn nodded, knowing she was talking about that girl Milly Jones who'd been lit on fire while still alive. The girl had danced at the club, but her death didn't have a damn thing to do with the Hathcock woman, although Quinn sure had liked her for it. Now she probably thought Quinn and the sheriff's office owed her a pass when another employee was found dead.

"This is a tough business," Fannie said. "I'm sure you understand we don't recruit a lot of Sunday school teachers and the local Jaycees to work here. People end up working for me because they don't exactly have a dynamite résumé. Can they bust heads? Can they shake their little shaved tails? That's all I need to know. I make money. They make money. What they do on their own time is their goddamn problem. If they want to suck it all up their nose or try and run with the big dogs, that's all about them. Don't try and push that shit off on me."

"Was Ordeen trying to run with the big dogs?"

"Goddamn it, Sheriff," she said. "You sure as hell don't stop. Do you know it's only about ninety-eight fucking degrees out here? I've already sweated a bucket talking to you out on this blacktop. Can we at least step inside where I can be treated like a law-abiding white woman?"

"Someone killed Ordeen Davis and shoved his body into a toolbox," he said. "They dropped him into the Big Black River. If it hadn't rained so much last week, I don't think we'd have ever found him."

Fannie's pale face seemed even more drained of color as she flicked her cigarillo onto the parking lot, mouth parting a bit as she took a long breath. "How'd he die?"

"I don't know," Quinn said. "His body's with Ophelia Bundren for the autopsy."

"You don't know?" she said. "Was he shot? Stabbed? Did someone beat the tar out of him?"

Quinn didn't answer or react, just kept staring at Fannie. She flared her nostrils, giving Quinn a hard-as-hell look, a thousand-dollar purse thrown over her shoulder and hands on her wide hips. She wet her lips and swallowed. "Do I need a goddamn lawyer?" she said. "Or are you gonna play fair?"

"OK," Quinn said. "Just tell me what you know about Ordeen."

"He's a nice kid," Fannie said. "I like him. But he was just an employee who did grunt work for me. How much do you know about your garbage man? Do y'all exchange fucking Christmas cards?"

"As a matter of fact, I do," Quinn said. "His name is Timmy Ray

Crawford. Goes to the church my sister runs and takes up the collection plate on Sunday."

She smiled with full red lips, her white teeth perfectly straight. She smelled good, like expensive perfume and nice clothes. No matter what folks said about her, Fannie Hathcock had the look and smell of the inside of a Memphis department store.

"You know, I sure miss Lillie Virgil," Fannie said. "Goddamn. She was just colorful as hell."

"I'd like to see Ordeen's personnel records, pay stubs, any video from the last few days he was alive."

"You ask a lot of a working woman," she said. "You do know tonight is Friday? I got two fraternity parties bussing in from Ole Miss. And a crew of doctors fishing for bass and crappie down on Choctaw Lake. They're expecting a real special night."

"I'm not leaving until I get what I need."

"How about we head inside, Matt Dillon?" Fannie asked. "It's burning up out here. And I promise my girls don't bite."

Quinn nodded and followed her toward the front door. It was red with a glass window up top that had been cut in a diamond shape. "Did I hear correct that you're a soon to be married man?"

"Yes, ma'am."

"Well, congratulations," she said. "You do know we specialize in bachelor parties? My girls would be tickled to give you a ride or two."

After being gone from society, the real fucking world, for twenty-three years, a trip to the local Walmart was like a gift from heaven above. Any goddamn thing you could think of was right in front of Heath Pritchard, there for the taking, with all the cash his nephews Huey and Louie had saved up by improving and building upon the Pritchard empire. He snatched up a couple bags of Oreos, realizing how many different damn kinds they made now: small ones, big ones, mint, hazelnut, red velvet, peanut butter, and even birthday cake.

"When the hell did they start making all these flavors?" Heath said. "These cookies sure would taste good going down, but, man, it would make you shit a fucking rainbow."

"Lots has changed," Cody said, pushing the cart, leaning into it with his forearms, his back hunched. "You need to get used to it."

"You know the strangest thing I've felt since getting out?"

"No, sir," Cody said, that buggy moving slow and easy. "But I'm sure you're gonna tell me."

"No need for you to be a fucking smartass," he said. "I'm the only family you boys got. Without me, no land, no weed, no goddamn money."

His nephew just lolled his big cow eyes over him, Heath just waiting for him to bring up that he'd killed that goddamn nigger and made a mess in their race car garage. But Cody didn't say nothing, just kept rolling on past the peanut butter and candy bars, Rice Krispie Treats premade and all ready for on-the-go snacking.

"Toilet paper," Heath said. "Too damn soft. Feels like I'm rubbing my ass on a cloud. Kind of miss that old hard stuff at Parchman. That paper could take the finish off a Buick."

He stopped to examine a box of Rice Krispie Treats, those fucking elves or fairies a-pickin' and a-grinnin' on the box. Snap, Crackle, and Damn Pop! Maybe they'd had that shit before he got busted, but he'd been so high most of the time he didn't notice. Besides, Tyler and Cody's momma sure could cook. He'd smoke up a mountain of that Pritchard weed, roll up his sleeves, and dig into the cookie sheet of whatever she'd baked up. She was a fine woman. Hard to know she'd smoked her goddamn brains out with that meth. That shit'll kill you.

A fat woman with giant ham-sized jiggly arms stared back at him and put a bucket of ice cream back in the freezer, scooting on away with her fat little child up in the buggy seat. Heath wanted to say, "Go on and git. Ain't no way you need to shove that Moose Tracks down your craw anyway." Not that Heath was down on fat women. He'd done rode a lot of them in his time when pickins were slim.

"How about some of them Tombstone pepperoni pizzas?" Heath asked. "And maybe a gallon or two of peach ice cream? Also could use me some more clothes. I don't want you to take no offense, but I'm getting tired of wearing your drawers. I kind of like to have some of my own underthings. Maybe some new blue jeans and undershirts."

"And a toothbrush," Cody said. "Some deodorant, too."

"That's all right, boy," he said, grinning, loving watching Cody's face when he saw those old yellowed teeth. "I been using yours all week. Used your damn washrag on my ass, too. I'm as clean as a tomcat's peter."

They wandered on over to the men's clothes and Heath found some stiff blue Wranglers, a pack of Fruit of the Loom tighty-whities, and a pair of decent shit-kicking boots. As he tossed the boots into the buggy, he took off his shirt and slipped into a black tank top that showed a bald eagle wearing shades and a U.S. flag for a do-rag that read 'MERICA. Nobody even looked as he ripped the tags off from the neck and just kept on moving.

"Good to be out of the g.d. house," he said. "Tired of drinking beer with Tyler sitting there watching that show with nekkid folks trying to live out in the woods. Why's he watch that shit?"

"It's called *Naked and Afraid*," Cody said. "It's supposed to teach you about survival."

"That's bullshit," he said. "That ain't survival. Your brother is sitting there with a hard-on just waiting for a wild titty to flop out of that fuzz box. I been around men for long as you boys been alive. It's all we think about. Eating and fucking. When I was y'all's age, I would've stuck my pecker in a light socket. Y'all don't have no rules or parameters in your life. No regulations or order, on account of your mom running off. Men got to have something to work with. Y'all sitting up all night long smoking weed, eating ice cream, and playing with those toy cars. It's like y'all gone wild, back to nature. Damn Huck Finn and Tom Sawyer, if them boys stuffed some weed into their corncob pipe."

"Can we go now?" Cody said. "I got my food. You got your supplies."

"I reckon," Heath said, reaching for a good baseball cap. He didn't care what kind. It was black and said LUCKY on it in glitter.

"We don't steal," he said. "Put that in the basket. Me and Tyler earn a living."

"Oh, hell."

"It's in the damn Bible," Cody said. "Plain as fucking day."

Heath tossed the glitter hat into the buggy as they made their way to the checkouts without no cashiers. When Cody used the scanner to check himself out, Heath was just flat-out amazed. The boy laughed at him and his old face colored a bit. He'd had about all the uppity, cocky-ass shit he could stand from those two boys. He knew more about racin', growin', drinkin', and screwin' than those little fuckers could ever imagine. Not sure when it would happen, but when the time was right, he sure needed to teach them boys a lesson, show them who is the king of the family hill. "Y'all check them filters this morning?" he asked.

"Yep."

"How about pruning?" he asked. "Some of those plants looking plenty ragged."

"Tyler took care of it," Cody said. "He's good at getting that growth started. I call him the weed whisperer."

They paid and pushed on through the automatic doors, out of the artificial coolness and into the heat of the Walmart parking lot. Cody had double-parked his Chevy in a far row so no one would scratch the white paint. He reached into his pocket to unlock the doors.

"When y'all gonna harvest?" Heath asked.

"Few weeks."

"And then what?"

"Sell it," he said. "What'd you think?"

"Where?"

"Uncle Heath," Cody said. "How about we not talk about this shit in public?"

"Suit yourself," Heath said. "Won't talk in the house. Won't talk at the Walmart. Where the hell are you boys gonna talk and explain how the business is being run? I got a right to goddamn know. You two little fuckers think you're tricky. But if y'all want to enter the big time, you need to follow my goddamn lead."

Cody stopped halfway down the row of cars. He didn't move, still hanging there with elbows on the push handle, eyes scanning the parking lot, ball cap down in his eyes. Somewhere, Heath heard the big dirty growl of some scooters rolling in. Sounded like a whole mess of 'em.

"You got that gun?" Cody said.

"What?"

"I said, you got your goddamn gun?"

"'Course I got my goddamn gun," Heath said. "I don't go to the shitter without it. You think I've gone soft in the head?"

"Get it," Cody said. "We got some damn trouble. Those motherfuckers tailed us here."

A dozen or so black-leather-and-denim-wearing fuckers on scooters blasted down the parking lot, roaring past the grocery cart and circling it like some snaggletooth sharks.

"Born Losers."

"Well," Heath said. "Sure. OK, then. Let's see what they got."

"I guess those booby traps didn't scare them none."

"Let's hurry this up," Heath said. "My goddamn ice cream's starting to melt."

"I'm done," Boom said. "Just cut me a check and I'll be on my way."

"Hold up there, son," L. Q. Smith said, fingers hooked into his skinny little belt. "You can't just skid onto company property, slamming on your brakes, and leave your rig parked like that. I heard what you said to the dispatcher. Those were some hurtful words. I'll have you know Earl is a Christian man who very much loves his mother."

"I said I'd do the job," Boom said. "I did the job."

They stood inside an open cargo bay, alone, after Smith had met him in the lot. Boom had jumped from the truck, tossed Smith his keys, and stormed on up to the main offices. Smith trailed behind him, telling him to stop, wanting to know just what had made him so gosh dang mad. When Boom tried to answer him in the Sutpen offices, Smith held up the flat of his hand and said this was more of a private conversation. He bought Boom a Mountain Dew from a vending machine and walked him into the empty bay. Some of the secretaries and men who worked the docks eyed them as they passed. But Boom paid them no mind. He didn't give a good goddamn who heard what he had to say.

"I told you I wasn't running anything that wasn't on the manifest."

"And I told you that you wouldn't," Smith said, hands in his fancy-ass jeans, green-and-white checked shirt wide open at the throat to show a diamond-crusted horseshoe hanging around his old saggy throat. "That's why I got you running these old cars back. That way you could see what we're moving and wouldn't be worried about a damn thing. I'm still telling you that was a simple and honest mistake on that last run. I don't know why they told you avocados when they meant electronics. I don't pride myself in mistakes, but there wasn't anything illegal about it, son. I appreciate you being prideful in your work, but this kind of loose talk and accusations can't stand if you want to keep on working for Sutpen. This company started back in 1968 and has twice been awarded Lee County Business of the Year."

Boom looked down at Mr. L. Q. Smith, with his rumpled checkered shirt and fancy loafers. He still had the face of a roughneck, with the deep-burned skin and the long mustache. He held out his hand and offered Boom a smile.

"Y'all welded hidden compartments onto three of those vehicles," Boom said.

"Son," Jones said. "I got no idea what you're talking about."

"I stopped off at a Home Depot outside New Orleans," Boom said. "I got a stick welder and opened 'em up. I know what you put inside. I don't mess with that shit. Ever."

The smile faded from under L. Q. Smith's droopy mustache. He folded his long arms over his potbelly and grinned in a different way than before, like they were both in on some goddamn hilarious joke. He nodded, thinking on it, color coming up from his throat and splotching the cheeks of his face. "I done bumped your ass to the front of the line," he said. "Jerry Colson said you got sand in your britches and would do a job without making no trouble. I guess ole Jerry was wrong. He's gonna be real sorry to hear that."

"Mr. Colson's a good man," Boom said. "He wouldn't run that garbage unless he'd been lied to."

"Little things," Smith said, fingering at his ear. "Little things can add up to big problems for a man. Jerry makes some runs on occasion for us. Nothing big, just up to Memphis or down to Mobile. I'm sure he'd hate to have those checks stop coming at his age."

"I'll take my check and get going," Boom said. "I'll let you know what I decide."

"You do that, son," he said, peering up at something beyond Boom's shoulder and nodding. Boom turned to see two men walk into the empty cargo bay. One of them was old and weathered, with long gray hair pulled into a ponytail. The other was a little taller, lean and muscled, looking like a cowpuncher, with shaggy brown hair. He'd seen them once before, working the big glass office beside Smith's. The guy with the gray ponytail had a billy club tucked into the back of his hand-tooled belt but moved empty-handed.

Boom watched the two men as he walked with Smith. He sure as hell didn't like their looks.

"Hate for you to miss out on a good-paying job," Smith said. "With your, um, abnormality. And I'll try not to take no offense to the accusations that you've made against Sutpen. You're a good driver and a valuable part of the team. You go on back to Jericho and think long and hard about what we're offering here."

"I heard you," Boom said. "Don't need to hear it again from these fellas."

"You hadn't met Mr. Taggart and Mr. Hood?" he asked. "They run Sutpen's. Took over when Old Man Sutpen passed away some years ago. Fine men."

The old ponytailed man cocked his head, studying Boom. The other cowboy-looking man just nodded in his direction. Neither of them spoke, offered to shake his hand, or moved to try and whip his ass. Not that either one of 'em could do it.

"All right, then," Boom said, feeling a little rush of adrenaline as he turned and walked slow and easy from the room, keeping his eyes on the two men hanging against the wall, waiting for L. Q. Smith to give some kind of signal. *Taggart and Hood.* He didn't know which one was which, but he sure as hell didn't want no more trouble.

Boom just wanted free of being some white man's punch, trucking his drugs and stolen shit across state lines. He'd rather go back to the County Barn and work under Skinner's cronies than spend the rest of his days in a federal pen like his buddy Donnie Varner.

"Look forward to hearing from you, son," L. Q. Smith said, loud behind his back, echoing on the metal walls. "We sure do value and appreciate your work here at Sutpen Truckin'."

What'd you peckerheads do with Ordeen Davis?" said the black-bearded, sallow-faced bastard sitting astride his Harley. "We come to ask you nice. And that shit ain't gonna happen twice."

"And who the fuck are y'all?" Heath said, not liking being addressed in that manner. But he knew full well these scooter boys had been sent by that Hathcock woman. His nephews had told him the whole story when some of the Born Losers hit that trip wire two days back, leaving scooter parts and a lone boot scattered across their private dirt road.

"Read the patch," the man said, pointing to his denim vest. The patch on his jacket read WRONG WAY. The man and his scooter were so damn close Heath could smell the cigarettes and whiskey on his breath. The man just hung there, sitting on his bike, and lit up a smoke.

"Your momma name you that?" Heath said. "On account of you coming out of the coot backwards?"

Wrong Way laughed hard, along with the two boys with them. They were all on the far side of the Walmart parking lot, close to where a few trees offered some shade. Heat waves shimmered up on the asphalt, scooter engines making ticking sounds after they set down their kickstands. "One of my boys got hurt real bad," Wrong Way said. "Y'all weren't very welcoming when we came out to your land."

"We didn't invite you," Cody said, standing tall behind their buggy filled high with little plastic bags. "Y'all were trying to sneak up on us."

"Ain't nothing sneaky with these pipes, boys," Wrong Way said. "Just coming to collect our friend, Mr. Ordeen. He came out to do some business with y'all last Saturday night and he never came home. We don't like that. We don't like that one bit. He ain't a Loser but part of the family just the same."

"My nephews were at the goddamn Possum Trot in Columbus last Saturday night," Heath said, puffing out his chest, making that bad-ass eagle on his tank top really stand out. "If your boy came to do some business, he sure wasn't looking for us. We got plenty of 'No Trespass' signs. We got every legal right to protect what's ours."

"Where is he now?" Wrong Way said.

"Boy, them bikes fuck up your hearing?" Heath asked. "We don't have no goddamn idea what you're talking about. Me and my fine nephew just come on out to Walmart to do a little afternoon shopping. Got some fucking Oreos you wouldn't believe. If you please, we need to get home and get our pizzas and ice cream into the deep freeze."

"Either you bring Ordeen back to Miss Fannie," Wrong Way said, "or we'll turn that weed farm into a funeral pyre. You hearing me, old man? We like watching shit burn. And it burns all the sweeter knowing it belongs to some sawed-off jailbird like you, Heath Pritchard."

"Well, shit," Heath said. "OK, then. I'm honored you know my name and didn't have to read it off my shirt. But I'd rather have you call me Captain 'Merica. A goddamn redneck hero who's come home from stinky, muddy, asshole-smellin' hell to protect what's rightly his. You get what I'm saying, Mr. Wrong Way? Or you gonna stand here and let my fucking peach ice cream turn to shit?"

"We ain't leaving till we get that boy," Wrong Way said. "Miss Fannie doesn't like folks who don't give her what she wants. In case you hadn't heard, Miss Fannie runs shit around here."

"Guess you're gonna go back empty-handed to that redheaded cunt," Heath said. "'Cause that nigger done came on to the wrong land. He's long gone. Y'all better forget his black ass and move on."

Wrong Way swung a leg over his motorcycle and reached into his leather satchel for a handful of chains. His two buddies followed, walking up shoulder to shoulder toward where Heath stood next to Cody and his Walmart buggy. Wrong Way pushed the buggy and Cody pushed back harder, nearly knocking ole Wrong Way off his boots. He shot a mess of chains down on Cody's hands just as Heath tackled him to the ass-burning parking lot. Those scooter boys laughing and yelling, spilling their fucking groceries and trying to wrap up Cody. Heath couldn't see the action but heard a sharp crack and one of those boys yell. Heath dug his knees into Wrong Way, punching that son of a bitch right in the throat, grabbing his melon head and pounding that shit to the asphalt. His palms were bleeding as he got to his feet, wiping them on his jeans and coming around for a boy circling Cody with the chains. The boy didn't see him and reared back, ready to strike. Heath grabbed the chains and wrapped them around the boy's throat. That Wrong Way fella crawling nearby, face bloodied. Heath pulled and twisted the chains until he rode that biker down to his knees, holding him there, whispering sweetly in his ear, "There, there. There, there, fella. Be a good boy and don't you move. Don't you move and you'll ride out of here."

Cody snatched up their plastic bags from their overturned buggy and crawled up into the white Silverado, letting down the windows and telling Heath to get his ass inside. "Damn, you know they called the fucking cops."

That boy Wrong Way had gotten up, stumbling toward Heath, motioning *Come at me* with his dirty fingers. Damn, Heath wanted it bad. He wanted to whip that boy's ass again so bad he could taste it in his mouth. He felt a tightness in his chest and down in his nuts as he walked forward, Cody yelling for him more. "Come on! Shit. I hear the fucking sirens."

Heath nodded before he turned, reaching for his gun, and shot Wrong Way in the thigh. The man let out a high-pitched scream that sounded just like an old woman's. Heath grinned real big, already tasting that sweet ice cream when he got home.

"Be seeing you, Wrong Way."

Heath heard the police coming now. Cody was already driving through the lot and Heath had to make a run for it and jump in the truck bed. Cody cut across the parking spaces and then doubled back fast toward those scooters. The hot wind felt good in Heath's face as his nephew squealed them big tires and went right for that upturned cart and those Harleys, riding that truck up and over them, some of those bikes and the buggy caught up under the truck, sparking on the blacktop, as they fishtailed free of the Walmart and headed out onto the highway. Heath fell onto his back in the truck bed, laughing like hell.

"Damn, that was fun," he said.

10

BOOM HELPED OUT AT THE RIVER WHEN HE COULD, SORTING donations into big plastic bins of canned vegetables, dried beans, peanut butter, fruit juice, rice, canned tuna and chicken, applesauce, and pasta. They kept freezers full of frozen chicken and beef, catfish donated from a farm over on the Delta, and on holidays, turkeys and hams that went first come, first served. Caddy often told Boom that she was never shocked by folks who damn well had the money but thought of The River as some kind of discount grocery store. But The River never asked for pay stubs, W-2s, Social Security cards, or food stamp vouchers. Caddy believed that those who showed up should get fed.

A wooden sign hung by the front door of the commissary, its burnt letters reading FOR I WAS HUNGRY AND YOU GAVE ME FOOD. I

WAS THIRSTY AND YOU GAVE ME DRINK. I WAS A STRANGER AND YOU WELCOMED ME.

Services on Sunday. Commissary open Tuesdays and Fridays.

Boom watched Caddy across the concrete floor, fluorescent lights buzzing overhead as she rummaged through big cardboard boxes of kids' clothes, finding a pair of Carhartt overalls for a little Hispanic girl. Caddy got down on her knees and held the overalls against the girl's small frame, sizing her up, and then handed them over to the girl's mother, who already held an armful of clothes. The woman was short and thick, dark and Indian-looking, in a threadbare cotton dress and tennis shoes.

Caddy had on a black SUN RECORDS T-shirt and some frayed cutoff jeans and leather sandals. She walked up to Boom while the woman gathered up the clothes into a black plastic bag. "Two church groups turned them down," Caddy said. "Wanted to see some identification. Asked if they were legal."

"That ain't right," Boom said. "What's it matter?"

"Every week I think we're not gonna make the next," she said. "But somehow we get what we need and keep the lights on. I don't think that's by accident. Like you. You just show up here with all that frozen chicken. How'd you know we were running low?"

"People like chicken," Boom said. "And I ain't too busy this week."

"You resting up from the road?"

"Gonna be a long rest," Boom said. "I think I'm gonna quit."

"Quit trucking?" she said. "Are you messing with me? I thought you loved the road?"

"It ain't what I thought," Boom said. "I'd rather go back to the County Barn. Fixing shit."

"You want to talk about it?"

"Nah," Boom said. "You got enough shit to deal with. You don't need to carry my damn water, too."

Boom lifted up a big box filled with the family's food for the week and followed them out to where they had parked by the creek. The little girl's big brown eyes followed him as he moved, looking up at his huge black shape and silver hand. Two more children hung out the windows of a battered blue Chevy pickup. There wasn't a single tree on the land, everything clear-cut and stripped, just a big wooden barn where they held the services, the commissary shed, and a half-dozen little shacks for the homeless or people in crisis. The name *The River* being some kind of joke, as most of the time their creek was just a dry gulch.

They stood together, Caddy's head barely meeting Boom's shoulder, as they watched the family drive away. Caddy turned back to the commissary to lock up as Boom wandered down the road to close the front gate. The Mexicans had been the last family of the day, Boom arriving just as she was about to shut down. When he got back, he saw Caddy sitting on the stoop of the metal building, smoking a cigarette.

Boom took a seat beside her. He could see the sun starting to go down over the creek and the cotton fields.

"Can't smoke at home," Caddy said. "Jason hates it. Last week, he threw my cigarettes in the trash."

"Can't fault him for it," Boom said. "Just looking out for you."

"My mother's on my ass, too," she said. "She quit last year and has taken up ice cream. Her freezer looks like a damn Ben and Jerry's."

Boom shook a smoke from the pack and lit up, taking a long draw, watching that big orange sun drop. He started thinking about that cotton around his property and how he should have gone in with his daddy this year. His daddy being such a hard ass that Boom wasn't sure he'd want help with the harvest.

"You hear about Ordeen Davis?"

Boom nodded. A plume of smoke hovering over them in the late-day heat.

"His poor mother," Caddy said. "Momma's cooking for the family now. Quinn's taking her over there tomorrow."

"You know I coached that kid when he played for Coach Mills?" Boom said. "Ordeen was tough. A hardworking kid but too slow for college. I don't think he saw a future outside football. Saw himself playing D1 and then going into the NFL. Ended up having to clean toilets for Johnny Stagg after graduation."

Caddy let the smoke out slow from her mouth. Her boots dusty, black dirt up under her short fingernails. "I heard they found the kid's body in a toolbox," she said. "What kind of person does something like that? Some true evil in this world."

Boom leaned forward, watching the beaten land around the church and that one goddamn tree hanging over the creek, all the mud and shit eroded from its roots. He wondered how the fuck that thing kept hanging on.

"You know he worked for Fannie Hathcock?"

Through the smoky haze, Caddy nodded. "Oh yes."

"Got me wondering," Boom said. "On account of what went on with Mingo—"

"That woman killed Mingo," Caddy said. "No two ways about it. I don't how she found out about him talking with us. But she did. And he just disappeared from Tibbehah County. Mingo would've let me know what was going on."

"I need to talk to Quinn," Boom said. "Today."

"What's the rush?" Caddy asked. "He's already been out to Vienna's and talked to that Hathcock woman. He said whoever killed Ordeen shot him in the back with buckshot, like he'd been running away. If she did it, Quinn will find out."

"That boy couldn't keep out of trouble," Boom said, ashing the cigarette on the edge of the porch. "I tried to make him go straight, make sure he got kicked loose from Nito Reece, but that boy was too far gone. He liked money and would do whatever the fuck it took to get it."

"Mingo was a good kid," Caddy said. "And I heard the same about Ordeen. Vienna's Place is a damn black hole in this community. How many girls do you think have gone in there and never come out?"

"Too much money coming through this broke-ass county," Boom said. "Ain't not everybody sees it. And they sure as shit can't touch it. But it's there."

"I know," Caddy said. "Too damn well."

Boom narrowed his eyes, looking toward the sun, feeling its last light warming his face. "Quinn needs to know a few more things about Ordeen," he said. "Might get my ass in some trouble. But won't be the first time."

"What do you know?"

"Same ole low-down, dirty-ass shit."

They'll be back," Tyler said. "You can't treat those motorcycle boys like some jailhouse bitch and not expect retribution. Those fuckers will be riding back in here full force next time wanting to burn us out. And you know goddamn well we can't call the law on them. This is some shit that needed to be handled with a little diplomacy."

Tyler was seated at the four-seat dinette set in the kitchen. Cody had brought home a family helping of Popeyes fried chicken, that twelve-piece bona fide meal with green beans, mashed potatoes, and a box of extra biscuits. A bunch of Keystone Light cans littered the table, most of them empty and half-crushed. A hand-painted sign hung by the stove read THIS KITCHEN IS SEASONED WITH ME-MAW'S LOVE.

"Diplomacy?" Uncle Heath said, reaching for a drumstick. "What the fuck do you think I was doing when I shot that greasy bastard in the leg? That's the only kind of talk those shit monkeys understand. You got to be the damn cock of the walk in this county or else someone is gonna ask you to touch your toes and drive it on home to Hong Kong and back."

"This ain't Parchman," Tyler said. "We run a business. We don't work under Parchman rules."

"No, sir," Heath said. "This is Tibbehah County and that makes it ten times worse. This place has always made Tombstone, Arizona, seem like Six Flags Over Georgia."

"We had the whole thing worked out with that Hathcock woman," Cody said, mouth full of mashed potatoes. "We had a deal that kept the peace."

"You keep thinking that," Heath said, "and someone will knock you boys upside your head while y'all are diddling with your peckers."

Tyler shrugged, searching for a fried chicken breast, thinking it was a fucking lie to call this a family dinner. Not a one of them even thought about saying a prayer, just reaching into the sack, snatching up those chicken parts like a bunch of mangy-ass dogs. What his momma used to call heathens before she got on the meth. Only Cody had on a shirt and that was on account of him having to go to Popeyes in person and fetch supper. His T-shirt read EASTBAY RACEWAY / WINTER NATIONALS, with a big ole orange sun and a couple palm trees. Tyler would do anything to be back down in Florida right about now, sipping on a frozen margarita and punching up some old Buffett.

"I don't like where this is headed," Tyler said. "This is a goddamn mess."

"Hell, I can straighten out that rear axle drunk and blind," Heath said. "Y'all will be ready to race this weekend at the Hooker Hood Classic. I promise you."

"Not with the goddamn car," Cody said. "We can fix the goddamn car."

"With them scooter boys?" Heath said. "Shit. They done run off with their tails between their legs. One of them bleeding like a stuck pig right there in the Walmart parking lot. That ain't trouble. That's just some good ole wholesome fun. We got back to the farm before the peach ice cream even started to melt."

"Maybe we should cancel the race," Tyler said. "Last time we left the property, we come home to you shitting the damn bed by killing that black boy."

"I saved y'all's ass," Heath said. "That Hathcock woman doesn't know a damn thing about our business, just to stay away from our goddamn foxhole. You understand? We don't need her approval to do business. Our business is our business. *Damn, son.* Ain't no different than a race. Look at the condition of your damn vehicle. You see that? Who was you racing against? That son of a bitch about ate your damn lunch?"

"Just some kid," Cody said.

"Some kid done this to you?" Heath asked. "Some kid did that to me and I'd put a bounty on his ass. I'd have him knocked up into the fence."

"Name's Booger Phillips," Tyler said. "He ain't but sixteen."

Cody shrugged, not looking like he gave two shits, and reached for a biscuit. He began to sop up the gravy and stuck the whole damn thing in his mouth. He chewed, watching the back-and-forth between Tyler and Uncle Heath, looking like he thought the whole damn thing was kinda funny.

"That woman ain't gonna be intimidated," Tyler said, using a chicken bone to point Heath's way. "She's gonna want her cut or to shut us down."

"A cut?" Heath said. "For what? What did that dang cunt do for us?"

"Shit," Tyler said. "You ain't never in your life met a woman like Fannie Hathcock."

"I don't care if she's Shania Twain with a solid-gold cooch," he said. "She ain't a Pritchard."

"Damn, old man," Tyler said. "Shania Twain? She's a hundred years old now. I'm talking Fannie Hathcock. That place out on the highway is a laundromat for the damn Dixie Mafia. You want to get into a pissin' contest with those fuckers?"

"Ain't none of those boys been in north Mississippi in a long while," Heath said. "Not since ole Buford Pusser knocked heads with a two-by-four. I ain't never had trouble with any of 'em."

"Well, times change," Tyler said. "That's just the cost of doing business in Tibbehah County. We don't get to make the rules."

"Shit on that," Heath said. "We got family. We got guns. And we got a whole lot of cans of whoop-ass. You can either run for the hills covering up your peter or you can stand up straight like a fucking white man and assess the goddamn situation. Why would you pay out to that bitch for growing your own damn weed?"

"'Cause she does business with Memphis," Cody said. "We want to sell up there, then we got to make the damn peace."

"And why the hell does this bitch get to make the rules?"

Tyler let out a long breath and tossed the half-eaten chicken to the center of the table. He stood, wiping his mouth, and cut the greasy taste by finishing the rest of the Keystone. "'Cause that woman and her people on the Coast are able to move a massive amount of shit up here that we couldn't get in a million years."

"Like what?" Heath said. "What's so damn precious?"

"Oh, hell," Cody said. "We don't know. Pills and shit. OxyContin. Heroin. Fucking Mexican meth. All that shit."

"And that separates y'all from the big dogs?"

Tyler looked across the table as Cody piled some more mashed potatoes on his plate and poured out a mess of gravy. He wasn't sure his brother had touched a bit of the spicy New Orleans chicken, always a man to just eat up them side items. Fine by him. Tyler only cared for that white meat and beer. He got up, wiped his hands on his blue jeans, and reached into the ice bucket for another can of beer.

"That ain't how we do business," Heath said, setting his hands palm-down on the table. "No way. It's gonna be the goddamn Pritchards running the show. Y'all want me to get you the keys to a pharmacy? Ain't nothing to it but to do it. I made a lot of friends in Parchman. One of them in Arkansas can get us about anything under this sun."

"Bullshit," Cody said.

"Call me a liar," Heath said. "Go ahead and do it, son. But I been running shit since before y'all was sucking your momma's little titty. This man I knowed? Fucking Doc McDuffie runs the whole Aryan Brotherhood in the Mid-South. Just sit back and make a grocery list and my buddy can roll trucks with more shit than y'all can handle."

"It's a lot," Tyler said.

"I don't know," Cody said. "This don't sound good, Uncle Heath."

Heath eyed them both. "Who's the buyer?"

"Used to be these two nigger brothers down in south Memphis," Tyler said. "Had a place called the Wing Machine before they got kilt, place all shot to shit. Now it's this old black man named Marquis Sledge. He operates a string of funeral homes, got back into it after those boys died."

"What'd I say," Heath said. "Everything old is new again. Can't believe that black bastard is still alive. He know me and you boys are related?"

Tyler said, "Never said either way."

"I bet he wouldn't mind if the Pritchards could handle all his damn needs," Heath said.

"Don't see why not," Tyler said. "Sledge hates working with Fannie Hathcock. He believes she was the one who got the twins all shot up. They weren't kin, but he'd helped raise those boys. He was real shook up about the whole thing."

"You don't want me in the same room with Marquis Sledge," Heath said. "I once tried to choke out the son of a bitch at a Western Sizzlin down on Poplar. I know business. Yes, sir. Doc McDuffie is one sharp son of a bitch. Y'all talk to Sledge."

Tyler drank some beer and stared out the kitchen window, the sun going down over the cornfields, row after row growing up high, green, and straight. He looked over at his brother, seeing if Cody would give him some kind of clue over what he was thinking. Cody just kept on munching on a biscuit, eyes far away, gazing at that setting sun.

"It's either let that bitch bleed y'all or get up off your fucking knees and walk like a man," Heath said. "What the fuck do you boys have to lose?"

Cody turned to look at Tyler, working something out of his back teeth with a finger. Tyler stared him down, waiting for him to weigh in on all this important family business. He just lifted his eyebrows and pointed at an open Popeyes box.

"Y'all mind if I take that last biscuit?" Cody asked.

Quinn got home at twilight, spotting Boom on his front porch. The big man sitting in his swing, moving back and forth under the colored Christmas lights, taking some time with Hondo, who sat beside him. Walking up the stairs, Quinn turned to his friend and asked if he wanted a cold Coors.

"Sure," Boom said. "Been a long-ass day."

Quinn opened up the old house, Boom and Hondo following, letting the screen door thwack behind them. In the kitchen, he snatched up two cans of Coors from the old International Harvester refrigerator and handed one to Boom.

"Didn't mean to sneak up on you," Boom said. "We need to talk."

"You know, I do keep regular hours at the sheriff's office."

"In private."

"You getting worried about being the best man?" Quinn said. "Don't worry. I won't ask you to sing. Or read any stupid speeches.

All you got to do is stand tall with me and make sure I don't bolt from the church."

"You bolt on a woman as fine as Maggie Powers?" Boom said. "Damn. Then I know you crazy."

Quinn agreed as they walked back out to the front porch, Hondo hopping up onto the swing. Boom and Quinn took the old rusted metal chairs, opening up the beers and looking out in the darkened pasture. In the shadowed half-light, he could see the dozens of cows and, far to the edge of the pasture, the two horses his father had abandoned. One of them was a pretty paint named Hooper.

Quinn propped his cowboy boots up on the ledge and sighed, glad to be home, reaching down and scratching Hondo's head. The dog's tongue lolled from his mouth, his black-and-gray patchwork fur covered in something that looked like mud but smelled like something far worse. Hondo just couldn't keep away from those cows.

"I was about to leave," Boom said. "Mary Alice said you left an hour ago."

"Stopped off to see Ordeen Davis's momma," Quinn said. "She's in some rough shape. Said she'd been praying that the county would shut down Fannie Hathcock's titty bar. She said she's sure whatever happened to Ordeen came about from Fannie."

"What do you think?" Boom said.

Quinn shrugged and drank some Coors, nodding a little. "About ninety-nine percent."

"And the other one?"

"I'd have to hear different," Quinn said. "All I know is where Ordeen was last seen and who he'd been working for."

"I saw that kid about a week ago," Boom said. "Maybe the same day he got killed. Over in Tupelo."

"Tupelo?" Quinn said. "What the hell's in Tupelo?"

"Where I work," Boom said. "He was over at the offices at the company I've been driving for. I didn't think much of it. I just saw him, talked to him for a little while about his momma and them. What he been up to. He said he was just over in Tupelo to pick up some rubbers and French ticklers and shit for Fannie. But after what happened, I figured you might needed to know."

"Appreciate that," Quinn said. "Something else to add to the time line."

"Only, there's more to it," Boom said, leaning forward in the chair, left hand playing with that silver hook, twirling it in his fingers, spinning it around. "That company ain't straight. I about quit today. They got me running stolen shit and drugs packed in little hidey-holes. I don't like none of it. I'm on the way out, man."

"Who are these people?" Quinn said.

"Outfit's called Sutpen," Boom said, turning his head toward Quinn, meeting his eye. "Got their operation right off 45 outside Tupelo city limits. Only man I'd known is this dude named L. Q. Smith. When I asked ole L.Q. what he tryin' to pull, he got all smart with me. He introduced these two mean motherfuckers he said were the real owners. They were named Taggart and Hood. Don't know shit about them. One of them, this old dude with a ponytail, carried a billy club in his belt like it was a pistol."

"He threaten you?"

"Shit, man," Boom said. "Them boys want to come up close and personal with some crazy one-armed nigger, come on."

"Was Ordeen picking up what you dropped off?"

"I don't know what Ordeen was really doing," he said. "That night, it was just TVs, electronics, and shit. But maybe. All I know is, I seen his ass there. And that place is dirty as hell."

Quinn finished the beer and placed the empty can down beside him. "How the hell did you get up with these folks?"

"Would you believe your Uncle Jerry," Boom said. "He's the one who recommended me for the job."

"Yep," Quinn said. "That sounds about like my Uncle Jerry."

"Hate to drag his ass into all this," Boom said, "but he might know something. Ain't no kid deserved to be killed like that. They threw away Ordeen like he was just some trash. That don't sit too well with me."

"This wouldn't be the first time Fannie Hathcock lost some hired help," Quinn said.

"Nope," Boom said. "Sure as shit wouldn't."

The cows made some mournful noises across the pasture, Hondo trotting off the porch and heading into the darkness to make the rounds. Quinn walked back for a second beer. Boom said one was enough for him. They sat there in silence for a bit, enjoying the warm breeze, the empty, quiet sounds of the hot wind through the trees. He and Boom could be together for a long while without saying a damn word, same as it had been hunting and fishing when they were kids. They didn't feel the need to fill that silence with a bunch of empty-headed talk.

"This place is a lot different from when you got back," Boom said.

"People in town said for me to burn the house down," Quinn said.

"Took us two days just to clear out your uncle's trash," Boom said. "Nothing good in here but some old records and guns."

"And a suede coat and a bottle of fine bourbon from Johnny Stagg."

Boom nodded, silent again for a while. Quinn drank his beer, watching Hondo, now just a flitting dark speck among the cows as he worked them a little, letting them know who was in charge. Nearly ten years Quinn'd been back and he wasn't sure he'd made a damn bit of difference.

11

QUINN AND REGGIE DROVE TOGETHER ONTO THE PRITCHARD property early the next morning, the gate wide open, welcoming them onto the land, passing all those NO TRESPASSING signs about not calling 911, BEWARE OF THE DOG, and how the best way to meet the Lord was to keep on coming. The sun was up, high in the pines, the gully running alongside the road choked with weeds and full of beer cans and paper wrappers. As they drove, the sunlight flickered through the rows of planted trees and through a big Confederate flag flapping from an overhead oak branch. A skull in the center of the Stars and Bars wore a cowboy hat and grinned with its big skull teeth.

"Real fine folks," Reggie said, riding shotgun with Quinn. "True Southern hospitality."

"Gate was open," Quinn said. "To me, that's the same as a welcome mat."

"Sorry if I don't believe you, Sheriff," Reggie said. "I've heard stories about these people, none of them good. These boys been on their own since they were kids, running wild, shooting guns and racing cars. I heard they're not real fond of black folks. I pulled one of those boys over last year for speeding and it was like I'd smacked him in the face. Watched his goddamn hands the whole time, boy mean and red-faced, looking like he was about to make a move. Never did. Took the ticket but never said a word but 'Yep,' 'Nope.' He tore that ticket from my hand and drove off. Pissed-off as hell."

"I'm sure he'll be glad to see you again," Quinn said. "Which one was it?"

"Damn," Reggie said. "I don't know. Hard to remember which one of those boys is uglier. It was the tall one with the beard, looking straight out of those Old Testament comics."

Quinn hit a curve in the dirt road and headed toward an old tin-roof house, not unlike Quinn's but only one-story and in some pretty sorry shape. The tin roof was rusted, the paint flaking, and the front porch sagging loose, busted and ragged. He slowed his truck by some old junk cars and trucks, a couple of Sea-Doos on the back of a trailer. Across from the ragged house was a brand-new metal barn with the side doors open. As Quinn and Reggie got out of the air-conditioning into the humidity, they could hear the high buzzing sounds of machinery and smell the oily smoke coming from the open doors. A radio was on, playing some of that modern country with the electronic beat, Auto-Tuned vocals, and an attempt at rap. The singer talking about a woman having a body like a back road. It was some god-awful shit.

As they headed into the garage, a stocky guy without a shirt holding a bottle of red Gatorade looked up from where he was cutting some sheet metal. He had goggles on top of his head, his muscled body covered in sweat, cigarette hanging from his mouth. Tattoos covered his back with checkered flags and angel wings. He looked to be in his late fifties or early sixties, with wrinkled, leathery skin and a bald head.

Quinn introduced himself. And Reggie.

"I know who y'all are," the man said, not getting up from the workstation. "I seen you on the cameras. Hard to miss that big star on the side of your F-150. That the V-6 or V-8?"

"V-6," Quinn said. "Got a Turbo Boost on it. Pulls all that I need."

"I heard those motors have improved," the man said. "Some dumb bastards can't get that V-8 sound out of their heads. They just want to growl them pipes but don't give a damn about performance. Performance is what it's all about. Just ask the ladies."

Quinn nodded and took a look around the shop, big and wide open, about thirty feet tall, with flags flying from the metal crossbeams. The concrete floor was spotted with oil stains covered up in cat litter, a handmade workbench strewn with tools and open bottles, gas cans, and oil filters. He looked over at Reggie, who was checking out a race car that had been taken down to the chassis, skeletal and sleek, a motor hanging nearby from some chains.

"I'm looking for Tyler or Cody."

"They ain't here."

"You know when they'll be back?"

"No, sir," the man said. "I sure don't. Can I help you boys with something?"

"Those boys drive a 2017 white Chevy Silverado?" Quinn said, knowing the answer. "Black Widow edition."

"Yes, sir," the man said, making some marks on the metal, looking down at his hands, and not seeming to pay a bit of attention. "They surely do."

"Do you know if they were at the Walmart yesterday?"

"No, sir," the man said. "I don't run their business. But I figure we all got to get to the Walmart once in a while. Only place I know where you can get toilet paper, Twinkies, and shotgun shells."

Quinn nodded at the man, waiting for him to look up from his work, and then looked over at Reggie, who stood by the wall, looking at dozens of gold trophies set on plastic storage racks. Reggie raised his eyebrows at Quinn, hand on the gun at his hip. The older guy finally looked up and stood, hitching up his tight blue jeans. They'd been tucked inside a pair of rattlesnake cowboy boots.

"Anyone ever tell you that you favor your Uncle Hamp?" the man said, cupping his hand and lighting a cigarette. Quinn studied the man's face. His smile broke into a wide grin, cigarette dangling from his lips. "Yes, sir. I knew your daddy, too. He was one crazy fool. I was there the day he jumped seventeen Pintos on his motorbike. Hell of a day. Baptist church gave out free popcorn and fried pies."

Quinn didn't say anything. He just watched the leathery man coming around the table, eyeing Reggie and then looking back to Quinn. He was thick and hard for an old guy, tough and muscled, with small black eyes and a tight brown hole for a mouth. When he grinned and coughed out some smoke, his teeth were small, ground-down, and yellowed.

"You're Heath Pritchard," Quinn said.

"Yes, sir," he said.

"Hadn't been told you were out."

"I done my time," he said. "Spent the last twenty-three years at

Unit 29 at Parchman, thanks to your Uncle Hamp. He'd been bird-dogging my ass for years until he finally found a way to get me."

Quinn knew the stories. He'd been in middle school when infamous outlaw Heath Pritchard got busted for growing fifty acres of marijuana between his rows of corn. People in Tibbehah still talked about him like he'd been some kind of Robin Hood, battling it out with the law and Johnny Stagg, keeping his little empire running until the sheriff's office burned his world to the ground. Most people still saying he'd been set up by the law, Uncle Hamp taking care of Stagg's business. Truth be known, Quinn wasn't too sure that wasn't true.

"Why y'all looking for my nephews?" Heath Pritchard said. "They take something from that Walmart? If they did, I'm good for it."

"Yesterday there was a fight in the parking lot," Quinn said. "Someone got shot. And we have a witness who saw your nephews' Silverado. They noticed the Pritchard Racing Team logo splashed on the side."

"You think my boys shot somebody?"

"No, sir," Quinn said. "But we're hoping they saw something. We believe some members of a local motorcycle gang were in town."

"You're talking about the goddamn Born Losers," Pritchard said. "Those are some mean hombres. They'd been stinking up this county since way before I went in jail. I thought y'all had run them out of town."

Reggie walked up to where the men stood, Pritchard looking over his uniform and then back at Quinn as if not believing what he was seeing. Quinn handed the man his card, telling him to have one of his nephews call him when they got back home.

Pritchard picked up the card, reading it with his lips moving, and then staring back at Quinn and then over at Reggie Caruthers. He licked his dry lips. "Sorry to hear about your uncle."

Quinn nodded.

"My hopes and dreams had been to come back to this town a free man and whip his ass."

Quinn stopped and turned so close to the man that he could smell the rancid sweat and testosterone on him, dusky, like some kind of wild animal. "And they would've put you right back into your cage."

"Maybe," Pritchard said. "But sure would've been goddamn worth it."

Quinn stood still close to Pritchard, not saying a word, just waiting for him to make a quick move. Instead, the man started laughing and laughing like he'd just heard an off-color joke in church. He even held on to his bare sweaty belly as he giggled as if he couldn't control himself.

"I'm just messin' with you, Sheriff. I'll tell my boys to give you a call. We sure as hell can't have no violence at the Walmart. That's just downright un-American."

"You checkin' in with your parole officer?" Quinn asked.

"Oh yes, sir," Pritchard said. "You better believe it, Sheriff. We plan to eat fried chicken and pray every chance we get. We're right as rain."

Quinn nodded at Reggie and they both walked from the garage, the bad country music turned up even louder. He stopped at his truck and looked out at the ragged property. The falling house, the tall metal barn, and endless rows of corn. They crawled into the truck and headed back out the dirt road.

"What the hell was that about?" Reggie said.

"Trouble," Quinn said.

"The smell of that man?" Reggie said. "Good Lord."

Black people get buried by black people and white people get buried by white people," Tyler said, stroking his bushy beard, hands in the back pockets of his Wranglers, looking around, trying to be cool about the meeting with Mr. Sledge. "That's how his family got so rich and owns half of south Memphis. Rib joints. Filling stations. Wigs and fucking weaves. His people been putting black folks in the ground since the Civil War and they been banking that shit ever since. Look at this place. It's like a goddamn fortress."

"It's creepy as hell," Cody said, looking around Sledge Funeral Home—WHERE DIGNITY AND RESPECT ARE KING—at all the open satin-lined coffins, gold-framed portraits of serious black men in suits and wide ties, and the wall-to-wall green shag carpet leading to the chapel and little private offices. The outside was nothing but sandstone and brick with a six-foot-high black iron fence surrounding the funeral home, a fleet of Cadillac limousines and hearses parked in the private lot.

"Hey, fucknuts," Tyler said. "How 'bout you just sit there, shut the hell up, and let me talk? You open your mouth and you're gonna piss this guy off. We need him to listen to what we came to offer."

"That ain't gonna happen," Cody said. "We're wasting our damn time. That's just some shit pie in the sky put there by Uncle Heath."

"Oh, is that right?" Tyler asked. "Mr. Sledge buys our product. He moves our product. He asks for more 'an we can give him. What's good for his black ass is good for us. I don't trust our crazy uncle any more 'an you. But shit, man. If Uncle Heath can deliver? *Wooh.* Man. That'd sure be something else."

"I don't trust Uncle Heath to flush the dang toilet."

"Let him do his part," Tyler said. "And we'll do ours."

An old black woman with gray hair wearing a black pantsuit walked up and led them into a big office without saying a word. Her perfume stuck around after she left, Tyler thinking she must really lay it on thick having to be around dead folks all day. He glanced around the office, a grandfather clock in the corner ticking off the seconds. There was a big ole desk with feet like eagle claws and a fat white leather chair behind it. The walls were that same dark paneled wood lined with glowing brass lamps and framed pictures of black people with big Afros and colorful clothes. The same thick green shag carpet covered the floors, with two very old and tall brass ashtrays by the plush white chairs where they sat. It was so damn cold that Tyler got goose bumps on his bare arms.

"I liked going to the Wing Machine better," Cody said. "Drop off some weed, get paid, and then get fed. The Bohannons were OK. I'm not so sure about all this."

Tyler stared at his brother as the side door opened and in walked Mr. Marquis Sledge himself, in his silky pants and silky shirt, unbuttoned too far down his old chest and showing off a thick gold chain. He wore big, gold-framed glasses, a straw hat like men wore in old movies, and kept a thin little mustache over his lip. The man had to be older than seventy, tall and thick, with wide-set eyes and copper-colored skin.

He shook hands with the Pritchard boys before taking a seat behind the desk and leaning back in his chair, giving them that *What you white motherfuckers want?* look but not saying a damn word. Sledge pulled a gold toothpick from his pocket and stuck it into the corner of his mouth, using his fat tongue to swivel it around, resting his hands on his belly.

"I know you're a busy man, Mr. Sledge," Tyler said.

"Gotdamn right," he said. "So why we got fucking Mississippi come to town? What you country boys want? Ain't y'all getting paid? Yes, sir. Mr. Sledge pays right and on time."

"Everything's fine," Tyler said. "It's good. We just wanted to talk a little new business."

"New business?" he asked. "Shit. You know I don't like being seen with white people. Bad for my reputation. If someone asks, you boys tell 'em that you come over to clean my gutters or fix the toilets or some shit. I don't want nobody talking about how Mr. Marquis Sledge is out shaking hands and making friends with a couple Cracker Barrel Slims."

Tyler looked over to Cody and Cody slouched into his seat, letting out a long breath. Cody had on a T-shirt with the sleeves cut off that said I GOT MUD IN MY BLOOD. A Dale Jr. ball cap down low in his eyes.

Sledge rotated the gold toothpick in his mouth with his fingers and leaned back into his white leather chair. "But that shit y'all got," he said. "That's some fine-ass weed. Folks loving that shit, asking me, 'Hey, Marquis. This shit come from fucking Hawaii?' And I say to them, 'Yeah, man. That shit come from Hawaii.' Because if they smokin' it up and thinking about volcanoes and hula dancers with coconuts on their titties, that's just good for business. Ain't no reason they got to know you trucking in that shit from down in *Petticoat Junction*."

Tyler glanced over at his brother's slouching and shot him a look for him to sit up straight, keep some eye contact with Mr. Sledge.

This man was the real sponsor of Pritchard Racing. Without him buying what they grew, they'd never have gotten out of all that debt. They were going to have to sell off the land, the garage, and their cars before he came along. Sledge saw him eyeing his brother and switched the toothpick into the opposite side of his mouth, leaning forward in the desk, clasping his hands together, and wanting to know what the hell they wanted.

"We got some problems in Tibbehah County."

"With the law?" Sledge said, rubbing his hands together. "Don't you be bringing that shit to my doorstep. No, sir. Anyone been following your ass? DEA? MBN? Damn, motherfucking FBI?"

"No, sir," Tyler said. "We got some trouble with the big boys down on the Coast."

"Oh, yeah?" he said. "The fucking Cornbread Mafia? Yeah, I work with those motherfuckers from time to time. I don't like it. But what other choice I got?"

Tyler looked to Cody and they both nodded back at Sledge. Sledge played with the gold toothpick, taking it from his mouth, examining the end, and then pointing it right at Tyler and Cody.

"Goddamn Syndicate," he said. "Those rednecks been wanting to shut down my Soul Train Line since the seventies. Never touched me. But, damn sure, how they tried. I thought we had an understanding, but that shit that went down last year? I got my own idea of what really happened."

"Sorry to hear about the twins," Tyler said. "They were always straight with us."

"You know I helped raise Short Box and K-Bo?" he said. "Their daddy used to do my embalming. Helped them get set up in that business down on EP Boulevard."

"Damn shame," Tyler said.

"Yup," Cody said, still slumping, looking at his dirty fingernails, grime and grit shoved up under 'em. "Dang fine folks. Christians even."

Sledge swiveled his chair around and pointed to a picture on the wall of two black kids in the middle of a sparkling brandy glass. Next to the glass was a red rose, the picture shellacked onto a square of cedar wood and turned into a clock. "I wouldn't gotten back into all this mess if those boys hadn't been kilt," he said. "Police say it was just some crazy men robbing the Wing Machine, but I always knew there was more to it. Those country-fried motherfuckers in Biloxi been wanting to put them boys down like mangy dogs for a long-ass time. I believe those robbers were just fronting for them, thinking they could cut out the fucking middleman and have all the grass and pills flow in straight from down in Old Mexico. Man, those boys knew how to wear their Sunday clothes. And they sure as shit knew how to make some goddamn wings. Set your asshole on fire."

"This woman giving us trouble doesn't want us doing business with you," Tyler said. "She wants to be your main squeeze."

"You talking about that Fannie *Hath-cock?*"

"Yes, sir."

"That's one tricky redheaded bitch," Sledge said. "She the kind of woman might be sucking your old ding-dong one minute and try and bite the motherfucker off the next."

"That's her," Tyler said.

"OK," Sledge said, picking up the toothpick again, working a space between his two front teeth. "Yeah? What's she trying to do to y'all? Working with the local law? Bring that heat on y'all's country ass?"

"She doesn't control the law," Tyler said. "Nobody does. The law is straight. She sent some dumb kid to our farm to spy on our business. After we took care of that, she sent the damn Born Losers Motorcycle Club to come and bust our heads."

"Y'all look pretty dirty," he said. "But your heads look OK to me."

"Our uncle shot one of them in the leg at the Walmart," Cody said. "And then we drove over their Harleys. Seemed to straighten things out."

"Well, well, well, boys," Sledge said, swatting the top of his desk. He started to laugh. "Those boys are gonna be gunnin' for your asses now. It ain't gonna end."

The Pritchard boys nodded together. Sledge smiled, adjusted his straw hat down in his eyes as he leaned forward, elbows on the tables, gold toothpick hanging in the corner of his lips. "And just what do y'all need from me?" he said. "*Petticoat Junction* might as well be a million miles from Memphis. I don't have no control."

Sledge working the shit out of that gold toothpick, thinking on things, trying to do what was best for Goddamn Marquis Sledge, King of the Memphis Mortuaries.

"We know how to cut Fannie Hathcock out of the Memphis pie," Tyler said. "We can take care of everything you need straight through us."

"Come on, boys," Sledge said. "Supply? Demand? I got one hell of a fucking demand. Sometimes you got to work with that devil bitch you know and all that shit."

"What if you didn't need her," Cody said, finally sitting up straight, looking a little blurry-eyed. "Or those boys on the Coast? What if Team Pritchard could meet and beat all y'all's business needs?"

Marquis Sledge clamped down on that toothpick. Hard to see his eyes with his glasses reflecting those lamp lights. Tyler waited, holding his breath, until he saw the old black man's face slide into a big, wide grin.

"Hmm," Mr. Sledge said. "Now, that's some shit I'd sure like to hear."

Lord have mercy," Jean Colson said. "That sure was a scene. I've never seen so much crying and yelling in my whole life. But truth be known, if something happened to either you or Caddy, someone would have to put my butt in Whitfield and throw away the key. I don't know how Danita does it, standing there all calm in the kitchen, holding hands and praying. She even took the time to thank me for bringing over that damn chili cheese casserole. That's a strong woman right there."

"I know," Quinn said. "I've had to eat that casserole."

"I know you're trying to lighten the mood," Jean said as they drove past Annie's Soul Food restaurant—known for the best fried chicken in north Mississippi—the old farm supply, and the VFW Hall with the newly installed old Patton tank outside in honor of Quinn's late friend, Mr. Jim. "You've got that dark Army humor like your uncle. But that was a rough, rough scene at the Davis house. Who was that woman they had to wrestle out of the family room and take outside?"

"Ordeen's sister."

"Did you talk to all of them?" she said. "The whole family?"

"I did," he said. "You always start with the family."

"And who do they think killed him?"

"Momma," Quinn said. "You know I can't talk about an active investigation. What kind of sheriff would I be if I started blabbing to my momma about all I'd found out on a homicide? You also don't want all this garbage in your head. This is some really dirty business."

"Poor ole Jean Colson," Jean said, hands placed neatly in her lap as she stared out the window, then brushing at the makeup on her cheek reflected in the window. "Just sit down with your Elvis records and your jug of white zinfandel. Don't you be worrying about a woman you've known for more than thirty years. Even when your son is the only one who can help her out."

"I'm doing my best."

"And what have you done so far?"

"Damn it, Momma."

"I really wish you'd quit using that kind of language, Quinn Colson," she said. "This isn't your Ranger barracks where y'all clean your rifles and spit tobacco on the floor. This is a polite Saturday drive with your momma after she's been trying to comfort a friend in need. I'm not asking you for none of that *CSI* stuff I see on TV with your black lights and microscopes. I'm just wanting to know are you gonna find out who killed Danita's baby."

Quinn swallowed, biting his tongue. He turned on the Jericho Square, a light haze hovering over the downtown. Several vendors had set up by the gazebo. Old men in overalls selling watermelons, tomatoes, and okra. One of them proudly displayed a mess of jams and jellies and Cajun boiled peanuts, advertising their business with a hand-painted sign.

"I don't think it's a secret who Ordeen was working for."

"That woman running that brothel by the highway?"

"Technically, it's not a brothel," Quinn said. "It's a rural gentlemen's club."

"And how many gentlemen show up to a place like that?" Jean said.

Jean had a particular kind of dislike for Vienna's Place, knowing her own daughter had danced in several places just like it in Memphis. There was so much guilt and denial that Quinn never mentioned it. But he fully remembered finding Caddy some years ago dressed in a Dallas Cowboys cheerleader outfit and grinding on men's laps for tips. Caddy hadn't forgotten it, either, and freely spoke about it—to their mother's intense discomfort.

"Who is this woman anyway?" Jean asked. "Fannie Hathcock."

"An opportunist," Quinn said, driving with two fingers, heading straight toward his mother's house on Ithaca Street, his police radio squawking under their conversation. "She took over most of Stagg's business when he left town."

"Oh, hell," Jean said. "Everybody knows that."

"Before that she ran a little motor court down at the Choctaw Rez," he said. "Good times for high rollers. Some folks I know in Oxford are pretty sure she works for some bad folks down on the Coast. I'm pretty sure she has some strong political pull with some men in Jackson."

"Like that repulsive a-hole Vardaman?" she said. "I heard him on the radio yesterday, dithering on about state's rights and how Mississippi was better off before the Civil War. He said women needed to get back to a more biblical interpretation of their role in society."

"Folks are betting he'll be our next governor."

"Lord help us," Jean said, playing with the gold cross around her neck. "Sometimes it feels like this state wants to take us back about a hundred years."

"People do love to bend the Bible," he said. "Hucksters and insane folks have been doing it for a couple thousand years."

Fannie didn't like the way the men looked. Or the way the two glanced around at everything in Vienna's Place except for the topless dancers working the pole, the buckets of cold beer and liquor shots, or the girls in bikinis and lingerie dishing it out and serving it up. She leaned into the railing from the second-floor darkness and looked down at them talking to each other, wishing right now she had Ordeen or Mingo to listen in and let her know just what they were saying. Ever since Vienna's had been hit last year, she'd been a little skittish, beefing up the boys at the door, watching the TV monitors a little more closely, and carrying a big fucking gun in her Birkin bag.

These two boys had a hard look about them. One was older, with gray hair pulled into a ponytail, and the other skinny and muscled, with a face that looked like it had been carved from stone. They leaned against the antique bar, shooting the shit, looking at all the action but really just watching the money flow around the big, wide-open room. She could see them watch the cash go from the sucker to the waitress, to the bartenders, and then back out to the bouncer and all the way up the spiral staircase to her roost. They'd been there for more than an hour. Each one of them had bought just one beer. Goddamn them. Didn't they know this was a two-drink-minimum kind of place?

The men spotted each camera in every nook and cranny. They watched the bartender slip the big bills into the safety box behind the bar. They saw the girls smile and giggle and slide tips up their coots. They were pros, watching all the action like kids at a midway.

Fannie was curious, firing up a cigarillo from her Dunhill lighter, blowing out the smoke from up in her perch, thinking maybe she should ask one of her toughs to make sure they didn't have a gun on them. That was the last fucking thing she needed was another robbery, more girls screaming and yelling, blood on her new carpet and more holes in her vintage bar. Or maybe they were just the law, although no law she knew around in Tibbehah

County. Maybe these were some feds who'd come down from Oxford to try to figure out just how Buster White and his boys laundered all that cash in this shithole county. They'd never see it. And even if they raised their badges, turned on the houselights, and shined the light on all that tanned skin, cheap-ass tattoos, and pools of sweat, they'd never find just how the hell everything moved slow, easy, and efficient through Vienna's. Fannie wasn't as dumb as Johnny Stagg. Only Stagg would've let one of his people keep a fucking leather-bound ledger like some old-time pharmacist.

"Miss Fannie?" Midnight Man said, calling up from the top of the staircase.

She ashed her cigarillo off the railing, down on the head of some old bald-headed fuck from the Delta, dollar bills splayed in his fat fingers like he was Howard Hughes. She turned to look at Midnight Man, barely seeing his face in the dim light.

"Some fellas at the bar want to see you," he said, in a voice somewhere between a grunt and a whisper. "Don't like their looks. One of 'em got a ponytail and smells like that old Aqua Velva. That other cowboy-looking motherfucker toting a gun under his T-shirt. I seen that bulge. Want me to go with you?"

Fannie looked down at her packed house and then over at Midnight Man's big sweating face and nodded. "Come on," she said. "Get a few more boys to watch that door. Make sure no one gets out of here alive this time. You hear me?"

"Yes, ma'am," Midnight Man said, smiling, only his teeth showing in the darkness.

Fannie leaned into her elbows farther, looking down at the floor, studying the man with the hard face, as she sucked on the end of the cigarillo, thinking maybe she'd seen the son of a bitch before. He was one mean-looking SOB in a black T-shirt and blue jeans, a silver belt buckle under a flat stomach. He had long, muscled monkey arms and longish brown hair like men used to wear back in the seventies.

His friend was a good head shorter, in a black V-neck tee and a tacky black leather blazer. Who the hell would wear leather in the middle of the summer? His gray ponytail stretched his redneck face into a tight, bony mask. As she put the cigarillo back to her lips, the taller of the two looked up at her and smiled just a little. Fannie knowing good and goddamn well he couldn't see her, maybe only spotted that glow of the cigarillo, thinking he was being cute. Maybe he had someone on the inside, explaining how Fannie liked to watch from above.

She turned and headed toward the staircase, making sure she stopped by the office and grabbed her Birkin bag. If either one of those boys decided to get cute, she'd turn each of 'em from a rooster into a hen with two quick pulls of the trigger. Fannie stubbed out the smoke on her desk, circled down the steps, and entered the floor. The working girls parted as she walked toward the bar, pulsing house music blasting from the speakers, as Fannie focused on those two boys, watching their hands, their eyes, the cocky-ass way they leaned back into the bar like a couple of cowpokes.

Midnight Man crossed his huge arms over his stomach, standing by if he were needed. The back of his T-shirt read VIENNA'S PLACE / COLDEST BEER & HOTTEST WOMEN ON HWY 45.

"You boys look a little lost," Fannie said. "Y'all might want to get closer to the pole. In fifteen minutes, two sweet Southern girls will wrestle for five hundred bucks and the chance to win a trip over to Tunica."

"Miss Hathcock," the craggy-faced man said, nodding. "Sure is good to see you again."

"Sorry," she said, tilting her head, studying his face. The older dude with the ponytail stood back, grinning, his hands in the pockets of that cheap leather blazer.

"Wes Taggart," the craggy-faced man said. "This is my buddy, J. B. Hood. Our mutual friend Ray thought we might be of service."

"Is that a fact?" she said.

"Yes, ma'am."

"Well, unless you can dance nekkid or make me a Manhattan, I don't have a use for you."

"We both can tend bar," Taggart said. "If that's what you need. But Ray said you'd been having some trouble with some local boys? You know Ray. He likes to keep everything running real clean and smooth. Hates when business gets interrupted."

"No trouble here," she said. "Not in Tibbehah County."

"I guess I was mistaken," Taggart said, tilting up the bottle of Bud and reaching into his pocket for a thick wad of cash. He had big hands and thick knuckles, like a guy who laid brick or had fought his way in and out of prison. "Best of luck, Miss Hathcock."

J. B. Hood glanced over at Taggart and shrugged, not touching his beer, completely full and beaded with condensation. His hard little eyes darted around Vienna's, he nodded as if deciding something, and walked away without another word.

"You mind if I call Ray?" Fannie said. "Make sure we're free to talk?"

"No, ma'am," Taggart said, grinning. "Not at all." He had black eyes and a cruel mouth. On his right wrist he wore a thick turquoise bracelet that would've given Burt Reynolds a hard-on.

Fannie stepped back, nodded to Midnight Man, who hadn't budged an inch, and walked back across the room and then up the spiral staircase. She called Ray on one of her phones and waited ten times before he picked up. "Did you just send Hopalong Cassidy and fucking Gabby Hayes over to Vienna's?"

"Didn't know they were coming," he said. "Not yet."

"Wes Taggart?" she said. "Fucking J. B. Hood? Who the hell are they?"

"Buster White's idea," he said. "Thought you might could use some help since your bikers got neutered. I told them you'd feel different. I guess they didn't listen to me."

"What are they?" she said. "A couple of Mississippi guard dogs?"

"Much worse than that."

"What do they do?"

"I don't think you want to know."

"The fuck I don't," Fannie said, tapping the top of her glass-top desk with her long red nails. "They were checking out my operation for damn near an hour before they asked to speak to me. I hadn't been that well inspected since the last time I got a Pap smear."

"I don't like them," Ray said. "And I sure as hell don't trust them."

"Then why the fuck are they in my place?"

"Christ, Fannie," Ray said. "I don't think there's a good way to say this."

"Say it, Ray," she said. "Christ. Just say it."

"Those boys are your new partners."

12

TWO DAYS AFTER CROSSING PATHS WITH HEATH PRITCHARD, Quinn drove twenty-five miles up the Natchez Trace and stopped off at a sacred Indian mound built a few hundred years after Christ. He parked his truck, stretched, and walked over to an empty viewing area, the mound maybe a hundred meters away, a gentle hill covered in green grass in a big old field bordered by a meandering creek. He set a boot onto the low brick wall and lit up the second half of his Undercrown, checking the time, knowing that Jon Holliday would soon arrive from Oxford.

A few cars passed over the next few minutes, kicking up some grit from the roadside. The Trace was a slow place for traffic, a winding road that had evolved from a buffalo trail to a Native American trading path to a route for pioneers making their way from New Orleans up to Nashville. Not far north of here, Meriwether Lewis had checked into an inn on the Trace and taken his own life in the dark wilderness. Quinn had always been intrigued by the story, as Lewis's family always believed he was murdered. Even from the earliest American times, the wilds of north Mississippi and west Tennessee were full of robbers, rustlers, and thieves. Not that shit had changed.

Quinn tapped the cigar's ash on his boot heel and watched a red truck pass, then a white SUV, and then two men on touring bicycles. A few minutes later, he looked up to see a black government-issue sedan pull into a space beside his F-150. A tall black woman got out and headed toward him. She had high cheekbones, dark brown skin, and wide-set large eyes. Her hair was big and bouncy, full of natural curls.

Quinn watched her walk, dressed in neat black trousers and a black sleeveless silk top. She made no effort to conceal the automatic holstered on her hip. "You must be Wyatt Earp," she said, squinting into the sun.

"How could you tell?"

"That Beretta on your belt and the cigar in your hand."

Quinn stood and smiled, blowing smoke away in the direction of the ancient mounds. It was hot that morning and he'd started to sweat under the starched cotton of his khaki shirt, an American flag on the sleeve and the shield of Tibbehah County on the breast pocket.

"A private joke with some of the folks in the Oxford office," she said. "You and Holliday made quite a team taking down Johnny Stagg's crooked old ass. Folks still talk about it."

"Is Holliday coming?"

"Got held up with some bullshit down in Jackson," she said. "Some assholes from Ohio came down to rally around a Confederate monument. But he sends his regards. I'm Nathalie Wilkins. Folks call me Nat."

She offered her hand and Quinn shook it. She smiled with both her greenish brown eyes and wide red mouth with big, perfect teeth. He'd heard her name before. Wilkins had been part of a north Mississippi task force, working for the DEA, focusing on drug running and human trafficking. Holliday had told him she might be joining them on the meet, as she'd been tracking the flow of drugs up from the Gulf Coast and might know a little about the trucking company in Tupelo.

"Y'all always meet out here?" Nat asked, scanning the wide green landscape and quiet curve of road where they stood. "Trying to get back to nature or something?"

"Kind of a tradition," Quinn said. "When Holliday was undercover, this was a place where we could talk in private."

"He told me that I could trust you," Nat said. "Said anything I know I could share and you'd be straight. Is that true?"

"Yes, ma'am."

"I did my eighth-grade history project on the Choctaws," Nat said, the cicadas making a high, wild clicking racket out in the tree line. "Did you know they believed these places were the entrance and exit to Mother Earth? That underneath that hill were all kinds of tunnels. It was the place the tribe emerged and where they'd return when they died. No telling how many old bones are in that mound."

"My old house is built on a mound," Quinn said. "When I was kid, I used to take a shovel to the hills. I found all kinds of arrowheads and pottery shards. My Aunt Halley hated it. She didn't see the sense in the digging, only that I made a big damn mess."

"This down in Tibbehah County?"

"Yes, ma'am," Quinn said. "Born and raised."

"Don't you 'Yes, ma'am' me, if we're gonna be working together," she said. "I'm from Memphis. Orange Mound proud. Did a few years in the service. Military Police, Afghanistan and all that. Came back home, got that degree, and got hired with Drug Enforcement."

"You married?"

"Do you see a ring on this finger?" she said, grinning. "Divorced. I married my high school boyfriend. How dumb was that? He couldn't deal with the hours and the attitude. Wanted me to have kids and keep house while he punched the clock at First Tennessee. How about you?"

"I'm getting hitched in two weeks."

"Damn," she said. "Good for you, Colson. What's she like?"

"Beautiful, smart as hell," Quinn said. "She's tough, too. Works as an ER nurse down in Tibbehah. We knew each other as kids but lost track until last year."

"Ain't that sweet," she said. "A real-life love story. Found each other again after all these years. Y'all probably used to climb trees and kiss under that Southern moonlight, making pledges of undying teenage love. So, how'd y'all connect again?"

"Her ex-husband was a bank robber," Quinn said. "He shot up a titty bar off Highway 45 and then he tried to kill me."

"Hate to say it, Colson," Nat said. "But you done fucked up trying to get a Hallmark Movie of the Week on that shit."

Quinn laughed, taking another puff on the cigar. A few more cars passed, moving north on the Trace. Nat grinned at him, letting him know she liked to mess with him. Quinn felt comfortable with her loose-and-easy style, no bullshit, and straight talk about business. She rested a foot up on the ledge where Quinn sat, looking down at him, watching his face like she was trying to figure out if he was playing with her on the bank robber stuff. "OK," she said.

"Now we're straight. How about you tell me about this informant you told Holliday about."

"He's a man I know and trust," Quinn said. "He spotted a kid named Ordeen Davis at a trucking company over at Tupelo a few weeks back."

"And what's that mean to me?"

"I found Ordeen Davis's body chopped up in a toolbox a few days ago," Quinn said. "Someone tossed it into the Big Black River. My friend let me know that this trucking company does a lot of dirty business. They move stolen goods, hijacked shipments, and drugs. He thinks they might be moving people in from Mexico, too. We've heard about girls getting caught up in human trafficking up to Memphis and over to Atlanta. Our source on all that disappeared last year."

"Dirty, dirty shit," Nat said.

"You bet."

"And dirty shit happens to be my specialty."

"I can introduce you to my friend," Quinn said. "He promised to stick around long enough to keep an eye out on this outfit. But he wants out fast. I don't want him mixed up in all this business."

"OK," she said. "I see what you're saying. But let me ask you this. Just how close of friends are y'all?"

"How about best man at my wedding."

"Oh, shit," Nat said. "And what's he doing for this trucking company?"

"He's a driver," Quinn said. "He's made a few runs for them over the last few months. The outfit forced him to make trips over in Houston and down on the Coast without knowing what he was hauling. He was on his way to quitting after he saw Ordeen Davis doing business there and then Davis turned up dead. He'd known

Ordeen since he was kid and has a personal reason for wanting to know the connection."

"And y'all think whatever Mr. Davis was doing got his ass stuffed into that box?"

"Yes, ma'am," Quinn said. "That's the working theory. He's been involved with some rough folks in Tibbehah County. I'm looking into them. But I don't know much about these people in Tupelo."

Nat Wilkins tilted her head and closed one eye to examine Quinn's face. Her big, bouncy hair shook in the hot, dry wind. "Y'all wouldn't happen to be talking about those fine people at Sutpen's Trucking, would you?"

"Now I know why Holliday didn't think we needed him."

"One white boy on this is enough." Nat reached over and patted Quinn's knee. "When do I get to meet this friend of yours?"

"Can you promise me that you'll keep him clear of this mess?"

"This man hauling for those mean-ass crooks in Tupelo?" she said. "Hate to tell you, Sheriff. But it's too damn late. His ass is already knee-deep in Shit City, USA."

It was three hours before the first heats and the Pritchard Racing Team—that being Tyler, Cody, and Uncle Heath—rolled into the west gate of The Ditch, Riverside Speedway, in West Memphis, Arkansas. Tyler knew the old man at the gate and they jawed a little about the condition of the track being too dry and way too slick, how many teams had already set up in the pits, and how the hot weather sure brought out those short shorts and tight tank tops on the ladies. The old man said he knew he shouldn't be looking, but once he stopped caring, they might as well put him in a pine box.

"That's one horny old coot," Heath said, as they drove slow away from the gate. "He should be ashamed of himself. Probably hands out butterscotch candy to his grandkids. But if that man's pecker hopped out of his pocket and started singing the 'Star-Spangled Banner,' he wouldn't know where to put it."

"Where'd that guard say to set up?" Cody said, driving their big-ass truck, making his way past all the other trailers and car haulers, looking back in the rearview to Tyler.

"Behind the pavilion area," Tyler said. "Back past the merch trailers where they got them jumpy houses and games for the kiddies."

"And where exactly are we supposed to find this Doc McDuffie?" Cody said, spitting gum out of his open window. "King of the Aryan Brotherhood and friend to the fucking white man?"

"Doc'll find us," Heath said. "He knows to look out for our trailer. Team Fucking Pritchard, all in big letters. Don't need to tell Doc nothin'. He's one of the smartest fellas I ever met. Knows all about politics, world affairs, read things in CIA files that make you shit your pants."

"Is this guy a medical doctor?" Tyler said. "Or is that some kind of White Power nickname?"

"Can't say," Uncle Heath said. "I don't know if Doc is his first name or his title. That's just what we called him at Parchman. He was always looking out for us, bringing in pills stuck into the women guards' coots. Sometimes he'd get a fucking pharmacy trucked in some fat man's butthole. If you were with the AB, you didn't worry about feeling no pain."

"You told me he was a real fucking doctor," Tyler said. "You said they called his ass Doctor Feelgood and that's how he could get his hands on all those sacks of pills from down in Mexico."

"Sure, sure, he's got connections in Mexico," Heath said, slumping down in his seat, craning his head around to look into the backseat at Tyler. "Down in Guatemala and Colombia, too. He did business before he got put in prison and moved down to Mexico after to live like a golden god."

"So why'd he come back to fucking Arkansas?" Cody said. "If he's such a damn big hotshot?"

"To move the dang pills," Heath said. "Shit, boy. Ain't y'all been listening to what I got to say? This man used to do lines with goddamn Pablo Escobar. You shoulda heard his stories about the women down there in Colombia with big ole brown titties and nipples big as silver dollars. They damn moved a mountain of coke from down in Colombia with some crazy-ass pilot who lived around here. Had a damn airstrip in his backyard."

"I seen a documentary on Escobar on the History Channel," Cody said. "He was one bad son of a bitch."

"And he's been dead for as long as Uncle Heath's been in prison," Tyler said.

Cody found a slot and drove in nose-first with the trailer hanging back toward the dirt road. The boys sat in the truck, the sounds of gunning motors and zip-zip of the air drill all around them. Heath lit a cigarette and reached to open his door. All the Pritchards piled out of the car and walked back around the trailer.

"That what happened to Doc?" Cody said, talking about the guy as if he knew him. "He get busted moving all that coke?"

"No, sir," Heath said, laughing. "Doc got all fucked up a few years back and stole some old boy's stump grinder. He rode that son of a bitch halfway across Arkansas before he got pulled over by highway patrol. He got caught with a baggie of weed and some of them fat-burning pills. Motherfucker was higher than a kite. Said he turned to the cop and admitted he'd taken the stump grinder but sure would appreciate them giving his weed back."

"This shit's not funny," Cody said. "We ain't got time for this."

"Doc McDuffie knows people," Heath said. "He gets us what we want, move that fucking product, and we won't need nobody's goddamn permission to run our own family business. Those scooter boys can blow it out their assholes."

Tyler hit the back door on a brand-new thirty-eight-foot Super Hauler, the ramp unfolding down like a fucking spaceship. He unfolded the ramp's extension into the dirt and walked on into the trailer, turning on the lights and making sure nothing shook loose on the drive up. Cody followed him on inside, checking the straps and tie-downs on the car, looking over the hood at Tyler. Uncle Heath had wandered off to parts unknown, toward the track pavilion where they were selling T-shirts and trying to get folks to sign up for cell phone service. One of those big blow-up figures that shakes and shimmies towered above all the jump houses and little kiosks offering all the free shit a redneck could handle.

Inside the trailer, Tyler hit the play button on his phone and the Bluetooth speakers started playing Jason Aldean. "Take a Little Ride." *"Been goin' round and round all day."* It was tradition. The Pritchard family anthem.

"Fuck me," Cody said.

"Goddamn it," Tyler said. "Goddamn it to hell."

"Maybe this Doc McDuffie is the real deal?"

"Pablo Escobar?" Tyler said. "Cocaine cowboy gets busted stealing a stump grinder?"

"You got someone else on speed dial who can bring in that many pills?" Cody asked.

"Either Uncle Heath comes through or our asses gonna get squeezed between the damn Cornbread Mafia and Marquis Sledge's gravediggers," Tyler said. "I don't know why we agreed to this. We done some stupid shit, brother, but this one gets the gold trophy."

"If it wasn't for Uncle Heath, we'd been dragged halfway to Tuscaloosa on those scooters," Cody said.

"And if it wasn't for Uncle Heath," Tyler said, "we wouldn't have goddamn Fannie Hathcock tail-grabbing our ass with those scooter boys in the first damn place."

Tyler felt his heart beating fast in his chest, his breathing narrow. He sure could use a little hit to calm things down, make the world move just a little slower to make sense of things.

"Knock, knock!" a voice called out. Uncle Heath stood at the mouth of the trailer with his arm around a fat man about a head taller than him, with a beard about as long and bushy as Tyler's and wearing a pair of amber-colored glasses. He had big meaty arms and a large belly swelling over his pants. His gray hair had been combed straight back like a television preacher and he wore a T-shirt that read, in big red letters, AMERICA FIRST.

"Hey, boys," Uncle Heath said. "I want y'all to meet Doc McDuffie. The best damn friend I ever had in Unit 29."

So what do you know about this Sutpen?" Quinn asked.

His Uncle Jerry sat across from him at a picnic table outside Mr. Varner's Quick Mart, Mr. Varner cooking barbecue on an oil drum that had been split in half. Varner had been smoking since early that morning and a low hickory haze hung under the old oak where they sat. As the men talked, Varner flipped the pork and half chickens over the grill, hissing and burning, a pleasant smell in the air.

Hondo had come with Quinn that morning and sat attentively at Mr. Varner's feet while he turned the meat.

"Mr. Sutpen's been dead for twenty years," Jerry Colson said. "The trucking company still uses his name. Yeah, I used to drive for them from time to time."

"You have any trouble with them?" Quinn said.

Uncle Jerry shrugged. He was a tall, thin man with a weathered face, prominent chin, and clear blue eyes. He had on a clean white T-shirt, bell-bottom jeans, and a CAT trucker's hat. Quinn had never seen him without it, although Uncle Jerry had retired about five years ago, spending time now doing a little gardening, a lot of hunting out in the Big Woods, and fishing on Choctaw Lake.

"What do you mean there, son?" Jerry said. "You mean about being paid?"

Quinn shook his head. "I mean, did anyone at Sutpen ever ask you to truck some things that made you uncomfortable?"

"Like driving a tractor-trailer full of Coors beer from Texarkana to Atlanta?" Jerry said, grinning.

"Sure," Quinn said. "Stuff like that."

Quinn had been working on a pulled pork plate with beans and slaw, Jerry having the Diablo sandwich with extra-hot sauce and some Golden Flake chips on the side. Mr. Varner didn't barbecue often, but, when he did, it was a special occasion. Quinn had promised to bring back a few extra plates for Cleotha and Reggie.

"Did they ever ask you to haul anything illegal?"

Jerry smiled wide and shook his head. "Now, am I talking to my nephew or to the sheriff of Tibbehah County?"

"You're talking to both," he said. "But, right now, let's just say your nephew."

"Damn Sutpen," Jerry said. "OK, son. What do you want to know?"

"Boom told me that you'd recommended him for the job?" Quinn said.

"Well," Jerry said, picking at his teeth a bit with his pinkie nail. "Me and ole Boom were at Shooter's, playing a game of pool and drinkin' a little beer. He told me all about the trouble he'd been having with Ole Man Skinner and those sorry bastard supervisors. He said he wanted to get back into truckin' and asked if I knew some folks."

"And you sent him over to Tupelo?"

"I told him I knew some local folks who wouldn't take issue with his arm," Jerry said. "A place he could make some good money fast. I figured Boom was a grown-ass man and knew what he was getting into, and if he didn't like it, he could get himself out. Figured working with crooks you knew was better than getting cornholed by some local good ole boys."

"But you knew they were crooked?"

"I never knew if I had a little extra on my truck," Jerry said. "And I have to be honest, I never really asked. You got to remember, son, I got my start running Colson shine. As long as I'm getting paid, I don't give a turkey about what I'm trucking. I just like to get paid well, on time, and Boom seemed to be hurting for some cash. Hadn't you ever cut a few corners? Maybe done something you weren't real proud of?"

Quinn nodded, thinking about his conversation with Maggie about Anna Lee, remembering that time when he'd first gotten back from the Rangers, wanting more than anything to get her back in his bed. And he had, breaking up her marriage, nearly tearing her family apart.

"So Sutpen's dead?" Quinn said. "You know who's running the company?"

Uncle Jerry shook his head and reached for his Dr Pepper. He took a few swallows and reached down to pat Hondo's flank. He looked up from under the bill of his ball cap and said, "I wouldn't get too involved with these folks," he said. "I think that if Boom's got trouble looking the other way, it's best just to move on."

"This isn't about Boom," Quinn said. "A young man was killed last week named Ordeen Davis. I'm pretty sure Ordeen was doing business with the folks at Sutpen. Just trying to get a better idea of who I'm about to deal with. I looked 'em up on the internet and couldn't find anything. The corporate records all go back to some holding company down in Gulfport."

Jerry's faded-blue eyes widened. Hondo sat on his rump and looked up at Quinn with his two different colored eyes, tilting his head, trying to look pitiful enough for just a bite of that barbecue. "I don't know who's doing what now," Jerry said. "But twenty years back, folks said Mr. Sutpen did a lot of business with a man named Buster White. That name mean anything to you?"

Quinn shook his head.

"You may want to check out the history books," Jerry said. "Buster was part of that state-line mob back in the day. He got sent off to prison some time back in Louisiana. But he may be back, and if he's still connected to those Sutpen folks, I'd sure watch my ass."

"Always do."

"These ain't some local yokels, Quinn," he said. "These are some real mean motherfuckers. Yeah, I've worked for folks like that. But at the end of the day, I just took a long shower and cashed my damn check. Not everyone wants to know who's buttering their bread."

Quinn nodded, watching Mr. Varner putting out some flames that had started kick up on the grill. He squirted some water out of a Gatorade bottle until the fire settled down.

"I done some things I'm ashamed of," Jerry said. "But I figure I wasn't hurting no one. And I was the one taking the damn risk. If I'm putting my neck out there, I sure didn't mind getting paid a little extra. In your job, you're not being asked to clean up all of north Mississippi. It ain't worth it, son."

"I prefer a little action," Quinn said. Hondo hopped up beside him and he handed him a little barbecue. He snapped it up fast and nuzzled close to Quinn, looking for more. "And don't scare easy."

"You are a true Colson," Jerry said. "You know, I used to run shine for your granddad. All the Colson brothers did, including your dad. How is that old so-'n'-so anyway? Is he at least coming to his son's wedding?"

"I haven't heard from Dad since he left town last year."

"Come on, now."

"Not a word." Quinn ate a little more barbecue and reached for the bottle of sauce Mr. Varner had left on the table along with a roll of paper towels. He poured out a little more sauce on the barbecue and took a big bite. The oak they sat under was big and old, the roots running deep up under the parking lot, buckling the hot asphalt.

"Your momma said something about him going to L.A.?" Jerry said. "He's a little long in the tooth and thin in the skin to be getting back into the stunt business."

"I don't think it was anything big," Quinn said. "He probably went back to that Old West stunt show they do at Universal Studios, playing the town drunk or maybe Cookie, the trail cook. Only thing he left were his two horses to feed and his last electric bill. You remember that old cherry-red Pontiac?"

"That was the one in that Burt Reynolds picture?" Jerry said, finishing the Diablo sandwich and wadding up the tinfoil. "The one where he and that other crazy-ass stuntman jumped over the river. He said it had been a rocket car and he'd converted it back."

"That was all more of his bullshit," Quinn said. "But, yep. Same car. He finally got that piece of crap running and, one morning, he just shagged ass."

Jerry set his jaw, nodding. He slipped off his CAT ball cap, played with the brim, and pulled it back onto his head, making a little *tsk*-ing sound. "I do love my brother," he said. "But he was a truly horseshit husband and father to y'all. I'm sorry about that."

Quinn looked over to see Mr. Varner forking a slab of ribs and turning it over on the grill, the meat hissing as the smoke blew off down the highway.

"He tried to make a go of a land deal in Tibbehah and the damn thing went bust," Quinn said. "I think he was embarrassed and didn't want to talk about it."

"And left his son holding a flaming bag of crap?"

Quinn nodded. "Yes, sir."

"That'd be my brother," Jerry said. "That man would jump out of an airplane with no parachute, run nekkid with his hair on fire, but he could never talk straight to you face-to-face."

Doc McDuffie was still hanging out, sitting in an easy chair by the pits with a bucket of Kentucky Fried Chicken in his lap, when Cody walked in from the infield and tossed his helmet onto the ground. Doc pulled a chicken leg from his teeth, wiped his mouth with his stubby little fingers, and said, "You were revving that damn engine way too high," he said. "Hell, I could hear it up in the grandstands. No wonder you blew your damn load."

On the eighth lap, Cody tried to take the lead on that damn

Booger Phillips and the engine bucked him, smoke and oil covering his face, nearly driving blind until he was off the track. Tyler had seen the whole thing, watching his brother from the fence line, close enough that he needed to pick the dirt out of his teeth. It wasn't his fault. Sometimes a car can just fuck a driver.

"I told y'all you needed a new engine," Uncle Heath said, handing Cody a red Solo cup filled with Jim Beam. "But don't you worry. We'll strip that damn car down to the lug nuts and build her up better 'an new."

Cody unzipped his fire suit down to his waist and slunk down in a folding chair, watching as they hauled his race car back out of the infield. Tyler took a seat next to him, not saying anything, knowing his brother was pissed as hell. This was a big race at The Ditch, the goddamn Hooker Hood Classic, and now that snot-nose little shit would be getting the gold trophy and one of those fine-ass Lucas Oil girls. That was like a hard swift kick in the nuts to the Pritchard boys.

The four men sat close to the fence, no one close to them, the sound of the engines keeping their business private. The next race was stock and already the boys were out there, testing the track, running their vehicles from side to side to warm up the tires, gunning the engines and testing the dirt. The stands were about half full that night, bright lights shining down on the dirt, the air smelling like corn dogs and burned rubber. Families with little kids holding American flags, old coots drinking beer and writing down the winners and losers, girls in cut-off jean shorts and cropped T-shirts trying to make their way into the infield and get a selfie with the drivers.

No one spoke for a long time, watching the green flag drop and the stock cars thunder off. After the fourth lap, McDuffie put down the bucket of chicken and said, "So you boys want to get into the pill business?"

Tyler and Cody nodded, not able to see Uncle Heath, who sat on the row behind them, cracking peanuts and yelling at the drivers. Doc McDuffie kept on watching the race while sipping on a Budweiser Tall Boy. The big bearded man had tattoos on his hands reading LOVE on his left knuckles and HATE on his right.

"Yeah, I know some people," Doc said. "But y'all need to be a little more specific about you want."

Tyler reached into his pocket and pulled out a folded piece of paper of the grocery list he'd got from Marquis Sledge. He passed it on to Doc, letting the old man lift out a pair of reading glasses and set it onto his thick nose, red and veiny. The man looked like a White Power Santa. He lifted his old fuzzy white eyebrows as his lips moved, reading over the words, took off his glasses, and handed the paper back to Tyler. "How about y'all come on and step into my office?"

The cars zipped around the quarter-mile track, hitting the gas and tossing up chunks of mud on the turns. The mud rained down on the bleachers, plunking down into Tyler's Solo cup. He picked out the mud chip and took a long swallow, following Doc McDuffie and Uncle Heath away from the track and back through the pits. The car had been dropped by their trailer and Tyler stepped inside the trailer for a moment to crack open a new beer and fill his cup. They headed on through the city of trailers, trucks, and race cars, some of the boys telling Cody "Tough luck" and "You'll get 'em next time," lots of handshakes and slaps on the back. They kept walking on out the gate and into the parking lot, where Doc McDuffie had parked a Mercedes diesel sedan. It was navy blue, with a lot of rust bubbling up on the hood, sun-faded and worn on the cab and on the trunk that McDuffie unlocked with a ring of a thousand jangling keys.

Inside, he pulled out an old hard-leather briefcase and looked around the half-empty lot before spinning open the combo and showing the Pritchards a bunch of bottles and baggies inside. "Y'all got the money?"

"This all you got?" Tyler said.

"Hell, boy," Doc said. "How fucked up do y'all want to get?"

Tyler felt his stomach drop as he shook his head and walked away from the big old Mercedes to the edge of the lot. Cody was right up behind him, barely listening to Uncle Heath dog-cussing that son of a bitch for not being straight with him. He handed Tyler the cup of whiskey and Tyler drained it before tossing the cup into the weeds. Over the speaker, they could hear the announcer talking with Booger Phillips, tonight's grand champion, the kid's high little voice trying to be all humble about it, saying it wasn't nothing but hard work and that winning is just part of God's grand plan for him.

"We'll get that car straight," Cody said.

"I ain't worried about the fucking race."

"I know."

"Listening to Uncle Heath was dumber than shit."

"Yep."

"We done worked too long and too hard," Tyler said. "What we grow. What we sell. That ain't nobody's business."

"He's our kin."

"Ain't no more kin to me than a monkey in the zoo," Tyler said. "And if we don't let him know his place, those Born Losers gonna be the last thing we need to worry about."

"There are other people."

"Who?" Tyler said.

Tyler heard a yelp and turned back to see Uncle Heath had slammed Doc McDuffie's fingers in the trunk. The man was convulsing and screaming with pain as Uncle Heath grabbed him by his white Santa beard and yanked his forehead down time and again to the metal.

"That's one way of doing it," Cody said.

"Man's got to learn," Tyler said.

Uncle Heath then started using the fat man's kidneys like a punching bag and snatched up the old scuffed briefcase, knocking him harder in the head and scattering all the pills to the ground. He was red-faced and sweating when he turned back to Tyler and Cody and said, "Come on. Let's go. We got to get that shit loaded up."

Tyler and Cody just stood there, watching Doc McDuffie blubbering and crying against the German car, his hands still trapped in the trunk. Plastic baggies and pill bottles all around him.

"Damn," Uncle Heath said. "You boys coming or not? Shit, we still got two more races to watch."

13

THREE DAYS AFTER THOSE TWO COUNTRY-AND-WESTERN dipshits showed up at Vienna's, Fannie drove over to Tupelo, to a trucking company off Highway 45 called Sutpen's, and left her Lexus out in the lot with the motor running. She knew it wouldn't take long to get her damn point across.

"Let's get a few goddamn things straight," Fannie said, after marching right through the cubicles and rabbit warren offices to a big glass office marked WES TAGGART, busting right in without so much of a tap. "I don't give a shit what Buster White told you, but Vienna's Place is not, nor will ever be, up for sale or free for the taking. That's my business. If you and Gabby Hayes want to flip burgers over at the Rebel and talk politics with farmers, be my guest. Y'all will be a big hit with all the toothless fuckwads wanting to make America great again."

"You want to take a seat?" Taggart said, looking a little amused, standing at attention by his desk in a tight black T-shirt with a pack of smokes in the pocket. He crossed his muscular arms over his flat stomach and watched Fannie with an annoying little smirk on his weathered face. "Could I get you some coffee or tea, Miss Hathcock? Maybe a cold Coca-Cola?"

"I didn't drive up to socialize," she said. "I damn well know what you and your buddy do and what you believe is going to happen down in Tibbehah County. But I just got off the phone with White. And after a supreme amount of good ole boy bullshit, he understands just what he is entitled to. I may operate the best damn whorehouse in north Mississippi, but I'm not anybody's punch."

Taggart grinned some more, big and toothy, his nose a little flat and misshapen, and sat at the edge of the desk. "No, ma'am," he said. "Never thought about that for one second."

"Then what was all that bullshit the other night with you two?" she said, so fucking mad her hands were shaking as she reached into her bag for her Dunhills and cigarillo case. "Y'all were casing Vienna's like you'd just bought the place at auction."

"Mr. White and I've been talking for a long while," Taggart said, rubbing his chin and ogling her titties as he spoke. "He just feels like you need a little help running things until we put out a few fires. It's in your best interest, Miss Hathcock. You need to settle down and just trust me on that."

"Trust you?" Fannie said. "Christ Almighty. I don't even know you and your damn *B.J. and the Bear* crew. And what kind of fucking fires can you see from over in Tupelo? The last thing I need is a couple ex-cons rolling up in their Cadillacs trying to tell me how to run my business because they were born with a pecker between their bowed legs."

Taggart leaned back a little and laughed, shaking his head, while

Fannie tried to kick on that five-hundred-dollar lighter but only getting a *click-click-click*. He reached into his tight Wranglers, hugging his goddamn package like it had sprayed on by Earl Scheib, and snapped open an old Zippo. Fannie took a draw and watched his hard face, still grinning, still amused by her discomfort and anger to the point she wanted to grind out that cigarillo right into his beady little black eye.

"Mr. White feels we're getting edged out up here," Taggart said. "By the blacks. And by a couple of young bucks and their high-tech weed operation. You know who I'm talking about?"

"Those dumb shitbirds couldn't find Memphis on a road map," she said. "They're just a couple locals giving me a headache. What's not clear about me saying that I got it all figured out?"

"That ain't what I'm hearing," he said. "My understanding is, they've been up in Memphis talking to Marquis Sledge's black ass about being his supplier and cutting us out of the picture. That doesn't sit so well with the boys."

Fannie blew out some smoke and tapped at the edge of his desk. "That's bullshit."

"No, ma'am," he said, standing up, adjusting his big turquoise belt buckle. "It ain't bullshit a-tall. How about you just sit down for a moment and we can talk through how all this is going to work?"

"You boys want to edge me out, you're gonna have to man the fuck up and come at me with a gun in one hand and your dick in the other, because I don't scare easily," she said. "And I sure as hell don't roll over on my back and spread my fucking legs. So what if those Pritchards are talking big-time shit and trying to make a name? Only thinking those boys know how to do is turn left for twenty laps. How you think they're gonna work with the fuckin' Mexican cartels through Houston?"

"I heard they got a new source."

"Where?"

"We don't know," Taggart said. "But me, you, and Mr. White are in this for the goddamn long haul. Without the bigger picture, Vienna's Place is just a snatch-and-titty money wash. How badly do you think Mr. White needs the aggravation your place has been giving him? You got the damn moralists raising hell with our friends in Jackson and then you got that fucking Wild West showdown from last year. You need to think about your value here. And if I were you, I'd be looking to make some good friends fast."

Fannie blew some smoke in his direction, her tongue roving at the edge of her mouth. Wes Taggart just smiled back at her with those hard black eyes. His eyes never left her tits until the gray-ponytailed fuck J. B. Hood wandered on in the door and looked left and right like a guard dog waiting to either bite someone or lift his leg. His jaw tightened and his left eye twitched a little as he tried to stare her down.

"Y'all all right?" J. B. Hood said. "Some folks heard some yelling."

"You ain't got any more caution than a blue-eyed mule," Fannie said, holding the cigarillo by the side of her mouth, doing her best Gabby Hayes. Hood didn't get her meaning, looking her over, and then back to Wes Taggart, wanting to know what the fuck he needed to do. Taggart just nodded to the door and Hood left, giving Fannie one last hard look.

"Let me put it this way," Taggart said. "What you got don't work without us. It never has. We've always been part of the deal even if you didn't care to acknowledge who we were and what we were doing for the boys. Who the hell do you think runs the chain from the Coast? Where the fuck do you think you get some of your girls? I got my part. You got your part. Fucking Ray has his part. We want what's best for all of us."

"I work for White," Fannie said. "Hired help is no concern to me. Whatever trouble I have in north Mississippi is under my watch. You just keep on riding that long white line and humpin' to please and let me handle my own fucking business."

"It's too late, Fannie," Taggart said, pushing himself off the desk, muscles flexing in his long arms. He walked up close to Fannie and she waited, even prayed, for him to lay one finger on her bare skin. Instead, he just stood there in the smoke and haze and smiled. "Buster White don't change his mind too often. So how about me and you just learn to play house?"

"Let's say I do," she said. "What's in it for me?"

The man smelled like the horse sweat on her father when he'd come in from weeks on the oil rig. No amount of Aqua Velva could cover it up. He looked down at Fannie and finally touched her right arm, Fannie yanking it away quick but not budging an inch in her Jimmy Choos. If he touched her again, she'd pull that pistol out of her purse and spread his nuts across the wall like a couple of cracked eggs.

"Everything keeps running smooth," he said. "You handle the women and let us handle the men."

"That's bullshit and you know it."

"Then who's gonna help you?" Taggart said. "That damn Choctaw kid from the Rez or that little ole nigger boy who got his lights shot out by the Pritchards? Seems like you're 0-and-2 in the employee department, Fannie."

Fannie held her breath, feeling the blood and heat flow to her face and her teeth grinding on one another. That man could toss off all his macho bullshit all he wanted, but mentioning Mingo was something that he'd never get back. She'd held her fucking nose, took care of what needed to be done, and didn't need some sweaty redneck telling her to understand the way the world turned.

"First thing, let's shut down that supply," Taggart said. "OK? The last thing we need is for those Memphis spooks to start going back on our deal."

She knew she was fucked. If this was what Buster White had decreed, it was either agree to work with these assholes in the meantime or get shut down real quick. White piled on that good ole boy backslappin' bullshit right up until the point he put a bullet in the back of your head or had you cut up and tossed into Lake Pontchartrain.

Fannie nodded, tossing down the cigarillo onto Wes Taggart's carpet and grinding it out with the point of her stiletto.

"My business is my own."

"Only when it ain't."

"We'll see."

"You've been in this business long as me, Fannie," he said, narrowing his eyes. "Nothing is permanent."

"I just hope you boys don't piss on the furniture," she said. "Y'all better be good and goddamn housebroken and don't shit the fucking bed."

"Oh yes, ma'am," Taggart said, swallowing, eyes wandering back down on her tits as he licked his lips. "We'll do our best."

"You're good luck already," Nat Wilkins said, sitting behind the wheel of her sweet-ass black sedan, Boom Kimbrough in the shotgun seat. "You see who that is?"

"I sure do," Boom said, watching as Fannie Hathcock exited the corrugated tin building of Sutpen Trucking, Inc., big white purse thrown over her shoulder, and got into her white Lexus and sped away.

"You a regular customer down there?" Nat said. "At Vienna's Place? I hear they got the coldest beer and hottest women in the Mid-South. Lap dances and all the chicken fingers a man can eat."

"Never been one for strip clubs," Boom said. "Whole lotta cash just for a tease. Besides, I don't go to bars no more."

"How come?" Nat asked. "You come to the Cross, Mr. Kimbrough?"

"Me and liquor used to be real tight," Boom said. "But we don't get along much anymore. I have a beer now and then. But I can't mess with that hard likker no more."

"I like a little cocktail now and then," she said. "Mojitos. Maybe a dirty martini. My ex didn't like it when I drank. He said it made me cocky as hell."

"So what's all this trucking business mean to y'all?" Boom said. "Don't see how much more I can help."

"Patience, Mr. Kimbrough," she said, grinning, tapping the wheel. "Damn name of the game. Fannie Hathcock in a meet with Wes Taggart? I can't say I'm surprised, but this is the first time I've seen those two together live and in person. Taggart is a two-time loser. Got out last year after fifteen years at Kilby over in Alabama. He'd been running some bingo parlors in Jefferson County and got in a little too good with the local law."

"I didn't deal with Taggart," Boom said. "Worked with a guy named L. Q. Smith. He's the front guy, a real aw-shucks kind of redneck. When I told him I wasn't good with running shit off the books, that's when that Taggart guy stepped in. Him and some nasty old dude with a ponytail."

"That'd be J. B. Hood."

"Why all these peckerwoods go by their initials?" Boom said.

"Makes 'em think they sound important," Nat said. "Or else it's just easier for their dumb asses to spell."

"Who's this J. B. Hood?"

"Cutthroat motherfucker," Nat said, reaching into her purse for a pack of chewing gum. She offered Boom some and he shook his head as she popped a piece of Doublemint into her mouth. "Killed a man when he was eighteen for talking back to his momma. Ran with some mean-ass brothers up in Memphis back in the day. He got charged with two more murders, but he wasn't convicted. Pretty sure he was button man for this guy named Bobby Campo who used to run the skin and money wash for the Syndicate before your Johnny Stagg stole the show. That man's been shooting, robbing, busting heads since Elvis watched women wrestle in their cotton panties."

"Did Quinn tell you about those missing girls?"

Nat, chewing on her gum, looked down at her cell phone. She tapped her long nails against the screen, hitting a fast reply, and nodded. "Sure did."

"Mexican girl named Ana Maria and a black girl named Tamika," Boom said. "Fifteen damn years old."

"Sheriff told me that you and his sister thought those girls got sold to Fannie Hathcock."

"That's right," Boom said. "I got told that straight by the pimp who turned them out. A nasty, pointy-eared motherfucker named Blue Daniels. Blue had no cause to tell me a lie. I banged his head into a door and bit off a piece of his ear."

"I like you, Mr. Kimbrough," she said. "You talk straight. Did y'all ever find those little girls?"

Boom shook his head, sitting there in the comfortable leather seats, feeling strange being in a parked car with a woman he just met. "Had someone on the inside of that Hathcock woman's titty bar," Boom said. "He told us that she'd put those girls on a truck. Said they were the same trucks that dropped off girls in Tibbehah County to work the pole or at these private parties that woman set up in the hills for rich men from up in Oxford and political types."

"Sheriff said that boy disappeared, too," she said. "Choctaw kid named Mingo."

Boom nodded. "Ain't nobody heard a word," he said. "There was no way Mingo would've taken off like that. Without saying shit. I think Fannie Hathcock got wise that he was tipping us off. I think she told him he'd better get far away from Tibbehah County. Or maybe she had him killed."

"That's about how it works with these people," Nat said. "They won't let anything get in the way of money or their own personal shit. You get in their damn way, fuck up that flow of money, and your ass is gone."

"Who are 'they'?"

"We call 'em lots of names," Nat said. "Dixie Mafia. Cornbread Cosa Nostra. The Good Ole Boys. The Syndicate. But they ain't that fancy. This isn't some *Godfather* shit with omerta and honor and all that. This is just some mean-ass rednecks who work together when the gettin' is good. It's more like a club of crooks than anything official. Been around for a long while. The people change. Some go to jail. Others die. After Katrina, they came back strong. Too much money flowing from Jackson down to the Coast. And now they got their eyes on Memphis, trucking all that shit up 55 or off Highway 45."

"Working with the cartels through Texas."

"How you know that?" Nat said, cutting her eyes over at Boom.

"Because I saw 'em," Boom said. "Couple of those cartel boys packed some shit in a car hauler. They wearin' these fancy-ass shirts and cowboy hats, carrying golden guns. Ain't no way they were just packing the trucks. They had a look about 'em. Real mean eyes, watching me to make sure I didn't make any trouble."

"You making trouble now," Nat said.

"How's that?"

"You're gonna help me shut these mothers down."

"No thanks," Boom said. "I've done my part. I done told Quinn. Now Quinn told you. Soon as we clear, I'm walking in there and turning in my keys to that big-ass truck. I don't need this in my life. I got straight. I didn't ask for this."

Nat reached into her purse and pulled out some photographs and handed them to Boom. He flipped through a few pictures, mug shots of a Mexican girl wearing a dirty tank top and a whole mess of makeup on her young face. One of her eyes had been beaten on, lid swelled up tight.

"You know her?"

Boom shook his head.

"That's Ana Maria Mata," Nat said. "The girl that you and Quinn's sister were looking to find. Quinn told me about her and I found out she'd been picked up in a sting in Cincinnati a few months ago. Some men up there had set her up with eight other girls. They had them in some broke-ass motel off the interstate running johns all day and all fucking night. Cop I talked to said Ana Maria might've run through twenty, thirty men a day."

Boom felt a cold break through his chest, his breathing tightened. He looked away from Nat and over at the loading docks at Sutpen's. Eighteen-wheelers coming and going out of the chain-link gates and blowing past where he sat still with a federal agent. He wished he was just back in his truck, doing his own thing, making his own time, seeing that world from behind the windshield. Way things were going, he'd never do that shit again.

"So?" Nat said.

Boom looked at her. She chewed her gum and studied his face for a long while, sitting there, cooling out in her government vehicle.

"Doesn't that inspire you or some shit?" Nat said. "Seeing a girl being taken from your hometown and run through the fucking wringer by these people? If you're thinking it's just some Mexican meth and a lot of stolen laptops, you just lying to yourself, Mr. Kimbrough."

Boom nodded and turned back to Agent Nathalie Wilkins. Ain't no denying she was a sharp, hard-ass, good-looking woman, with that silk style and that loose, bouncy hair, worn natural and wild. He studied her high cheekbones, greenish eyes, and ripe mouth. Everything about her was precise and tight as hell. As she worked that gum waiting for him to answer, the whole car smelled of sweet mint.

"OK," Boom said.

"OK what?"

"How about you just call me Boom?"

Quinn and Maggie sat together in the small hospital cafeteria a little after dinnertime, Maggie just getting out of surgery and changed into a fresh pair of blue scrubs. Quinn had brought her a Styrofoam shell full of fried catfish, hush puppies, and fries from Pap's. She ate while he drank some bad coffee from the vending machine, wishing he'd brought his own. The stuff tasted like it'd been brewing for the last two weeks, as thick and tasty as a quart of used motor oil.

"Slick night," Maggie said. "Already had two accidents brought in. The last one was pretty horrible, bad leg breaks. Teenage girl slid off Jericho Road and hit a tree. Truth be known, she's lucky to be alive."

"I was down there with Kenny," Quinn said. "I got there after the ambulance left but we had to get the car pulled out. Looks of it, I thought she'd have a hell of a lot worse than a broken leg."

"The girl was small," she said. "Must've thrown her back into the seat. Where did she take a hit?"

"Whole front end got crunched up to the dash," Quinn said. "Windshield was busted out. Lot of glass. I bet she got pretty cut up."

"She'll have a few scars on her face," Maggie said. "Not too bad. Lots of glass on her forehead. She was lucky as hell not to get some of it in her eye."

"What time are you getting off?"

"Midnight," she said. "Double shift. Don't worry. I got Brandon set up with Mrs. Tidwell. She said he can stay until I get home. All that woman does is sit around reading *The National Enquirer* and watching *The Golden Girls*. Her stupid kids never come see her."

"I'll pick him up."

"You don't need to do that," she said. "What if you get called out?"

"He can stay at Momma's tonight," Quinn said. "Jason's over there and they've been working on bringing back our old treehouse. Momma got them a bunch of stuff to fix it up like Caddy and I had it."

"That's sweet, but—"

"But nothing."

Maggie worked on the fish, stripping the bone from the meat, pulling off the tail and eating the crisp part like a potato chip. Quinn recalled when they used to fry catfish with the heads on and wondered when that stopped. Maybe folks started to worry about their meal looking at them. Maggie kept eating, looking like she hadn't had a thing all day.

"Are you getting anywhere on that murder?" she asked.

"A little," Quinn said. "I've learned a few new things that might help."

"I may be able to help you on something else," Maggie said, smiling, looking pleased with herself. "Did y'all ever charge anyone with that throwdown at the Walmart?"

Quinn shook his head. "Pretty sure some local turds got into it with some bikers. But we don't have a victim. And no one has exactly wanted to step up and name names from anyone who runs with that crew."

"What if you had a name?"

"That'd help."

"A man came into the ER two days after the trouble," she said. "Someone had stitched him up but it was a real mess. Looked like he'd done it himself with some fishing line and a sewing needle. He had a bad infection and needed to get flushed out and cleaned up. Doctor tried to get him to stay, but he got some meds and took off."

"Look like a gunshot wound?"

"He said he got shot in the ass with an arrow while hunting."

"Who was he?"

"I can get the name, Social, and address for you," she said. "All I know is, one of the nurses said she'd seen him a few times at the Southern Star. She said his name was Lyle and he rode with the Born Losers. You know him?"

"Yep," Quinn said. "He's an old friend. Had some run-ins with him in the past."

"Well," Maggie said, her face looking as big and bright as a kid's. Her big green eyes, freckles, and devilish-looking grin making her seem even younger. "Guess I earned my dinner."

"Yes, ma'am," Quinn said. "All the catfish you can eat. Only problem is, those boys disappeared from Tibbehah last year. I have five outstanding warrants on them. I've been looking for Lyle for a long time."

"Where do you think they went?"

"That old clubhouse has fallen in on itself," Quinn said. "I heard they got a new clubhouse in Memphis down on South Lamar. Hadn't had a big reason to go and find them. Maybe now I'll check it out."

"How about you bring Reggie along?"

"You worried I might get shot before the big day?" Quinn said.

"Damn straight."

"Might help us get out of this button soup wedding we go going on," Quinn said, shaking his head. "Every day the pot just gets thicker and thicker. My momma adding folks. Your momma adding folks. Diane Tull wanting to bring in more folks for the band. Catfish, barbecue, and tofu. I get shot and we could get married right in the hospital. When it's time to say 'I do,' you'd just have to push the button on the bed and raise me up."

"That's not funny," Maggie said. "I don't like you joking about stuff like that."

"Only way to do it," Quinn said. "In the Rangers, if you couldn't laugh about getting shot up, blown up, or killed, you'd damn near drive yourself crazy. I can't tell you how hard some of us laughed after we'd get in some tight spots. I never knew anyone with a blacker sense of humor than folks trying not to die every day."

"How 'bout you bring Reggie?"

Quinn nodded and stirred the coffee. He hadn't touched it. The smell alone had been enough to wake his ass up. "Thought about reaching out to Lillie," Quinn said, looking up from the slick surface of the cup. "It's been a while. And I figured the Marshals might have a lead on Lyle and the Losers."

Maggie's face brightened. "Even better."

14

IT SEEMED THAT TYLER SPENT MOST OF HIS LIFE IN THE garage, on the track, or deep down in the grow barns pruning weed. He'd learned that pruning was maybe the most important step, beyond just the planting and running the irrigation system. You had to take your time when using your shears on new plants. Tyler liked Fiskars, they cut quick and precise, making sure you didn't shock the plant too damn fast. Today he was mainly looking for dead growth, low-hanging buds in grow trailers. The Pritchards had four grow rooms buried out back of the old barn, having spent four years of their lives putting together a whole new world, a series of bunkers and tunnels underneath their property. As he worked in the ultraviolet glow of the overhead lamps, box fans keeping the air moving deep down in the cool ground, he snipped off a few of the low-lying branches, making sure to give the strong growth and energy to the branches getting the most light and air.

In the grow rooms, they had all kind of shit planted in irrigated buckets: FLUID, SUPER SILVER, STAR KILLER, ALIEN RIP, COCO, HALF GOOEY, GRIZZ, and their special, STAND ON IT. He and Cody could handle most of it. Sometimes they brought in some trusted buddies to help them out, folks they knew would absolutely never say a word about how they'd outwitted the damn DEA, with all their flyovers of the Pritchard property not being worth jack shit. Most of the time Tyler ran the grow side of things, pruning, checking on the new plants, testing the water quality. Cody was the harvest man, taking the buds to the drying room, racking 'em up on plastic coat hangers and drying them out for a few weeks. Once that was done, they knew a couple girls from down in Starkville, Ag students and party chicks, who'd ride up and help them package. That was the fun times when they'd put on the music and watch all that money just pile up in baggies on the table.

Cody walked into the grow room and called out to him.

Tyler was sitting on an overturned Home Depot bucket while he worked. He waved with the shears in his hand and told him to come on.

"Uncle Heath never came home," Cody said. Tyler looked down at his feet to make sure he'd put on those booties to keep the work space clean. "I wouldn't give a good goddamn except for he took my truck and stole fifty dollars from my wallet. Said he was horny and thirsty and not to wait up."

"Did he tell you he was taking your truck?"

"Figured he was gonna take that old Ford," Cody said. "Not the damn Black Widow. I'm about getting sick and tired of that son of a bitch thinking that he owns everything on the property. He even sits on our damn commode like he's king of the land, reading *Juggs* magazine and laughing at the jokes they put in back. Don't have an ounce of shame in that man."

Tyler nodded, careful as he reached into a bushy plant to snip off some wasted branches, a few dead leaves. It was cool and comfortable down here, the gurgling of the water tanks, the woosh of the fan. Not a bad place to spend your time. Lots of times he'd smoke it up before he opened up the hatch, put in some earbuds and listen to some Jamey Johnson or Chris Stapleton. Just chill out, do the work without even thinking on it.

"We could use an extra hand down here," Tyler said. "If we're gonna keep up production and keep racing."

"Sure would be great if Uncle Heath worked," he said. "But prison did something to that man. All he wants to do is lay around and sleep and watch TV, talking about how good the colors are now, trying to find MMA fights and titties on the satellite."

"He's an old man," Tyler said. "Twenty-three years is a long time being gone. Got to be a real mindfuck coming back to cell phones, flat-screen televisions, and grow houses like we done built. You know?"

"C'mon," Cody said, scratching at his cheek, walking down the long line of plants, fingering the branches, inspecting the work Tyler had already done. "You want that son of a bitch gone same as I do. Only your problem is, you didn't fall asleep in church when Momma used to take us. You think kicking that man to the fucking curb is some kind of dang sin."

"He ain't gonna go," Tyler said. "Not easy."

"Have you forgotten what it was like building all this shit down here?" he said. "Working that backhoe in July, driving them Conex containers down from Memphis. Welding all that shit together like a motherfuckin' Erector Set. Shit, yeah. This is all our house. Every damn seed down here. And I don't need our worthless momma's worthless brother stinking up our goddamn universe."

Tyler set down the shears next to the bucket. He stood up, looking down on his shorter, yet older, brother, and nodded. He pulled at his beard a little bit, finding a little bit of ash stuck in it from smoking a blunt after breakfast. Standing there, he could see it all, from the first churn of the soil to dropping them Conex containers down in the holes, linking it all up with sheet metal, running pipes, water from the well. All the damn expense of filtration systems, cattle tanks, grow lights, buying seed from all the way in goddamn Napa Valley, California. Yes, sir. There was something particular and shitty as hell about Uncle Heath showing up one night and expecting to be Mr. Hot Shit 1993 like he'd stepped from a fucking frozen time capsule.

Tyler stood there, thinking, mind swirling on things as he played with the beard. "OK," Tyler said. "I'm not doubting you. I'm just asking what the fuck do we do about it?"

"He works for us," Cody said. "Not the other way around. If he tries to make some trouble, we get rid of his ass."

"That's some hard-ass Old Testament thinking there, Cody Pritchard," Tyler said, picking up the shears, feeling the handles and springs working in his hand. *Clip, clip, clip.*

"Tell me you ain't been thinking the same goddamn thing," Cody said. "Goddamn Doc McStuffins and his fucking box of pills? Shit, man. What's wrong with that son of a bitch? If we don't get someone to cover our ass quick, we're fucked five ways from Sunday."

"I'll talk to Sledge," Tyler said. "Maybe he'll let that shit ride for a while?"

"Ain't a damn chance in hell."

. . .

Those turds out of Tupelo would come over tomorrow, put their feet up on her fucking furniture, and take over everything Fannie had worked nearly twenty years to build. She'd done her goddamn part, everything Ray and Buster White had asked. From taking over the shit show at the Rez, making it into a first-class cooze parade until the chief wanted his cut, to driving on up the highway to Tibbehah to clean up Johnny Stagg's mess in this godforsaken county. Fannie had rebuilt a goddamn lean-to barn called The Booby Trap into one of the finest T&A beer joints in the Deep South. She never as so much got a thank you from White or any of the boys, just damn grunts on the phone questioning her on the night's take or the cash exchange with the blacks up in Memphis. But this thing? The deal with Wes Taggart and his ponytailed fuckwad buddy, J. B. Hood, hit her right where she fucking lived.

"Want another, Miss Fannie?" Midnight Man asked.

It was nearly nine, Fannie sitting at the edge of that old weathered bar, waiting for the house to really open up for the night. Why the hell not? She motioned for another half gin, half grenadine special with extra ice, plenty of cherries, and a slice of orange. It was sweet and burned and hit the damn spot, making her feel steady and confident, that long brown cigarillo in her fingers burning down to her immaculate nails. Thinking how to out-fuck a man who did twenty years in Angola with a smile on his face, working his scams and business from behind bars, getting the guards to smuggle in TVs and cell phones, goddamn Oysters Rockefeller from Antoine's and whores from the Mississippi coast. She'd heard Buster White didn't give a goddamn whether it was male or female, switching to either side depending on his mood. He spent most of his teenage years over in reform schools in Alabama, learning to survive with his fists and his mouth, working for nickels and dimes and chocolate bars until people got real comfortable with him and he'd put a knife right in their gut. She'd known that swamp creature for most of her adult life and knew he didn't have any more loyalty to her than some of the cats she fed out by the dumpster.

"How's that?" Midnight Man said, motioning to her drink.

"It's fine."

"Need more cherries?"

"I said it's fine."

Fannie had always done for Fannie, but when it came to the good ole boys, she figured doing her business, being professional, would get her a seat the table. Instead, it got her a tap on the ass and more bullshit until Buster White decided to take away her keys and turn her into some kind of glorified greeter. She didn't have much. Not so much of the cut or the overall action, but the deal had been for Vienna's. There was no end for the need of tits and pussy and there was no damn reason it had to be skanky and dirty. She did good for those girls. Kept them neat and clean, bought them clothes, made sure they got what they deserved. Every other week she got them tested with a gyno brought in from Grenada. These boys, Taggart and Hood, would turn Vienna's into a Wild West clap trap within weeks.

Fannie sucked down the drink, kept an eye on the time, and watched the door, just waiting for those sonsabitches to come in, smiling and happy, loving they just got the damn front door keys to all the pussy they could stand.

She drained the glass. Motioned again to Midnight Man. *Bring it on.*

"You sure, ma'am?"

"Did I stutter?"

Yes, sir. Fannie did for Fannie. Vienna's was fucking hers. It was her grandmother's, built on basic Southern principles of hospitality, hot women, and full-tilt liquor. This fucking business had already taken two of her boys down with it and if she showed a damn bit of weakness, they'd take her along, too. Either way, she might be fucked. But if she rolled over on her back for these boys, she knew Buster White wouldn't have a goddamn lick of respect for her.

She needed to find the way to flush the toilet on these two turds and show that north Mississippi and that little cut-through to Memphis was all fucking hers. She drank some more, tapped the ash off the cigarillo, and thought about how she'd been outsmarted by a couple of kids with dirty fingernails and a truckload of body odor. She had the cooze. They had the weed.

"Midnight Man?" Fannie asked.

"Yes, Miss Fannie?"

"You know anyone who can get in touch with the Pritchard boys?"

Midnight Man looked down at the empty drinks in front her, passing a little judgment. But Fannie looked up at him, clear-eyed as hell and thinking of a few things.

"Sure," he said. "I do."

"I want you to set something up," Fannie said. "Soon as you can."

"Just what you thinking, Miss Fannie?"

Don't worry," J. B. Hood said, sitting up in the cab with Boom Kimbrough as Boom made a midnight run down to Biloxi for an unknown pickup, deadheading it down to the Coast. "I'm not going to ask you about your fucking arm. I'm sure you get enough of that shit already."

Boom nodded, following that long white line on Highway 45 deep into the night, down through Waynesboro and on through Buckatunna, skirting the Alabama state line. L. Q. Smith had told him he'd have an adviser on the next run, not real specific about what was being observed or why. But when Boom got to the Sutpen office to pick up the truck, he saw the same old gray-ponytailed motherfucker who'd eyed him after he'd asked about the shit they'd put on his truck. The guy didn't say a word, even when introduced by Smith, just hopped up in the passenger cab and lit up a smoke. Talking about Boom's arm was the first damn thing he'd said since leaving Tupelo.

"I was in 'Nam," Hood said. "Just a kid at Khe Sanh, where we had the damn shit shelled out of us for five months. I saw up close and personal the meat grinder of that war and still don't know what the fuck we were trying to do. The only thing that kept me going was a pinup of Nancy Sinatra sitting on a big pile of combat boots in her bikini. Many a night I took the dog for a walk just thinking about her long, bare feet. That woman had such great-looking toes."

Boom nodded. His left hand steady on the wheel, downshifting with his hook as they ran through the flashing yellow light, passing a Chevron, an Exxon, the First Baptist Church of Buckatunna. A big sign at the church said GIVE THE DEVIL AN INCH AND HE'LL BECOME YOUR RULER.

"I don't know why a woman's feet just always did it for me," Hood said, keeping on. Boom not asking for more. "I don't mean that I'm some kind of pervert. I don't want to lick them clean or nothing. Or have her stick her toes up my ass. I just think feet are sexy, is all. The first thing I look at when seeing a woman? Toes. Don't care a thing for short, stubby little ones. I like them long, lean toes, nice little painted nails. I used to date a woman from Shreveport who had toes as long as a monkey's. She could pick up a cigarette with them and pluck the damn thing in her mouth."

"Where we headed?" Boom said, his own voice sounding strange to him as he hadn't spoken for a long while. He just wanted to get down to business and get this creepy-looking motherfucker out of his cab. His truck reeked of cheap aftershave and cigarettes.

"Just drive," Hood said. "When we hit I-10 at Mobile, I'll tell you which way to go."

Boom kept on rolling. He didn't mind the talking but would prefer the radio. Most of the time, his music kept his mind right and sharp, focused as the miles clicked away. He and Quinn liked that old-school country music, but he also kept *Enter the Wu-Tang*. Something told him that J. B. Hood's old, countrified ass wouldn't be into *"Shame on a nigga who try to run game on a nigga."* Boom glanced over at Hood as he drove, knowing he had a loaded .357 Magnum down in the space between the seat and door. He wasn't sure exactly what Smith and the boys were trying to run on his ass, get passed through him, but the old guy riding shotgun was making him nervous as hell.

"Whatever you see down here," Hood said, leaning forward in his seat toward the glass, clearing off a smudge with his fist, "don't be asking me about it. Just like I'm not asking you about your fucking arm and how it all went down. What we got to do down here, the run, don't mean nothing in this big ole world. All you got to do is go where I say, stay in the cab while we load up, and drive this rig on back to Tupelo. I heard you had some ethical issues driving back from Houston last time? I don't need none of that."

"Then why am I driving?"

"Call it baptism by fire," Hood said. "If you were so goddamn offended by what you were doing, you would've quit. But you and me are the same. We don't give a good goddamn about the job, long as it pays. And, for the record, I don't care how black you are or how many limbs you got. I learned that over in The Shit. We're all headed down into the ground and you might as well have a hell of a ride on the way."

"You really believe that?"

"What's that?"

"That there ain't nothing else in this world?"

"I can't see no farther than the headlights," Hood said. He laughed, lighting up another cigarette, the cab filling with smoke. "Beyond that, it's dark as hell."

"Light cuts through all that mess."

"Goddamn," Hood said. "Please don't tell me you're gonna witness. Better men and women have tried, and, to be real honest, man, I just don't give a fuck."

"Hard thinking."

"Just keep your eyes on that blacktop and your mouth shut," Hood said. "And we'll get along just fine."

Hood pulled a pistol from his pocket and checked the magazine. The gun looked like a toy to Boom, but he knew it could kill a man just the same. "When the racket starts," he said, "all the wailing and crying, knocking on the walls, just keep driving. When you hear screaming and yelling, just drive."

"What the hell are we driving?" Boom said. "Cattle?"

Hood let down the side window, hot wind blowing through the cab. He spit and looked over at Boom with those sleepy, dead eyes. "Of a kind."

15

"I'M HAPPY FOR YOU, QUINN," LILLIE VIRGIL SAID. "I REALLY am. About time you got married or folks might start to whisper. A grown man, pushing forty, living way the hell out in the country in a big ole house with no one but a cattle dog to talk to. You need a woman, or a person, to civilize you, make you not seem like some kind of Boo Radley with a buzz cut and a badge."

"You know, people have been talking for a while," Quinn said. "They say they always figured you and I were going to get hitched."

"Christ Almighty," Lillie said. "Can't a man and a woman be fucking friends without people thinking they want to bump uglies together? I love you like a brother. But, like a brother, the thought of getting nekkid with you makes my flesh crawl a little."

"Appreciate that, Lil," Quinn said. "That's awfully nice of you."

"You're welcome," Lillie said. "Now we got that out of the way, just what the fuck do you want?"

They stood outside the Clifford Davis/Odell Horton Federal Building in downtown Memphis, where Lillie had been assigned as a U.S. Marshal soon after leaving Tibbehah County.

She was a tall woman, about Quinn's height, but maybe taller today in some fancy black shoes that went with a fitted black blazer over a gray top. She had on jeans and wore her MARSHALS SERVICE badge around her neck. Her unruly brown hair pinned down in a bun and a brand-new Sig Sauer on her hip.

"Nice-looking gun," Quinn said.

"Little present to myself," Lillie said, patting her hip. "The judges didn't like me carrying a rifle around the courthouse. I think it's because they have small dicks and I intimidated them."

When Lillie left Jericho, she'd originally planned to go back to the Memphis PD, where she'd started her career out of Ole Miss. But the Marshals had offered more money and better hours for her to spend with her daughter, Rose. Also, Quinn was pretty sure she liked saying she was a U.S. Marshal. Kicking in doors and chasing fugitives was pretty much Lillie's speed.

"Did you get the warrant I sent?" Quinn said.

"We already had Wrong Way on file," she said. "*Fucking Lyle Masters.* I thought we'd run his ass far away from Jericho."

"Not far enough," Quinn said. "He came back and got into a throwdown at the Walmart."

"Now, that's class," Lillie said. "That's the goddamn Olympic pinnacle of shitbirdism. Who was he fighting?"

"The Pritchard boys and their uncle," Quinn said.

"You're not talking about Heath Pritchard?" she said. "The really bad seed?"

"Yep," Quinn said. "Heath Pritchard got paroled from Parchman two weeks ago. He came back to spend some quality time with his nephews."

"Hamp used to talk about him," Lillie said. "Lots of stories. There was zero love lost between those two. Did you know he vowed he'd kill your uncle when he got free? He didn't happen to mention that to you?"

"About getting robbed of the chance?"

Lillie nodded.

"I tried not to listen," Quinn said. "Prison seems to have messed up the wiring in his head."

"I doubt he was a stable genius to begin with," Lillie said.

A streetcar passed by the federal building on Main, no one on it but the driver, headed on toward the Pinch District and the Pyramid. Quinn leaned against a big round planter filled with flowers but designed as a barricade in case someone tried to make an Oklahoma City–style run at the feds. The flowers were a bright purple and white, Quinn thinking that he needed to do a little work at the farm before Maggie and Brandon got completely moved in. Maybe he could stop at the Farm & Ranch on the way home get some petunias and impatiens.

"That's sweet Heath Pritchard is back with his family," Lillie said. "Those Pritchard boys look like the spawn of Charles Manson if he fucked some of those *Hee Haw* honeys. Did they get messed up bad by the Losers?"

"Here's the thing," Quinn said. "Wrong Way was the victim. He got shot in the ass by one of those boys."

"Terrific," Lillie said. "Some good old-fashioned drug shit."

"Probably. Maybe something more," Quinn said. "But if I don't make some arrests, the locals are going to start writing letters to the editor at *The Tibbehah Monitor* about how I'm not doing my job."

"Rednecks don't like people to fuck up their Walmart time."

"Nope," Quinn said. "They sure don't. Second only to church."

Lillie grinned at Quinn and he smiled back. It was good to see her; they hadn't been together since she'd left for her Marshal training. They'd left on good terms, Quinn knowing that she was a hell of a lot better, and bigger, than Tibbehah County. The only reason she'd come home after working in Memphis was to take care of her dying mother, who'd passed years ago. It was only a matter of time before she broke free, expanding her horizons and searching to take down more shitbirds outside Tibbehah.

"I'm supposed to be chasing down a nineteen-year-old Vice Lord who robbed two banks and nearly choked out his baby momma," she said. "Now you want me to look for Wrong Way's sorry ass?"

"Up to you," Quinn said. "I couldn't be in Memphis without saying hello. Maggie and I hadn't heard back whether you'd make the wedding. Sure would like you to be there."

"That's what phones are for," Lillie said. "You know what? I think you just wanted me to come with you to fuck with Wrong Way. You would've felt guilty doing it alone. Having too much fun at the new Born Losers clubhouse breaking shit."

"Is that a fact?" Quinn asked, squinting into the bright light high overhead.

"Nothing changes, Ranger," Lillie said, slipping on a pair of gold aviator sunglasses. "We're still on the same side. Just ninety-nine miles are between us."

"You know where we can find this new clubhouse?"

"What part of U.S. Marshal don't you understand?" Lillie said, hands on her hips. "I didn't do seventeen weeks of training at Glencoe to just come home, sit on my ass, and google shit."

"Sure is good to see you, Lil," he said. "Been too long."

"Stay here," she said. "I'll be right back."

"I'm driving."

"No shit," Lillie said. "But I left my favorite shotgun up in the office. Those Loser boys have some hard motherfucking heads."

Fannie hated goddamn chickens. She hated their smell, their nasty feathers, their beady little eyes, and the way they cocked their head when they stared at you, scratching and scraping in the dirt. When she pulled up to the Pritchards' house and barn, a fucking flock of them, or whatever you call a mess of chickens, gathered by her freshly waxed Lexus. They clucked and pecked in front of her as if they expected her to emerge from the leather and air-conditioning tossing out milled corn. Instead, she scattered them with the pointy toe of her Italian boots, being fucking careful of where she walked in all this nastiness. The Pritchard compound was a goddamn mess of redneck boys gone wild. Hollowed-out race cars, old trucks, Sea-Doos, and trailers with flattened tires lined the drive up to the house and big metal barn.

She figured the barn was where they were growing the weed until she looked through the big open bay door and saw one of the brothers working on the engine of a car. He stood up, shirtless and wearing flowery pajama bottoms and cowboy boots, and headed her way, holding some kind of engine part in his hand, cleaning it with a dirty red rag.

"Well, hello there," he said. He was tall, with a bushy beard, some kind of weird-ass sleeve tattoos on his arms. "Didn't know you was stopping by so early, Miss Fannie."

"Figured it was high time we met."

"Mmm-hmm," the boy said, setting down the rag and the part on a tool cart. "We met once before at Vienna's Place, but I don't expect you to remember."

"Is that a fact?"

"Yes, ma'am," he said, smiling with some yellowed teeth. "You told me to quit dancing on your fucking furniture or you'd make sure my pecker would never get pulled again in the VIP room."

"Sorry about that," she said. "Common problem. Didn't mean anything by it. Besides, we don't even have the VIP room anymore. Can't serve champagne with the girls' coots on full display."

Pritchard pulled at his beard with his dirty, oily fingers. His arms long and skinny, framing a caved-in boy's chest and a small potbelly. "Them Holy Rollers in the county don't want us to have any fun, do they? I don't think I've had a better time 'cept for when me and my brother went over to Six Flags in Atlanta and nearly died eating cotton candy. You sure do provide the entertainment."

"Appreciate that, kid," Fannie said. "Which one of the Pritchards am I talking to?"

"I'm Tyler," he said, glancing over her shoulder, something catching his eye.

Fannie turned to see another boy about Tyler's age, shorter and rounder, with lots of brown hair and wild eyes. He had a shotgun up in the crook of his arm, walking slow and easy, being followed by those fucking chickens and a mangy-ass dog.

"And that's Cody," the one named Tyler said. "We weren't expecting you to come alone since you had that colored fella call on us."

"Midnight Man?" Fannie said, smiling. "Nope. This is a private conversation. I wanted us to meet outside Vienna's and discuss our recent misunderstanding and fucking failure to communicate."

"You ain't never wanted to talk to us before," the boy, Cody, said behind her. "First time you sent that Indian kid to tell us our business. The next time you sent goddamn Ordeen Davis to come spy on our land. Who else you got coming?"

"Just me," Fannie said. "Do you boys mind if I smoke?"

She couldn't imagine smoking a cigarillo inside their race car shop would do a thing but improve the smell of the grease, chickenshit, and body funk. The kid wouldn't put down the shotgun, circling her, watching her as he started to walk backwards as if she was about to pull her gun from her Birkin bag or shoot a high-powered laser out of her pussy.

"Y'all have anyone else in the rafters?" Fannie said, pulling out a cigarillo, setting fire to it, and looking up to the crossbeams where they'd hung some Confederate and race car flags.

"Go get Uncle Heath," Tyler said.

"He's asleep," Cody said.

"Then wake his ass up," Tyler said. "He needs to be in on this and listen to whatever this woman has to say or what she's peddling."

Peddling. Every rich white woman in a fancy car must look like the goddamn Avon lady to these fuckwads. She smoked, moving forward, past Tyler and over to the tool bench. It looked like they'd taken apart an engine and spread out every part along some slatted two-by-fours polished smooth with a thick varnish. Ten years ago, she'd taken the company of a well-known NASCAR driver who'd been on Wheaties boxes and underwear commercials. She'd been five years his senior, but that boy didn't get any satisfaction from her working girls, being someone who lived for speed and curves and liked to be left gasping and spent on the floor of their motel room.

Tyler shot his brother a hard look and Cody finally lowered the shotgun, not looking thrilled about it. He stood there for a long moment, gun hanging limp in his right hand, scratching his ass with his other. He had on a blue T-shirt that read SHAKE 'N' BAKE that hung down nearly to his knees. His legs were thick and squatty, with big calves and no shoes. Without another word, he turned from the barn and went walking up to the old house with the rusted tin roof.

"He don't trust you," Tyler said.

"No shit."

"I don't trust you, neither," he said. "You send Ordeen to spy on us? Or fucking shoot us?"

"If I'd wanted to shoot y'all, I would've sent someone much better."

"Guess it don't matter much now."

"No," Fannie said. "You boys took care of Ordeen. That matter's finished."

"Except for the law."

"That's between you and me," she said. "Unless y'all been running your damn mouths."

"Is that why you're here?" he said. "You want us to know where we stand in Tibbehah County. Like when you sent those biker boys to come whip our ass?"

Fannie shook her head and blew out some smoke. She looked up, admiring all the trophies and flags and motivational shit spray-painted on discarded racing car hoods: YOU CAN'T LET ONE BAD MOMENT SPOIL A GOOD ONE; IF YOU HAVE EVERYTHING UNDER CONTROL,

YOU AIN'T MOVIN' FAST ENOUGH; DON'T MATTER IF YOU WIN BY AN INCH OR A MILE.

"Y'all got a real can-do attitude," Fannie said. "Real spunk. I like that bullshit."

"Them bikers were lucky to only get shot in the ass," Tyler said, standing there in his kiddie PJs and Walmart boots trying to be tough. "Next time, they'll end up like that black boy."

"You won't have any more trouble," Fannie said. "I fired Wrong Way and those boys. What I want to discuss is between me and you, Tyler."

"And my family," he said. "Whatever you got to say needs to be heard by all of us. But let me tell you something right here and right now, Miss Hathcock. We're not stopping what we're doing or slowing down none. I don't care how much money you're offering to buy us out. This is our fucking land. And our fucking product."

Fannie held the cigarillo close to her face as she brushed at her chin with her thumb, nodding. She turned to see the short one, Cody, walk in with one of the ugliest creatures God had ever put on this Earth. Short, bald, and muscled, with skin so dirty and tanned that he looked like old leather. He had nothing on but blue jeans. No shirt. No shoes. He couldn't get served at the goddamn Waffle House, but here she was, about to talk shop with the worst Tibbehah County had to offer.

"Can we sit down somewhere?" Fannie said. Not liking the way the three men had approached her, looking at one another like a bunch of coyotes, two of them holding guns while all she had was a smoke.

"What the fuck do you want?" said the old man. "I know'd who you represent and don't want shit to do with those folks. Pritchards work for ourselves. We're independent owner-operators."

Fannie smiled, nodding toward the mouth of the barn, to the sunlight and somewhat-fresh air outside by the chickens pecking around a mudhole. "Good," Fannie said. "That's just what I wanted to hear."

The two boys looked at each other as the old man continued to stare. But all three of them followed her out, goddamn single file, to a waiting porch at the old house. Settling in on rusted metal chairs, the Pritchard boys waited, curious as hell at what she possibly could have to say.

Did you have to break the damn jukebox?" Lyle Masters, aka Wrong Way, said to Lillie.

"I didn't break it," Lillie said. "I just busted it. Send me the fucking bill."

"Yeah, with one of my boys' heads," he said. "That's just not right. Look at him sitting over at the bar, bleeding like that. Don't you know it's not fair to beat on a drunk man? We've been up all damn night."

Lillie looked over at Quinn and shrugged. He wasn't sure if she'd tripped the guy because he'd touched her back or because she hated the music blaring from the box. It was playing some old Mötley Crüe, "Looks That Kill." Lillie hated hair metal about as much as Quinn hated that bro country shit.

As soon as they'd walked into The Busted Shovel on Summer Avenue, all eyes were on them, no one mistaking him or Lillie for anything else but law enforcement. Lillie carried a pump Winchester. Quinn wore his Army-green Tibbehah sheriff's cap and Beretta on his hip. But as they scouted the room for Wrong Way, most of the bikers and their women did their dead-level best to make sure they didn't care. Except for the fat man in the leather vest who put his hand on Lillie, asking if she'd like to give him a slow lap dance.

Lillie pulled him forward by his neck and tripped him at the same time, sending him falling forward, knocking his head hard on the jukebox. The room went silent, Wrong Way coming out from the bathroom, zipping up his fly. Seeing that it was Quinn and Lillie, he put his hands up and started to laugh as he recognized them both.

"OK," Wrong Way said. "I forgot a few court dates. But my lawyer got it all straightened out. They got me back on the docket. No need for y'all to come all the way up here from Tibbehah."

"Oh, I live here, Lyle," Lillie said. "I'm a Marshal now and I can come and visit you boys here at The Dirty Shovel anytime I please. What night is margarita night again?"

"Shit," he said. "That just freakin' sucks. And it's The *Busted* Shovel, woman. You know, like a Harley Shovelhead? Don't you know nothing about bikes?"

There were about eight bikers sitting around the room at little tables and up at the bar. None of them wanted to make eye contact with Quinn or Lillie. Six men, counting Lyle, and two scroungy and tired-looking women with toothpick arms and skinny legs under short denim skirts. The light was dim, with lots of smoke hovering around the neon beer signs and stuffed dead animals by the whiskey bottles. All roadkills. Possums, skunks, armadillos, and squirrels. One of the armadillos was on its back drinking a Lone Star, the ultimate insult.

"Can you turn the music up?" asked a woman at the bar. She held her head in her hands as if she was nursing a bad hangover. "Damn."

Lillie just glared at her. She turned back around fast.

"You were just down in Tibbehah County," Quinn said. "You got into a mess with the Pritchard boys and one of them shot you."

"Hey," Wrong Way said, showing his palms. "C'mon, man. You know we've been out of Tibbehah for more than a year. Don't you remember what the hell happened to us at that snatch bar? Most of my boys were carried out in trash bags."

"I'm not asking," Quinn said. "And we're not here to bust you. Way I see it, you were the victim."

Wrong Way's mouth hung open, unable to process what Quinn was talking about. He looked from Lillie back to Quinn, shaking his head. His long black hair had been cut off at the shoulder, black beard combed into a V. He looked like he'd just stepped out of the Pirates of the Caribbean ride at Disney World, only with more denim and leather.

"I don't know what to tell you," Wrong Way said. "Call the DA's office. You'll see. I got new dates set on my appearance. Wasn't my fault anyway. We were just trying to get a wheelchair for a cripple friend. I didn't know we had to pay for the damn thing."

"I don't know what you're talking about," Lillie said. "And I sure as shit don't care. How's your ass doing, by the way?"

Wrong Way walked to the edge of the bar for an open bottle of Jack Daniel's and took a nice long drink, his Adam's apple working up and down as he swallowed. He wiped his mouth and turned back to them. It wasn't even ten o'clock in the morning. No one spoke. No one moved. Quinn didn't think any of the Born Losers had ever seen Wrong Way being so damn hospitable to the law in his own bar.

"My ass fucking hurts," he said. "Nearly got gangrene or some shit. Had this dumb-ass doctor in Eupora take out the bullet and he did a shit job. Nearly killed me."

"Which Pritchard shot you?" Lillie said.

"You really gonna pay to get that jukebox fixed?"

"Sure," she said. "Right after I sit here all goddamn day and run checks on every turd in this bar. I'm sure all of y'all want to get clean with your criminal records, moving violations, and such."

"You believe this?" Wrong Way said, pleading with Quinn. "We moved all the way out of Tibbehah County and I turn around and it's back to the old Wild West showdown with you and Calamity Jane. Can't a white man catch a goddamn break?"

"Which Pritchard shot you?" Quinn said.

"And you'll leave me the hell alone?"

"I don't care for people getting shot at the Walmart," Quinn said. "Makes me look bad with the locals."

"C'mon, Sheriff," Wrong Way said. "We was just arguing over the last Barbie doll on the shelf. I wanted to get one for my grandbaby and one of those Pritchards wanted to fuck the damn doll."

The Born Losers all started to laugh, including the woman who had the hangover. She started to snort, then looked uneasy at the way it made her feel, and clasped her forehead back into her hand. She upturned a beer and gave the side-eye to Lillie.

"C'mon now, Sheriff," Wrong Way said. "How about we all just let it go?"

Lillie reached for her phone. She looked over at the exit and Quinn headed that way, the bikers looking uneasy and nervous. He watched their hands, keeping the whole room in focus. If any of them started to shoot, he could snatch up his Beretta and clear the room quick.

"I'm not scared of him," Wrong Way said. "If that's what you're thinking. I just don't want to go to court. Have to wear a fucking tie. Make you get up early in the morning. That shit lasts forever. Goddamn murder trial."

Lillie's eyes widened, lifting her chin at Quinn. Quinn moved across the room, still keeping all the bikers in focus, watching Wrong Way, but making sure no one else moved, either. The light was dim, small hanging lamps weakly flickering over a scuffed and dirty linoleum floor of black and white squares.

"Who'd they kill?" Lillie said.

"Fucking Ordeen Davis," Wrong Way said. "Don't come into my bar, break my jukebox, and try and fuck with my mind, too. I ain't stupid. I know why y'all are here. But I'm not a good witness. All I know is what Fannie Hathcock told me. She wanted me to squeeze those country squirrels to find out what happened to her boy. Hell, I didn't know he was dead till after I got shot in the damn ass."

"Why'd they kill him?" Quinn said.

"Don't know," he said. "Y'all will have to ask Fannie that."

"We're asking you, fucknuts," Lillie said. "I can still make a call to Memphis PD. Make this a very unpleasant day for your scooter boys and these two fine young ladies."

"I don't fucking know," Wrong Way said. "Fuck me, man. She sent Ordeen down to the Pritchard place and he never came back. I wondered why she didn't just call the law. But seeing you both in operation again, I'm starting to remember what it's like to have a hard-on pressed into your ear."

"And when you asked about Ordeen," Quinn said. "One of them shot you."

"The old and crazy one," Wrong Way said. "Heath Pritchard. Used to be some big swinging dick back in the eighties, raising a hundred acres of weed. Or at least that's what I heard. Sure would like y'all to nail that son of a bitch."

Quinn nodded to Lillie, Lillie stepping back from Wrong Way. The space was dark and quiet, a slow buzzing from the neon signs over the bar. A gentle hum of fuzz coming from the jukebox with its cracked glass. The man Lillie had tripped looked up from the bar, holding a rag to his bloody head.

"We'll be in touch," Quinn said, walking out with Lillie.

"Watch your ass, Sheriff," Wrong Way said. "I hadn't been able to shit straight since I ran into that sawed-off little fucker."

Ma'am," Heath Pritchard said. "Can I offer you a little breakfast? I was just about to fry me up a steak with some runny eggs. Cody, did you clean the skillet after Buckshot licked it clean last night?"

Fannie stood against the porch railing, watching the two brothers and the misshapen man talking. "No thank you," she said. "I haven't had all my shots."

"Wouldn't be no trouble," Heath said. "Fine-looking woman like yourself. Doing what you do. You better keep your strength up."

"And what exactly do I do?" Fannie asked.

The Pritchard boys looking down at their beaten porch, unable to stop the shit coming from their uncle's mouth.

"From what I hear, you're the damn cock of the walk at that titty bar," he said. "You rule that fucking roost."

The old man had her there. She nodded, tipped the ash of her cigarillo, and leaned slightly against the railing. The tall one with the beard scratched at his bare stomach as they sat there, the other one looking up with quick, mean eyes as the uncle looked her over like she just might be some good eating herself. As she took her hand away from the railing, she gathered some flaking paint in her fingers and had to brush them onto her skirt.

"I don't want to buy you out," she said. "I want to work with you boys. I want to sell what y'all grow."

"And why would you want to do that?" Cody asked. "Out of the goodness of your black heart?"

"Would you shut the fuck up and let her talk," Tyler said.

"Yeah, shut up, Cody," Uncle Heath said, grinning like an idiot and still looking her over. "Where'd you get that dress, pretty lady? Sure is tight in just the right spots."

Fannie crossed her left ankle over her right, pushing down the edge of her skirt. She figured if she didn't cover up a bit, the old man just might start salivating. Somewhere out in the barn, a rooster started to crow and the old man giggled, a nice little private joke between them.

"What kind of deal did y'all work out with Sledge in Memphis?" she asked.

"We ain't got no deal," Tyler said.

"Come on, now," Fannie said. "That's not what I'm hearing."

"Way we figured it," Uncle Heath said, "we can talk to them niggers just same as you. That man's tired of y'all selling him seeds and stems from south of the border. He got a taste of some of that Pritchard product and there was no looking back."

"Our weed?" Cody said, shaking his head, spitting over the railing. "Shit. What are you talking about, old man? We might got a deal if some of us could hold up our fucking end."

"Don't worry about my end," the uncle said. "Y'all just keep on growing and stacking and we won't need nobody else. I got my people. Prison contacts. We don't need this woman coming on our land trying to tell us how to run our business."

Fannie smiled, enjoying hearing the squabbling between them. The short brother was really pissed off at the uncle. He looked so damn mad, she half expected him to blow out his damn spine with the shotgun set on the porch swing. The old man muttering something to himself about how ole Doc had been a mistake but he got other people who'd come through for them all.

"You got the weed," Fannie said. "But the fucking pharmacy is closed. I know. I know what Sledge needs and what he expects and I know you boys only got half the fucking grocery list. Is that right? Or am I wasting my time coming down to *Green Acres* and talking business?"

"Loved that show," Heath said. "That pig was smart as a whip."

Tyler started to nod, seeming to be the only Pritchard with a bit of sense. She only wished he'd change into some normal clothes and maybe take a fucking shower. The smell of those boys coupled with the fucking chickens was going to send her straight back to the Golden Cherry Motel for a nice long bath.

"Why you doin' this?" Tyler said. "You don't need us. We killed one of your boys. And shot another. Why would you want to share your stash with us? I know our weed is good, but it ain't that damn good."

"Maybe I don't like my arrangement," Fannie said. "I think every person on this porch is about tired of getting cornholed when we turn our backs. I could use some new partners. And I can get right for what you promised Sledge."

"Woman," Heath said. "You try and cut out those good ole boys on the Coast and they'll come for you and for us. I don't want no part of that shit. I know who Buster White is. And I know you're just the person sucking his ding-dong and tickling his nuts."

Fannie watched the cigarillo burn in her long fingers, admiring the little manicure she'd gotten up in Southaven after her meet with Ray. She clicked her nails against the rail, looking at the dirty faces of her sorry-as-hell options. "Not if they don't know what hit 'em," she said.

"That's crazy talk," Uncle Heath said. "You know that?"

"We make Marquis Sledge happy for a few weeks," she said. "Deliver what you boys bragged on what you could get. And then we open up some new lifelines out west. Fannie Hathcock and the Pritchards."

"Aren't you pissed about what happened to that Davis boy?" Cody said. "I mean, damn. He was one of your Employees of the Month."

"Y'all did what need to be done," Fannie said. "I was wrong. I should have never had him on your land. A man's land is his kingdom."

"That's goddamn right," Uncle Heath said. "See? See I told you boys. That nigger had no business stepping foot on our goddamn property. I was in my damn rights as an American."

"I know I'm just some dumb fucking redneck," Tyler said. "But that sounds way too generous, ma'am."

"I'm gonna make you earn your keep," Fannie said, lifting the cigarillo to her lips. "Y'all are gonna have to go and get it."

"How's that?" Cody said.

"Come again?" Uncle Heath said.

Tyler, again being the smartest, kept his hick mouth shut and reached into his pajama bottoms to scratch his nuts while he thought on the offer.

"Y'all race cars?" Fannie asked.

"Damn straight," Tyler said.

"Any good?"

Cody started to laugh and shook his head. "Ain't nothing we can't race and win," he said. "We would've won the fucking Hooker Hood Classic up in West Memphis on Saturday if our engine hadn't blowed up."

"And you can drive anything?" Fannie asked.

"Hell yes," Tyler said. "Just what are you thinking?"

"What if I said I happen to know where and when, down to the fucking minute, the next truckload of Mexico's finest pharmaceuticals will roll through this godforsaken county?"

"I'd want to know what's that mean to us," Cody said.

Uncle Heath got it, standing up, laughing, rubbing the back of his neck, grinning like a damn fool. *"Oh, shit,"* he said. "*Oh, shit.* I sure always did love me a redhead."

16

"HOW BAD WAS IT?" NAT WILKINS ASKED.

She sat across the sidewalk from Boom at a rest stop just over the Alabama-Mississippi line. Boom had been driving back a load of car batteries from Birmingham when she called, coming out to him rather than waiting for them to meet in Tupelo. She looked serious and professional, tight as hell in a cream silk top, flared black pants, and that natural hair all styled and bouncy. Wilkins had brought two more agents with her, two young dudes in T-shirts and jeans, who checked the trailer while they spoke. All of 'em trying to assure Boom that no one had followed and that no one was watching.

"Bad," Boom said. "Hood didn't tell me much. Just gave me directions to that warehouse I told you about. The place smelled like dead shrimp, rotten as hell, half the roof falling in. They had twenty girls waiting there. Told me to stay in the cab while he and four other guys pushed them up into the trailer. Told them to take a piss now or hold it for the next five hours."

"Did you know the men?" Nat asked.

"Nope."

"Did you find out there they were taking the women?" Nat said.

"Nope," Boom said. "I drove them as far as another warehouse outside Ripley. They pushed them out of the truck and Hood told me to go on and head back to Sutpen's. They had another driver down there. I got the feeling they were headed north."

"Why?"

"There was talk about getting the girls out somewhere in Kentucky," Boom said.

"Were the girls black, white?"

"Asian," Boom said. "Three or four of them were Hispanic. All of them didn't speak a lick of English. Hood didn't say a word about it, but they looked young as hell to me. Little bitty girls, carrying sad-ass little purses and backpacks. They didn't look like they had any idea where they were headed or what was going on."

"Chinese?" she said. "Vietnamese? Mexican? Guatemalan?"

"Miss Wilkins," Boom said. "Only two places I ever spent much time is Mississippi and Iraq. All I can tell you is that these girls weren't from around here. They were real young, couple of 'em maybe not even teens. And scared. Some of them crying. Saw one of those boys down in Biloxi slap the shit out of one kid. Took everything in me not to grab that motherfucker by the throat with my prosthetic and toss his ass against the wall."

"Glad you didn't," Nat said, smiling at him. Trying to make him feel a little better about what he'd seen and done. "Or else they might've killed you and we'd never known what was going on."

"Still makes me feel dirty," Boom said. "All of this is nasty as hell. Drugs is one thing. Running young girls up from the Coast . . . Where they taking them? What will they end up doing?"

"You really want to know?" Wilkins said.

Boom didn't answer. He had his own ideas, hearing things that Mingo had told him about girls who came to work at Vienna's or were sent on down the line to Memphis. They didn't care any more about those girls than rabbits locked up in a hutch. That's the way they'd do it, set 'em up in some apartment building, old motel, and then start selling their time online, the way they had with Ana Maria and probably Tamika Odum, too. He wasn't surprised folks were pimping out kids, but it got him thinking about all the men out there wanting this kind of shit. How many sick motherfuckers were out there keeping this kind of action going?

"You OK?" Nat said.

"Yeah," Boom said. "I'm fine."

She looked up and the two young agents walked down the pathway toward the rest stop. They shook their heads, saying the truck was all clean, heading back to the black SUV they'd parked behind his rig.

"Told you," Boom said. "Interstate batteries. Nothing more."

"And what did you drive over?" Nat said.

"Goddamn frozen pies," Boom said. "Refrigerated truck full of sweet potato pies they say were better than your momma used to make."

"My momma never made sweet potato pie," she said. "If my momma cooked sweet potatoes, we had yams with some collard greens and chicken."

"You know it," Boom said. "My momma could cook like that, too. Before she got sick, she did all that stuff at the church. Worked with Ordeen Davis's momma there, too. Lot of good, strong women at the church. My daddy is a deacon, but it was the women who ran the place."

"You trying to tell me how much you value and appreciate a strong black woman?"

Boom scratched under his chin, trying not to smile but not helping himself. He liked Nat Wilkins's company, even though sitting here in the dark with two federal agents going through his damn load was maybe gonna get his ass killed. That woman had a style, a confidence about her that sure made him smile. "Oh yes, ma'am," he said.

"You still go to church?" she said. "I like a man who's got his priorities straight."

"I left my old church," Boom said. "Stopped believing after I got home from Iraq. I hit the bottle and some other shit real hard. Lots of folks praying for me, trying to cast those fucking demons out. But it didn't do no good. I also was told I couldn't eat catfish and pork. I spent my whole life having to sneak that shit over at Quinn Colson's house. Now I find myself a grown-ass man and I want to eat some barbecue when I want it."

"And you're back with the Lord?"

"Yes, ma'am," Boom said. "We got straight. I got services at this place called The River. Lots of folks who got themselves clean. White folks who love that old-timey white gospel and country music. But it's black, too. Lots of Mexicans. Ain't nothing to it but folks who want to show a little respect and gratitude for being alive. I ain't trying to preach to you. But it's all right. You should come with me sometime."

"I'd like that," Nat Wilkins said.

"Sorry there wasn't any cocaine or anything in my truck."

Nat stood up, lifted her chin at him, and narrowed her eyes.

"They giving you a little break. Maybe seeing what you'll do. If they feel like you made that run to Biloxi and didn't do shit, they'll loosen up. Those boys will trust you with something bigger."

"And then what?"

"You do it," she said. "And you do it again. And then when we got it all set up and right, we take those peckerwoods down."

"Again and again?" Boom said. "That ain't for me. I'm tired of this mess."

"This is the most we've ever found out about Sutpen," she said. "Do I really need to sit here and insult your fine intelligence with a pep talk?"

"Might help."

"What if I promised to go to church with you one Sunday?" Nat said. "All nice and proper, when all this shit is over. Nice little gloves, a big ole hat. Maybe show some leg if your church allows that kind of thing."

"That sounds like entrapment, Miss Wilkins."

"Just a little longer," Nat said, reaching out and touching his shoulder. "I promise."

Quinn found Heath Pritchard that night on the Square, drinking beer in public and checking out the high school girls walking under the old oaks. The trees and the gazebo by the veterans' monument had been strung with little white lights. One of his deputies had followed Pritchard from his property out to the farm supply and then Reggie tailed him over to Varner's Quick Mart, where he'd bought a case of Natural Light. For the last thirty minutes, Reggie said, Pritchard had just been sitting on a park bench trying to talk up teenage girls, offering them a beer or a sip of whiskey from a brown paper sack. It was hot, Quinn sweating through his stiff uniform shirt, the young girls on the Square wearing next to nothing.

"There's a law about drinking in public," Quinn said.

"Oh yeah?" Heath Pritchard said. "Yeah, I think I heard something about it. I ain't drinking. Just carrying home some groceries."

"I've been watching you drink for the last ten minutes," Quinn said. "And trying to solicit teenagers to go get in your truck."

"Oh, hell," Pritchard said. "Just having me some fun. Besides, ain't you the law in the county? You ain't the law in Jericho."

"I'm the law everywhere."

"Well, goody for you," Pritchard said. "How about you just sit down and share a beer. I'll tell you some stories about your beloved old Uncle Hamp that would make a goat puke. I have to admit something. The other day when I said I used to dream about killing him? I said I was kidding. Well, I wasn't kidding. I would've loved to have been the man who pulled that trigger. Real sorry that son of a bitch did it himself."

Quinn didn't react. Folks like Pritchard got off on it. They liked to see people's nerves as loose and jangled as their own. The man looked drunk as hell, red-eyed and smelling of whiskey even from several feet back. Quinn just stared at him, waiting, before he said, "You didn't seem to have any trouble shooting Lyle Masters."

"Who the fuck is Lyle Masters?" Pritchard said, not giving a damn and reaching into his sack for a beer. He drained the whole thing and tossed the can at Quinn's feet.

"Goes by the name Wrong Way," Quinn said. "You shot him in the leg and then your nephew Cody ran over those boys' scooters. If I were you, I wouldn't be showing my face in public for a while. The Born Losers have a long memory."

"Fuck me," Pritchard said. "Those boys can come on and try and git it. I'll shoot that fella again. In fact, I'd fucking love to."

Quinn watched the small, wiry man, hunched over on the bench, as two girls in short shorts, tank tops, and flip-flops walked toward the gazebo. Pritchard followed them with his eyes, tongue licking at the side of his mouth like he was savoring some forgotten flavor. "They sure do grow 'em up good in this town," he said. "I close my eyes and think what it must be like to taste one of them. Must be like spreading apart an Oreo and licking out that cream fillin'."

"Come on."

"Come on?" Pritchard asked. "You taking me in for what?"

"Public drunk," Quinn said. "And for attempted murder."

"I didn't attempt jack shit, Sheriff," Pritchard said. "Use your fucking head. If I wanted to kill that mongrel, I would've shot him right in the damn head. Ain't nothing but a warning shot. Besides, I got my dang rights. Those boys rolled up into the Walmart lot looking for trouble. They threatened my little nephew. They threatened me. All I was doing was trying to get back to my fucking property and eat some ice cream on the porch. I'm gonna enjoy my damn summer, relaxing and loving every damn minute of life. I didn't go twenty-three years in Parchman to have some damn criminals on scooters try and tell me what I can and can't do. I got my rights. Way I see it is, it's you that's done wrong. Ain't you supposed to keep the fucking peace?"

"You got that gun on you right now?"

"Fuck, yeah," he said. "Or ain't this America? I have my damn rights."

"Not as a felon," Quinn said. "Raise your hands. And stand up."

Pritchard shook his head. It didn't look like he'd shaved in the last few days, more stubble on his face than on his head. His brown little mouth hanging open as he breathed, all ragged and slow, like he was thinking on his options. Heath Pritchard wasn't a quick thinker. But he looked like he had a slow burn on some mean ideas. Quinn watched every movement, waiting for him to go for the gun or try to run for it. Either way, he wouldn't get far.

"Can I at least finish my fucking beer?" he asked.

"Give me the gun."

Pritchard smiled, trying to look all coy and funny, smiling a little bit. "Shit," he said. "How about you try and come get it? I can't have Hamp Beckett's little damn nephew harassing my ass on the Square. Taking away my damn rights."

Quinn nodded, took a long breath to steady himself. "Two seconds."

"Till what?"

"Till I knock you on your ass, Pritchard," Quinn said. "Grab that gun and put you under arrest."

Pritchard wet his lips, sticking the empty can back in the paper sack. He stretched his arms out on the bench, like everything was cool and easy, and began to watch a car circling the Square. A bunch of young girls hanging out a truck window, yelling to some boys who'd parked down at the gazebo. "Damn youth is wasted on the young," Pritchard said, grinning with yellowed teeth. "Am I right?"

Quinn snatched up Pritchard's right arm, yanking him to his feet, and forced him down onto the walkway. He took a little .32 from Pritchard's back pocket. The man strong as an ape, trying to wrestle his arm free, but Quinn already had a knee to the man's spine, finding cuffs on his Sam Brown belt and clicking them on Pritchard. "Goddamn motherfucker," Pritchard said. "You goddamn piece of shit. I knowed my rights. Don't you touch me. Don't you dare touch me."

Quinn reached for his phone and called in to dispatch.

"Can't a man protect himself in this town?" Pritchard said. "You just as dirty as your damn uncle, looking out for a fucking motorcycle gang. Those turds working for the fucking Dixie Mafia."

Quinn got down on his haunches to speak more privately with Heath Pritchard. Some of the kids on the Square, stopping their socializing, began to pay attention to the free show. Quinn waved a few back, speaking in a low, direct voice.

"This has to be a record," Quinn said. "You've already shot two men since you've been out."

"Two?" he said. "What the damn hell. You're a fucking crook just like your uncle."

"Two of my deputies are headed to your place right now," Quinn said. "You wouldn't happen to have a twelve-gauge lying about?"

"A twelve-gauge?" Pritchard said, laughing, face flush to the concrete path. "Everybody in Mississippi has a twelve-gauge. More common than a damn Walker hound. What kind of man doesn't want to protect what he's got?"

Quinn took off his ball cap, curved the bill in his fingers, and set it back onto his head. "Is that why you shot Ordeen Davis in the back?" he said. "That's how this whole damn story started. Right?"

Heath Pritchard didn't answer for a bit, as Quinn heard the sirens coming up on the Square.

"Naw," Pritchard said. "This goddamn story started before you had your first wet dream. Back when your dead uncle sided with fucking Johnny Stagg."

I hope you understand this is the way it's got to be from now on," Wes Taggart said, sitting at Fannie Hathcock's desk, counting down Fannie's money. "Me and J.B. can handle the shutdown.

You can head on home early, maybe get you a little more beaut sleep."

That last little bit wasn't meant as an insult, more of a gentle tap on her ass as they sent her on back to Cordova, where she kept a mainly empty three-bedroom condo. Wes Taggart didn't even look up from her glass-top desk as he ran a handful of sweaty one-dollar bills though the counter, the cash smelling of cherry body lotion and cigarettes.

"You sure you don't mind?" Fannie asked.

"Not at all," he said. "Me and Wes run a lot of clubs in our time. Beer joints, titty bars, even a seafood restaurant in Mobile. Don't you worry a bit. We got this thing."

"That's awful nice of y'all," Fannie said. "Working so hard like this."

Taggart stacked the cash, wrapped it in a paper band for a hundred, and then scooped up another big handful, his eyes tilting up at Fannie from beneath that stringy brown hair. It looked like he hadn't changed his goddamn style since 1979. Basic boy's cut, running down to his eyebrows and hiding his ears.

Fannie smiled down at him. "J.B. told me you'd grown a little fond of Twilight."

The cash counters shuffled through the pile in a quick whir, Taggart grabbing the neat stack and wrapping another hundred. "She's a nice young lady," he said. "Just trying to give her a little direction and advice."

"Did she tell you about her two babies?" Fannie said.

"She told me some of it," Taggart said, scribbling down some third-grade math notes on a legal pad, leaning back in Fannie's leather chair, nodding. "She's a tough young lady. She told me she wanted to be a marine biologist one day. That girl sure has a thing for dolphins."

"Don't I know it," Fannie said. "I saw the tattoo."

"I have to hand it to you, Fannie," he said. "I been in thousands of strip clubs. Me and J.B. both. But we both were saying how you got some of the finest-looking girls we've ever seen. All of them clean, polite—"

"Young," Fannie said. "Fresh."

"Not a damn dog among them," he said. "I'm gonna talk to Buster White and tell him what a damn fine job you're doing. You sure got an eye for talent. It's not just that you bring those fresh faces. The things those girls do? Holy moly. The way they work that pole I'd have thought I was in Vegas at that Circus du Soleil."

"That's sweet," Fannie said. "I do my best."

Taggart leaned back farther in that chair, the springs squeaking and popping, and placed his dusty pointy-toed boots up on the glass, nearly knocking over a pile of twenties J. B. Hood had gotten from the three registers at the bar. There were coffee cups filled with cigarettes and ash, a half-eaten hamburger and cold fries in a Styrofoam shell. For some damn reason, the man had brought up a suitcase, living down here for the last two days, washing up in the girl's changing room and sleeping on the office sofa. Something in the air had changed. Instead of Dunhills and Chanel No. 5, the office smelled like man funk and cheeseburgers.

"I'm glad you're OK with the new arrangement," Taggart said, hands behind his head, his arms muscled and veiny. He had a hawk nose, looking like it had been busted a few times. "Me and J.B. worried you might give us some pushback after that first night."

"Well," Fannie said. "Y'all sure did surprise me. I wish Buster or Ray had given me a little warning."

"I think there's some good opportunities for you in Memphis," he said. "We've just took over some of Bobby Campo's old properties. I checked out that old club on Mount Moriah. It's a little dusty, got some black mold in the kitchen. But the carpet's not too worn out and it still has those birdcages where the girls can dance and put on those lezzie shows. I also spotted this old Pyrtle's fried chicken joint on Poplar that might could get converted."

"I appreciate you looking out for me," Fannie said. "I know we all just want to make sure the boys are happy."

"Don't you know it," Taggart said, ashing the cigarette on the cold cheeseburger. "I can already see where me and J.B. might make some improvements. First thing I'd do is knock out that old wooden bar and put in something a little more modern, with some mirrors and neon. I'd also expand our VIP room. I don't have to tell you that's where the churn really happens. Get those boys in, fleeced, and back out on the floor."

"Might have some trouble with the locals on that one," Fannie said, smiling, her cheeks starting to ache. "They shut down the lap dancing for now."

"We can take care of that," Taggart said. "We heard about the Baptists around here. They might be right with the Lord, but there ain't a man alive that can't be trapped with good whiskey and pussy."

"Amen to that," Fannie said.

Fannie took a seat on the edge of the glass desk, watching Taggart writing down more figures and raking up another big pile of crumpled cash to the counting machine. The cigarette hung from the side of the mouth, making him look like a Marlboro Man gone to seed. She'd checked up on Taggart from some friends in Tupelo and over in Birmingham. He was a pretty simple man, too. Got into some trouble a while back in Alabama cruising the shopping malls with a circuit judge who had a modeling studio in his basement.

Fannie watched as two of her girls, Twilight and CoCo, walked up the spiral staircase and peered into the open door. Twilight favored Britney Spears before the bitch went crazy and shaved her head. Big brown doe eyes and natural titties so big she had to order special bras from the internet. CoCo was tall and black, her skin like milk chocolate, with a lean, athletic body, small titties, and wide hips. The best goddamn dancer at Vienna's, she could pick a man's pocket while hanging upside down and humping the pole. Both of them had on matching pink bikinis and tall, clear plastic heels.

"What's this?" Taggart said, dropping the money in his hands and pulling the cigarette from his mouth.

"A little prize," Fannie said. "You've been working two days straight."

"I know your rules, Fannie," Taggart said. "And I gave you my word."

"Consider it work," Fannie said. "Since you and J.B. are wanting to open the VIP room back up, you might want to take it for a little spin. There's only one way to experience it, see how we might make a few improvements to your liking. Maybe see things from a man's perspective?"

If fucking Wes Taggart had been a dog, he'd have been slobbering all over her desk. He eyed those two girls, black and white, smooth skin and long legs, like they were a couple of T-bone steaks. Fannie looked to CoCo and gave her a little secret wink, CoCo walking all sexy and confident in those six-inch heels over to Taggart and sitting right in his lap. Twilight joined her, standing behind him and rubbing his shoulders. As if caught awake in a dream, Wes Taggart shot a mean look up at Fannie. "Come on, now," he said. "You think I'm that dumb?"

"What's that, Wes?"

"I gotten my lap rode thousands of times," he said. "I can't be controlled by my pecker."

"You're a smart man, Wes Taggart," she said. "You got me there."

"Then again . . ." he said.

"Never hurts to make friends with the bossman," Fannie said, watching as the girls pulled Taggart up to his feet, his cowboy boots sliding off her glass desk.

"Leave me to the count," he said, getting to his feet. CoCo started rubbing him between his legs, priming his old cowboy pump, being led away down the spiral steps and into the VIP room. He gripped Twilight's ass, right below the tattoo of a dolphin flipping in front of a sunset.

"Let me know about those improvements, Wes," she said.

After they left, Fannie felt like her face was frozen from all the fake smiling. She walked back into the office, shut the door, and reached for the beat-up Samsung phone he'd left behind. It was one of those cheap-ass, pay-as-you-go phones, something to bust up and toss out when you're done. Fannie used them, everyone in the Syndicate did. They liked that they couldn't be tracked and traced by feds, and were seldom kept beyond a week or two. So damn short that Taggart didn't even bother to set up a passcode.

She sat down at her desk, cleared a spot in the mess, and began to scroll through the dumb bastard's messages.

17

BOOM HAD BEEN ON THE ROAD FOR FIVE HOURS, FROM Houston, after waiting nearly a day at some crummy-ass Motel 6 across the road from the warehouses. They'd loaded him up at eight at night, the rig fueled and ready to roll, and he hit Baton Rouge at midnight, stopping off to piss and grab a cup of coffee, then back on the interstate. He'd heard from Nat Wilkins twice already, saying they were all over Sutpen's and would bust in right after he made the delivery and got off the property. He was damn glad all this shit was about to be over, but, man, he sure would miss the road. Nobody was gonna hire a one-armed driver that had worked for an outfit with its name all over the news.

He'd probably have to go back to the County Barn, make good with Skinner, and work under his people, fixing trucks, changing tires, hauling in broken gravel spreaders and backhoes. He'd done it before and would do it again. The dashboard of his truck glowed a gentle blue, Boom checking out his speed, rpm's, fuel, making some mental calculations on where he'd stop next, although the damn computer would remind him every step of the way. His blue dot moving along the GPS on Interstate 10 through Louisiana.

He liked this part of the country, loving just the sound of the names the places he'd passed through in the night: Turtle Bayou, Rose City, Lake Charles, Breaux Bridge, the Atchafalaya River. He liked those big road signs, too: GOD BLESS TEXAS, BLUE LIVES MATTER, TIGER TRUCK STOP (SEE A LIVE TIGER!), SURPRISINGLY SMOOTH C.C.'S COFFEE, VISIT LARRY FLYNT'S HUSTLER CLUB, EVANGELINE MAID BREAD, and YOU CAN'T HOLD HANDS WITH GOD WHEN MASTURBATING. That last one being a good one, always making him laugh, lots of billboards being put up by God or folks who thought they were talking direct with Jesus Himself.

All that landscape, bright lights, and color so different from when he was driving trucks in Iraq. The trick driving back then was not falling asleep or running off the damn road because you didn't see nothing but sand and desert, only your lights shining twenty feet ahead. The driving into nothing, heat and the horizon, did shit to your head, your perspective, and direction. Nothing but talk between you and your boys keeping your mind alert, letting your ass know you were still on Planet Earth.

Right outside McComb, Mississippi, birthplace of Bo Diddley, the burner phone they'd given him started to buzz in his pocket. He picked up, hearing that gravelly countrified voice of L. Q. Smith telling him to cut on over to Interstate 20 when he hit Jackson, that there were some highway patrol stops around Grenada and that they needed him to keep on to Okolona, where he could refuel and wait around for the new drop-off location.

"What about Tupelo?" Boom asked.

"You're not going to Tupelo, son," he said. "Not tonight."

"Where am I headed, then?"

"You'll know when I know," Smith said. "Just don't drive that rig nowhere near Sutpen's. We got some feds on our ass. Spotted two of them bastards taking pictures not far from our gates."

Son of a bitch. Boom hung up, picked up his own phone, and called Nat. Three rings later, she picked up.

"They onto you," Boom said. "What y'all got planned ain't gonna happen."

Tyler Pritchard was watching an old VHS tape of the time he and Cody were on *America's Funniest Home Videos.* He hadn't seen it in a long time, the tape starting to wear out from all the views and the nearly twenty years that had passed. The picture was grainy, an electric fuzz at the bottom, but it was clear as day watching their dead stepdaddy trying to teach them baseball. He had him and Cody out back of their trailer, Cody with the bat and Tyler doing the pitching. Their dumb-ass stepdaddy, drunk on his tenth beer and a half bottle of Beam, stood a little too close to Cody, making sure their momma had them on the video, and got the everliving shit knocked out of his nuts. Tyler wasn't sure if the old colors were playing with the picture, but it sure looked like their stepdaddy turned green as he pitched over and fell on the ground, their momma setting down the camera sideways and running for his dumb ass.

Damn, if Tyler didn't snicker a bit every time he watched it, snorting some weed smoke out his nose, all on their fifty-inch Sony at three o'clock in the morning. He hadn't been able to sleep. Uncle

Heath had bonded out of jail that morning and was wired, keeping them up till midnight to play poker and then making them watch *Young Guns 2* until he started to snore in his chair, a cold Popeyes chicken leg in his hand. *"Goin' down in a blaze of glory . . ."*

Tyler got up and turned off the TV, careful to rewind the tape back to the beginning. He wondered what would happen if he lost it or the damn thing broke. Maybe those folks at *AFV* had a damn library of the greatest nuts shots of all time. He knew they'd had thousands of folks knocked in the cojones with garden rakes, golf balls, and nunchucks, but, goddamn, watching his mean-ass stepdaddy taking a Louisville Slugger to the balls was, well, just damn perfect. What some folks might call therapeutic.

The front door and back screen doors were open as Tyler walked up to the five computer screens set on an old desk, popping the keys, checking the cameras along the dirt road, the race shop, and down into the grow rooms. He carefully looked at the detailed image of each one, amazed at how damn good cameras had gotten in the last twenty years. You could make out the detail on a leaf of a plant. Watching that old video, he didn't think he could really see his stepdaddy no more through all the grainy fuzz. Probably the only image left of the dumb bastard besides some Polaroids his grandmomma gave them at the funeral.

Tyler wandered on in his bedroom, flopping on his back, checking through some texts between him and that girl Rhonda that he'd met at the MAG down in Columbus. She'd sent him some pretty damn good pics of her in a bikini, modeling her tan skin and bright smile in the bathroom mirror. Sometime last night—hell, he couldn't remember, on account of being drunk—he'd asked her to show him her titty. And she'd just responded with a winky-faced smile. He didn't know whether that meant *Hold on, it's comin'* or *Go fuck yourself.*

He tossed the phone on the bed and closed his eyes, trying to get some sleep, when the phone started to pulsate. His ringtone playing "Copperhead Road" as he pressed ACCEPT and told whoever the hell it was to get to talking.

"You boys know your way to Okolona?" a woman said.

"Who the fuck is this?"

"It's happening," the woman said, telling him the address of some truck stop off 45. "Those bastards are moving more pills tonight than a goddamn Walgreens."

Boom filled up and parked away from the pumps by a gathering of eighteen-wheelers resting and waiting before getting back on the highway. He locked up the cab and headed on into the truck stop, a little place called Smokie's, made to look like an old-time general store, with stonework and unpainted wood. As soon as you walked in the door, a life-sized statue of John Wayne greeted you at the candy display, caught in mid-draw with a pack of Twizzlers in hand.

He used the bathroom and sat up on a stool by the kitchen counter, everything made out of corrugated tin and barn wood. He looked up to the daily specials on a chalkboard and decided to go on and get right down to breakfast, asking the waitress for two sausage biscuits and a large Mountain Dew.

She wanted to know if he'd like some American cheese on those biscuits and Boom just looked at the woman like she'd gone crazy. Only a damn fool puts cheese on a biscuit.

Nobody was in the truck stop besides two waitresses, a cook, and the young girl working the register in the convenience store. Some folks would filter in and out, but Boom was pretty much alone in the restaurant. A television hung on a far wall playing goddamn *Gomer Pyle, U.S.M.C.* Boom remembered his daddy watching that show in reruns, Gomer always fucking up and getting yelled at by the Sarge. His daddy making a point about how much damn fun they were having on the base while all the other Marines had gotten their asses shipped off to Vietnam. That was before his daddy's conversion, when he was still on that Kools and Crown Royal diet, heading out to the clubs at night, stepping out on his momma, doing whatever he could to get off their land and find some action in Tibbehah County.

But he was a good man now. A deacon. A man of God who hated the smell of liquor and wouldn't think twice about telling you about it. Like the man put it, he'd "Come to the Cross."

"What's your problem with cheese?" asked the waitress, an old white woman with dyed red hair that showed a big split of white down the center part like a skunk. She had ruby-tinted glasses on and big gold hoop earrings.

"Just don't like cheese, is all."

"We got other stuff," she said. "I can make you a plate of eggs if you want."

She said eggs like it started with an *a*. Looking tired, she sat down beside him at the stools, noticing the hook for a hand but not finding the right way to ask about it. Boom used his left hand to eat, resting the elbow of the prosthetic on the counter, glancing up to see Gomer Pyle trying to untrain a Marine German shepherd.

"That was a funny show," she said.

Boom nodded.

"Don't make 'em like that no more," she said. "Nothing but sex, violence, and trash. You could watch that with your whole family. I think that's what's wrong with folks out there today. I got that DirecTV and, Lord, the things I've seen on my screen, I wish I could wash my damn eyes out."

"Maybe you should unplug your TV," Boom said, drinking down some Mountain Dew. Not a damn bit tired after being on the road for nearly seven hours. He felt like he could make a run up to Chicago and back and not be the worse for wear.

"Can't," she said. "Got to watch my stories. Did you know *Days of Our Lives* has been on more than fifty years? That's got to make it the longest-running show in history."

Boom nodded, finished up his biscuit. Gomer Pyle being told to not get too close to the dogs, they were trained to attack strangers. Gomer being Gomer, he just couldn't figure out why those nice doggies could be so mean.

The woman reached into her apron and pulled out a vape pen, blowing out some steam that smelled like cinnamon. She nodded as she exhaled, looking down at his hook. "You in the service?"

"Yes, ma'am."

"Wasn't like TV," she said. "Was it?"

Boom shook his head, glancing down at the screen of the phone Sutpen had given him, waiting for it to ring, so he could head on down the road. He looked up to see a hand-painted sign by the fried pies that read SAVED BY GRACE. Boom looked back to the woman, who rested her hand over his steel hook.

"I dated a boy in high school who went over to Vietnam," she said. "I sure did love him. Sometimes when I'm feeling sorry for myself, I wonder what my life would've been like if he'd come home and I married him. Maybe I wouldn't have made all those damn mistakes, having to turn my life around at fifty-five."

"Yes, ma'am."

"He was a fine young man," she said. "When I heard he'd been killed at the Hamburger Hill, my legs went out from under me, fell right to the floor."

She pulled on the pen again, blowing out some steam, her mind somewhere way off in time, thinking on things as you do at four a.m. "Where you headed?" she said.

"Don't know," Boom said, studying that hand-painted sign a bit more, looking like someone local had made it, ripped a piece of old wood right off a rotten barn.

"Ain't that your rig out there?" she said.

"Yes, ma'am."

"And you don't know which direction you're headed?"

"No, ma'am." Boom shook his head. "Wish I did."

Fuck me," Tyler said.

"We can't jack his ass here," Cody said. "They got ten trucks all around that trailer. We wouldn't get a mile down the road without Johnny Law hightailing it after us. And that Freightliner don't run like no race car."

"Son of a bitch."

They'd parked their white Chevy away from the pumps, down in some deep shadow by a road off the highway. They'd watched as the big black driver had locked up the rig and gone on inside the building. From where they waited, they could see him through the window, sitting up at the counter, talking it up with some old redheaded woman. It almost looked like they were sitting there praying over a plate of food. There was something damn familiar about that man, but Tyler couldn't quite make out his face.

"We can't do it here," Tyler said.

"Well, if we can't do it here, we can't do it nowhere," he said. "Where did that Hathcock woman say he was headed?"

"Ripley," Tyler said. "Those good ole boys got a compound up there. They got spooked by some kind of trouble down in Tupelo. But I ain't gonna jack him up in Ripley, neither. You know how many peckerheads gonna greet that truck with shotguns, just waiting for someone to ride on up and try to take that whole shipment off their hands."

"Wait," Cody said, sitting in the passenger seat and holding up the flat of his right hand. "Wait just one goddamn minute. We can't jack him here. And we can't jack him at those crooks' place. Then we're gonna have to get him somewhere between them two points."

"We got a big truck," Tyler said. "But we ain't gonna be able to run no Freightliner off no fucking road."

"What if he has to stop?" Cody asked.

"Like a roadblock or something?" Tyler said. "Maybe on that old two-lane?"

"Use your fuckin' head," Cody said. "We make that big rig peter out somewhere down the road and we swing on in behind his ass when he's got to stop."

"I can't get to that truck's engine without someone seeing me," Tyler said. "And I sure can fuck it up, but not with no time delay."

"What about if we put water in his tanks?"

"He just filled up," Tyler said. "Besides, if that did work, how the fuck are we supposed to move that trailer? With a Chevy Silverado?"

"OK, smartass," Cody said. "You tell me how we do it, then."

"No water," Tyler said. "I ain't doing nothing I can't fix. Not under five, ten minutes, once we get things under control."

"Then what?"

"Hold up," Tyler said. "Hold up. *Jesus Christ.* I can't hear myself think."

"It's got to be the damn fuel."

"Maybe the air line."

"Cut off the air to the tank?" Cody said. "*OK. OK.* Sure, man. I like it. Maybe tie that tube. How long you think you can drive like that before the gas tank sucks up all that air?"

"I don't know."

"Will it work?"

"I said I don't fucking know," Tyler said. "But I'd give it twenty, thirty miles. That gas ain't gonna flow into that engine, and that old black boy will have to pull off and check on things. That air will vacuum out the tank, just like pouring out a jug of milk."

"And we slide on behind him and offer help," he said. "Like a couple redneck Samaritans."

Tyler nodded, thinking on it from behind the wheel. He pulled at that long-ass Moses beard, deciding this felt like the right plan. Right as fuckin' rain. "Sorry for calling you fuck brain," Tyler said. "You can be right smart when you want to be."

18

BOOM COULD MAKE RIPLEY IN A LITTLE UNDER AN HOUR, scooting up to New Albany and then hitting Highway 15 north toward Blue Mountain. He'd been to Ripley plenty of times, to the First Monday sale, where they sold everything from antiques to tools to hunting dogs, both bred and stolen. Boom paid his tab, tipped his CAT hat at the old waitress, and headed on out to the door, the slash of light shining over the pumps leaving his rig in shadow. As he headed across the open lot, little red and yellow lights glowing on the parked trucks, he checked to see if anyone was around before calling up Nat Wilkins on his private phone.

"Ripley," he said, giving her an address.

"We make arrests in Ripley and we might as well kiss the Sutpens good-bye."

"They onto you anyway," Boom said. "What the hell's it matter?"

"We're not just after what you're hauling," she said. "We want their records, cell phones, to interview everyone who works there. It ain't just drugs. It's girls, pills, stolen shit. You trucking that stuff in to Sutpen's place made our warrant work. You ain't trucking into Sutpen's and that warrant is dead."

"And my black ass is hanging out in the wind," Boom said. "I feel like a goddamn pimp, bringing this stuff up to Ripley. I'd just as soon dump this shit in the Mississippi."

"Come on, now," Nat said. "You know how this all has to work. Be patient, Boom. Be cool."

"Be cool?" Boom said. "Yeah, sure. But y'all ain't the ones behind the wheel."

You know who that is?" Cody said.

"Yep."

"That's fucking Boom Kimbrough."

"No shit," Tyler said. "How many big one-armed niggers you know up in north Mississippi? I didn't see it when he walked in, but I see it now. Ain't nobody said nothing about Boom driving that rig."

"Son of a damn bitch."

Tyler watched Boom use his good hand to take hold and hop up into the cab, then he turned back to his brother. "Why's it got to be fucking Boom?" he asked. "He'll know it's us. I ain't doing this shit."

"You know what Uncle Heath would say?"

"Uncle Heath can suck my damn balls," Tyler said. "I ain't killing Boom Kimbrough to hijack some pills for Fannie Hathcock. You remember how he come through for us when we blowed out that engine that time? He machined the block, crankshaft, and cylinders back like it had come straight from the factory. Boom's a goddamn artist."

"Yeah," Cody said. "I remember."

"This ain't gonna happen."

"Unless he don't recognize us."

"Come on, now," Tyler said. "We knowed that man since we was kids. How many damn times has he helped us out, sitting around the County Barn talking racing and cars. Ain't Boom a big Dale Jr. fan? Hell, we was just shooting pool with that son of a bitch a few weeks back."

"I still don't know how he shoots pool with one damn arm," Cody said. "I'm not even sure it's legal, way he sizes up that goddamn cue in that hook of his."

"'Course it's legal," Tyler said. "And we ain't fucking with no Boom Kimbrough."

Cody crawled into the back of the truck, rooting all around through the junk they tossed there: a mess of car parts, crates of oil and beer cans, dirty T-shirts, old paper sacks from Sonic, and maybe a few women's panties. He sure as hell hoped Cody didn't come back with a pair of some girl's panties, wanting them to disguise themselves with goddamn cotton lace hip-huggers.

"I know what you're thinking," Tyler said. "But it ain't gonna work. Let's just head on back and talk to Miss Hathcock straight. She'll understand. We can wait for another time. Boom can't be driving that shit for Sutpen's every night."

"And who's gonna talk to Marquis Sledge?" Cody said. "As the good ole boys come up from behind us and fuck us long and hard in the asshole. *Nope.* We can't wait. None of the damn shit can wait."

Cody reached up between the two front seats and handed Tyler a couple of those neoprene face masks they had to wear when racing down in Florida. In the summer, it got so damn dusty, you'd about choke out after the fifth lap. These were some good ones, all black, with a damn skull as the face. They looked like those things scuba divers wore under their goggles, only with a little mouth piece that filtered out all the dust and dirt.

"That'll work," Tyler said.

"Hope you fucked up that tank right."

"I plugged up both of 'em," Tyler said. "I used that Pro Seal putty. Goddamn Boom Kimbrough. You think someone's just fucking with us? Maybe that Hathcock woman wants to see our asses get killed."

"Man's got to eat," Cody said. "But I never saw Boom as the criminal type. Ain't he real good friends with the sheriff?"

"Best friends," Tyler said. "They'd known each other since they were kids. I heard that when they were in school, those two stole a damn firetruck. Both of them had the choice of either jail time or going in the service."

"And Boom comes back with one arm."

"And Quinn comes back to being sheriff."

"That's just fucked up, man," Cody said. "Can't blame the man for wanting to be on the other side of Johnny Law."

That Freightliner's engine started knocking right as Boom turned up on Highway 15, the dawn starting to come up on that twisting road to Blue Mountain. Boom was already trying to figure out the problem, the cab shaking and shuddering, wondering when the last time that truck had some basic maintenance, someone with half a brain checking on the wear to the rings and valves. Whatever was going on, he was losing a lot of power, the truck straining to go up that next hill. And he had a full tank of gas. Could be the liner seals, bearings, or the pistons. The goddamn combustion timing was most definitely off. If he could just get on up to Ripley, he could park the son of a bitch and get gone. He had no interest in looking at the problem or fixing it for a fucked-up company like Sutpen. He just prayed to the Lord he could make it a few more miles.

"Come on, baby," he said. "Come on."

Last thing he needed was to be standing on the side of the road with a trailer full of pills and dope. His dick in his hand as the highway patrol rolls up, wanting to know the trouble. Maybe DEA would come through. Nat Wilkins was kind and sweet, with that perfect smile and big bouncy hair. But sometimes life didn't go like that. Ain't nobody wants to be your friend when that shit hits that fan.

High beams flicked up in his rearview. Boom turned on his hazards, letting down his window and reaching out to motion the car forward. It was five in the morning and there weren't many vehicles on the state highway. But the damn car, Boom now seeing it was a big white truck, didn't speed up, only kept on hanging there behind the trailer, lights up on high.

The engine kicked under the hood, Boom wanting to stop off and check things out, but also noting the time. L. Q. Smith expected that delivery in twenty minutes, and if Boom could just ease up on that engine a bit, maybe coast down some hills, he could hand over the rig and get the hell out of there.

The light flickered a grayish blue through a planting of small pines, and up over the reddish brown dirt of a clearing, some machines left vacant up into a logging site. The truck behind him flashed its damn lights again, this time trying to pass. Boom motioned them forward again, the engine kicking like a goddamn mule almost like it was out of gas, rpm's falling low and hammering quick and fast till the damn thing died. He was on a straightaway now, coasting, after cresting the hill, a long shot of blacktop in the first light as he slid to a stop. His hazard lights blinked as he parked off on the side of some cleared property. A big sign planted up on the cleared land that read GO TO CHURCH OR THE DEVIL WILL GET YOU!

Boom stopped and slammed his good fist into the steering wheel, locking the brakes and engaging the pressure with a long hiss. He looked down at his GPS. He only had eighteen miles to go to the address of that land they'd given him up in Ripley.

He looked back in his rearview and saw that white truck that had tried to pass had stopped.

Boom reached for his door handle and hopped down to the ground.

The air smelled of fresh pine cuttings and the early-morning heat off the soil. No cars coming his way as he walked back to the truck, ready to tell them everything was fine and dandy, before getting on the phone to Smith, telling him to come get his fucking truck and his black ass out of here.

"It's good," Boom said. "It's all good."

And then the truck's doors opened and two men in black T-shirts with the sleeves cut off got out, both of them wearing goddamn skull masks, looking like Halloween come to town.

"Boys," Boom said. "I'm fresh out of candy."

The boy with the shotgun crooked his head in the skull mask and studied Boom for a second. "How 'bout you hand over them keys and we'll be the fucking judge of that."

. . .

As Tyler and Cody had followed Boom Kimbrough up to New Albany and then onto the back highway toward Ripley, Cody wanted to make it real clear that the two of them weren't thieves.

"This is a one-time deal," Tyler said. "We show Sledge that we can deliver and then we put it on Miss Hathcock to figure out the rest."

"No way, no how," Cody said. "We don't kill. We don't steal. We don't covet thy neighbors' wives."

"Only neighbors we got is livestock," Tyler said. "And I sure as hell don't covet no cows."

"I read about some woman down in Calhoun City who had relations with her dog," Cody said. "They arrested her ass."

"For what?"

"Damn cruelty to animals," Cody said. "What do you think?"

"How do you know she was being cruel?" Tyler said. "What if the dog liked it?"

"It wadn't how you think," Cody said. "This old gal weighed about two-fifty and entrapped the poor animal with a jar of Skippy peanut butter."

"That's sick, boy," Tyler said. "Real sick."

"And the reason she got put in jail."

"We ain't going to jail," Tyler said. "We're nothing but a couple of farmers carrying on an old family tradition. If that jug-eared midget from Alabama hadn't gone to Washington, we'd be just about to be on the legal side."

"George Washington," Cody said. "Goddamn Thomas Jefferson. All of 'em grew and smoked weed. You tell me the difference between what we do and them fat cats down in Jackson who drink up whiskey with a straw. Sweating their fat asses off in church because some preacher tells them they can't drink, can't screw, when that's all they're doing while talking up family values. What are we doing but taking care of our damn family?"

"Big liquor don't want the competition."

"No, sir," Cody said. "Sure don't. What we're growing may be illegal. But what they're doing is downright immoral."

The red lights on the trailer ahead of them started to flicker, Tyler slowing down a bit, the truck looking to have real trouble just getting around that next hill. "I'm gonna pass his ass," Tyler said. "See if we can't get him to slow on down, help him out with his problem."

The sky was a pinkish blue at the top of the hill, nothing coming at them in the opposite lane. Tyler sped up, keeping up with the truck, watching a big black hand appear from the driver's window, telling them to go on ahead.

"What do I do?" Tyler said.

"Keep moving," Cody said. "We can catch him down the road."

As Tyler saw the hazard light flicker from the cab, he let off the gas, sliding back behind the truck and following it up and over the hill until it got maybe a few hundred feet onto a straightaway and slowed to a stop by a logging site.

"Here we go," Tyler said.

"We ain't thieves."

"Nope," Tyler said. "Just headed off road a little bit. Now, put on that fucking mask and hand me the shotgun."

Right after they asked Boom for the keys to his rig, the two men stood still beside the trailer, not a single vehicle coming and going on Highway 15. Boom had his hands up, the shorter of the two boys coming up on him holding a cordless drill and searching into Boom's empty pockets when he didn't answer. The other boy in the skull mask stood a good bit taller, a mess of tattoos trailing down one forearm. Boom couldn't see much of the tats, but he saw crossed checkered flags and a big blue Chevy symbol that looked familiar as hell.

"Why you boys doing this?" Boom said.

"Shut the hell up," said the shorter one.

"You want this rig?" Boom said. "Take it. I ain't gonna stop you."

"'Course you ain't," the taller one with the beard poking out said. "'Cause you ain't holding the gun."

"No," Boom said. "Because I don't want what's inside."

Neither of the boys answered, Boom still keeping his arms up, nodding to the trailer. He could hear the bugs and crickets out in a grassy field between the road and the long stretch of pines. The earth had been dug away in large sections, leaving little squares of dirt looking like slices of cake. The GO TO CHURCH sign sat on one of the slices, sitting up maybe five, six feet from the dug-out pasture.

"Go on," Boom said. "*Git.* Keys is in it."

"Follow me," said the tall boy with the shotgun. "That's it. Come on. Right back behind the trailer."

"Mister," Boom said, not taking a damn step. "You gonna shoot me, shoot me where I stand. 'Cause ain't no goddamn way I'm stepping behind my truck for y'all to cut me down like some dog."

The shorter one with the drill had already run off from Boom and he could hear the high whine and boring into some metal. The tall boy with the gun just stood there, dropping the barrel while they waited, a couple cars passing and sending grit up into Boom's eyes. Whoever saw them didn't seem to take no mind that his hands were in the air and talking to a guy in a skull mask. Just another day in the piney woods of north Mississippi.

The door slammed. And then the engine sputtered and kicked and finally chugged to life. Boom wondered what those boys had done to get him started again or if they'd played with that engine somewhere back on the road, probably Okolona, while he was watching *Gomer Pyle* and talking about lost time with that old waitress.

The tall boy walked up on him, shotgun loose in his right hand, black T-shirt fluttering around his waist, a bushy beard spilling out from under the mask, as another car hauled ass by them. Boom could make trouble, try to wave someone down, but he didn't like the odds of that boy in the mask raising up that gun and blasting his ass.

"It ain't far back to New Albany," the skull man said.

Boom looked down at the tats covering his right arm. HEROES OF DIRT TRACK RACIN'. He closed his eyes for a moment and took a deep breath. *Goddamn Pritchard boys.* Dumber than dog shit.

"Y'all know who owns this truck?" Boom asked.

"I look like I give a damn?"

"Hard to say," Boom said. "Can't see your face."

"Shut the hell up."

"You boys watch yourself, now," Boom said, hands still raised, watching Tyler Pritchard's eyes from behind the mask. "These good ole boys own this truck don't play."

19

A FEW HOURS AFTER THEY LOST CONTACT WITH THE TRUCK and that black boy driving the rig, J. B. Hood walked into an empty Sutpen warehouse, where he found Wes Taggart stacking and counting barrels of bourbon. They'd taken the lot off the hands of some friend up in Kentucky, thirty-year-old Pappy Van Winkle, that most thought had been destroyed after a court case. But he and Wes had arranged to have it brought down to Tupelo, where they parceled it out to some of their friends. Wes scooped an old barrel up on a hand truck to drive down to a Jackson for a state senator named Vardaman.

"What the fuck happened?" Wes said. "I mean, Jesus H. Christ. Last I heard, he was gonna meet you over in Ripley."

"He never showed," Hood said. "Just got a call from the driver at a Waffle House in New Albany. He claims that his rig tore up on

Highway 15 right before he got hijacked by two fellas dressed up for Halloween."

"That sounds like some bullshit right there," Taggart said. "He just happens have some trouble with his rig and two boys just happened to wander by and jack his ass. How the hell did they get the trailer? They bring in a new rig?"

"Nope," Hood said, watching Taggart lean against the hand truck. Looked like he'd been working a while stacking those barrels, nearly sweating through his T-shirt. "Driver claims them thieves got it started right back up."

"See, that's the thing that don't make no sense, J.B.," Taggart said. "Who was driving for us?"

"Boom Kimbrough."

"Boom Kimbrough?" Taggart said. "Well, fuck me. What the hell did we expect?"

Must've been twenty more barrels of Pappy set up in a pyramid display in what they called the party room. They had extra TVs, stereos, jewelry, fucking mink coats, women's shoes, hunting rifles, and boxes of cigars from Cuba. When the boys needed some folks in Jackson to move on in the right direction, they called up Wes and J.B. to sweeten the pot a little.

"Did fine with me the other night," Hood said. "Didn't have no trouble bringing those slants and Mex poon up from Gulfport. He didn't seem to give two damn shits about what we were hauling long as that cash was waiting for us when we switched trucks."

"I don't like him here." Taggart said. "Who the fuck hired him anyway?"

"Smith," Hood said. "Said he was buddies with ole Jerry Colson. Smith says he didn't expect any trouble with his ass on account of him being a cripple."

"I just wish the son of a bitch had at least tried to fool us," Taggart said, hoisting up the hand truck, the veins bulging in his forearms and biceps as he scooted it toward the open doors of a cargo van. "It's like he was laughing at us while we was getting cornholed."

"I don't buy that shit he got engine trouble," Hood said, reaching for a cigarette in the front pocket of his black shirt. Going full-on Johnny Cash today with black shirt, black pants, and pointy-toed black boots. A woman at the old Vanelli's bar, before it burned down, told him that he looked slim and tough with that gray ponytail. He never forgot that. Although that woman had turned out to be a real piece of trash, giving damn Wes a blow job in the parking lot after she'd been dancing with Hood all damn night.

"Go get him," Taggart said, laying the whiskey in the van and slamming the doors.

Hood let out a lot of smoke and nodded. "Figured on that," he said. "I said for him to wait for me at that Waffle House off 78. Told him to go and get his hash browns scattered, smothered, and covered."

"I'm gonna scatter his damn ass he don't tell us what happened to that fucking rig."

Hood squinted through the smoke, looking out the big cargo doors into the Sutpen trucking lot, all the trucks coming and going. Loading up and dropping off shit from all over the country, most of it legitimate goods getting distributed out to north Mississippi and on into Memphis. He looked at his watch. Nearly noon. He'd told Kimbrough he'd be by to pick him up more than an hour ago.

"How's it goin' with Fannie Hathcock?" Hood asked.

"Good," Taggart said, hands on his narrow hips. "She's a crafty bitch, I tell you. Last night she brought by some young girls to work my crank. I told her she could dish out the pussy as much as she wanted, but I wasn't goin' soft on her."

"You?" Hood said. "Turning down some gash?"

"Hell no," Taggart said. "You think I gone crazy? I screwed both of them back in that VIP lounge. We ate chicken fingers and drank cheap champagne after. I even think that one white girl, Twilight, is sweet on me. Has a tattoo of a damn dolphin doin' flips right over her cooter."

"Maybe Fannie was just trying to be friendly," Hood said. "Now, that's a woman I wouldn't mind taking on sometime."

"That bitch would break you in two, J.B.," Taggart said. "Don't you ever turn your back on a woman like that. You let her know her place, let her know who's boss, and she'll act right. I figure I just about got her redheaded ass trained real good."

"How were the chicken fingers and champagne?" Hood asked, ashing his cigarette on the concrete floor.

"Goddamn delicious."

Appreciate you picking me up, Quinn," Boom said. "Ain't no way I'm gonna get in the car with those country-fried killers."

Quinn nodded, taking the Natchez Trace back down to Tibbehah County. It was a bright blue, cloudless day, both truck windows down, the stereo playing Waylon's "Slow Rollin' Low." They drove through the rolling green hills, copper-colored creeks, and deep-shadowed woods. The hot air smelled clean and fresh, Hondo's head hanging out the back.

"What'd they say when you said you'd been hijacked?" Quinn said.

"Told me to sit my ass at that Waffle House and order me up some hash browns."

"Hash browns?"

"Like I said, these some strange motherfuckers," Boom said. "Anybody with some sense gonna get some grits. Besides, I just ate back in Okolona. Had two sausage biscuits."

"And a Mountain Dew," Quinn said, taking the next turn. The Trace bright and green after some recent rain, up and down the hills under the shaded sections of oak branches, pockets of bubbling natural springs. Quinn had wanted to take Brandon and Jason up this way for a while, hunt for some arrowheads on the site of an old trading post.

"You talk to Agent Wilkins?" Quinn said.

"You mean Nat?" Boom said, leaning back in his seat, every few minutes glancing in the rearview like maybe they'd been followed back in New Albany. "Yeah. She knows I'm done with all this shit. Ain't but one person those motherfuckers gonna blame and that's my black ass. You think they're gonna have me trucking anything more than a load of Pop-Tarts after I lost that load? Even if I wanted to stay on, help out our friendly feds, they wouldn't have me. I'm gone."

"They can't blame you for getting hijacked."

"Wanna bet?" Boom said. "Especially when they find out who jacked my ass."

Quinn turned to look at him and then cut his eyes back on the road, taking on the next bend, hitting a straightaway, south toward home.

"You really want to know?"

"Hell yes, I want to know," Quinn said. "You could have gotten killed."

"Naw," Boom said. "They wouldn't kill me. Them Pritchard boys like me too damn much. Ain't no one else in Tibbehah County who'll work on their engines good as me."

"Son of a bitch," Quinn said. "Was the uncle with them?"

"Just Tyler and Cody," Boom said. "Both of them thinking they real smart wearing these masks like they wear under their helmets. Didn't even bother covering up their arms. Tyler Pritchard has some real specific tattoos about his heroes of Dirt Track Racing."

"Retribution for Fannie Hathcock giving them trouble?"

"Sure sounds like it," Boom said. "If you're saying the Sutpen's boys are friends with Fannie."

"Not me," Quinn said. "That's what Nat Wilkins and her people say. Ordeen was the go-between with those boys and Fannie. How come all this shit's got to come on back to my doorstep?"

"Lucky, I guess."

Quinn kept on driving, passing by a turnoff for the Owl Creek burial mounds, Waylon wanting to know *"Are you ready for the country / Are you ready for me."*

"Good song for the wedding," Boom said. "You think Maggie's ready for your country ass after all that time she spent in Nashville?"

"To quote Burt Reynolds—" Quinn said.

"As you most often do."

"'It depends on what part of the country you're standing in as to just how dumb you are.'"

"I didn't say you were dumb," Boom said. "Just asking if Maggie is ready to throw all in with the hunting, fishing, cigars, and whiskey."

"I consider myself a Southern gentleman."

"She ain't gonna let Hondo sleep in the bed no more," Boom said. "You *do* know that."

Quinn looked in the side mirror, Hondo's head hanging out the back window, still panting into the hot June wind. "We'll work on it."

"You do that."

Quinn didn't like where all this was headed, Boom trying to be real cool and low-key about getting a shotgun pulled on him while delivering a truckload of drugs to Ripley. "Do you think these people can tie you to the Pritchard boys?"

"Only if someone tells them who took that trailer," Boom said. "And I ain't saying shit."

The Pritchards drove straight on to Memphis, running that rig through the gates of an old warehouse down from the Kellogg's factory, the smell of baking Frosted Flakes in the air. As Tyler got out of the Chevy and met Cody by the trailer, he noticed the big red Kellogg's sign, written in cursive neon, shining in the early afternoon. Cody lit a cigarette and walked up onto an abandoned dock. Looked like some homeless folks had made camp there, lots of refrigerator boxes, sleeping bags, and old clothes strewn about. Cody paced up there on the docks, checking the time, while Tyler looked at that gate hanging open off that chain-link fence, waiting for Marquis Sledge's people to go ahead and show and take this shit off their hands.

It was hot but cool in the shadow of the old building, everything quiet down in south Memphis, the cereal plant chugging out steam from the smokestacks. Tyler had heard that sometime back some old boy got so tired working in the factory that he'd unzipped his pants and pissed in the cornflakes. He didn't think he'd eaten a box since but sure could understand how you'd grow tired of someone all over your damn ass.

"What if Sledge asks where we got all this?"

"He won't," Tyler said.

"But if he does?"

"I'll tell him to mind his own goddamn business," Tyler said.

"And what are we gonna do with this rig when we're done?" Cody asked.

"Shit," Tyler said, craning his neck to look up at his shorter brother. "Leave the damn thing where you parked it. Let's get our money and get on back to Tibbehah."

Cody drew on his cigarette, his LUCAS OIL cap far down in his eyes. He sucked on that cigarette, deep in thought, Tyler knowing he had something on his dang mind but wouldn't just speak up.

"What the hell is it?" Tyler said.

"Nothin'."

"Bullshit," Tyler said. "Say what you're thinking on."

"You don't have trouble with Fannie Hathcock not wanting her damn cut?"

"No," Tyler said. "She didn't do jack shit."

"She done told us the route of that truck," he said. "Now, why the fuck would she do that? Because she thinks we're just so goddamn handsome?"

Tyler took a deep breath, shaking his head, his brother always wanting to be the one to piss in his goddamn cornflakes. Cody hopped down from the loading dock onto the asphalt. The back lot filled with rusted oil drums and old gas pumps, a pile of rotten old sofas and mattresses that needed burning.

"She knowed we was in deep with Sledge," Tyler said. "And she knowed she'd done fucked up sending Ordeen Davis onto our land. It was a kind of peace offering, a damn olive branch, to get on your good side, so she could be the main distributor of Pritchard weed."

"Bullshit," Cody said. "You think that goddamn woman's ever done something nice for the hell of it? That's the kinda woman takes what she wants."

"I didn't say it was for the hell of it," Tyler said. "I said she done it to get on our good side, make things work until we can figure out how we can truck in our own shit, expand the family business like Uncle Heath was talking about."

"But she's fucking her own damn people."

Tyler looked at Cody. He could barely make out his brother's beady little eyes, the son of a bitch making a little bit of sense. He stroked his beard with his right hand, thinking on what that woman done and some of the reasons and ways she might be trying to fuck the Pritchard boys. Tyler was just about to tell Cody that they needed to sit down with the woman at Vienna's, try to lay out all the terms and specifics of their partnership, when he spotted a line of black hearses turning into the gated yard, moving fast as hell and kicking up dust on the hot streets.

The passenger door of the first hearse flew open and goddamn Marquis Sledge stepped out. Surveying the abandoned lot in a double-breasted maroon suit with a high-collar white shirt and a purple tie, looking like that black bald dude on the *Family Feud*. As always, he had the damn gold toothpick hanging out of the corner of his mouth, turning back to see the three hearses stacked up behind him. Nobody else got out of the vehicles except him, walking forward, not smiling or offering his hand, just looking up at the rig and saying, "Y'all boys better be straight with me," he said. "That's a whole lotta shit you promising."

"More shit than y'all can cram in them death buggies," Tyler said.

Sledge swiveled the toothpick around, grinning a little. Walking past Tyler and Cody to the rear of the trailer. He knocked on the back with his knuckles. "OK, boys," he said. "Let's see what country done brought to town."

Boom was flat-ass worn the hell out. Driving to Texas and back, having to wait around on those Sutpen boys in Okolona, and then getting jacked in the damn booger woods and having to walk five miles to a goddamn Waffle House. Boom had left his truck in Tupelo, Quinn dropping him at J.T.'s to get a loaner and then finally heading home. It was still hotter than hell at seven in the evening, windows down in the old truck he'd taken, a '65 Ford with the twin I beam that he'd always admired on J.T.'s lot. J.T. always said he was gonna restore the son of a bitch but never got around to it. He hit the road onto his family's land, nothing but the green plantings of cotton all across the bottomland, little cut-throughs, ditches, and a long stretch of dirt road to his cabin, a place that been built by his grandfather Lucas. Only one room with a kitchen hanging off the back, but his grandparents had raised eight kids in that house, so he didn't figure he needed to complain. His house was an authentic Mississippi shotgun shack, moved from the original location, sagging a little bit on the porch. But it was clean and simple and, since he'd gotten home from the service, a decent place to live. He liked the calm of it, being right there in the center of all that bottomland, not a house or big road to be seen for miles.

He parked the truck off to the side by his propane tank, the original laundry line still running out back, two wooden crosses with baling wire between them. He reached into his backseat and got out the six-pack of Coors he'd bought at the Piggly Wiggly, icing it down in a cheap Styrofoam cooler on the way back. He felt for one of the cans, not cold enough, but not warm enough to wait. He popped the top and sat down in one of his chairs, his porch not quite twenty feet across.

He planned to sit here and drink down that whole six, watch that sun go down over the bottomland, and then head on to bed. He felt his eyes get heavy, sitting there, just thinking about that long sleep that was about to come. Tomorrow, he'd get up, brush that beer smell off his breath and go see his daddy about picking up some work bringing in the cotton, and maybe, just maybe, he'd go see Ole Man Skinner about getting his job back. He knew the old man would make him grovel, make him ask real nice about getting some work, although he knew for a goddamn fact they couldn't keep a good mechanic the County Barn.

He deserved better hours than they'd given him. He deserved more money. But like his grandfather Lucas used to say, *"Wish in one hand and shit in the other and see which one gets full first."* That was just like old Lucas, straight shooter, no bullshit, one of the first black men in Tibbehah County to own a decent chunk of land since Reconstruction. Sometime back in the seventies, he'd organized a group of black cotton farmers to get fair pay at the scales. Nearly got himself killed in the process, but the man got what he set out to do.

That first beer of the evening sure was good. Didn't matter that it was a little warm, just nice to be home, kicked back and leaning into that chair, the sun a big orange ball coming down on the flat of the land. Looking so big and perfect, Boom felt like he could just reach out and grab it.

Boom heard the car before he saw it. Looking down the dirt road, he saw a black SUV kicking up dust behind it, maybe a half mile from his shack. He stood up to stretch, finishing the beer, and reaching for another. He held the can in his hook and cracked open the top with his left, taking a big sip, looking to see who might be coming his way. He hoped like hell it was Nat Wilkins, leaving her a detailed message about how he was out, but wouldn't exactly mind if she came over to his porch to discuss the matter a little further.

He walked inside and went through his drawers for a clean white T-shirt, slipping it over his head and walking back out just in time to see the vehicle slow to a stop about ten yards from his house. It was a Chevy Tahoe and looked government as hell with the clean shiny paint and the tinted windows.

Boom took another sip of Coors and smiled in the direction of the Tahoe, being a little surprised as both doors opened. He wished Nat had come on her own and maybe he could have talked her into getting a little food on the Square.

But he didn't see that broad smile and bouncy black hair. He only saw two ugly white dudes step out of the car. Goddamn Wes Taggart and J. B. Hood. Both of them walking on up to the porch, fast as hell, holding aluminum baseball bats.

He knew he could either try to lock those boys out and call for help. Or face them head-on.

Boom took another sip of beer, crushed the can in his hand, and stepped off the porch. "OK, motherfuckers," he said. "Let's talk."

20

ORDEEN DAVIS'S MOTHER TURNED TO QUINN, REACHED OUT for his hand, squeezed it tight, and said, "What have you done about my boy?"

The first thing that came to mind was *We're working on it*. But that was about as good as saying they had a few leads. Which wasn't true at all. They had the word of an outlaw biker and some possible prints off the Husky toolbox where they found Ordeen's body. Not nearly enough to get at the Pritchards. And in the short time Quinn had Heath Pritchard at the county jail before he bonded out, he wouldn't say a damn word.

"I'm trying, ma'am," Quinn said. "I promise to do everything I can."

"Quinn Colson," Pastor Davis said. "If I may speak directly, sometimes everything ain't worth jack shit."

"Yes, ma'am."

"Someone killed my baby," she said. "Shot him the back—"

Quinn started to speak, as no one was supposed to talk about details of Ordeen's killing until someone was charged. But she held up the flat of her hand, shook her head, and kept going. There was no way he would try to stop a confident black woman from speaking her mind, let alone a woman like Danita Davis, who commanded a ton of respect down in Sugar Ditch. If a supervisor wanted to win her district, he had to appease Pastor Davis and make sure her people's needs would be addressed.

"Chopped up my baby's body, put him in a box, and tossed him into the Big Black River," she said. "Now, I don't believe in revenge. An eye for an eye. Old Testament stuff. But I do believe with every ounce of my being that there will be justice for Ordeen."

"Yes, ma'am."

"Do you hear me, Quinn Colson?" she said. "I known your mother before you were even born. Used to look out for your crazy Uncle Van when he had that pizza shop on the Square. Tended to your father when he busted up his leg after he tried to jump between two buildings downtown. How is your daddy anyway?"

"Gone to California."

"God help him," Pastor Davis said. "But you see what I'm saying? I need more than what y'all are giving me. I can't get by, my day-to-day, take care of my church, without knowing someone is out there looking out for my family."

Danita Davis was a small brown-skinned woman with silver hair and high cheekbones. She held herself like a teacher about to whack you upside your head if you weren't paying attention. Her large brown eyes taking you all in, watching all your movements, your breaths, making sure you were being straight with her.

All he could think of saying at the moment was "I promise."

"If you don't," she said, "that says to me that you don't believe Ordeen has any worth at all. I know what he was doing. But I also know that boy used to be something more and was gonna come back to the Cross real soon. Me and him talked about it. He was on that dark path, lost as he could be, confused, but he was coming back. Lord."

She began to cry. This was the part that always made Quinn sick, trying to distance himself from a victim's pain but at the same time still be a damn human being. It was ten times tougher when you knew the victim and the family. Pastor Davis had been around his whole life, was on a first-name basis with his mother, not to mention what she did for his dad when she worked at the hospital. He thought back on a time he had to sit with the mother of a Ranger from his company. He'd been shot in Kandahar and it had been weeks, long after the funeral, before Quinn was back stateside and could make a personal call. The woman didn't want to talk, she just wanted him to sit with her. And he did, for several hours and long into the night.

"I'll find out what happened," he said.

Pastor Davis nodded, sitting across from Quinn on a royal-blue sofa, pictures of her three children in gilded frames above her head. Her home was a simple brick ranch house, looking pretty much the same design of the place he grew up in, only it was down in Sugar Ditch and on ReElection Road. Down here, this home up on a hill was a damn palace.

"I never quit telling Ordeen that the Lord loved him," she said. "I don't blame anyone but myself for the path he followed. I think leaving school the way he did, without a diploma, without any scholarship offers, made him turn on the church. At first, he'd miss a service, and then two services, and then he started to run with

Nito Reece. I kept on telling him the Lord loved him. No matter what he'd done, no matter where he'd gone, he could always come back to Jesus."

"Yes, ma'am."

"You believe?" she asked. "Don't you, Quinn Colson?"

That was a hell of a complex question. And a more complex answer. But he nodded, not wanting to get into a theological discussion with a pastor who'd just lost her son.

"You know the story of the Prodigal Son."

"Yes, ma'am," he said. "I do."

"I always expected Ordeen to come back home," she said. "You know, lost and then found? I never, ever was willing to think he'd strayed too far from me or the Lord. Whatever he was doing was on his own time. He'd always come back if I needed him, started showing up some Sundays. But I saw that fat money roll he'd flash and those clothes he wore. Only thing didn't change was that car he drove. Taking on Nito Reece's old ride. Why do you think he did that?"

"Guilt," Quinn said. "I think he figured what happened to Nito might've happened to him, too."

"Coach Bud Mills," she said. "The Devil comes in all shapes and forms. I think when all that happened with Nito, that really pushed Ordeen too far. That's when he got in with that Hathcock woman. And I prayed for him every day. I never stopped praying for him. No matter how he told me he was all right, fine, just hustling for that money, I knew. I'm not a fool. I'm a grown-ass woman. I know what goes on at those places."

Quinn nodded.

"Don't just 'Yes, ma'am,' 'No, ma'am' me, son," she said. "Give me something, Sheriff. What did you find out from that Hathcock woman?"

"She says she doesn't know," Quinn said. "She says Ordeen came to work, did his job, and left for the night."

"And you believe that white woman?" she said. "I stood behind her one time at the Fillin' Station and I'll tell you all that expensive perfume can't mask that evil."

Quinn watched Danita Davis wipe her face with a kitchen towel. She'd been cooking supper when Quinn had knocked on the door, just doing a nightly wellness check to make sure she was doing all right. He could smell the neck bones on the stove, blackberry cobbler cooking in the oven.

"There was a print," Quinn said, knowing he shouldn't be letting the information out, but the words coming.

"Where?"

"Inside that toolbox," he said. "We sent it off to Batesville. It might be something. But we don't know yet."

"You stay on it," Pastor Davis said, standing. "Don't you let it go. Keep pushing on that Hathcock woman. She may not have done it. But everybody knows she knows who did. That place should've been shut down a long time ago."

"That woman has a hard time telling the truth," Quinn said. "Sometimes I don't know if she understands the difference between right and wrong. Not much I can do to her as long as she follows the law."

"What did Paul say?" she said. "All things may be lawful. But not all things are expedient."

Nat Wilkins knew she'd probably pushed Boom too damn far. But this was the first time they'd ever had someone inside at Sutpen's. Two years ago, they'd had an illegal working to load the trucks in Gulfport and six months ago had this secretary in Tupelo who'd had a come-to-Jesus moment and suspected they weren't doing the Lord's work. But everything was so damn compartmentalized that they would never be able to shut down all the shit they were running. They might get them on moving some drugs, but those good ole boys would lawyer up and blame it on the driver. If they wanted to make a federal case on those boys, they'd need all of it. They'd need wiretaps, they'd need multiple runs of drugs and girls, and they'd need Boom, and maybe a few more like him, to testify against those crooks. From the sound of Boom on her voice mail, she was pretty sure she'd just blown her best damn witness.

It was dark by the time she hit the Tibbehah County line, already trying Boom several times but not getting an answer, and not really expecting for him to pick up. She knew where he lived, and if she were to get him to sign back on for one more run, she'd have to have her say in person. Besides, the man was kind of growing on her a bit. He was tall, big, and handsome, with a strong jaw and a real man's style. She liked his cool, relaxed way of talking, easygoing manner, and that simple Southern charm. Her ex had been a real piece of work, a moneyman, a banker, who wanted a football team of babies and for her to finish going through her career phase and stay at home and tend to family business.

Marcus P. Jarrell projected some type of success, but underneath that thousand-dollar suit he had legs like a chicken. Strip away that cocky swagger and he wasn't nothing but a scared little boy. Damn Boom Kimbrough probably never even owned a suit, wouldn't know what to do with a martini, straight up, extra olives, but the kind of man who was good with his hands, knew how to fix things, make her feel like a woman instead of Marcus's momma.

The thought of the time she wasted on Marcus's narrow little ass just pissed her off as she turned off the highway and onto the county road to Boom's place. Man, he said he lived in the country, but this was damn countrier than country. The GPS got to be wrong because it was taking her right into the middle of a cotton field, nothing but row after row of that green cotton, the evening light fading to a bluish black. The wheels of her Explorer wiggled slightly over gravel and mud, Nat thinking maybe she needed a four-wheel drive to get through this mess. Her headlights shone down the long road until she finally saw tiny lights on some kind of small building.

As she drove closer, she saw it was an old-time tin-roof shack, like something from old sharecropping days, with colored Christmas lights hanging from the porch. An old blue pickup truck was parked outside. Her headlights shone across the porch and into the house.

She left her engine running, not sure if she had the right place, and stepped up onto the porch. Looking inside the screen door, she didn't see anyone or hear anything as she knocked. The lights were off and she could barely make out a small kitchen, a small gas stove, and a small circular table. Nat knocked again and called out Boom's name.

When she moved to the side, more light spilled into the kitchen and she saw a trail of blood. Her heart went up into her damn throat as she opened the door and reached for her gun, not sure who might still be hanging around. She didn't get two steps in when she saw Boom's big body lying on the kitchen floor, not moving a bit, face bloody as hell, his good arm hanging at some kind of crazy angle.

"Boom," she said. "Boom. Come on, now."

She got down to her knees, closing her eyes against what she saw, her stomach turning. She put her ear to his mouth.

His eyes were closed. But he was still breathing.

. . .

Fannie had tried to tidy up the office a bit, find the glass of her desk under all that trash, while Wes Taggart had disappeared for the afternoon. But the son of a bitch was back that night, heading up the spiral staircase and slamming the door, stripping off his T-shirt and walking over to her bar sink to start to wash up.

"Honey," she said. "You think you might go outside to hose off? That's where I wash my crystalware."

Wes didn't even turn to acknowledge she was in the room as he used his wadded-up black T-shirt to mop over his forearms and under his pits. He tossed the shirt down to the floor, splashing water up into his face and combing back his long brown hair with his fingers. He kicked off his boots and walked over to her leather sofa, laying down and staring at the ceiling. Without so much of a glance in her direction, he said, "Get me a whiskey."

Fannie wasn't so much pissed as kind of amused by the situation. She picked up the phone and told Midnight Man to bring up a bottle of Jack Daniel's and a setup. Fannie stood and walked over to him, noticing a little dried blood on his blue jeans.

"Looks like you had a hard day at the office."

"There's only one way of dealing with some folks."

"Peace, love, and understanding?"

"And when that don't work," Wes said, "got to try a fucking Louisville Slugger."

"Did I ever show you my framing hammer?"

Wes didn't answer. Fannie walked back behind the desk and pulled out her sixteen-ounce hammer she kept in her handbag. She waved it in his direction and said, "Sometimes the customers won't listen to reason," she said. "You try and make them understand to keep their fingers and peckers to themselves. But you boys just can't control your appendages. I once had some local painter who tried to grip one of my girls like a bowling ball. I shot this thing right between his eyes just to get his attention."

"That's real sweet," Wes said. "You got any cigarettes?"

"I don't think we have the same taste."

"It don't matter," he said. "Just give me whatever you got."

Fannie placed the hammer back in the purse, right near her pistol, and pulled out her cigarillo case, hating like hell to waste a Dunhill on a shitbird like Wes Taggart. He couldn't tell fine Turkish tobacco from a pack of American Spirits. But she wandered over on her tall heels and plucked a dry smoke into his lips. He looked up at her from the sofa, under his shaggy bangs, almost like he expected her to light it for him. She'd rather hold his damn pecker while he took a piss.

She tossed him her lighter and he caught it in one hand as J. B. Hood came on into the room, crowding the office, stinking it up with his ancient testosterone and Aqua Velva. The old ponytailed fuck had a cheeseburger in his hand, getting real comfortable about helping himself in the kitchen. He walked across the room and sat right on Fannie's desk, ketchup running down his chin, as he chewed with his mouth open. "You order up a bottle of whiskey, Wes?"

Taggart didn't answer.

"That old boy's blood sure was flying," he said, dabbing the ketchup off his chin. "That one eye snapped shut quick. He came charging like a goddamn bull, thinking he was gonna knock you to the ground. But you damn swung that bat like fucking Jose Canseco, I swear you busted half his ribs right then and there."

Wes turned his head and stared at Hood. "Can you please shut the fuck up for two seconds?"

"Why?" he said. "Don't tell me you feel bad about what we done."

"Me and J.B. had some trouble," Wes said, turning his head to Fannie, firing up her cigarillo. "One of our rigs got hijacked up around Blue Mountain. Pretty sure one of our drivers set the whole thing up."

"'Course he set it up," Hood said. "Ain't no way some thieves just passed by as he was having some mechanical difficulties. That nigger was in cahoots with those sonsabitches."

"I told you I don't care for that word," Fannie said.

"'Sonsabitches'?" Hood said, snickering. "Ain't you all politically correct. Can't say 'bitch,' can't say 'nigger.' Everyone is so goddamn sensitive about saying the right word. Makes a white man feel like he's walking on eggshells."

Fannie walked over to Hood, nearly toe to toe, as he sat on the edge of her desk. She reached down for a napkin and dabbed some either blood or ketchup off his elongated forehead. He didn't respond, only kept mawing up that last bit of the burger, talking about how that never in the history of America had the white man ever been a more endangered species.

"Do you know who took the truck?" Fannie said.

"Nope," Wes said. "Driver said they were wearing masks. But hell if he didn't work with a couple boys."

"What'd they get?" Fannie said, tilting her head, seeming to be interested as hell.

"Better off you not knowing," Wes said. "Why don't you just go make sure the cooze is shaking it down on the floor, baby? We've already lost enough goddamn money for one night."

Fannie nodded and left the room, closing the office door behind her with a tight click. Through the cracks, she could hear Wes starting to tear J. B. Hood a new asshole for being so goddamn stupid for agreeing to hire some old boy who was best friends with the sheriff. "What the fuck were you thinking?"

Fannie couldn't help but smile as she passed Midnight Man on the spiral staircase, going down, as he was headed up.

How bad is it?" Quinn asked.

"I'll skip the normal bullshit about trying to calm you down and make you feel better," Maggie said. "Because it's bad. He's got nine cracked ribs, a broken arm, and a fractured skull. He's stable but in some really rough shape."

"Is he conscious?"

"Barely."

"What do the doctors think happened? How'd somebody do this?"

"You want the medical explanation?" Maggie said. "Or the straight stuff?"

"What do you think?"

"Someone turned Boom into a damn piñata," she said. "Beat him senseless with something hard and left him for dead."

Quinn let out a long breath, standing there in the hospital hallway with Maggie. Maggie looked at him, hands on her hips, green scrubs splattered with blood. She was trying to be tough, control her emotions. But Maggie wasn't like Lillie and her mouth quivered a little bit as she spoke, trying to keep eye contact, be professional, and relay the news as best as possible. Down the hall, Caddy, his momma, and Luther Varner sat in the waiting room, hoping that Quinn would come back and let him know what was going on. The whole way to the hospital, driving damn-near eighty miles per hour, he'd been thinking Boom was dead. The bastards from Tupelo came up here and got him.

"Can I see him?"

"You don't want that," Maggie said. "Not now. Besides, doctors have sedated him. He's in a deep sleep. They do that sometimes with trauma patients when it's too much to take."

Quinn didn't know what the hell to say, staring over Maggie's shoulder at an old woman trying to walk down the hall with an IV drip. He felt his eyes blur with hot tears as he clenched his jaw and his fists, hanging somewhere between sadness and absolute rage. He needed to talk to Nat Wilkins. These federal people had fucked around long enough and needed to clean house of all these bastards.

"You OK?" she asked.

Quinn nodded, but his face broke slightly.

Maggie cried, shook her head, and wrapped her arms around him, Quinn just hanging there in space, hands loose and useless at his sides, unable to damn move. These people had come into their county, their home, and beaten his best friend to a pulp. His right hand clenched and unclenched at his side.

Quinn rubbed his face and walked back to the waiting room. Caddy and his momma huddled together on some chairs, watching a fuzzy television playing some old episodes of *Bonanza*. Hoss and Little Joe at the local saloon, watching a couple toughs in an arm-wrestling contest.

Luther Varner, all wiry muscle and bone and leathery skin, looked up from the television set. His eyes were red, weary, and tired as hell. "Is he dead?"

Quinn stood over the three of them, crossing his arms and shaking his head. "He was beaten up real bad," he said. "He has some broken bones and a nasty crack in the head. The doctors have him stable and medicated. He's asleep. His dad and a couple of his cousins are with him now."

"Thank God," Jean said. "Thank God."

Caddy dropped her head into her hands and started to say a silent prayer, her lips moving as she stayed quiet with her eyes closed. Her face was red and chapped, streaked with tears.

Maggie had followed him, walking up, standing with Quinn, and placing her hand on his back. He didn't know what else to add, except to comfort his family and friends and then figure out where Nat Wilkins had gone and just what she planned on doing about it.

"Why?" his mother asked.

Quinn looked over to Maggie and shook his head. He swallowed and found his mouth and throat too damn dry to speak.

"Someone robbed him," Maggie said. "Nobody knows why. They found him unconscious at home."

Luther Varner got to his feet, the old Marine's eyes and jaw hard, looking Quinn dead in the eye. "My ass is sore as hell," he said. "I hate sitting around."

Quinn nodded at them all. "If something changes, Maggie will let y'all know," he said. "I better be getting back to the office, find out what I can, before Boom wakes up."

Caddy and his mother nodded. Luther stepped up close to him, reaching around to give Quinn a big bear hug. As he did, he whispered into Quinn's ear, "When you find these fuckers, you damn well better call me," he said. "Don't you dare have all the fun yourself, Sergeant."

Uncle Heath was so damn excited to see the boys back home that he forgot to put his pants on. He stood in the kitchen, pacing back and forth, in nothing but a pair of Fruit of the Looms and his rattlesnake cowboy boots. He loved hearing every damn detail, from how Tyler figured out how to block the airflow on that truck down to wearing those neoprene masks with the skull faces on them. He had his hands on his hips while he walked, looking probably like he had in the Parchman yard, muttering and talking to himself, grinning and slapping his thigh when he heard something he liked. "And what'd that mean ole nigger up in Memphis say?" Heath said. "I bet you he about nearly shit his damn britches."

"He was real happy about it," Cody said, going to the freezer for some Jäger he kept there and setting it down on the kitchen table. "They got all the shit transferred to their vehicles and gone before we could even shake hands on the deal."

Heath stopped pacing. "But you did?" he said.

"Did what?" Cody asked.

"Shook hands on that fuckin' deal?"

Cody kind of shrugged and poured out some Jäger into a couple of old jelly jars, each one with a different Pokémon character on it. Tyler held his up to the light to see old Bulbasaur just as Uncle Heath smacked Cody upside the head and said, "Did you or didn't you?"

"Fuck me," Cody said.

"I sent y'all up to trade with them niggers 'cause I thought you could handle it," he said. "Don't you ever show a weakness to a gosh dang black. Someone like Marquis Sledge will cut you boys up like a porterhouse with dippin' sauce on the side."

Tyler took a final swig of his Jäger and reached for the bottle for another shot, running his tongue around his teeth, savoring every last bit of that green licorice taste. "Since when was it you that sent us anywhere?"

"Don't you get smart, boy."

"We did what we did to save our ass," Cody said, rubbing the back of his skull. "You done fucked us with ole Doc McStuffins. I don't see we had any damn choice but take Miss Hathcock's advice."

Uncle Heath looked down at the floor, shaking his head at this whole damn sorry situation, as he reached into his tighty-whities and scratched his nuts. "Calling out your blood and calling a gosh dang whore. You know that woman's probably sucked on more hot dogs than a stray mutt at a carnival."

Tyler sat direct across from his brother at the dinette. Cody hadn't touched his shot, reaching for a plastic baggie on the table and rolling him a joint. This pressure, all this tension in their family abode, was getting too damn much for him. The light above them was one of them old-fashioned ice cream parlor fixtures, scattering different colors over them; red, blue, yellow. A damn candy kaleidoscope.

"Boys, I done my time," Heath said. "Twenty-three years scheming and dreaming, thinking on shit I done wrong and done right. You can't fuck with that kind of knowledge. Better than having a Ph.D. from a fancy school up North. What I'm trying to tell y'all is, don't get used up there. Y'all are in the goddamn driver's seat. The Pritchards the ones doing the damn work, growing that weed, hijacking them trucks. Making sure everybody in north Mississippi comes to the party locked and damn loaded."

"This thing this morning," Cody said. "Me and Tyler talked about it. That was a one-time-only deal. We ain't in the business of robbing folks."

Tyler nodded, knocking back his second shot. Heath loomed over the table, his right eye twitching a little, Tyler not sure it was from the harsh light or he was having some kind of brain fart. He reached across the table and drank right from the bottle.

"I bet Marquis Sledge asked about me this time," he said. "Didn't he? Recalled some of that shit we got into back in the day."

Tyler shook his head, Cody lighting up the joint and taking a big puff. He pulled it in and let it back out slow, not doing that thing some folks do, try to hold it in for as long as they can. That didn't give you no more of a high than just smoking that weed normal.

"Let me see the money," Heath said. "Where's the g.d. money?"

Tyler lifted his eyes to Cody, giving a little shake of the head. Cody didn't react, taking one more slow draw on that weed, his eyes growing red and soft. Relaxed as hell.

"Don't you tell me you handed over a truck filled with enough pills to fuck up a whole damn Kool Moe Dee concert and not get paid," Heath said, yelling now, spit flying off his thin little lips. "Goddamn it, boys. Thought I raised you two better 'an that."

"How you figure you raised us?" Cody said, laughing like hell, the humor of it just bubbling on up from his gut. "You been in the joint 'bout as long as we been alive. You talking about those words of wisdom you passed onto us at family day at Parchman? Them things like *'Don't you fuck a fat woman or your life is over.'* Or telling us all about how our real daddy was a real piece of shit and we needed to stay close to our momma, that Pritchards did for Pritchards and never trust no one else."

"That's it," Heath said. "Exactly. So where's the damn money?"

The money was in four different Nike duffel bags they'd buried in the compost pile behind the barn. Tyler and Cody figured the last place that son of a bitch would look would be a place where he could actually do some goddamn work. Tyler looked down at the tattoo on his right forearm, RIDE FREE OR DIE, with a damn tire skid across his skin.

"That Hathcock woman's got our cut," he said, lying through

his damn teeth and not feeling a bit bad about it. "We can pick it up anytime we want. Just didn't want no trouble with the law headed on back from Memphis."

Uncle Heath smiled, standing there in his underwear, like he was cool with the situation until he wasn't. Just as Tyler reached again for the Jäger, he flipped that fucking dinette set end over end, scattering the weed and liquor, tromping out of the room in his snakeskin boots. "Y'all get our money by morning or I'll handle that damn redheaded bitch by myself."

The front screen door thwacked shut behind him.

Cody hadn't moved from his seat, joint still in his fingers. He looked at Tyler with wide eyes, serious as hell, and then, not taking it anymore, started laughing like a hyena. "Who the fuck is Kool Moe Dee?" he said. "Christ Almighty. That fucking ole man has lost it."

21

QUINN ROLLED UP ON THE OXFORD SQUARE A LITTLE AFTER noon the next day, not getting a bit of rest from the night before, checking in with the SO and spending the rest of the time at Boom's bedside. He still hadn't woken up when Quinn received the text from Nat Wilkins, wanting to talk in person.

He found Wilkins and Jon Holliday in the shade of the three big oaks in front of the old courthouse, the Confederate soldier statue high on a pedestal and facing south. Wilkins and Holliday sat together on a park bench and stood up as he got close. Holliday offered a firm handshake and Wilkins a hug before sitting back down. The courthouse didn't seem to be in session and they were pretty much alone, the two feds walking over from the federal building a few blocks away. Nathalie had on a black pantsuit and Holliday wore blue jeans and a long-sleeved dress shirt that covered the tats he'd gotten while serving in the Special Forces. His head was shaved bald again and he wore a tight black beard and thin black sunglasses.

Quinn sat down and leaned forward, elbows on thighs, facing them. "OK," he said. "What do we need to do to get 'em?"

"We need Boom," Holliday said. "Nat and I were with the prosecutors all morning. Our CI can't talk and what we've collected so far isn't enough for the feds. We've been tracking those trucks for a good long while. But a lot of what we have is speculation, some wiretaps, but you know how the prosecutors want it. All wrapped up with a nice bow before they get down to issuing indictments."

"I want those motherfuckers' heads more than anybody," Nat said. "Been wanting those boys for a long time. Even more after what they did to Boom. But we want all of them. We want Taggart, Hood, and their friends down on the Coast. If we bust up in Tupelo now, we ain't getting nothing but the hired help."

Quinn nodded. He rubbed his temples and pulled out half of an Undercrown he'd started early that morning. He clicked on his Zippo and got it burning.

"Don't tell me Boom smokes those nasty things, too," Nat said.

"On occasion," Quinn said.

"OK." Nat smiled. "I can work on that. My daddy smoked those Hav-A-Tampas. Laid back in his La-Z-Boy, watching the Atlanta Hawks. Loved him some Dominique Wilkins. Now he's all about the Grizz. All that grit and grind."

"We spooked those good ole boys in Tupelo," Holliday said. "They saw us watching that trucking company. Boom said it himself, said they saw our agents taking photos. Did you know one of them, Wes Taggart, was down in Tibbehah County with Fannie Hathcock?"

Quinn shook his head, not surprised to hear it.

"Wouldn't you like to see that woman gone?" Nat said. "All these people work for Buster White. Taggart and Hood, several crooks over in Tunica and down on the Coast. And I know I don't have to tell you about that fat sack of shit. Let's say we take down Sutpen Trucking. Well, OK. But, damn, if there are six more companies just like 'em across three states."

"Those boys beat my friend senseless," Quinn said. "Y'all sit around and talk. I'll talk to folks in Lee County. I'll charge both of those men with attempted murder."

"What if Boom can't recall what happened?" Holliday said.

"He'll recall," Quinn said. "You say one of them is over at Fannie's place? Glad to go pay a visit and arrest his sorry ass."

"Don't forget how long it took to get Johnny Stagg," Holliday said. "We both had to be patient as hell, meeting when we could, acting surgically when there was no other choice. But we got DEA, FBI, and ATF all over this. You know how much I love to kick in doors with you, brother. But let's hit them when they're looking the other way."

Quinn looked up from the ground. "That's now."

"How's that?" Nat said.

"They have more trouble than just the law," Quinn said. "Boom didn't tell you what happened yesterday morning. Did he?"

Quinn looked at Nat, with her delicate brown face under a lion's mane of natural hair. She stared back, her face softening, looking a little worn out, with red-rimmed green eyes.

"Boom got hijacked," Quinn said. "They must've believed he was in on it and went to teach him a lesson."

"I thought it was because he quit on them?" Nat said. "When he called me, he said he was done with the whole mess and walked away from Sutpen's."

"Those Tupelo boys have bigger problems," Quinn said. "They're getting ready for some kind of war in north Mississippi. They had a ton of shit on that truck Boom was hauling and someone knew what was on it, where he would be, and when he would be there."

Nat nodded, knowing almost all of it, but not what happened on the road to Ripley.

"I want us to hit that trucking company," Quinn said. "As the sheriff of Tibbehah County, I'm asking for assistance in the raid along with Lee County Sheriff's Office."

"You want to hit Sutpen's?" Nat said.

Quinn nodded, drawing on the cigar, taking it from his mouth and ashing it on his boot heel. "As soon as possible."

"Brother," Holliday said. "That's a tall order. Putting all our asses on the line."

"You know Boom," Quinn said. "You know who he is to me? Right?"

Holliday nodded slow, not liking at all where this was headed, listening to some redneck sheriff trying to tell him how to run his business. He finally turned to Quinn and said, "Sure would be good to know who robbed those boys and why."

Quinn grinned. "I know who did it."

"How?"

"Because Boom recognized both of them," he said. "Y'all ever heard of some weed-growing grease monkeys named the Pritchard boys?"

Nat shook her head, a slick black purse in her lap. "Should we?"

"Oh yes, ma'am," he said. "They've done more in a day to disrupt that Gulf Coast Syndicate than we have in years."

. . .

Truth be told, Maggie Powers had always been a little intimidated by Lillie Virgil. Not because of her height, that she was a U.S. Marshal, or that she cussed worse than any Marine Maggie had met at Camp Lejeune. It was that she'd always had a tight bond with Quinn that wasn't exactly romantic but reminded her a lot of her ex-husband's relationship with his fellow Marines. They shared something from being in gunfights, stakeouts, and investigations that she and Quinn would never have. Standing there in the hallways of Tibbehah General, she watched Lillie walk right up to her, look her dead in the eye, and say, "Don't you dare tell me he's gonna die."

"He's not going to die," Maggie said.

"Don't you bullshit me, Maggie Powers," Lillie said. "I supported you and Quinn's whole whirlwind romance while this whole town's tongues were wagging. I didn't give a good goddamn that your ex was a true rotten piece of shit bank robber or that Quinn latched onto your cute little ass so damn fast it made my head swim. But if you're lying to me, I swear to you I will return that fucking toaster oven I bought for y'all at the Williams-Sonoma outlet and six months of frozen steaks I bought online."

"Boom's busted up," she said. "But he's not in a coma. And he's strong as hell."

Lillie's jaw muscles clenched, a vein throbbing in her forehead. She opened her mouth as she raised a finger but didn't say a word, holding back that torrent of expletives that made her famous.

"Did you know I bought a goddamn silk dress for your wedding?" she said. "Jesus."

"Can you sit down with me?" Maggie said. "Let's get a cup of coffee. I can explain what I know."

"Goddamn, you are Quinn Colson's wife," she said. "Sit down, let's get some fucking coffee, talk it out, while this county falls into a sea of shit."

Maggie placed a steady hand on Lillie's arm, feeling the tension and the quivering. She watched as the tall woman swallowed something back, tears welling up in her eyes.

"Do you know who did this?"

Maggie shook her head.

"You know," Lillie said. "Just like Quinn. But neither of you will tell me because I sure as hell will start shooting and ask questions later."

"Quinn is in Oxford."

"What the fuck is he doing in Oxford?" she said. "Only thing up there is pussy frat boys, trophy wives, and federal agents."

"He had a meeting."

"Goddamn, sonofabitch," Lillie said, pounding a fist on the concrete wall.

Some folks looked up from the nearby nurses' station and Maggie held on to Lillie's arm, trying to talk in a smooth, reassuring voice. She was used to it, spending half of her day helping doctors do their jobs and the other part talking down shell-shocked family members. "Come on with me."

"I ain't taking two lumps of sugar while Quinn's tracking down the people who did this."

"I'm sure he won't do anything without talking to you," Maggie said. "He said y'all had a hell of a time in Memphis."

"You don't know the half of it," she said. "Did he tell you I put some dumb ass's head through a Wurlitzer?"

Maggie steered Lillie down the hall toward the cafeteria, having her take a seat while she bought two coffees. Lillie just sat there, long legs stuck out straight from her chair, hands in her lap, staring straight ahead as if catatonic.

"Can I see Boom?"

"It's only family right now," Maggie said.

"Maggie," Lillie said, slowing lolling her head in her direction. "I sure appreciate the crappy coffee. But you should know there's not a person in this hospital from orderly to candy striper who can keep me away. I am Boom's family."

"OK."

"Don't lie to me."

"I promise," Maggie said, reaching out to squeeze Lillie's fingers, holding her there. No one was in the cafeteria besides the old woman working the register. Maggie didn't say a word for a long while, just trying not to look over at Lillie, who started to cry.

"Tell me about that toaster oven," Maggie said.

"Ten fucking preset functions," Lillie said, wiping her face. "And it comes with a goddamn nonstick pizza pan."

"Fancy."

"OK," Lillie said, standing, not touching her coffee. "Enough bullshit. How about you take me to Boom?"

What the fuck kinda music is this?" Heath Pritchard asked.

"It's Drake," the stripper said. "'God's Plan.' You know his record label gave him a million bucks to shoot this video and he gave every penny away. Took some young girls from the projects to Saks and got them a full-on makeover. Had block parties and bought people groceries."

"Man's got about as much business sense as he's got talent," Heath said. "This shit sounds like talking over a computer farting."

The girl laughed, taking the twenty he'd offered in his teeth, and scooted back to the pole, circling and circling. *"Bad things. / It's a lot of bad things . . . They wishin' on me."* Heath leaned back into the huge leather chair in the dead center of Vienna's Place, feet up on the edge of the stage, a handful of cash in his fist. Every so often, he'd show the girl what he had, flicking through each of them bills. Felt good as hell to be back out of jail again. He only spent a few hours in there for that BS charge of public drunk and illegal gun possession. That high-dollar lawyer he got said the attempted murder charge wouldn't never stick. He had every goddamn right to carry a fucking pistol. And that damn sheriff didn't even know what it was like to see Heath Pritchard drunk.

The girl moved up toward him on her knees, reaching back and taking off her red bikini top. She tossed it at Heath's face, him catching it and setting on top of his head like a hat, using the cups over his ears and tying the string up under his chin. Young girls always liked it when he played funny, showing them he wasn't no different from them. He wasn't some fuddy-duddy old man but could get down and play on their level. He moved his head along with the music, acting like he was digging it, fanning those twenties in his right hand. Damn, he was having one hell of a time.

When the girl scooted her butt up to him, shaking that ass in a way that he'd never imagined in his whole life, like Jell-O on a silver platter, he asked her if Miss Fannie Hathcock happened to be around. The girl, now on all fours, turned her head back to him and motioned up to a catwalk overlooking the stage. Up there, Heath saw the curvy shape of a woman and the glow of a cigarette butt. *"Bad things . . . They wishin' on me . . . God's plan, God's plan."*

Heath had to hand it to this woman, this sure as hell was a real step up from Stagg's ole Booby Trap. He remembered going to the Booby Trap and watching a woman nine months pregnant working that pole. Now, every person had the God-given right to make a dollar, but watching a woman all swole up with child was a little much. He recalled being just a little bit scared that he was gonna see a little hand reach down out of her cooter and snatch up a dollar bill.

"What's so funny?" the stripper asked. She was a bleached blonde wearing a lot of that trashy eye makeup, her skin the color of tanned horsehide.

"Thinking on how Miss Fannie sure runs a class joint," he said. "I used to come here back when it weren't nothing but a big metal barn with flashing lights and smoke machines. Girls used to stand up on a plywood set between two sawhorses, dancing to fucking Axl Rose. Y'all got nice polished floors, high-dollar Hollywood lights, and a bar that looks straight out of Tombstone, Arizona."

"Miss Fannie said she bought it from Kansas City, Missouri," she said, sliding up to Heath on her knees, topless and shaking them titties, and now nearly nose to nose. "They had it shipped piece by piece. She sure don't like anyone trying to dance on it. That's one of her big rules. *'Don't you even think of dancing on my antique bar.'* She's got real serious rules like that. Miss Fannie is a true professional."

"What's them other rules?" Heath said, glancing up again, seeing that shapely feminine form in the dark lights, smoke flowing from the woman's mouth into the stage lights shining down on the dancer.

"'Whatever you do, don't try to hide money in your twat.'"

"Where I been, folks sure knew how to work their orifices," he said. "Cell phones, candy bars, dang cocaine. Can you imagine being so hungry that you'd want yourself a Snickers bar that's been shoved up some nigger's butt?"

When Heath looked up again, the woman up on the catwalk was gone. His personal stripper going around the maypole again, time after time, wearing nothing but a sparkly red G-string and the tallest damn shoes he'd ever seen in his life. When Stagg was running the place, the girls didn't have nothing on but their smiles. He liked all the stained wood, brass, all-around fine look to the place, but he'd trade it all in a New York second to see a woman buck-ass nekkid.

Heath reached up and smoothed down the scales on his rattlesnake boots, having just oiled them before coming to town. When he'd got 'em back at Parchman, some of the scales were so dry they about flaked right off. But he'd got them conditioned again, pulling them on, along with a new pair of Wranglers and that 'MERICA shirt he'd gotten at the Walmart. He wore a red do-rag over his bald head, growing himself a little beard since getting out, dying it black again with some Just For Men in Jet Black. The color may have been too much, as it looked like he'd taken a damn Magic Marker to his face, feeling like a smaller version of old Randy "Macho Man" Savage.

"You mind taking your fucking feet off my stage?" a woman's voice said behind him.

When he turned, Heath Pritchard stared up at Miss Fannie Hathcock herself, tall, wide-hipped, and big-breasted, wearing some kind of wraparound dress that looked like a cheetah print. The woman's red hair had been piled up high on her head, and she rested a slim hand on her hip while lifting a man's cigar up to her lips.

Heath lifted up a hand. "Take my hand, Miss Fannie."

The woman blew smoke direct into his eyes. "Why?"

"'Cause I just want to tell folks I been touched by an angel."

She walked past him and kicked his legs off the stage, the stripper, scared now, reaching out and snatching the bikini top off his head and heading back into the back room. He looked up, laughing while she took a seat on the cocktail table, nearly knocking over his Beam and Coke.

"My barman said you wanted to see me."

"Yes, ma'am," Heath said. "You're doing business with my nephews, which means you're also doing business with me, Heath Fucking Pritchard."

Fannie just stared at him, her eyes having that nice sleepy, sexy look.

"Sure would love to see what you got goin' on underneath that *Mutual of Omaha's Wild Kingdom*," he said. "But, then again, I just want that fucking money we're owed. Now that the Pritchards and you are in cahoots."

"I have no idea what you're talking about." she said. "I don't owe you boys a thing."

"Hmm," he said. "I sure wonder what ole Buster White would say about you fucking him over? I used to play spades with his cousin when I was in Unit 29. Bet he'd be real happy to hear from me."

I want you to come pick up your trash," Fannie Hathcock said, pacing her office with her cell phone up to her ear. "I don't like to get threatened in my own place."

"Shit," Tyler said. "We didn't know where he was at."

The lights were off overhead, pulsing dance music coming in through the cracked door and through the floor. She could still smell the stink of J. B. Hood's fucking cheeseburger and Aqua Velva in her office. "You didn't send him?"

"Hell no, we didn't send him," Tyler said. "He said he was going to Sonic to pick us up some hot dogs and tater tots and that was damn well near two hours ago."

"He's run up a two-hundred-dollar bar tab," Fannie said. "He told me since we were now partners that everything should be on the house for you Pritchard boys."

"Goddamn, I'm sorry," he said. "Me and Cody'll come get him. How drunk is he?"

"As a fucking goat," Fannie said. "He had two girls in his lap telling each of them he was gonna marry them. Kept on insulting my DJ for trying to keep up with the times. He threatened to kick his ass if he played any more Drake. Tossed forty dollars into his face and told him he didn't want to hear nothing but AC/DC and Guns and Roses."

"Uncle Heath is a real G N' R man," Tyler said. "I bet he wanted 'Welcome to the Jungle.' That was his theme song back when he was racing. They called him The Scalded Cat."

"I know who he is," Fannie said, spewing smoke from the side of her mouth. "And what he's done. I know he's some kind of Austin Powers fuckhead from the eighties who's come back and sow his wild oats. But what you boys and I have does not, and cannot, include his worthless ass. Do you understand me? He's drunk as hell, shooting off at the mouth about people down on the Coast with whom I do business. He keeps talking like that and someone's gonna end up quick and dead and I can tell you it's not going to be me."

"Just kick him out," Tyler said. "We're on the way."

"Did y'all tell him that you gave me what Marquis Sledge gave you?"

The line went quiet for a few seconds. She could hear the boy's rangy breathing coming from the other end.

"Because he has it in his pea-sized mind that I owe y'all some money."

Again, a long silence. Nothing but breathing, a little coughing, and then the boy trying to make up some kind of crazy-ass excuse on the fly.

"You got to take care of this," Fannie said. "I didn't bargain for this crazy son of a bitch in our deal."

"Yes, ma'am," he said. "Yes, ma'am. Won't happen again."

"Goddamn right it won't," Fannie said, closing her eyes, finally sitting down into her office chair and taking a deep, long breath. "You want to keep that supply chain running with your buddy Sledge? You need to limit your dependents."

"Come again?" Tyler said.

"Either you kill that son of a bitch," she said, "or I will."

22

"DO YOU REALLY THINK THEY'LL SHOW?" LILLIE ASKED.

"They said they would," Quinn said. "I took them at their word."

"Do I need to remind you they're feds?" Lillie said. "Remember what we used to say about trusting those kind of people?"

"Aren't you one of 'em now?" Quinn said, reaching forward to grab his thermos of coffee. "A U.S. Federal Marshal?"

"Oh, fuck," she said, reaching for the badge hanging around her neck as if seeing it for the first time. "You're right. I am."

Quinn and Lillie sat in his truck outside a Love's Truck Stop in Tupelo. It still wasn't light, but Holliday and Wilkins promised to bring some folks to help them out. Quinn had already squared things with Lee County to shut down the roads around Sutpen Trucking and assist with any arrests. He unscrewed the top and poured more into his travel mug, etched with the insignia for the Tibbehah County Sheriff's Office.

"You getting nervous?" Lillie asked. Her shotgun situated between her and the passenger door.

"Nope," Quinn said. "How many times have you and I done this?"

"Not the raid, Ranger," Lillie said. "I'm talking about your fucking wedding. You could raid these shitbirds' trucking company drunk and blindfolded."

Quinn drank some coffee, staring out at the open lot, waiting to get word from the feds on what time they were showing up. And what time they'd coordinate converging at Sutpen's, which was only a few miles down 78 and then south on 45 for a few exits. "I wouldn't say I'm nervous," Quinn said. "More like settled to the idea."

"I bet that makes Maggie's heart really pitter patter," Lillie said. "Settled into getting married."

"That's not what I mean," Quinn said. "I mean Maggie and I are grown-ass people with a lot of life experience before deciding to do this. We've been talking about it, kind of playing around the idea, since not long after we met. We both know what we want. I guess we're just pretty much ready to get the bullshit over and start living."

"You really should put that on a Hallmark card, Quinn," Lillie said, laughing. "I love you. Now, enough bullshit. Get to work, woman."

"It'll be work on both sides," Quinn said. "Both of us haven't had the best of luck with some of our previous relationships."

"That's the biggest goddamn understatement I've ever heard." Lillie had a dark blue ball cap down in her eyes, a black linen shirt with the sleeves rolled up to her elbows. She wore that new Sig Sauer on her hip just in case the shotgun didn't make the proper impression. "You know what I thought of Anna Lee and her mind tricks. But out of respect for your upcoming nuptials, I'll keep my mouth shut for once."

"Appreciate that, Lil."

"No sweat."

They didn't talk for a bit, Quinn checking messages on his phone, keeping in touch with Cleotha at dispatch. Last night, three kids had robbed the Dollar Store off Main Street, getting away with two hundred dollars and all the Tennessee Pride Country Sausage they could carry. Security cameras got the whole damn show. Deputy Cullison recognized two of them and they'd already been picked up that morning at Tibbehah High's summer school. Two wrecks and a woman who kept calling 911 saying someone was using black magic on her.

"Any word on Boom?" Lillie asked.

"If his condition changes, Maggie's got me on speed dial."

All through the night, they'd done their best to keep their minds off Boom and on prepping the raid, going through the priors of J. B. Hood and Wes Taggart. Lillie had found a few warrants in Alabama for Hood and she gladly offered to come down from Memphis and assist locals in his capture and then transport him back to Birmingham.

"That's a good woman, Quinn," Lillie said. "She stayed with me and Boom almost all yesterday, laying out everything she knew without an ounce of bullshit. I guess getting shuttled around to all those Marine bases only made her tough as hell."

"She knows what she's signing up for."

"What about Brandon?" Lillie said. "How's he gonna deal with y'all getting married? New house, new family? All of that crap?"

"He's a tough kid," Quinn said. "He knew his daddy was

screwed up long before his folks got divorced. He saw things I wouldn't wish on any boy that age. I think he's hoping for some calm and quiet. I'll do the best I can. I've taken him and Jason up to Tishomingo to hike, taught him a little about turkey hunting this spring. Plan to get those boys on Choctaw Lake this summer."

"That's very Andy Griffith of you, Quinn."

Quinn drank some coffee as Lillie started to whistle *The Andy Griffith Show* theme song. A few more minutes passed until four black SUVs wheeled into the Love's parking lot and idled in front of the McDonald's. Quinn's cell phone began to ring, Nat Wilkins's number flashing on his screen.

"I sure loved that show," Lillie said. "But I'll never know why Barney and Andy didn't take out ole Ernest T. Bass. That asshole was always coming to town and throwing rocks through windows."

"You got to see this," Cody said.

"In a minute," Tyler said, checking the pH levels in the tank, the water filter gurgling away down in the depths of the family operation. If you didn't get the goddamn water just right, you'd poison every damn bucket they'd been growing for weeks. "And take off your damn boots. You're tracking dirt everywhere, man."

"Just come on over to the monitors and check this shit out," Cody said. "The old man has fucking lost his mind."

"Did he ever really have one?" Tyler said, setting down the test kit and walking through a long row of hearty and healthy plants sprouting high from orange buckets. The light in the grow room glowing a weird purple as he trailed Cody back into the second trailer, where they'd set up a bank of monitors.

"Look at that," Cody said. "Just look at what he's done."

Tyler leaned forward, taking off his rubber gloves, and saw Uncle Heath get out of a big-ass Dodge 2500 with chrome rims about the size of a kitchen table. The truck was so damn jacked up, the short little bastard had to hop down into the dirt, circling the truck, running his hand along that smooth black paint. He strutted around that truck like a banty rooster with a ten-inch pecker.

"Where'd he get that?"

"Fuck if I know," Cody said. "How about we ask him?"

They climbed up the ladder and through the hatch into the bright sunlight in the old barn. Cody headed out toward the dirt road that separated the racing garage from the old homeplace. In the middle of the lot, Uncle Heath had the radio blasting in the truck, playing "Sweet Child O' Mine" loud as hell. Closer they got, they saw some towheaded woman the color of a fucking Oompa Loompa hanging out a back window, singing along with goddamn Axl Rose.

Tyler walked straight on up to Heath and said, "What the hell is this?"

"Well, it ain't a skateboard," he said. "Got the truck, tag, and title out the door for seventy grand. Ain't that something?"

Cody looked at Tyler, his jaw clenching. His brother turned his head and spit as Tyler looked hard at their Uncle Heath. The man was shirtless in nut-hugging jeans and his snakeskin boots, waving at the piece of trash up in that truck.

"Finally made it to the Sonic," Heath said. "The truck was too damn big to park by the speakers. I had Candy up there get you boys some breakfast burritos. Did y'all say tots or fries? I can't remember shit after getting so fucking high last night."

Tyler couldn't think of damn thing to say as he shook his head. Looking over at Cody, he could tell his brother was just about to launch himself on Uncle Heath and beat his ass, both of them knowing what that motherfucker had gone and done.

"Where'd you get that kind of money?" Tyler said, grinding his teeth.

Heath gave a shitty little smile while he scratched at his cheek. The woman up in the cab dancing along to the music, looking down at all the boys as she pulled up her T-shirt to show them her fake titties, shaking them like they was at a puppet show.

"Funny-as-hell story," Heath said. "Someone had gone and throwed that cash into that manure pile out back. Figured as no one wanted it, I might as well put it to use."

"Momma was right," Tyler said, Cody walking up, standing at his side. "You really are the family turd that wouldn't flush."

"Come on, now," Heath said. "You boys need to think on things, put everything in perspective. I went to talk to Miss Hathcock last night and straightened out our whole relationship. I sure am sorry to think my kin would be so goddamn almighty foolish as to deliver a truck full of fun up to them black folks without getting paid."

"That's our money," Cody said. "You motherfucking little garden gnome."

"And this is my land, my house, my garage, and, by default, also my damn operation down there in the depths of Hades," he said. "You starting to understand the picture? I had to walk through things with Miss Fannie, but the bitch now knows Heath Pritchard is again the fucking cock of the walk of Tibbehah County. Even tossed in Miss Candy up there to keep me company on my victory lap and return to business. You boys better start understanding the hierarchical relationship on our family land. I run things. Y'all either grow or steal what we're gonna need for Miss Fannie's grocery list. I run the thinking shit. Y'all got it now?"

The woman up in the truck cab started to beep the horn, waving down to Uncle Heath, her boobies jiggling each time she mashed it and giggled.

"Y'all wouldn't happen to have some dang rubbers in the house, would you?" Heath said, grinning a yellowed smile. "I done already run through my whole pack."

Tyler looked across at Cody. Cody spit into the dirt again, looking up at his brother and giving him a serious-as-hell nod. Getting rid of this sorry motherfucker was long overdue.

Up on the roof of the Peabody Hotel, Fannie could pretty much see all of Memphis, the snaking path of the Mississippi River, the humpback bridge over to Arkansas, and all those squat little brick buildings sloping down the water's edge. Her great-grandmother once ran a brothel around here a long time ago, somewhere on Gayoso Avenue. That's when girls wore long skirts, blouses up past their necks, and waited in the parlor for men to choose which one they wanted to take to a back room and screw. Somehow that old-time arrangement was a lot more honest than acting like men gave two shits about watching a girl twirl around a brass pole.

Fannie had been on the terrace for a while with Ray, waiting for those numbnuts from Tupelo to show up, hearing they'd been run out of north Mississippi with their tails between their legs. Ray said it was that black trucker who'd planned the job and later turned them in to the feds. He just couldn't get over ole Wes and J.B. being screwed in the ass like that.

"That driver's good buddies with the sheriff," Fannie said. The wind up on the roof making hell of her perfect hair today. Only a few people on the terrace milling about, standing by the iron barriers, looking out over the Mississippi or down south to where the Delta ran flat and clean to Vicksburg. "Everyone in Tibbehah knows that. I wouldn't have hired that fella to wash my dishes."

"The feds are gonna bust apart Tupelo," Ray said. "But they shouldn't have put the beatdown on that black fella. Not right now. Not so damn fast."

"Agreed. That's just sloppy," Fannie said. "Those old boys have a temper on them. Beating up the sheriff's buddy? That's a pretty damn bold move, but stupid. Colson wasn't taking that sitting down."

"Just what do you know about him?"

"The sheriff?" Fannie said. "I've pretty much told y'all everything you need to know. He's a goddamn Boy Scout. Doesn't seem to be like the rest. I offered him all the pussy he could eat for his bachelor party. Can you believe he didn't even consider it?"

"Doesn't matter," Ray said. "They won't get nothing at Sutpen's. Those boys cleaned the hell out of that facility. They spent the last twenty-four hours loading every computer, file cabinet, and scrap of paper that could be used against us. The law might file some wild charges about running drugs and women, but it won't stick."

"Unless that driver, Boom Kimbrough, comes to."

"He won't be talking for a long while," Ray said. "You got to give Hood and Taggart that. They sure know how to lay down the damn law."

"Fists ain't brains," Fannie said. "Fuck me, Ray. Those peckerwoods are gonna get us all marched into the courthouse in Oxford to explain how we run illegal pussy in five states and supply the blacks in Memphis with their chronic and OxyContin."

Ray stepped an oxblood loafer up on the edge of the terrace, looking out across the river to Arkansas. A long bank of dark clouds rolled in from the west. He straightened the cuffs on his seersucker suit in a pinkish hue. "I think it's gonna rain."

"And we got a damn shit storm on our hands, if we don't handle it," Fannie said. "This whole damn corridor's been shut down because Sutpen Trucking fucked up, from 45 to 55 and on over to the Delta. I appreciate the old boys' club law of rewarding every damn crook with a swinging dick. But this bullshit never happened until Wes Taggart decided to put his feet up on my desk and started blinding his brain with more free cooze than he could handle."

"He's screwing your girls?"

"Two at a damn time."

"Can't be having that."

"You know, Ray," Fannie said. "I don't really give a good goddamn, if he'd do his job. But when he starts acting like a bitch, throwing a little temper tantrum and going after my fucking sheriff's buddy, we better step back and consider that maybe Buster White doesn't understand this neck of the booger woods like we do."

Ray nodded, turning to see Taggart and Hood emerge from the

elevators by the Skylight Lounge and head out onto the open terrace. Both of those boys looked more worn out than normal, dressing like they'd just left a shit-shoveling competition down in Yalobusha County. Ray placed his right hand in his pocket and waved them forward. J. B. Hood had on a SUN RECORDS ball cap with that gray ponytail sticking out the back. Both of them in jeans and dirty T-shirts, hotel security probably thinking they were headed on up to the roof to fix an AC unit.

"They did it," Taggart said, shaking his head. "Feds busted into Sutpen's an hour ago, harassing our people, saying they have warrants for me and J.B."

"For what?" Ray asked.

"That goddamn sheriff thinks we tried to kill his nigger friend," he said. "And he's got some kind of smart-mouth woman Marshal with him. She's got some outstanding warrants on J.B. that go back about fifteen fucking years. Some bullshit about him running some kind of pyramid scam on some old folks."

Hood didn't say a word. He just hung back, checking out a couple college-age girls leaning against a rail in summer dresses kicking up with the wind. Hood's lack of respect wasn't wasted on Ray, who looked across at Fannie and simply lifted his chin.

"Next shipment goes through the old airfield we own in Tibbehah," Ray said. "I don't want you boys going close to Sutpen's until we can get our lawyers to pan for some gold in this shit show."

Taggart nodded, getting his redneck ass called on the carpet, while Hood kept on watching the young girls, wiping his greasy hands on the thighs of his jeans and repositioning his ball cap lower in his eyes. Without them seeing, Fannie reached back and ever so lightly touched Ray's back, feeling the cool, dry material of his seersucker jacket flapping in the wind. He knew Fannie was there for him and for the whole goddamn Syndicate. The wind whistled briskly over the river and across the terrace of the old hotel.

"Y'all make this work," Ray said. "Hear me? Jesus Christ Almighty. Just get it done and get our asses moving again."

23

RAY DECIDED TO STAY OVER IN MEMPHIS, GETTING A SUITE at the Peabody, where they could sit and dine in private, discuss details, without anyone listening in. Fannie knew the score, Ray bringing up the champagne and chateaubriand, moving on to the sitting room after for brandy and cigars, not giving a damn about the hotel's smoking policy. They'd talk business and old times, until he get bored with both and he'd stand up to refresh his drink, moving behind her and placing his hands on her shoulders. He'd start to massage her until her head dropped back and he'd kiss her full on the mouth. Times like these went on and on, going back twenty years, when her titties were a little higher and you could bounce a silver dollar off her ass and hit the fucking moon.

They'd done it again and Fannie awoke sometime around midnight, both of them naked and sleeping like dead folks. She crept her way off the bed and to the closet for a robe, making her way back to the sitting room and finding a half bottle of Moët & Chandon Rosé. She refilled her glass and moved to the window to stare out at the ballpark, the Redbirds playing a late game, and the bright lights blazing down on Union Avenue.

She heard Ray stir from the bed and, being an older gent, head to the bathroom. She drank a little, looking out at the city lights, as he came into the sitting room and poured out some whiskey. He sat down in a big overstuffed chair, sinking into the cushions with his drink, his silver hair mussed and wild.

"I didn't plan on that," he said.

"Of course you did," Fannie said.

"Of course I did," Ray said. "Christ, that was good."

Fannie toasted him with her champagne glass and joined him in the little grouping, sitting in an identical chair. She enjoyed being back in a civilized place, being around some fine furnishings and service. It was nice to know she could just snap her fingers and have another bottle sent up or have her suit brought down to the cleaners for a pressing.

She looked down at the trail of clothes—her black bra, black panties, Ray's white boxers—leading to the bed.

"We should probably stop this," Ray said.

"Why?" Fannie said, crossing her legs, robe opening up just a bit.

"I'm twice your age."

"What if I said you haven't slowed down a bit?"

"I'd say you were blowing sunshine up my ass," he said. "In a year or two, I have some action like we just had and you'll be standing over my grave. God, Fannie. The things you do. You just kind of get me going and find a way to hold me there as long as you want."

"Aw, shucks," Fannie said. "How's the whiskey?"

Ray toasted her back. It was dark in the suite, a little light shining through the curtains from the downtown buildings and the ball field. Ray fingered at his gray mustache, wiping away the whiskey, giving her a long, wistful smile. "I don't like this business."

"Me, neither."

"And I don't trust those boys," Ray said. "Not one goddamn bit."

Fannie lifted her chin to listen, taking a breath and sitting up straighter in the chair, the robe falling off most of her left thigh. Ray noticed, taking a long swallow of his bourbon.

"I think Taggart might've tipped off those guys who hijacked that truck."

Fannie didn't react, only listened, looking down at those tiny bubbles fizzing to the top of her glass.

"He was the only one knew the route," he said. "Mr. White's people told Taggart and Taggart only. He beat up that black truck driver to throw us off. Hell, the driver didn't even know which direction he was headed twenty minutes before he was hit."

"Damn," Fannie said.

"Keep that to yourself," he said. "OK? Mr. White would shit a brick. I don't know what I'm gonna do."

Fannie sipped the champagne, playing with the sash around her waist.

"You didn't see or hear anything?" Ray said. "When he was at Vienna's? Talking about those trucks and where they were headed."

"Wes didn't say much to me other than to go fetch him a drink or a girl."

"Bastard," Ray said. "Fucking redneck bastard."

Fannie nodded, pressing her lips together in thought, and told Ray to stop worrying tonight. All their problems would be right there in the morning where they left them. She pulled at her sash and opened her robe, setting down into the big plushy chair, arching her back and spreading her legs wide. A perfectly trimmed red landing strip between her thighs.

"Oh, God," Ray said. "I think one fine day you just might kill me."

Quinn didn't get back to the farm until late, hitting the little bridge over Sarter Creek, with Hondo meeting him at the road, barking to announce his arrival. The lights were on upstairs and he hoped Maggie hadn't waited up. He knew she worked another day shift tomorrow, trying to bank up her hours before taking off five days for their honeymoon. He parked his truck and squatted down to rub Hondo's ears, Hondo seeming a little confused and inquisitive as to why he'd been left at home all damn day.

But today was pretty much all Tupelo. After they couldn't find Taggart and Hood, the feds produced a warrant based on information Boom had already given them. They opened up trailers and cargo bays, blocking the chain-link fence while they interviewed every last employee. By the time Quinn and Lillie left, the docks were swarming with men and women in black shirts that read either DEA or FBI. They hadn't found a thing besides a lot of empty offices and vacant rooms that looked like they'd been recently cleared. The special agent in charge who'd come down from Oxford wasn't pleased and let it be known to Quinn.

Lillie whispered to Quinn that the man could go fuck himself and took off on the search for J. B. Hood, learning he may be back in Memphis.

Quinn walked up the front steps with Hondo, the porch

glowing with the multicolored Christmas lights that stayed up all year. Several new plants and freshly planted flowers decorated the ledge, Caddy and his mother getting ready for their rehearsal dinner.

The front door was open. Quinn pulled at the screen door, trying to be quiet walking into the house. Although he was pretty sure Hondo had woken up everyone in a five-mile radius.

He set his keys in a ceramic bowl in the entryway and unclipped his gun and holster from his belt. Looking up the staircase, he saw Maggie headed down, looking sleepy-eyed and beautiful in one of his old T-shirts from Camp Rhino in Afghanistan. He'd helped liberate the airfield as a young Ranger back at the very start of the war.

Quinn smiled at her, Maggie walking up to him and sliding her arms around his neck, kissing him hard on the mouth.

"I tried waiting up."

"I had some business to tend to at the office," Quinn said. "County bullshit doesn't stop while I'm away. Wish it would. You'd think someone could stop trying to rob filling stations without a getaway vehicle."

"Reggie found them?"

"Oh, yeah," Quinn said. "And we had to get them processed before I could leave. That and we had a water line bust in the jail showers. I had to get a plumber up at midnight."

"How'd it go in Tupelo?" Maggie said, looking up at him. She wore her hair down and loose, a long strand covering her cheek and mouth.

"Terrible," he said.

"What happened?"

"The men who beat up Boom were gone," Quinn said. "And knowing we were coming, they trashed the place. I don't think we left the feds a thing and that made the special agent in Oxford pretty upset."

"It's not your fault."

Quinn nodded. "How's Boom?"

Maggie gave a weak smile and slowly let go of his neck. She swallowed and reached for Quinn's hand. "He's still not awake," she said. "That's not good. But not unexpected, given what his body's been through."

"He's been through worse," Quinn said.

"I'm sure he has," Maggie said. "But the human brain isn't built to take many blows like that."

"What's the doctor say?"

Maggie's eyes wandered over his face as she held his hand and led him toward the kitchen. She sat him down and Quinn leaned forward in the rigid chair, snatching off his ball cap and tossing it down on the floor. He hadn't slept for nearly thirty-six hours, always priding himself on not needing much to get by. He thought back on the empty raid and those boys slipping loose after what they'd done. Why the hell they'd blame Boom for the Pritchard boys' doing was beyond him.

"Are you OK?"

Quinn didn't answer, feeling something like nausea and heartache pass through him. He heard the screen door open and thwack shut, Hondo wandering into the kitchen, looking up at Quinn and licking the tears from his face before Maggie could see them.

"We can postpone the wedding," she said. "I hope you know that."

He nodded. Maggie reached into the refrigerator for a Coors and popped the top, setting it before Quinn.

"Damn, Quinn," she said. "You look like hell."

"I need some sleep," he said. "Tomorrow I need to call on the Pritchards. They've stirred up too much trouble."

"I thought you had the uncle in jail?"

"Bailed out the very next morning," Quinn said. "His nephews paid ten grand cash to get him out."

"They must really love him."

"Or they recognize a fellow member of their species."

Quinn looked down at the cell phone, at a text from Reggie saying he'd gotten everything squared on the plumbing. The inmates could finally get showered in the morning. He drank down half the can of Coors and set it on the table, looking up at Maggie. Standing there in his threadbare T-shirt, long bare legs, and hair flowing over her shoulders, she was a welcome sight.

He reached for her long fingers and pressed her hand to his cheek. Maggie smiled, her freckled pale skin slightly flushed from the sun, her mouth bowed and pouty. She pulled him to his feet and kissed him. Quinn felt unsteady on his boots for a moment, the way she'd always made him feel, with his heart racing and his breathing grown quick. He kissed her some more, Maggie reaching back and smoothing his short hair, wrapping her arms around his neck. "I'm so sorry," she said.

"It's gonna be fine," he said. "Boom will be fine."

He followed her upstairs, where Brandon had fallen asleep in their big bed. He was dressed in pajamas and clutching an old WWE figure Jason had given him. Quinn recognizing the ugly little toy as The Undertaker, one of Jason's all-time favorites. Maggie bent down to pick him up and carry him down to his bedroom.

"He can stay," Quinn said.

"Are you sure?" Maggie asked.

"Of course," Quinn said, sitting at the edge of his bed and taking off his boots. "We're a family now."

Hondo trotted upstairs and jumped up to the foot of the bed, circling a few times and making himself comfortable. He yawned and looked suspiciously up at Quinn with his two different colored eyes, not sure if he was going to have to move from his usual sleeping spot.

"All of us," Maggie said, switching off the lamp, leaving the room in shadow.

Tyler and Cody kept to their business, replacing their worn-out 640-horsepower with a Battenbilt 867-horsepower, an all-aluminum, absolute beast of an engine. They'd been running strong all damn night on Red Bull, pills, a few joints—what they called a hippie speedball. The weed mellowed them out but sometimes made them lazy as fuck. The Red Bulls kept their energy up and they finally got the engine into the car, priming the new oil pump before that first start-up. You better get oil pressure right off or you were screwed.

They had the big bay doors open on the garage, blasting some AC/DC CD that they'd found in some of the shit their momma had left. *"Tailored suits, chauffeured cars / Fine hotels and big cigars . . ."*

Cody was kind of dancing around the engine as he worked, both of them excited as hell about this new motor they had shipped all the way from Rocky Mount, North Carolina. Cody promised Tyler that he could race this weekend down in Loxley, Alabama.

And after all the damn shit they been through, he couldn't wait to get back behind the wheel.

"You think Uncle Heath might want to take a look?" Cody asked.

"If he ever gets back from dropping off that damn whore at the titty bar."

"She wasn't too bad," Cody said. "Never seen a woman eat that much in my whole life. She ate two Hunt Brothers Pizzas from the filling station and a half gallon of ice cream."

Tyler pulled on the joint and passed it to his brother when he stood up from working on the engine. Cody took a long draw.

"I think she was on some shit," Tyler said. "She had them real red, glassy eyes. Kept on telling me about how she'd seen a UFO when she was a toddler. Said she'd drawn this spaceship with crayons and her momma got real scared 'cause she'd seen the same thing in her dreams."

"Uncle Heath knows how to pick 'em," Cody said.

"Sure does," Tyler said. "Said she was absolutely, one hundred percent positive that aliens had visited down in Shubuta, Mississippi. I mean, if you were a higher fucking life-form, why the fuck would you fly to Shubuta? From a million light-years away."

"That's an evil goddamn place," Cody said. "Gives me the creeps every time we roll through."

Tyler admired the way their car was taking shape again. They'd replaced most all the side panels with decals from their sponsors and a big #17 on the side. Cody handed the joint back to him, that AC/DC shaking the whole damn shop as they heard the growl of a big truck pulling up outside.

The engine went silent and a door slammed. Cody looked up

at Tyler and then screwed on the carburetor filter. With its new engine and most of the chassis covered, the car looked sleek as hell. Tyler couldn't wait to get her out on the track, racing and drifting, lap after lap.

Tyler looked up at the old Valvoline clock on the wall, coming up at one in the damn morning, as Uncle Heath wandered into the shop. Cody turned down the music and leaned against the workbench, a big screwdriver in hand, watching Heath head toward their car.

"Honey, hush," Heath said, checking out that new engine. *"Whoo-fucking-wee."*

Tyler passed on the joint and his uncle took a long draw, nodding, holding his breath, until he slowly let it out. His head bobbed with another one of them old-time songs, "Highway to Hell." Tyler recalled his momma telling them that she'd gotten rid of all her rock 'n' roll records long ago, as they carried the voice of Satan. Their mother had also ripped apart that damn house when they were little boys, looking for anything made by Procter & Gamble, showing them the moon-and-thirteen-stars logo, saying their executives dabbled in the dark arts.

Heath had on a brand-new pink T-shirt, nearly hanging down to his knees. On the back it read SEE Y'ALL AT VIENNA'S PLACE. A curvy cartoon woman in an old-time pinup pose.

"Nice shirt," Cody said.

"If you buy a dozen lap dances, you get one for free."

"How much did that cost?" Tyler said.

"Oh, hell," Uncle Heath said. "I don't rightly know. Somewhere's around five hundred bucks. But worth every damn nickel, I'll tell you what . . . Y'all cranked that baby yet?"

"Not yet," Tyler said, walking over to the race car and waving his hand over that beautiful aluminum Battenbilt. "Figured the leader of our clan should have the honors."

"This mean we're goin' racin' this weekend?" Heath said, grinning.

"Oh, hell yes," Tyler said, noticing how Uncle Heath had tucked his jeans into the tops of his rattlesnake boots. "Go on. The pump is primed and ready."

Heath nodded, grinning a little, leaning down into the open driver's window for that mash start. *"No stop signs / Speed limits / Nobody's gonna slow me down."* He looked back for a moment and gave the boys a thumbs-up, pushing that button, the starter kicking, chugging away.

He crawled back out and walked over to the engine, reaching for the throttle, pulling it, making that engine whine and growl.

"Seems like that timing is a little off," Heath said.

"I don't hear it," Tyler said, eyes shifting over to the workbench and his brother.

"Come on, now," Heath said. "Hand me that there strobe."

Cody reached for the strobe light and passed it to him, Uncle Heath turning and leaning down to look at the engine. His breath smelled like the inside of a whiskey barrel, slurring his speech as he spoke, wobbling a little on those fancy boots. He reached back and revved the engine, looking up at the boys with a *Didn't I tell you?* look on his face. Cody walked up beside Tyler and behind Uncle Heath, pulling that .44 Taurus they kept in their glovebox.

"Something just ain't right," Uncle Heath said. "You boys really don't hear that shit?"

Cody pushed the barrel to the back of Heath's skull. And as the engine revved higher and higher, he pulled the trigger.

. . .

"Whatever you do," Wes said, "keep your fucking mouth shut."

"Where are we?" Twilight said.

"Just stay in the damn truck and I'll be right back," Wes said.

"I'm not staying out here by myself," she said, trying to look a little scared and surprised. "Out in the damn booger woods. I've seen those movies where the boyfriend says, 'I'll be right back,' and then some crazy asshole in a ski mask pops up behind her with a machete. Don't even think about it."

Twilight's real name was Tiffany Dement, born and raised down in Laurel. But Miss Fannie had liked the way Twilight sounded a lot better. Plus, she already had three Tiffanys. Twilight Tiffany thought the name suited her, and maybe she'd add a little more detail to that dolphin tattoo to fit, maybe get an orange sunset sky inked behind the palm trees.

"Won't take but a second," he said. "I got some business inside."

"What the hell are all these buildings?" she said. "Way the hell out there?"

"You be a good little girl," he said. "And when I get back, Daddy'll get you a surprise."

"Come on," she said. "You promised you'd take me back with you to Memphis."

"I will," Wes said. "They got that Crabfest going on at Red Lobster and you can eat until you damn near bust."

"And then what?"

"I got to pick up a buddy and then all of us will drive down to the Gulf," he said. "Stay a few days at the ole Beau Rivage down there. I heard that Blue Man Group is doing some shows."

"What the hell's the Blue Man Group?"

"Baby, it's the craziest shit you ever saw," Wes said. "These dudes with shaved heads, skin painted blue, dancing to music and banging on shit. They got confetti and streamers, flashing lights, and one big goddamn butterfly."

"Can't wait," she said, the whole thing sounding like a snoozefest for old folks. "How long can we stay?"

"Might be a while," Wes said. "Your momma and daddy waitin' up for you or something?"

"They never did," Twilight said, Wes reaching over and patting her bare leg. She'd been back in the VIP room giving some hand action to a chicken hauler out of Kosciusko when he'd come for her at midnight. All he said was to pack up all her stuff and come on. She'd only been twenty minutes from closing time but wasn't surprised a bit to see him. Wes sure couldn't get enough of Little Miss Twilight.

Wes crawled from the black Tahoe and walked toward a building that looked big enough to fit an airplane inside. She waved to him as he turned back and then watched as he disappeared through a side door.

Twilight didn't wait a beat to reach into the console of the truck and pull out the cell phone she'd been told about.

She scrolled through it and then used her own phone to call Miss Fannie. Everything was just the way she'd explained it to her. Miss Fannie was good about things like that, knowing which way the world sure turned.

Fannie took the elevator down to the Peabody's lobby, no one around at three o'clock in the morning. Even the ducks that swam in the marble fountain were up on the roof sleeping off their day. The ceiling above her went up for two floors, huge chandeliers and a fancy gilding overhead, with intricate designs in the woodwork. She leaned back in a chair by the elevators, admiring it, as she called up the Pritchard boys to see if they'd taken care of business.

"Yes, ma'am," Tyler Pritchard said.

"That's good," she said. "But don't get rid of him just yet."

"Why?"

"I need proof of fucking purchase," she said.

"And how the hell do we keep him?"

"Put his nasty old ass on ice."

"We got a damn race this weekend," he said. "Down in Loxley, Alabama. We won't be back till Monday."

"Not now," Fannie said. "Y'all got shit to do."

"We just put a new engine in our car," he said. "Shipped all the way from Rocky Mount, North Carolina. Cost five hundred dollars just to get it here. Besides, I think it's best if we leave town for a little bit. Considering our complicated family situation."

"Today," she said, "a truck will be running straight from Houston, Texas. It'll make a stop down in Meridian at the Magnolia Truck Stop. Do y'all know that place?"

There was silence and a little breathing before Tyler spoke again. "It won't be like last time," he said. "This time they might be waiting on us."

"Let me worry about that," Fannie said. "Y'all just get that fucking truck."

24

THE DAY BEFORE HIS WEDDING, QUINN WENT WITH HIS mother and little Jason down the road a few miles to pick some flowers. Maggie was pretty damn clear about not having old, boring arrangements from a florist on the Square and preferred just having cuttings from Jean's rosebushes. Maggie liked the idea of having something from the home where Quinn grew up. Her mother was bringing up some canna lilies from her place down in Mobile. The only problem was Jean had run out of blue hydrangeas halfway through decorating the church. She called up dispatch and had them place an emergency call while he was out on a wreck. Cleotha, chewing gum, saying over the radio, "You better call your momma, Sheriff."

A half hour later, he found himself out at the old Spratlin place, a house that had been abandoned as long as Quinn could recall. The white paint flaked off from the old wood, most of the windows broken out, and the doors stripped from the hinges. Quinn held the bucket while Jean harvested the biggest hydrangea bush he'd ever seen, tucking the bright blue flowers into the water.

"I think Miss Spratlin would be pleased," Jean said. "When she was alive, she had the most beautiful flowers and plants. She grew tomatoes the size of softballs. But look at what her kids did. Just left her lovely little house out here to rot. I hope you'd never do that to me."

"Nope," Quinn said. "I'd sell the house and Caddy and I'd pocket the money. We already agreed to put up all your Elvis stuff on eBay. That may be worth more than the damn house."

"That's terrible," Jean said, taking some more cuttings from Jason, who was slicing off flowers with the pocketknife Quinn gave him. "Awful. It's nearly a hundred degrees and I'm out here tromping around this old place for your wedding. Don't you even think about selling my Elvis records. Those are for little Jason. You hear me?"

Jason grinned and patted Quinn's back, whispering, "Don't even think about it, Uncle Quinn. If anybody gets to sell all that shit, it's me."

Quinn was glad to hear Jason joking with him. They'd had some long, tough talks back in the spring when he found out Quinn was getting married. He grew a little defiant and cold. Jean had been the one to realize Jason was jealous of Brandon, fearing he'd lose his uncle for good now that he was getting a son. Quinn had done his best to let him know nothing was further from the truth.

"Don't we have enough flowers?" Quinn asked.

"Let me walk around back and see what else might be left."

Quinn nodded, his radio set on the steps of the old house, cool under a big oak with roots that had busted apart a concrete walkway.

He set down the bucket and headed into the house, dozens of doors and two fireplace mantels set in the center of the building waiting for a pickup that never came. One end of the house, in what looked to be the kitchen, had fallen in, a large tree branch growing through what used to be a window. The air seemed even hotter inside, thick and humid, and a great place for snakes to nest. Quinn heard his mother's steps following him inside. He looked about for any slithering shadows.

"Is this all we leave?" she said.

Quinn set his hand on his mother's shoulder as she looked at the broken floorboards, the old flowered wallpaper coming unglued from the walls. He tried to imagine what it was like when a family lived here full of love and energy.

"I never saw a woman more house-proud than Miss Spratlin," Jean said. "She used to sell jellies and jams on the Square. Her husband used to come with her until he got cancer and died. *Oh, Lord.* When was that? Maybe before your daddy and I even got married. They raised fancy chickens and sold rabbits around Easter time. And, God, look at this place, falling in on itself. Their children ought to be ashamed of themselves."

Quinn nodded. He thought he should find out who owned the property now; maybe pull out a few of these old doors and the mantels to replace the ones in his house that weren't original. He liked the idea of the farm being the way it was a hundred years back, before it got all cobbled together.

"Uncle Quinn?" Jason said, calling out from the yard.

Quinn walked out and down the steps, Jason holding out the police radio. "Miss Cleotha's trying to reach you."

His cell phone started to go off on his hip, the sheriff's office number flashing on the screen.

"What is it?" Jean asked, up from the porch as the phone started to ring.

"I'm not sure," Quinn said. "But let's load up those flower buckets. Looks like I better head back to town."

I can see why Uncle Heath liked this truck," Cody said. "This display is sick, man. The way the interior lights up all blue with all this damn tan suede and real wood. Limited grille. Limited wheels. This fucking thing is a custom truck right off the fucking lot."

"We can't keep it," Tyler said.

"Oh, hell yeah, I'm keeping it," Cody said. "I read they call this Dodge the Tungsten Edition because that's a high-dollar kind of chrome. All that silver on the grille and the wheels? That's all tungsten metal. Same shit some folks wear as rings and jewelry."

"I'll buy you a damn belt buckle," Tyler said. "I think after we show the body to Miss Fannie, we drive this son of a bitch deep into Choctaw Lake with Uncle Heath in the toolbox just like we left Ordeen."

"Oh, come on, man," Cody said. "We got every right to keep this truck. He paid with our cash and we just say, 'We don't know where he went.'"

"How's it gonna look, fuck brain?" Tyler said. "With me and you driving around in our uncle's new ride after they find him dead?"

"They won't find him."

"They damn well found Ordeen," Tyler said. "Use your fucking head, man."

Tyler kept his eye on the truck moving on ahead of them,

moving out from Magnolia Truck Stop in Meridian and heading north on 45 just like Miss Hathcock had told them, rolling on through Lauderdale, Scooba, Wahalak, and Shuqualak. Tyler started to get a little worried. It only took that last truck about twenty minutes to start to slow down, but this damn truck, a big ole hoss Mack Titan, shining black paint with that gold bulldog on the hood, hadn't even sputtered. A shame that Cody got to drive the big semi again—he won the coin flip—but at least Tyler would get to play around with that Dodge truck a bit before they deep-sixed it back in Tibbehah.

"Glad it's not Boom Kimbrough."

"Can't be Boom Kimbrough," Tyler said. "Didn't you hear?"

"Hear what?"

"Someone beat the hell out of him," Tyler said. "Put him in the damn hospital. I heard he nearly got his damn brains beat out."

"Shit," Cody said. "Who the hell would do something fucked up like that?"

"I don't think it's gonna work," Tyler said, looking at his watch. "He's been driving nearly thirty minutes. That gas flow should've started to peter out back at Shuqualak."

"It's happening."

"How do you know?" Tyler said.

"Because we sealed that tank tighter than a preacher's butthole," Cody said. "Ain't no air getting into there. That diesel will quit flowing. Just be cool. It's coming."

"What happens if that son of a bitch breaks down in Starkville?" he said. "We can't jack his ass in the city limits."

"It's Starkville, man," Cody said. "Them people fuck cows in public."

Tyler watched the truck for another two miles, neither of the boys saying a word, until he saw the brake lights flicker and black smoke pour from the exhaust stacks. He leaned forward to the glass, Cody starting to slow down, watching as the truck's hazard lights flickered on. The truck slowly rolled down the highway, coming to rest by a stretch of cotton land, not a son of a bitch around except for a few trailers up around the next bend.

"Hell fucking yes," Tyler said.

"What'd I tell you?"

"Who the fuck sealed them tanks?" Tyler said.

"You were the one doubting your work."

"Shut the hell up and pull on that mask," Tyler said. "I'll tie that driver's ass up behind the rig and toss him in the bed. Good thing it's got that nice cover on it."

"First class all the way," he said. "This ain't no work truck. This is like a four-wheel-drive limo. Smooth as hell."

"We ain't keeping the truck," Tyler said. "Shit."

They waited for a minute for the driver to get out of the cab. They could see a man's face in the rearview look back a few times but not move. Cody honked the horn, trying to get him on out of the cab so they could snatch him up. "Aw, hell," Tyler said. "I'll walk around the other side. I'll aim that shotgun at his head and that'll get that fucker moving."

"What about the masks?"

"Pull it down when you get close," Tyler said. "You don't want to go and spook him."

"Where the hell's he gonna go?"

"He might lock the damn doors and call the law," Tyler said. "Just act nice and friendly and I'll walk around to the other side."

Cody pulled the neoprene mask onto his head, wearing it like a ski cap. Tyler did the same. As they waited a second, Tyler unwrapped a piece of Dubble Bubble. Everything looked slow and easy through his sunglasses as he got out of the cab and walked careful and slow with the shotgun held behind his right leg. "Come out, come out," Cody said, snickering.

"Shut up, shithead," Tyler said. "I told you to be cool."

"Oh, hell," Cody said. "Just having some damn fun. Don't be a dick."

Just as they were about to split off on each side of the trailer, they heard the rough clanking of metal.

The trailer's double doors flew open and four men with guns jumped out and started to shoot. Tyler and Cody were already running back to the Dodge when the bullets peppered the side doors of the pickup and shattered the windows.

"Motherfuckers," he said. "Motherfuckers tricked us."

They looked at each other across the floorboard of the truck, hiding with the doors wide-ass open. Without a word, only nodding, Cody reached up to where he left the keys and started up that son of a bitch. Neither of them had time to shut the doors, the doors just kind of flying shut as Cody drove off blind, steering under the dash until they hit the highway.

Soon as they got clear, Cody busted out laughing.

"What's so funny?"

"Most fun I've had in a while, little brother," he said. "Goddamn. How the fuck do you think they knew we were coming?"

"This was a bad idea," Tyler said, scooting up into the seat, the windshield looking like goddamn Swiss cheese. They rolled fast and hard down the blacktop. Highway patrol would be on their damn ass in a few minutes. "Trusting that mean-ass bitch. What the hell were we thinking?"

"Why do you think she'd fuck us?" Cody said.

Tyler let down his window, his heart racing hard, sweating like hell. "Maybe we should've wondered why the hell she wanted to keep us around. We done what she wanted."

"And what's that?"

"Fucked up the damn system."

Tyler looked into the rearview and saw two SUVs racing up fast behind them. Neither of them looked like the law, but they were coming up behind as Cody was driving damn near ninety. "They're coming."

"Who?"

"Fuck if I know," Tyler said. "Just get us the hell out of here."

Quinn walked into the sheriff's office break room and waited for his other deputies to gather at the beat-up old table in the center of the room. Reggie Caruthers, Dave Cullison, Art Watts, and Kenny were all on duty for the day. Two more coming in special since Quinn had gotten the news from Batesville.

"I don't want y'all to breathe a word of this," Quinn said. "But we got a match on those toolbox prints. And I got a warrant for the arrest of Heath Pritchard for the murder of Ordeen Davis."

The deputies nodded, none of them being all that shocked to hear it, as there had been talk about what Quinn had learned in Memphis from Lyle Masters. Heath had also been a jailhouse turd for the twenty-four hours he'd spent under the hospitality of the Tibbehah County Sheriff's Department. He'd thrown his food against the wall, tore up his bedsheets, and pissed all over the walls. Kenny himself had taken an instant disliking to the man, wondering why Hamp Beckett didn't finish the damn job twenty-five years ago.

"I want to approach this with extreme caution," Quinn said. "A man like Heath Pritchard doesn't have a damn thing to lose. Not to mention, he's in a guarded compound with his two nephews. I don't think either one of those boys are going to freely cooperate. Just remember the situational awareness we discussed at the shoot house. Y'all got it? We move and communicate. If these good ole boys so much as fart in our direction, you know what to do. Anyone have any questions?"

Reggie raised his hand.

Quinn nodded at him. "Yes, sir."

"I heard they got dogs out there," Reggie said. "You know how I hate dogs, Sheriff. Especially pit bulls."

"Only dog I know about is that old Walker hound."

Reggie nodded, seeming to be satisfied with it. Quinn leaned into the desk, everyone standing over the table crowded with boxes full of files, maps, and empty coffee mugs filled with cigar ash. Quinn looked over at Dave Cullison, who studied one of the maps of the Pritchard land, nodding, seeming to be in deep thought. He was a medium-sized guy with thinning brown hair and glasses.

"What's up, Dave?"

"When I was a school resource officer, I got to know those boys pretty well," he said. "Tyler's not a bad kid. I think under different circumstances, he might've been a solid citizen. Great at math, science. But his brother is another story. That boy flies by the seat of his damn pants, a real hothead. He won't take kindly to us showing up to take his uncle away."

"Like I said, let's do our best to arrest Heath Pritchard without incident," Quinn said. "But my first concern is y'all's safety. Keep your damn eyes and ears open. We take it to the Pritchards fast and mean and don't give them a chance to think about any other options. That's five against three. I kind of like those odds."

Reggie looked up from the table and nodded, rubbing his chin. "Yeah," he said. "I'm ready. But, damn if I don't miss Lillie Virgil up in the hills with her Winchester."

"You can't do that," Cody said, running that Dodge Ram Tungsten to damn near a hundred miles per hour, farmland racing past their windows. "You can't be shooting at folks on Highway 45. I sure as hell ain't cut out for no prison."

"I'd get off on Highway 14 and scoot our asses through the Tombigbee Forest," Tyler said. "They're gonna try and shut our asses down the closer we get to Starkville."

Their back window cracked. A side mirror splintered into a dozen fragments.

"Goddamn son of a bitch," Cody said, standing on it now. The engine howling, bucking forward, taking them up to the damn redline. Tyler would never admit it in a million years, but he was glad Cody was driving. That boy would drive that truck until it was rode hard as hell and put up wet, the engine giving out before he would.

"Did you get a good look at them?" Tyler said.

"I started running when you did," Cody said. "I wasn't gonna ask no questions with those cocksucking commandos jumping out with AR-15s."

"They weren't taking no chances," Tyler said.

The window cracked again, both Tyler and Cody hunched down in their seats, Cody so fucking low he could barely see over the fucking wheel. Running that big-ass truck flat out, flying past other cars unlucky enough to find themselves in a Wild West shoot-out in east Mississippi.

"Who are those guys?" Cody said.

"How the hell should I know?"

"They sure knew us."

"Miss Fannie said they work for some bad folks down on the Gulf," Tyler said.

"And who the fuck does she work for?"

"I said I didn't ask."

"That might've been a good start," Cody said. "Shit, Tyler. What if Uncle Heath was right?"

"'Bout what?" Tyler said.

"That we were two JV turds in the big leagues."

Tyler could see the HIGHWAY 14 sign coming up quick on the right, his brother, not giving a damn about turn signals, turned the other way, crossing the southbound lane and kicking up dirt. The truck flew down an embankment toward the highway that would lead them deep into a National Forest. If they could get out that way, they could get home.

Cody smiled when they got about a mile down the road, checking the rearview, that beautiful Dodge truck shot to shit. "Damn," he said, laughing. "That was close as hell. We're good."

Tyler looked back in the busted rearview, steadying his breath, seeing the grille of an SUV racing up behind them, going faster than any street legal truck should travel. "Cody."

"Yeah," he said. "I fucking see 'em."

"Guess they want their shit back real bad."

"Real bad," Cody said. He floored it, Tyler holding on to the passenger door so not to get knocked into the backseat. The shooting started back again. The rearview mirror shattered into pieces and fell from the truck onto the road.

"Who are those guys?" Cody said.

"Shut the fuck up," Tyler said. "You done already said that."

"What do we do?"

"Like always," Tyler said. "Drive like hell and don't ask no more questions."

Quinn had just spread out the aerial map of the Pritchard place on the hood of his F-150 when a big black truck came blowing past him and the deputies at the gate to the Pritchard land, not stopping, not hesitating, just busting right through the cattle gate and leaving in a plume of dust.

Quinn looked up from the map. "Or," Quinn said, "we can pursue those shitbirds and take their asses down right now."

They'd parked in the shade of a big oak, maybe three hundred meters from the entrance to the land. Whoever had busted through the gate hadn't seen the grouping of law enforcement vehicles or simply didn't give two shits.

By the time Quinn snatched up the map and reached for his shotgun on the hood, two SUVs came racing down the highway, fishtailing behind that black truck, running through the wide-open gate.

Art Watts, muscly with blond shaggy hair, looked over at Quinn. "That was Heath Pritchard's truck," he said. "That's the one I told you he paid seventy thousand in cash for at the Dodge dealership."

Quinn nodded, heading around to the driver's side, Reggie opening up to ride shotgun. Quinn cranked the truck and handed Reggie his gun. Reggie checked the load and snicked it closed. The other deputies piled into two other sheriff's office vehicles and U-turned toward the old Pritchard place, Quinn thinking on his Uncle Hamp and the famous time he'd had here long ago.

He reached for the mic and called into Cleotha.

"We need assistance from highway patrol and Lee County," Quinn said, giving her the address of the trouble. "And Cleotha? Call up Maggie and tell her I'm gonna be a little late to the rehearsal."

"She's gonna have your ass, Sheriff."

"Ten-four," Quinn said and then pressed the mic button again. "How about we keep this channel clear of personal business?"

25

"RIGHT NOW, I WISH WE HADN'T KILLED THAT SON OF A bitch," Cody said.

"Uncle Heath had it coming," Tyler said. "If it hadn't been us, it'd been someone who didn't appreciate his special brand of bullshit."

"And how does that make it better?"

"Don't make it worse."

They'd run the Dodge inside the race shop, closing the big bay doors and locking them from behind. Cody reached into a little hidey-hole under the workbench and snatched up an AR-15 with a big-ass drum clip. That gun could spit out a hundred rounds before you could cover your damn peter. Tyler headed on over to the tool racks stacked with Rubbermaid containers, searching for some shotgun shells for his Remington, pouring a few into his hand while staring up at a framed picture of the Pritchard boys racing go-carts up in Memphis. Both of them wearing matching helmets decorated with Confederate flags. Cody had lost his two front teeth.

"Ain't nobody gonna miss this race," Cody said. "Damn ten grand purse and the return of those Lucas Oil girls with the big tatas. A big time in Lower Alabama."

"I don't know," Tyler said. "Maybe we should just call the sheriff. This is our damn land. They don't have no right to be here."

"Don't matter," Cody said. "I think we lost 'em back in the Tombigbee Forest."

"You keep thinking that, Cody," Tyler said. "Maybe that dream'll come true."

They heard dirt spewing and car doors opening, slamming shut, engines continuing to run with feet crunching on the gravel. For the first time all day, maybe forever, Cody looked a little scared, his face growing pale. Someone started to shoot at the garage locks, the big bay door echoing like a steel drum.

"Come on into the briar patch, motherfuckers," Cody said, placing the AR up to his shoulder. "We'll scatter your damn nuts across the back forty."

"We're fucked," Tyler said.

"Nope," Cody said. "We're gonna shoot our way down into the grow room. Ain't nobody can get through that metal hatch."

"Ordeen Davis did."

"That's 'cause you left the goddamn door open," Cody said. "I'm talking about sealing our asses down there and watching the whole show from the TVs. We got enough Twinkies, Ding Dongs, Keystone Light, and weed to last us until the Seventh Seal is opened and those seven bugles sound."

"Why the fuck not?" Tyler stroked his beard, holding the Remington in both hands, his pockets so fat with shells he could barely walk. "C'mon. Let's do this shit."

"When they don't find us," Cody said, "they'll think we're long gone."

"That's a damn big piece of real estate between here and the barn," Tyler said. "How many boys they got in those two Tahoes?"

"Don't matter," Cody said. "Might as well be the whole goddamn Bolivian Army."

Tyler swallowed, looking around the shop, their race car sitting pretty at an angle, ready to roll onto the trailer for the big night down in Loxley. *The Deep South Speedway.* Women in bikini tops, short shorts, and after they won, a long white beach and ice-cold beer. They needed some real-world Jimmy Buffett shit after what they'd been through.

"Maybe we should stay right here," he said. "Protect the car."

"Those boys can bust through those doors with their trucks," Cody said. "It's time to take it to the fucking barn, brother."

"Hey, man?" Tyler said, looking over at Cody's side, bright red with blood. "What the fuck? Are you bleeding?"

Cody touched his stomach, looking down at his slick palm. "What do you know?" he said. "I guess I am."

Dispatch, this is Tibbehah One," Quinn said. "We're at the Pritchard place on Chicken Roost Road. We've encountered a gunfight with half-dozen subjects on each side. Handguns and semi-autos involved. How are we coming with MHP and Lee County?"

"On their way, Sheriff," Cleotha said.

"Ten-four."

There was a long silence and then the click of the radio, Cleotha back on the mic: "Miss Maggie said for you to take your time."

"That's good," Quinn said. "Because we are about to engage. Over."

"You think Maggie'll believe this?" Reggie said, grinning. Quinn knocked the truck into gear and headed down through the busted gate into the Pritchard property. "Her sitting at the church, ready to rehearse, and you not showing? I was really looking forward to that barbecue."

"Barbecue's tomorrow," Quinn said. "Tonight was catfish, catered by Pap's Place."

"Son of a bitch," Reggie said. "I sure hate them Pritchard boys."

At first, Boom thought he was back in Iraq on a helicopter with that medic who shot him full of morphine, then coming to a few days later at a field hospital outside Baghdad being told he was one lucky man even though he'd left his goddamn arm somewhere outside Fallujah. He could taste that blood and sand in his mouth, sense his hand and arm even though it had been gone a long time. He didn't think much on it, just tried to push himself off the bed, when he heard a woman's voice telling him to be still. The woman wasn't that Army medic on the chopper or a doctor at the field hospital or anyone back at Walter Reed where that shrink talked to him about the "new normal." This was a voice he damn well knew but couldn't see her worth shit, all the images coming through damn double like looking out the wrong end of some field glasses. *Maggie Powers.*

"Be calm," she said. "You're fine. You're gonna be all right."

"What happened?"

Last thing that came to mind was driving home from New Albany with Quinn, waiting around damn near forever at that Waffle House. He thought about it, trying hard as hell to remember, but nothing more came to him. Time had just kind of stopped.

"You got knocked around pretty good," she said. "Doctor's on his way."

"Where we at?"

"The hospital," she said. "Just lay back, don't move. Don't stress yourself."

"I feel like I'm gonna puke."

"Deep breaths," she said. "Close your eyes. Breathe deep."

"Breathe deep?" Boom said. "Shit. Yeah, OK. Where's Quinn?"

Boom's mouth felt as dry as paper. He had to close his eyes. The double vision was making him sick as hell. If he didn't move, didn't look, he could tolerate it. The sheets smelled like Lysol and bleach, everything air-conditioned and cold as hell. He moved his left hand a little, wiggling his fingers, and then his feet and toes. Make sure he hadn't lost anything else. He thought of that rolling and running in the big truck, the Humvee, a big goddamn explosion and electric silence and pain so fucking deep that everything in his brain shut down.

"Did I miss it?" Boom said.

He felt Maggie's cool hands on his cheek, laying back, feeling useless, not being able to see, some of his hearing muffled.

"What's that?"

"The wedding," Boom said. "Did I miss y'all's wedding?"

"Tomorrow," Maggie said. "Don't you worry. Everything is going to be just fine."

"Quinn's a good man," Boom said. "You know he loves you?"

"I know," she said.

"And he won't quit?"

"Rest easy," Maggie Powers said. "Lay back."

Boom felt Maggie's hands leave his face, touching his left arm, squeezing, as more voices filled that little room. Prodding, poking, feeling the tubes strain all around his body. "Quinn don't know how to quit," he said, eyes closed. "We'll get those motherfuckers who did this."

"He knows," she said.

"Me and Quinn don't know another way."

What amazed Tyler most was that the damn highway patrol hadn't been on their ass the whole way back to Tibbehah. Those bastards were never around when you needed them. Only in your rearview if you were five miles above the speed limit or if they knew you'd just left a beer joint, maybe with a little likker on your breath. He figured the space between the shop and the old barn was only about thirty or forty yards, not even half a football field. There couldn't be more than a half-dozen boys from those two black SUVs and they'd be seriously distracted when Cody opened up with that AR-15 with the big-ass round clip.

"Are you sure you're OK?" Tyler said.

"This ain't shit," Cody said, holding a dirty rag to his side. "I'm right behind you. Ain't nobody comes on our land and tells us what to do. You see this thing? Fucking hundred rounds. I'll turn those sonsabitches into ground chuck in a few seconds."

Tyler headed on over to the side door, duck-walking the last ten feet or more, in case someone was peeping in the glass. He looked out and saw the corner of the barn, the old faded building leaning hard to the right. It was nearly five o'clock, but it felt like when they'd been racing all damn day. Tyler had nearly sweated through his T-shirt, jeans dusty and dirty and rolled up high over his old cowboy boots.

Cody's white T-shirt was red and sticky with blood. He waited by the bay doors with his AR in his left hand and right finger on the button to open up the shop. "Go on," he said. "Run. You can't shoot worth two damn shits."

Tyler nodded from across the big shop, turning the dead bolt to the back door. He ran like hell.

There was yelling and shooting behind him as he raced toward the deep shadow of the barn. Then he heard the long, sustained chattering of Cody unleashing that gun, sounding like those sonsabitches were being fed into a goddamn buzz saw. He got halfway to the opening when he felt something tear in the back of his leg, taking him down to his fucking knees, seeing red as he limped, dragging that busted leg into the darkness.

Not until he steadied himself on an old horse stall did he realize he'd been shot, too. Even in deep shadow, he could see the dark red blood pooling onto the powdery dirt floor. *Son of a damn bitch.*

He gritted his teeth and spit, dragging his leg over to the hatch, slapping it wide open and crawling on inside. He flicked on a switch to light up the passage down into the ground, holding on to the rungs with his hands, smelling the wet, musty earth below.

Quinn left his truck to block the narrow dirt road and headed out into the woods with Reggie, keeping coms with the other deputies, who waited for instructions, lights flashing all the way down the Pritchards' private road, more help arriving soon. The last thing Quinn wanted to do was run his deputies right into the mess. As he learned a long time ago back at Fort Benning, never be in a hurry to go and get shot. Assess the situation, get the damn intel, and then make a good decision on how to shut it down.

"That don't sound too good," Reggie said.

"Nope," Quinn said. "Looks like the Pritchard boys have more trouble than just us."

"Who do you think were in those SUVs?" Reggie said.

"Two options," Quinn said, swatting away a few branches, jumping over a narrow ravine, holding his Winchester pump. "But considering those boys weren't on motorcycles, I believe it's the Syndicate. They've come to get what's theirs."

More gunfire, a few shotgun blasts and the *pop-pop-pop* of rifles. Quinn used the shotgun's barrel to push away the brush and branches, moving in closer to the family compound, spotting the sun glinting off the tin roof of the house.

"Can I ask you something, Sheriff?" Reggie said. Both of them onto a cleared stretch of woods, hitting what looked to be some kind of old trail. They picked up the pace, moving into a slow jog toward the action.

"Yes, sir."

"We're going to head into a dangerous situation," Reggie said, "to save a couple peckerwoods. And their uncle, who was the one who killed Ordeen Davis."

"I'm hoping we're about to engage with the boys who put a beatdown on Boom."

"And snatch up Heath Pritchard in the process," Reggie said, walking beside Quinn. He held a Colt M4 as they ran, the barrel aimed down toward the ground. "Make him answer for Ordeen."

"Maybe," Quinn said. "But if it's the Syndicate, we may already be too late. Let's just try to hold them down until MHP arrives."

"Love to meet the men who did that to Boom."

The gunfire revved up, fully automatic weapons slicing through the air in what seemed like an endless barrage that finally left the woods and the property in a weird, electric stillness. They were to the edge of the tree line, with a clear view of everything that was happening. Two black SUVs parked crooked, the bay door to the race shop wide open.

"Me, too," Quinn said, kneeling down, trying to get a sense of the numbers. "Just don't leave me alone with them in the interview room."

"I wouldn't trust those folks, either," Reggie asked.

"It's not that," Quinn said. "After what they've done? I don't trust myself."

Tyler dragged himself through a series of grow trailers, everything still and silent below the earth, making his way toward the safe room where they kept the security cameras and supplies. He'd already tied his T-shirt around his thigh but knew they had some gauze and duct tape in a toolbox somewhere. Maybe he could clean out the wound with some Jack Daniel's they'd left down there the other night.

He slapped on the light and flipped open a toolbox to grab some supplies. The bottle of Jack was just where he left it, in the deep freeze with Uncle Heath. He and Cody had a few swigs in his honor before placing him inside, tucking the bottle into his arms, a peaceful smile on the old man's face. Or at least they told themselves that, trying to feel better about the whole goddamn rotten situation.

Tyler took a long-ass swig before pouring it across his leg. It stung so damn bad that he drank the rest of the bottle before reaching into the kit for the gauze. He pressed it tight to his wound as he looked up at the monitors, which showed the property from about every angle, from the front porch of their house on into the shop, and into every grow room watching over their weed.

He started to roll the duct tape around his leg, pulling it tight as he could, feeling like the Jack Daniel's wasn't gonna cut it, gritting his teeth together as he saw Cody's back from the shop camera. He was firing off a bunch of rounds from that AR, moving forward out of the garage.

Everything soundless and in black-and-white, like some kind of old-time gangster movie.

He looked up, catching the feed from the telephone pole outside, watching Cody shoot three dudes with guns and then tear the shit out the front of those two SUVs. He was laughing the whole time he was doing it, reminding Tyler a hell of a lot of William H. Bonney in *Young Guns*, loving every second of that crazy-ass destruction.

"Get 'em," Tyler said, standing up, a pain shooting through his leg, but hobbling forward. "Hell fucking yeah."

He tore off his shirt and reached into a box of some of their merch, Team Pritchard Racing. The T-shirt read DOING IT OUTLAW STYLE, with a logo of a man in a black hat, a red bandanna covering his face. They stole it off the internet from the Skoal Bandit car that ole Harry Gant used to drive, their stepdaddy showing them his races on videos he'd taped of the Winston Cup from a million years back. Tyler made his way to the sink and washed his face and the blood off his hands, hobbling back over to the monitors to fetch his gun and head back to the hatch to let Cody down into the rabbit hole.

Three men were down on their backs, SUVs all fucked up, as Cody kept walking, knocking loose that big drum and reloading with some magazines from his pockets. As he moved, something caught Cody hard and fast in the chest, knocking him back on his ass.

Tyler screamed, not believing that high-pitched sound came from his own mouth. He got up so close to the monitor that he nearly touched it with his nose.

An old man with a gray ponytail stepped out from around an SUV and kicked Cody hard in the ribs, looking around the property before moving to their race shop.

Tyler ran from the room, screaming, holding the shotgun and trying to get back up to the surface. He felt like he was walking at the bottom of a pond, unable to take a fucking breath.

Wasn't the Pritchards," Boom said.

It was just him and Maggie again. The two doctors had left, saying that he needed to head back for more tests, and with some solid luck maybe might get some Jell-O for dinner. Maggie helped him raise his bed a little. He was still hooked up to a heart monitor and IV, some fucking tube stuck out his nose and down in his pecker.

"What happened?" Maggie said.

"Two white dudes," Boom said. "They run that trucking company. Quinn knows."

"Cleotha called me and said he was going to be late," she said. "We have the rehearsal at the church tonight. Something big must be going on."

"You think Quinn went after those boys?"

"He was about to arrest Heath Pritchard," she said. "That's the last I heard."

"Damn," Boom said. "They're coming for those boys."

Maggie looked at him. "Who?"

"Those Pritchard boys jacked my ass," he said. "Stole my whole damn truck and everything in it. That's why they came for me. These men in Tupelo thought I'd thrown in with the goddamn Pritchards. Now they're coming to kill those boys."

"You don't know that," she said. "Just hang tight until Quinn gets here."

"God help them," Boom said. "These are some nasty folks. You tell Quinn that. Tell him to watch his damn ass."

Maggie stood, just looking at Boom, the phone already in her hand, dialing. The ringing went straight into voice mail.

Quinn moved from the tree line with Reggie Caruthers, getting to the edge of the old house when the man with the ponytail came around and shot Cody Pritchard right in his chest and off his feet. There were three more bodies on the ground between those SUVs and the race shop. Quinn didn't see Tyler, only another man join the guy with the gray ponytail, the gray-headed man looking to be in charge as he pointed for the other one to circle around back. Quinn nodded to Reggie, who disappeared to the back of the house, coming at the old barn from the other side.

Quinn found a good spot to work from the old house's porch, two brick pedestals near the front steps. Quinn slung the shotgun off his back and covered Reggie.

The older man toed at Cody's body and then turned, spotting Reggie, raising his gun as Quinn blasted the shotgun, jacked in another shell, and blasted again. The ponytailed man ran for the second vehicle, Quinn yelling for him to stay down. A half-dozen shots followed from in the garage as Quinn reloaded and slung the shotgun to his back, reaching for his Beretta, waiting for the man to stick his head out.

About sixty meters separated Quinn from the dude with the ponytail. He heard two quick shots from behind the shop. After a long minute of silence, Reggie came over the radio to say one man was down. That left the man by the truck and the shooter in the garage, only them and Jesus Himself knowing what had happened to the remaining Pritchards.

Quinn heard a car door open and Quinn shot at the SUV, shattering the side windows. He picked up the radio and told Reggie about the second shooter in the race shop, and for deputies to shut down everything coming out to Chicken Roost Road. The black SUV started and reversed fast, Quinn emptying out his clip into the back window. It sped off toward the shop, the other shooter jumping into the truck while Quinn reloaded and moved from the porch into the yard, following the SUV, walking with purpose and firing for the tires.

The Tahoe fled in a big cloud of dust and fishtailed into the curve and toward the county road. If the highway patrol hadn't showed to block off the road, he wasn't so sure they could stop them.

Quinn holstered the Beretta and slung the shotgun back into his hands, moving past the bullet-riddled SUV and the four dead men, moving with caution into the half-light of the race shop.

He stepped onto the smooth concrete, his eyes adjusting to the light as a motor grumbled to life, the engine gunning hard and fast.

Quinn fired off two big blasts as a green race car came speeding toward him and jumped out of the way as it shot past, out of the shop, onto the dirt, and following that SUV onto the main road.

Quinn lifted the mic as Reggie ran into the garage and saw him lying on the ground. "Shut down the damn road," Quinn said into the radio. "Two cars headed your way."

Quinn and Reggie ran for the bend in the road and saw his F-150 crossways in a ditch, a pattern of deep tire ruts where the SUV had knocked it out of the way. They jumped into the truck, hit the four-wheel drive, and after some dirt spewing behind them, came up onto the gravel. They drove through the Pritchards' gate past a disabled sheriff's car and a path wide enough for an SUV and a race car to make it through. "Son of a bitch."

"They gone," Reggie said.

Quinn hit the lights and siren on the truck, following the blackened tire tracks on the asphalt, heading east, while Reggie called in details of the dead.

"Heath Pritchard?" Quinn said.

"Never saw the son of a bitch," Reggie said. "That was Tyler in that goddamn race car."

26

THERE HAD BEEN A TIME AT THE BEACH WHEN TYLER HAD wanted to kill his brother. It was the exact damn moment he knew that he could never race like him, that he didn't have the lack of fear, the flat-out craziness of Cody. They'd been racing go-carts down in Gulf Shores, trying to impress this bowlegged girl from Wetumpka, Alabama, with their racing skills. The girl watching from the fence as they were running neck and neck on this old wooden track, rolling up into the sky on these big spiral ramps and coming fast and hard down a hill, hitting that sweet turn. Tyler had been damn sure he had him when his brother nosed his way to the inside and knocked the everliving shit out of him, throwing him hard into the concrete wall, breaking the thread-worn straps holding him back, and sending him tumbling and rolling across the asphalt. He'd broken his arm and bloodied his nose and face, the bare legs in those jean shorts scraped up as hell. But, goddamn, Cody didn't stop, racing up the ramp and not slowing until he'd finished that last damn lap.

Tyler got the girl, though. She gave him some titty underneath the pier later that night, his arm in a cast and his legs and arms covered in bandages. Cody told him that it was his own damn fault for driving that close to the wall and, if he'd had any nuts, he'd have tried to beat him on the inside of the track.

Cody was like that. And now Cody was dead.

Tyler felt the hot wind in his face, running their car to more than a hundred, redlining that son of a bitch, no wall to hit and no turns to take. Only a straightaway past the Jericho Square and on out toward the highway, the Rebel Truck Stop, the Golden Cherry Motel, an Exxon station. He saw the taillights of that Tahoe turning north onto 45, thinking they could come on their damn land, kill his brother, and get the hell out of Tibbehah County.

He didn't know who these people were. And he didn't care.

They'd killed Cody. And now he'd do what Cody would've wanted. He'd knock their damn dicks in the dirt. Tyler stood on that pedal, aiming for the SUV's right front panel as it sped up onto Highway 45. He rubbed against the side of the truck, the panel of the race car shearing off like an apple peel. He hit their ass again, trying to send those boys down into the off-ramp, but they kept on going, the race car too damn light against the SUV.

They were side by side, Tyler seeing, smelling, and tasting everything as they rolled up on Highway 45 toward Tupelo. The man had a squared-off head, chapped red skin, and nubby little ears. He lowered the window and raised a gun toward Tyler.

Tyler reached down beside him and clutched the Remington pump while steering with his left hand. He balanced the gun on the sheet metal cover of the passenger side and steadied the barrel, running flat out at one hundred and ten. He had to slow a bit to get beside those fuckers again, running two wide and door-to-door down the highway, just as he blasted the driver. The Tahoe slowed a bit, Tyler thinking hard on crazy-ass Cody sending him into the wall at the beach, crazy-ass Cody knocking the shit of their dumb stepdaddy's nuts. That was the Pritchard way. You goddamn knocked your enemies' dicks into the dirt.

He raced hard in front of the Tahoe, cutting right across the highway, the truck ramming him so damn hard that his head flew forward, the truck sending the race car tumbling down the fucking embankment, over and over. Tyler's goddamn lights went out at some point, and he came to hanging upside down like a goddamn space ape in the cockpit.

Tyler Pritchard tried to get free just as quick as he could and find that Remington pump to finish the fucking job.

Holy shit," Reggie said. "You see that?"

Quinn picked up the mic and called in the mile marker, a few details of the damn mess he saw broken apart down the side of Highway 45. Fenders, broken lights, shattered glass everywhere. The highway patrol had set up a roadblock a few miles down the road and Cleotha said they were now heading back. Quinn slowed the F-150, sliding off to the shoulder, he and Reggie getting out fast. They walked down the embankment sideways, looking at the green race car turned upside down and the black SUV lying on its side, hazard lights flickering, as they approached.

Quinn had his Beretta out. Reggie moved with him with his Colt as they watched Tyler Pritchard, bloody-faced and crazy-eyed, crawl from the flipped-over race car, looking like a stuck turtle, holding a shotgun. The boy was in some serious shock.

"Better think on it," Quinn said. "Put that shit down. Now."

Tyler looked to Quinn and Reggie, hearing the highway patrol sirens screaming as they headed south to the wreck. He held the shotgun loose in his right hand as he staggered, the sun a swirl of orange, yellows, and blues to the west.

"I'm sorry about Boom Kimbrough," Tyler said. "That wasn't our doing."

Quinn nodded. "I know," he said. "Put down the fucking gun, kid. I really don't want to shoot you."

"But he will," Reggie said.

"What about Ordeen Davis?" Quinn said. "Y'all shouldn't've done that."

"That's my Uncle Heath," Tyler said. "We were racing at the MAG down in Columbus that whole night. Christ Almighty. All me and Cody wanted to do was smoke a little weed and drive real fast. What's the matter with that?"

"Sorry about your brother," Quinn said. "Put down the gun."

"Me and him used to be famous," Tyler said, laughing a little. "Went all the way out to Hollywood, California, to try and win ten thousand dollars for knocking our stepdaddy in the nuts. People thought we were real cute and funny."

Quinn had the Beretta on him, finger on the trigger. He took careful aim, Tyler Pritchard stumbling forward, glassy-eyed and mumbling, "If you ain't on the gas, I'll be kicking your ass."

. . .

The sheriff was gonna shoot him. And that was fine by Tyler. *Go ahead, take his ass out.*

Everything was fucked. All of the damn work they'd put into the land, the weed, the deals, and the racing. Fucked up by that redheaded bitch out on the highway. If only goddamn Uncle Heath had just stayed in Parchman.

"Shoot me," Tyler said.

The sheriff and his black deputy didn't answer, both standing tall and tough, holding their guns on him.

"Go ahead," Tyler said. "Don't matter. You know you want to do it. Kill the last of the wild-ass Pritchard boys."

"Where's your uncle?"

"Dead," Tyler said. "They're all dead. Except my momma. And she just moved to Tampa."

The cops didn't shoot. So Tyler decided to give Johnny Law a little nudge in the proper direction and lifted up that shotgun. That got those boys going, both of them shooting at his ass at the same time. His bloody leg gave out and he fell, the bullets whizzing overhead. As he flipped onto his back, looking up at the bright orange sky, he thought, *Ain't it funny how that shit goes down?*

He turned his head to see the eyes of that fucker with the ponytail, openmouthed and deader than hell. A pistol loose by his open hand. Those law boys shot the old man over his damn shoulder.

"Goddamn son of a bitch," Tyler said, screaming, surrounded by his wrecked race car and busted-up car parts scattered along the hill. The sun going down slow and easy behind the back of those two damn cops. Every patrol car in north Mississippi speeding up to him with lights and sirens firing. The tall brown grass on the embankment blew every which way in the hot summer wind. "Ain't shit going my way."

Two hours and twenty minutes later, somewhere around 2100, Quinn headed back to the Pritchard property. Tyler Pritchard had been taken off by ambulance and Reggie Caruthers hitched a ride with one of the MHP boys back to the sheriff's office. He couldn't wrap his head about all the paperwork and inquiries that were about to follow. He'd been back and forth to Maggie for the last hour, Maggie running through the wedding rehearsal with Jason standing in. She said Jason had done pretty good, doing a decent imitation of Quinn, refusing to say anything else but "Yep" and "Nope" to the pastor. Everyone got a real kick out of it. Now they were listening to bluegrass and eating fried catfish at the farm.

He didn't tell her that he'd just killed a man on the side of Highway 45. A twice-convicted felon named J. B. Hood from Birmingham, Alabama. Or that in the overturned vehicle, they'd found two baseball bats flecked with blood. Quinn had taken both as evidence, placing them in the back of his truck.

There was a lot of activity down at the Pritchard house as he rolled down their old dirt road, federal agents already swarming across the property. Bright lights showed from the big racing shed. Quinn parked his truck, speaking to a couple DEA agents, one of them pointing over to Nat Wilkins, who stood at the edge of the old house, talking on her cell. Her bouncy hair pinned tight to her head, a DEA windbreaker covering a black pantsuit.

"Boom woke up," she said.

"I know," Quinn said. "My soon-to-be wife is his nurse."

"You mean that white girl with the long hair and all those freckles?"

"Yes, ma'am," Quinn said. "That's her."

"She's nice," Nat said. "Smart and pretty. You did real well for yourself, Sheriff."

"What'd Boom say?"

"He IDed Hood and Taggart," she said. "We got warrants out for both."

Quinn placed his hands on his hips, nodding. "Might can help you find J. B. Hood."

She looked at Quinn, arching her eyebrows. Before he could explain, one of the DEA agents he'd met at Sutpen's Trucking came jogging up, breaking into the conversation, out of breath. "We got something under that old barn," he said, pointing. "You just won't believe all the shit we just found."

"Want to take a look?" Nat asked, grinning.

"Damn straight," Quinn said.

27

"I FIGURED THEY'D FIND OUR LITTLE BUSINESS," TYLER Pritchard said, talking to Sheriff Colson at the hospital. They'd spent most of the night digging buckshot out of his ass and legs, sending up a grief counselor to talk about Cody while he was handcuffed to the bed. "I left the hatch wide open when I ran out. Should've covered the damn thing up."

"That was a hell of an operation, Tyler," Sheriff Colson said. "Must've taken a long time to bury all those bunkers, set up all those lights and the irrigation. Real impressive."

"Took us a couple years," Tyler said. "I learned pretty much how to run the whole system off YouTube. Me and Cody got to where we could run most of it."

"What about the harvesting and packing?"

"We sometimes hired a crew of Mexicans from over in Yalobusha County," he said. "Blindfold them and drive 'em over in a van. They done good work. Don't know why folks have so much trouble with Mexicans. They work their fucking tails off. Do jobs that no white man would tackle. I respect that shit."

The sheriff stood over his bed. The deputy, a nice man named Dave Cullison, had left them alone to run down to the cafeteria for some breakfast. He'd been talking a lot about heaven, trying to make him feel better. The deputy saying that there was even a place up there for his brother, Cody. And that maybe Cody was at rest now, hanging out with Jesus and the Apostles up in that big dirt track in the sky, maybe teaching those boys how to drift in those tight turns. Tyler wasn't sure he believed all that. But the talk made him feel a little better.

"Sorry about Cody."

Tyler nodded, laying back in the bed. Somewhere in the night, a nurse had turned on the television. Goddamn *Maury Povich Show* going with no sound, some fucking three-hundred-pound whore with MONIQUE CONVINCED 16TH DNA TEST WILL FIND CHILD'S FATHER running across the screen. People are just fucked up as hell in this old circus world.

"We didn't ask for none of this," he said.

"Maybe y'all shouldn't have hijacked a truck owned by the Syndicate."

"Is that who those fuckers were?" Tyler said, his head lowered down, staring up at the ceiling now. "Hot damn. I sure am glad you shot that old bastard instead of shooting me."

"You're welcome," Sheriff Colson said.

"He killed Cody."

The sheriff nodded, standing there, not looking like himself in a black suit and tie, like he was headed to senior prom or somebody's funeral. Tyler didn't study on it too long or ask many questions. He knew where the hell he was headed. He'd become an old man in the federal prison, hoping to Almighty God he survived the work and time without coming out like Uncle Heath. Used up, worn out, bitter as hell, with his brain shriveled like an old piece of fruit.

"I need to talk to you about Ordeen Davis," the sheriff said. "You told me your uncle killed him."

"That's right," Tyler said. "Me and Cody were racing. We didn't even know Uncle Heath had come home from Parchman. Nobody even thought to warn us. He shot that old boy right in the back."

"You got anything to prove that?"

"Check with the MAG," Tyler said. "They all knew Team Pritchard."

"ME's having a hard time pinpointing the time of death," Quinn said. "Given the condition of the body and all."

"I knew Ordeen Davis," Tyler said. "I wouldn't kill him. Uncle Heath was meaner than a goddamn water moccasin."

"How'd Ordeen get into that box?"

Tyler swallowed, knowing he was fucked but not being so almighty stupid as to tell the sheriff about watching Uncle Heath taking those sheet-metal cutters to Ordeen's body or helping him toss that toolbox into the Big Black River. Tyler didn't say a word, just kept his damn mouth shut.

"We found a mess of prints," Quinn said. "You want to tell me if we'll find a match to you and Cody? Y'all weren't in the system before. But now—"

"Do what you want," Tyler said. "We didn't touch that boy. That's all Heath Pritchard's business."

"We found your uncle," the sheriff said. "Down in the grow room."

"Is that a fact?"

The sheriff nodded. "Someone had shot him in the back of the head."

"Damn shame," Tyler said. "Those Syndicate folks don't play."

"Looks like he'd been down there for at least a day or so," the sheriff said. "Someone shoved him into a deep freeze with a bunch of pizzas and cartons of Bluebell ice cream. He was holding an empty bottle of Jack Daniel's. You think he drank that himself?"

"I want my damn lawyer."

"Feds got you good, kid," the sheriff said. "And I don't give a damn about what happened to Heath Pritchard. That looks like a family matter to me."

"How about you talk to my lawyer?"

"You got a lawyer?"

Tyler didn't answer, trying not to react, just watching that fat woman on TV jump out of her chair and run over to a skinny little black man and bitch-slap him right in the face. A couple of Maury's guards grabbed her by her ham-sized arms and pulled her back to her chair.

"That's about all I got, Sheriff," Tyler said. "They took a lot of metal out of my ass and I lost three pints of blood yesterday. Not to mention I got to figure out how to wrangle a funeral for my brother and my uncle while my ass is chained to a bed."

"You got to give me something more on Ordeen Davis," Quinn said. "Or we'll get you for your uncle."

"Goddamn, Sheriff," Tyler said. "You really think I got something to lose?"

I bet that dickweed didn't say jack shit," Lillie Virgil said, standing outside Boom's hospital room. Boom slept hard, but he'd been awake for a lot of the morning, making jokes and not shedding any tears that J. B. Hood had passed on to that big truck stop in the sky.

"He says his uncle killed Ordeen Davis."

"Yep," Lillie said. "That's what he'll say. The Duke boys completely innocent in this whole mess while wild card Uncle Jesse came back to Jericho with bloodlust."

"You know what?" Quinn said. "I believe him."

"You know what I think, Ranger?" Lillie asked. "I think all the flowers and sponge cake and bullshit makes you want to give the world a hug."

"You look nice," Quinn said.

Lillie nodded, wearing a simple black dress, her wild brown hair pulled back into a neat bun. She had a white rose pinned to the dress's neckline and looked odd without her Sig Sauer at her waist. She'd handed Quinn a cup of black coffee as they'd walked down the hall, both of them wanting to check on Boom one more time before heading to the church.

Lillie crossed her arms over her chest, standing there in the open hallway, nurses and doctors heading on to surgery or recovery. Babies being born, old folks dying, broken bones being set, and people taking treatment for all kinds of diseases. Quinn wondered how Maggie got through this every damn day without it starting to wear on her a bit.

"Appreciate you taking Boom's place as my best man," Quinn said. "He and I agreed there was no one else for the job."

"I know I talk tough," Lillie said. "And, for the most part, prefer to wear pants. But I do draw the line at getting called a man. There are a lot worse things I'd rather be called."

"How about best woman?" Quinn said.

Lillie bit her lip, hugging herself more closely around the waist.

She looked down at her feet and up at Quinn, smiling into his eyes. "I'd like that," she said. "Fits me to a T."

I want all this shit out of here," Fannie said. "All of Taggart's garbage, beer cans, cigarette butts, his damn clothes. Keep the doors open and burn some fucking candles in here. It's gonna take a long time to get rid of that smell."

"Where'd he go?" Midnight Man asked, his big round body moving about the office, pitching trash into a black plastic bag.

"Where else?" Fannie said, lighting up a cigarillo to start the exorcism of Vienna's. "Down to the Coast with that dumb bitch Twilight, trying to suck the ding-dongs of the big boys down there before he gets taken for that long, last Cadillac ride."

"You think they'll kill him?"

"Maybe," Fannie said, waving away the smoke. "I don't care. Just clean up this shit and quit asking so damn many questions."

Fannie left Midnight Man alone and headed out to the railing looking over the bar. It was early—they wouldn't open up until three—and both doors were wide open, letting in a little fresh air while the air conditioner pumped in the cool. She liked the way the old-fashioned bar shone after a good polish, the big plushy chairs neatly grouped around the stages. The floors were swept, toilets cleaned, and everything was in order again until tonight, when the truckers would pull up their rigs and the frat boys would drive down from Ole Miss and the shots would be poured and the titties would jiggle to get that nice flow of cash going again.

She watched as Ray entered through the front door, looking around the empty stages and down to the VIP room, finally figuring it the fuck out and looking up to Fannie's roost. He smiled and gave

Fannie a wave. He looked sharp and cool in black pants and a pink shirt, real old-school Memphis shit he bought at Lansky Brothers.

"I got your message."

Fannie looked down at Ray and blew smoke out into the open space over the stages.

"It's yours," he said. "They agreed."

She nodded and headed to the spiral staircase, turning around and around until she met Ray at the bar. He'd already started to help himself, reaching for a bottle of Blanton's and two clean glasses, pouring out a double for each of them.

"What about you?" she said.

"I'm too old for this shit," he said. "I got grandkids down in Florida."

"What did Buster say?"

"Not much," Ray said, smoothing down his white mustache. "He's not the type to admit he fucked up bringing in those boys. But when I told him you could get straight with Sledge and Memphis . . ."

"He was fucked."

"Well," Ray said, lifting the bourbon to the overhead light and admiring the rich color. "Yeah. Pretty much. He only asked one thing."

"Not to go after Wes Taggart."

"I wouldn't say that name for a while," Ray said. "If it's all the same. Taggart's not the worry. That's all over now."

"Then what?"

Ray leaned his head to the side and raised his big brushy eyebrows, holding the whiskey as if about to make a toast. "They didn't just send Taggart and Hood here to watch over you," he said. "They were sent to do a little housecleaning around this county."

Fannie didn't answer, ashing her cigarillo on a tray on the bar. She leaned into it with her elbow, watching Ray's face.

"You know about this goddamn election coming up?" he said. "You know how much damn shit around here is riding on it?"

"Of course," Fannie said. "Do you know how many coochie parties I've arranged out at that hunt camp? I've given more to this goddamn race than anyone. What they call sweat equity."

"They want your local sheriff neutered or gone," he said. "They're all leaving it up to you to decide which way to go."

"And that's our fucking deal?"

"That's the deal."

Fannie nodded, picking up the big square-cut glass, raising it to Ray, touching glasses, and then both of them taking a big sip. "Well, goddamn," she said. "All he had to do was fucking ask."

Quinn and Lillie stood together outside the Calvary United Methodist Church, Lillie complaining under her breath how her underwear was riding up her ass. Everyone already inside, seated and waiting, Diane Tull and the Tibbehah Bluegrass Boys ready with bass, fiddle, and mandolin. Diane Tull pulled out her daddy's old Dobro special for the occasion. "I know you think it's gonna happen," Lillie said. "But I'm not going to cry. Women who cry at weddings just make me want to puke. All that *Steel Magnolias* bullshit. Do you have any idea how much I hate that fucking movie?"

"I appreciate you doing this," Quinn said.

"I only came for the barbecue," Lillie said. "Can't turn down all this free food and good music. Not to mention you made Rose the flower girl and I had to come anyway."

"She looks beautiful."

"Sometimes I forget the world of shit and pain she came into," Lillie said, looking at her reflection in the window. "You ever think about that? Where we found her? The filth of that place? Sometimes I can still smell it. You and me chasing all those shitbirds out of Tibbehah County."

"We had us a time."

"It's not over, Ranger," Lillie said. "The Southern shitbird isn't exactly an endangered species."

"I want you to find Wes Taggart."

"I will."

"And Boom wants to testify against him."

"Maybe he'll get lost on the way to the courthouse," Lillie said. "Mississippi roads have a lot of potholes, might shake his ass out of the van."

"You wouldn't do that," he said. "That's not our way. That's too damn easy."

Lillie shrugged. "So this is how it all goes?" she said. "You get married, you have a ready-made kid, and you settle into life on the farm. Just promise me that you won't go all soft on me. I think that's the one goddamn thing I couldn't take. Taking in the chamber of commerce meetings, glad-handing the supervisors, eating up caramel cake with the Garden Club."

"What the hell do you have against caramel cake?"

She held out a little box to him, tied with a blue silk ribbon. Quinn took it, holding it, and Lillie told him to go ahead and open the fucking thing. He pulled at the ribbon and opened the top, finding a tarnished silver star inside. TIBBEHAH COUNTY SHERIFF. '74.

"It was your Uncle Hamp's," she said. "I found it in his desk after he died. It's the same one he wore when he first became sheriff. I think it's high time you have it."

"Jesus, Lil."

"I couldn't admit for a long time what he'd done to this place and himself," she said. "Don't let the shitbirds tarnish what you got. You keep on doing your damn job."

The music started up inside the church, the first strains of "You Are My Sunshine," a personal favorite of Quinn's mom and Caddy and the signal to come up to the altar.

"Yes, ma'am," Quinn said, slipping the old star into his suit pocket.

"You fucking better," Lillie said, whispering, pushing open the door, all heads turning to the side of the pews toward Quinn and Lillie. "Memphis ain't but ninety-nine miles away, Ranger. And if you fuck up on your job, on Maggie, or any of it, I'll be all over your ass. Now, get in there and marry that girl."